W9-AMS-139

wild horses

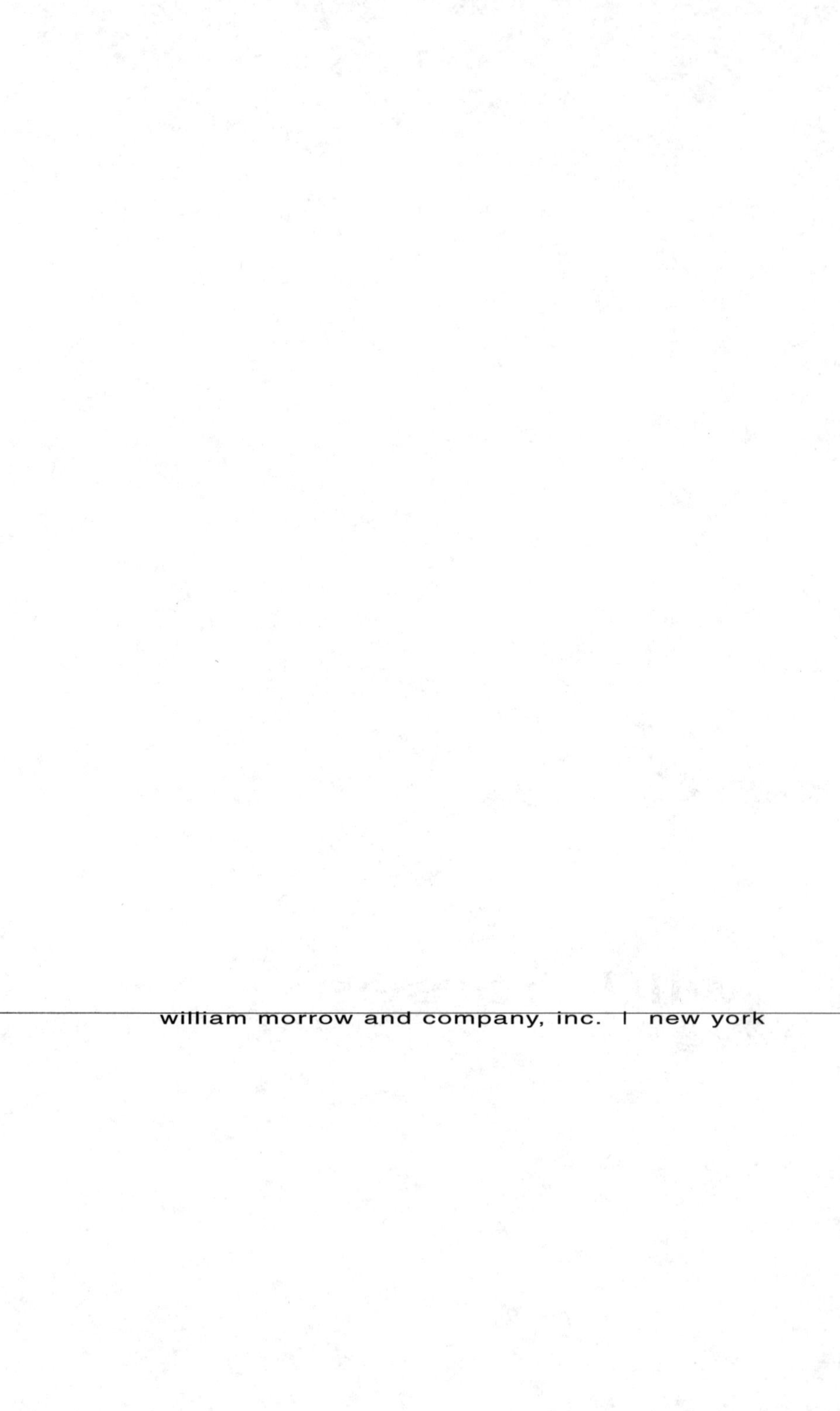

william morrow and company, inc. | new york

wild horses

brian hodge

a novel

Inquiries should be addressed to Permissions Department, William Morrow and Company, Inc., 1350 Avenue of the Americas, New York, N.Y. 10019.

It is the policy of William Morrow and Company, Inc., and its imprints and affiliates, recognizing the importance of preserving what has been written, to print the books we publish on acid-free paper, and we exert our best efforts to that end.

Library of Congress Cataloging-in-Publication Data

Hodge, Brian, 1960–
Wild horses : a novel / Brian Hodge. — 1st ed.
p. cm.
ISBN 0-688-16527-3
I. Title.
PS3558.034196W5 1999
813'.54—dc21 98-30361
CIP

Printed in the United States of America

First Edition

1 2 3 4 5 6 7 8 9 10

BOOK DESIGN BY DEBBIE GLASSERMAN

www.williammorrow.com

This one's for Wildy,
for sending those blues
from so far away, yet
still loud enough to be heard

Acknowledgments

Many thanks to Dolly (and love, but of course), for time and space; to Howard Morhaim, for knowing a good thing when he saw it; and to Paul Bresnick, for *buying* a good thing when he saw it.

Also, to my fellow wayfarers on the Grapes of Wrath Tour, especially Amy, whose heinous and inexplicable breach of gamblers' protocol has been worth far more in conversational value than the cash she made me lose, and to a certain management-level casino employee who for obvious reasons prefers to remain anonymous.

And, most mysteriously, to the Bluesman, for delivery.

Gambling is inevitable.

—1976 Commission on the Review of
the National Policy Towards Gambling

Crime is to the passions what nervous fluid is to life:
it sustains them, it supplies their strength.

—the Marquis de Sade,
Juliette

wild horses

chapter one

She should have known eight months ago, when they moved to Las Vegas, that it was a mistake, the stuff of which rough roads and blood clots were made. Omens filled the air that day. A freak storm showered down that afternoon, to send tourists and natives alike into disgruntled fits of despair, unnoticed only by the most inveterate gamblers at their tables. Worse, a throat infection kept Wayne Newton offstage that evening, plunging Boyd into a deep indigo funk that lingered for days.

Wayne Newton. Just which level of Dante's Hell had she fallen into here? To Allison, root canal sounded more appealing, but it had meant a lot to Boyd: Wayne Newton, throwing down big tips for watery drinks, doing the whole tacky Vegas routine up and down the Strip for one grand evening before settling in as residents and Boyd's dream job of blackjack dealer extraordinaire—his way of announcing to Nevada at large, "We have arrived!" The master plan ruined, then, courtesy of a strep infection.

Secretly, she had rejoiced.

"If we'd moved here twenty-five years ago," Boyd lamented, "I bet we'd've killed Elvis ahead of schedule."

Allison recalled frowning. "We were only six years old at the time," she'd said, but she knew what he meant. Some people carried with them their very own plagues, wherever they went.

Typhoid Boyd—it had a ring to it.

He'd proposed a few weeks later, the presence of all those quickie wedding chapels eating away at his oversexed brain. She'd had the good sense to say no . . . not yet, at least, an amendment sutured on only to soothe the sting of rejection while she hoped Boyd would otherwise forget all about it.

Love *should* figure somewhere into the equation, of this she was certain, and with equal certainty Allison Willoughby knew that she didn't love Boyd. Was unsure she'd ever loved anyone who had stood much over four feet tall. There had been no shortage of opportunity during her fourteen years on the run from Mississippi, most of the men arrayed in a stepping-stone succession that implied a monogamous disposition. But each had been, admittedly, a stopgap measure to fill intermittent gaps in her life; there was something just too horrible about living alone for very long.

Paradoxically, apartments seemed noisier when they weren't shared. She would lie awake at night, listening to creaks and pops surrounding her, each made by a footfall from long ago, when eager breaths once whispered like an ill wind. Every shadow evoked the ghost of a visitor whose face remained as sharp as a razor's cut; they had come to her nocturnally, those visitors, with numbing frequency and intentions she'd not wholly understood, knowing only there was pain and shame involved.

After a time she'd not even needed faces anymore; could tell them apart from smell alone, variations on a shared group scent that could even today make her gag whenever she caught a whiff of anyone too similar. The fermented testosterone stink wafting down from above had been heavier than their bodies.

Of course she'd never told Boyd any of this. A guy like Boyd, give him a little leverage, sooner or later he'd have to use it.

That Vegas mentality again.

No wonder he was doing so well here.

. . .

When after nine months together she noticed signs that Boyd was exploring options elsewhere, it came as no surprise. Allison had long recognized that women were to Boyd Dobbins's soul what oxygen was to his lungs, and should someone put a gun to his head demanding he give up one or the other, he'd honestly need time to think it over. Women were goddesses, and Boyd overflowed with undying worship.

To hear him tell it, she was the loveliest woman on earth—maybe of all time. Her hair was spun flax, and her eyes emeralds. Her nose was perfectly buttoned, the dusting of freckles across her cheekbones adorably childlike, given lie only by those taut haunches and belly, shoulders and breasts. A daily litany, this; she had become the sacrament of his new religion. Meanwhile, the mirror showed her the crinkled birth of crow's-feet around her eyes and a tush that screamed for longer rides on her bicycle. It cost Boyd credibility, left Allison feeling it was inevitable that he would fall for the charms of a goddess more radiant still.

As Boyd so obviously had.

The perfume scent clinging to him when he came back late each night from the casino was a simple matter to brush aside: He dealt winning hands to bouncy, squealing women—was he supposed to fight them off when they wanted to hug him? Not when the objective was to keep them at the table long enough to lose their winnings back. Yet what were the odds these affectionate women were, night after night, all wearing the same scent?

And he'd also been leaving earlier each day. Not that she'd ordinarily be likely to notice. His shift began at four in the afternoon, overlapping hers at Gingerbread House Day Care by two hours. One day's chance failure to raise him on the phone before he left turned into a second, then a third, and a pattern was established. It was getting to be a game—pin the tail on Boyd.

Then there were the smaller signs that would never hold up in a court of law, only before a vigilante jury of her peers: women wronged by Boyd, by the world's Boyds, who understood feminine radar and trusted its infallibility.

When it came time to force the truth, Allison left work hours early, claiming a doctor's appointment. Her male supervisor was a nitpicker skilled at bookkeeping, with little talent for relating to children or the women who took care of them. A yeast infection, she'd begun to explain, and he hadn't wanted to hear another word.

Her commute home was ordinarily made on two wheels. With only Boyd's car between them, she bicycled to work, never minding it; it helped keep her legs toned. Today, though, she'd planned ahead, borrowing the car belonging to Doug Powell, the quizzical-looking doughboy who managed their apartment building. Earlier this summer she'd found and returned a zippered vinyl bank pouch stuffed with rent checks and cash after Doug had dropped it near the Dumpster. He owed her, all right. When she reminded him of it this morning and demanded the car, he'd surrendered his keys with a half-eaten pear in one hand and a Superman comic in the other.

Wearing a breezy sundress and sandals, Allison kept watch over Boyd's Dodge Daytona from across the alley and down one parking lot. She'd pinned up her hair to get its hot mass off her neck and took frequent drafts from a bottle of Gatorade, trying not to touch anything. Doug's Toyota had the smell of a forgotten basket of laundry, the feel of a petri dish. Bored earlier, she'd peeked inside the glove compartment to find a bag of Halloween candy bars, melted out of their wrappers into a runny volcanic blob.

Sweating, she fanned herself with a comic book from the backseat. Summer had been murderous, and early September a broiler. Las Vegas was the hottest place she'd ever been, worse by far than the sultry Mississippi summers in which she'd grown up. There, at least, a verdant earth would welcome you, lush grass easing misery as you sank into its cooling layers. But here? They'd taken the desert and paved it. The sun ricocheted off as though the entire ungodly slab of city were a giant reflector. It baked your brain, kept you from thinking straight; left you in a low-grade delirium in which you actually believed you could beat the system and go home rich. He'd chosen well, Bugsy Siegel had.

After ninety minutes of watching, Boyd emerged from their building in his blackjack togs and his annoying gigolo strut. A quarter past two, more than an hour before he needed to leave. Tucked under one arm, a laptop computer brought from his aborted career in Seattle selling swimming pools, hot tubs, home spas. He'd mostly used it for sales calls, a slick multimedia brainwash designed to shame suburban families into admitting how dreadfully empty their lives were without a hole in the ground.

Curious. He hardly needed a computer at the casino—twenty-one wasn't *that* tough to count to.

Boyd's Daytona was a glaring beacon, lacquered as red as a fire engine. She heard the electronic chirp as he used his remote to kill the alarm, then trailed after him at the end of the alley.

He led west on side streets, then cut south onto Las Vegas Boulevard, the Strip. Come nightfall, this would turn into ground zero, enough lights to trigger headaches even in the blind; a holocaust of glare and flash, a gaudy riot of smeared colors each trying to strobe brighter than the last, and under it all, the desperate and the naive out swimming the seas of neon.

As Boyd held an unswerving course, she began to think he was only heading into the casino early. The Ivory Coast was one of Las Vegas' newer complexes, south of Caesars Palace, designed to give the impression of stepping into the antiquated days of British colonialism; Kipling's "Gunga Din," with slot machines. The concept seemed quietly racist. A pair of doormen flanked the main entrance, looking like soldiers who'd slaughtered the Zulu nation, wearing jodhpurs and red jackets with shiny black belts and boots, white pith helmets, and wooden antique rifles held at port arms.

Inside the lobby lunged a taxidermied bull elephant, cheaply bought and alarmingly old, seventy years if a day. During the grand opening a tusk had rotted loose and crashed to the floor. Casino security had immediately been deployed with cash to buy up all amateur videos of the calamity.

The Ivory Coast came and went. Boyd cruised past the wedding-cake castle of the Excalibur, then the phony Sphinx and glass pyramid of the Luxor, and the Strip was behind them. Eventually he turned west, led her to some condominiums, a dozen buildings competing for the shade of half as many trees. While he parked in the shadow of a building overlooking the pool, Allison darted to another stretch of the lot and waited. She heard the chirp of his reactivated car alarm, then Boyd was stepping light and easy, the laptop under his arm.

And look at him. Just look. Walking up there like it was prom night and he was taller. Pressed white shirt. Gelled hair, shiny black. She knew when she got home she'd find the bathroom sink sprinkled with trimmings from his cheesy little mustache.

He ascended an outside stairway and stepped off at the second-floor deck. At the first door, Boyd ignored the doorbell in favor of jauntily banging knuckles.

Allison soaked in every detail: the door opening inward, Boyd blocking her view of the other woman as they kissed, but she could see a shoulder-length sweep of hair, red, *too* red, the face unseen and her arm worming around Boyd's waist, hand dropping to squeeze his tight ass as though checking a melon. And the idiot, he nearly dropped the computer. He rushed at the woman with encircling arms while kicking the door shut behind them.

Allison left the Toyota and detoured into the tiled pool area, an oasis reeking of chlorine and lotions. Bodies lay inert and scattered, a few energetic ones stroking through the water. Her gaze settled on a fiftyish man lying regal atop his chaise longue. Skin like cured leather. From baked forehead to shriveled toes he gleamed a deep mahogany.

"You look like you're out here a lot," she said.

He eyed her over lavender aviator shades, his flat response weary of well-intended warnings: "And . . . ?"

"And you look like you probably notice who comes and goes."

He softened. "It helps pass the time."

She thrust before him a picture, peeled from her billfold's flip

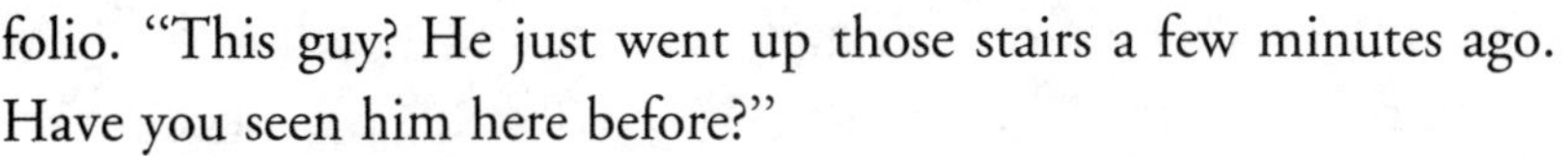

folio. "This guy? He just went up those stairs a few minutes ago. Have you seen him here before?"

Mr. Mahogany gave the picture a neutral glance. "And what's my answer worth?"

She moved her thumb to reveal herself at Boyd's side, one sunny afternoon at Fisherman's Wharf, the two of them laughing as they watched merchants sling fresh catch of the day. Arms looped around one another's shoulders, eyes bright with adoration and toothpaste-ad grins. A moment they'd coerced a stranger into immortalizing; evidence they could have been happy, there had been potential.

"It might be worth a good fireworks show."

Mr. Mahogany nodded. "Let me put it like this: He knows his way up those stairs by now. Capeesh?"

Allison thanked him, then traced Boyd's footsteps, wondering how often he'd come home with the dust of this place on his shoes. A glance up at the door gave her the number, unit 230, and a pause by the mailbox most of a name: DeCARLO, M.

The name was hazily familiar. On first coming to Vegas, Boyd had been unable to get work along the Strip, where the competition was downright Darwinian. Instead he'd hired on at a lowly grind joint downtown called Cactus Dirk's. Hadn't even been there four weeks when the flash and dazzle of his dealing caught the eye of someone out scouting table talent, and so he'd been lured away to the Ivory Coast. Something about that stroke of luck recalled the name DeCarlo.

Up on the deck Allison found that DeCarlo, M., was quite the horticulturist. A mobile garden up here, with hanging baskets and laden plant stands. What kind of person grew cactus, anyway?

Allison tried the knob—locked. No satisfaction would be had from knocking or ringing the bell. They would most likely ignore it. So she appropriated the largest clay pot from its stand. The fronds of a fern tickled her arm as she stalked to the edge of the balcony and hoisted the pot overhead. She heaved it and watched it plummet toward Boyd's car, then fracture egglike at the front of the roof, with a thick ceramic crunch and the tortured buckling of sheet metal. Black soil showered over red lacquer while a jagged lightning strike of cracks speared down through the windshield, the fern resting limp in the center, like a fallen flag. The alarm blared shrilly.

She waited, arms crossed over her breasts, while down at the pool a grinning Mr. Mahogany shot her a thumbs-up salute. Allison turned at the fresh commotion at door 230. The door banged open and out he flew, Boyd shirtless and breathless, trying to stumble his way into black slacks and having an ungainly time of it. He'd forsaken underwear for speed.

When he saw her, he put on the brakes, skidding on the wooden planks, backpedaling in bare feet, wide-eyed and confused while he held his pants closed with both fists: Boyd, caught. Despite the mustache, he looked very boyish, but it was more than his lack of stature. It was the total dearth of lines creasing his forehead. Of course not. Boyd worried about nothing.

"Oh, uhhh," he quavered, and she could see him tossing every conceivable alibi into the air like a box of puzzle pieces in hopes they might land in a cogent pattern. "This is a bitch, this is a bitch"—with fierce shakes of his head, as if this could *not* be happening—"this is a bitch . . ."

Allison glanced at the open door, feeling a sluice of chilly central air. "This isn't what it looks like, right, Boyd?"

His face tensed with hope.

Through clenched teeth: "You can explain *every*thing, can't you?"

"Well, babe, you *know* I can, if you'll just give me a chance."

Her hands raised in the air, summoning thunderstorms. "You know how bad this looks, but there's something I'm missing, isn't there? I have to be mistaking this for something else, don't I?"

"Well now, Allie, you know you've got this tendency to jump to conclusions." His composure leached back with a sly smirk, and *why* hadn't she seen what a worm he was before now? "There's a bigger picture, you know . . . in the grand scheme? I don't blame you one bit, but . . ." He was on the move, shuffling to the edge of the deck, drawn by the piercing wail from below. "Now if you'll just put down that cactus, I'm sure—"

He froze at the railing, staring down at his car, his mouth unhingeing with a silent scream, and then the real thing: "Allie? *Allie?* Allie! Oh, Allie!" Her name yelped over and over.

Movement drew her eye to the open doorway, where the redhead came out in a shorty kimono that hit her at midthigh. DeCarlo, M., this must be, showgirl-leggy and showgirl-long, but obviously a showgirl retired, Boyd's senior by ten years minimum and taller by an inch. Mean-eyed now, her face was rouged flint, sharply angled and interrupted too soon to have been rejuvenated by the flushed dewy glow of sex. Her dyed hair was a bundle of stressed copper.

"Can't you shut that fucking thing off?" she shouted, pressed both palms over her ears.

"What's your problem?" Allison shouted back. "You can't hear yourself age?"

The woman flinched with a genuine terror of years. Her mouth downturned into a vicious snarl; a finger pointed in warning.

"You put my cactus down, you hear me? You put it down right where you found it—" Switching targets in an eyeblink, "Boyd? Boyd! What are you screaming about?"

"My car, *look at my car,* Madeline!" he cried. "It looks like she hit it with a wrecking ball!"

Madeline went striding across the deck in a waft of Chantilly Lace and Virginia Slims, fuming under her breath. She clutched the wooden railing. "My *fern*!"

Madeline DeCarlo went on the attack, the kimono flapping to expose a pocked jiggle of slack-muscled tummy that contrasted with her toned legs. Allison slashed in self-defense with the cactus, but it had no heft, the pot plastic and spewing clumps of sand. She missed, Madeline leaping aside with dancer's grace, a hard and embattled elegance about her.

Allison's next swing tagged Boyd on the right shoulder and

brought a howl of anguish, and still he was begging for a chance to explain; they never learned. She hurled the pot to the deck, grabbed the others as quickly as she could, and flung them down as well at the irresistible targets made by those four bare feet.

And then she darted between them, her fury spent, moving with impunity because she was the only one with shoes. She walked as tall and straight as she could, beneath that brutal sun, crossing the lot to applause from the swimming pool.

She'd met Boyd nine months ago at a charity fund-raiser for a children's hospital—Casino Night, a guaranteed crowd-pleaser with Seattle's philanthropic finest bellying up to the tables to buy bankrolls of play money. The first thing they lost was perspective. Winning was still everything, even if their wagers weren't worth the paper they were printed on.

Allison had gone as a representative of the day care center where she worked, its donation to conscripted labor. Chosen for what—legs? figure? experience handling unruly children?—then sent forth in garters and fishnet stockings, short skirt and push-up bra. Most of her hair was gathered back, the rest falling in wheat-blond twists past her neck. Her oval face tarted up with more makeup than she'd ordinarily wear in a month. She humored the tight-vested pack of coronaries-in-the-making while they puffed cigars and played high rollers, delivering their drinks like a harried pro.

Boyd, on the other hand, stood behind his blackjack table with an unassailable authority. His black slacks were sharply creased, his shirt was white as an angel's robe, and his bow tie was not a clip-on. A lacy garter, dark bordello red, was cinched around each biceps, and he'd waxed the tips of his mustache, their angles jaunty, devil-may-care.

If she hadn't known better she'd've guessed that a steamboat had delivered him directly to the wharves, straight out of 1880.

He had a knack, had Boyd, plus a crowd around his table to testify to his skills. Boyd Dobbins possessed a near-telekinetic command over each card that he dealt. When he gave them a flick of his wrist, the cards didn't merely skitter across green felt—they glided. They seemed to hover, then settle wherever he wanted with a precision defying natural law. He could deal a quick round of blackjack, five hands, and align each second card perfectly atop the first. He would ask who was Catholic, then deal their hands in the shape of a cross. Even the losers were applauding the show.

"Wher*ever* did you pick that up?" Allison asked, genuinely curious, during a rare lull in the action.

"Zen," deadpanned this dealer savant. "*Be* the card." Then an amiable shrug, and his shoulders flexed nicely beneath his shirt. While he could stand to be taller, it was no dealbreaker; although if she found out he slicked his hair down the middle in real life, it would be a severe setback.

He elaborated: "You've heard how all the great jazz and blues greats are supposed to've slept with their instruments?"

She arched an eyebrow. "*You* sleep with a deck of cards?"

"It's a . . . a spiritual thing."

"And from a distance," she said, jousting, "you looked like a grown-up."

"So you've never once, as an adult, slept with your childhood teddy bear."

He had her there. "It was a floppy dog named Roscoe. And he was a lot more cuddly than any deck of cards."

"Oh, I'm sure he was. Then again, nobody ever tipped you because you were good with Roscoe, did they?" Smug as an indicted politician, he produced a green bill that he'd wrapped tightly around his finger. His *middle* finger. "Deal a few winning hands for play money, and get the real thing. Not bad, huh?"

Allison told him how lucky it was that he had cards to sleep with, for obviously without them he'd be sleeping alone. Wondering why, moments later, when going back to reload her drink tray, she had bothered to check his ring finger. . . .

Unencumbered.

Yet he proved oddly chivalrous later. Allison doing her duty, delivering frequent gin-and-tonics to a man with a face like florid dough and a habit of dropping a humid hand to skim over her rump. Patting firmly, oh so avuncular; thank *you,* little girl. Lecher. She let it pass the first time. He was drunk, after all. She fought against impulse the second time, a kill-urge uncoiling within, a dragon awakening in its cave. She could taste the fire on her breath. Could anticipate his lecher's scalp peeling away from his skull with one brutal swipe of her hand.

The third time he groped her, Allison's breath locked in her throat, the world constricting to the point of this moment. Her hand gripped a bottle from her tray. He'd never know what hit him.

Before she could lift for the windup, she saw Boyd's hand flash, a single card leaving his thumb and fingers as a martial arts throwing star might leave a ninja's hand. The card's edge cracked across the bridge of the man's nose, the sound sharper than she would've imagined, and her own hand was stayed.

"Oh, now would you look at what I've done?" Boyd gushed with apologies while the rest of the deck went spilling from his hand across the green felt table. "Sir, I'm *so* sorry, I'm on medication for the seizures, but sometimes one sneaks up on me."

The groper wobbled in his chair, eyes watering, and after he massaged the bridge of his nose he stared at his fingertips. "I'm . . . bleeding," he said in a frightened slur.

Boyd apologized again, sparing a discreet wink for her, then assured him it wasn't bad. Allison stared with vindication at the thin tributaries trickling like red tears down either side of the man's nose.

"Don't unnerstand. I'm—I'm a—I'm a"—groping the table now instead of her ass—"*hemophiliac!*"

Towels and ice compresses were rushed to the table, and there was more than one doctor in the house, plus a besotted priest who hovered nearby in case he was needed for last rites.

Allison was able to hold it off until she made it into the ladies' room: a spell of trembling so bad it verged on convulsion. And she hated what she saw in the mirror. That red-lipped whore's face, not even her own idea, made up for someone else's amusement. Just like very old times.

She could so easily have killed that man. Hemophilia aside, she might still have killed him—hit him with the bottle, then hit him again with what remained, then gone after him with the jagged stump. He would bleed and bleed and bleed, and the worst of it . . . ?

It would not really have been him she was killing.

Did Boyd have any idea what he was preventing, or had he only gotten lucky? She left the bathroom knowing it didn't matter, and that he at least deserved a thank-you.

Back outside, the crowd at Boyd's table had quadrupled in size, and she was told that her services were no longer required for the night. For having done nothing? After realizing that he wouldn't bleed to death her groper had turned vindictive; had done some talking, some finger-pointing. Already making pretzel twists out of the truth, let's blame that low-class woman and her trailer-park morals. It was sound strategy.

Boyd had received a similar dismissal, and the two of them left at the same time. Allison found herself feeling much younger than thirty-one; younger and ashamed. Back there? It was *her* fault, all of it, the blame deep as marrow. She carried guilt as she might carry an ugly, malignant child conceived by rape: hating it, knowing nevertheless that it was hers and always would be. It had suckled from her for too long to be given up now.

It was early winter in Seattle, the city blanketed with fog and clinging mists. Corkscrews of wind whipped around corners. She couldn't hold her coat tightly enough about her. The wind carried on it the basso drone of a ship's horn, from another world a few blocks away, a deep and mournful sound that conjured spirits of departure, with farewells made obsolete. Sometimes you just wanted to *go,* and answer to no one.

"I have this suspicion that career opportunities here just got really limited for me," Boyd said. "But there's always my contingency plan." The cards were in his grip; he shuffled them with one hand. "Vive Las Vegas."

Before leaving, he'd taken paper towels to his scalp, scrubbing away a slick of grease and leaving wet clumps in its wake. His hair looked like roadkill in the rain.

He lamented further: "That good old boy network, you're not in the loop, screw up once with one of them and they'll ream you for sure. I might as well grab my ankles right now."

"Don't you think you're exaggerating? He *will* live."

"Yeah, that's the problem. I don't know, maybe I should follow politics a little closer," Boyd Dobbins sighed. "How was I supposed to know that fat chucklehead was a state senator?"

Hours after their relationship's cactus-strewn finale, she drank sweet, syrupy Southern Comfort, alone in the apartment. Boyd at the casino, or maybe having his shoulder tended by a nurturing side of Madeline DeCarlo unglimpsed earlier. Allison held a glazed stare on the TV, some old movie hypnotic only for its presence.

When Boyd came home after midnight she was still awake, if in bed and pretending otherwise. When he stepped into the darkened bedroom, the only sound his quiet breath, something sad rode upon it, sad and heavy and final. Then he turned away.

She was still awake hours later when the deep breaths of his slumber reached her from the sofa, and she followed them into the living room. Anger began to surge all over again, fueled by the bourbon, while her blurry gaze settled on the dining table and the laptop computer he'd been toting around earlier. She'd completely forgotten about that.

Havoc for havoc—just how much *did* she plan to wreak on his life? Did it stop at car and shoulder? Not by a long shot. A moment later the bourbon had her flipping up the computer screen, turning the machine on. She browsed file names to learn what he might've been up to lately, but made little headway. His games, his e-mail,

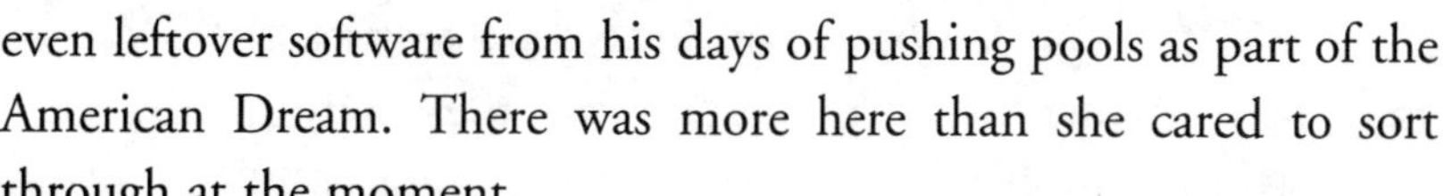

even leftover software from his days of pushing pools as part of the American Dream. There was more here than she cared to sort through at the moment.

It was an evil temptation, too powerful to resist. While Boyd slept she fetched a carton of floppy disks, then launched the data backup program and copied in compressed bulk the laptop's entire inventory of files. For the coup de grâce, she tracked the pointer up to pull down the menu of commands under the heading **Special,** and selected the most ominous: **Dump.**

The screen confronted her with a bold, boxed-in warning, last chance to back out: **Erase the Hard Drive?**

"Damn right," she murmured, and keyed **Yes.**

While Boyd's computer embarked upon its internal slash and burn, she hunted for a notepad and a pen.

Morning came down hard, later than usual, Allison clueless in hungover sleep until the phone rang: her boss. Admittedly her work ethic wasn't what it should be this morning. She begged a sick day, and only when she hung up, too warm in a flood of late-morning sun, did she notice what was missing. Little things, and not so little: most of the CDs, hers as well, except the ones that Boyd detested; the stereo, TV, and VCR; all of his clothes; more, a full carload's worth.

But she had awakened to worse days than this, and it helped to realize that her heart still beat as strong as ever, and that while Las Vegas lay beyond the windows it wasn't going anywhere. It would not follow. She could leave it behind like a prison cell.

When the agitated knocking tattooed her door late in the afternoon, the last person Allison expected to see was Madeline DeCarlo. Red hair gathered smartly back, she wore the familiar tailored blazer from the Ivory Coast.

"All right, where *is* the son of a bitch?" Madeline snapped.

Allison began to laugh, wondering if Boyd had been stringing along the both of them. If there'd been a third woman, or if he'd simply chosen to begin again, wherever, alone.

"You're too late," Allison told her. "And he took the TV, so it must be permanent." She pointed toward the empty stand.

Madeline fumbled with a cigarette that took six flicks of her lighter. Turning to go, she glared, then couldn't resist one last attempt at inflicting a wound.

"What that weasel was doing to you nights for the last nine months?" she said. "Looks like he just did it to me for over seven hundred thousand dollars."

Allison tried to mask her bewilderment at how Boyd could be involved with this kind of money. "I knew it had to be something like that." Looking Madeline up and down with dour appraisal. "But just between you and me? I think he probably deserved more."

Then she slammed the door.

chapter two

"Imported beers, definitely. Drink American, piss American, that's my motto," said the bartender. Then he hunkered grinning across the bar. "Especially all that dark German shit. You can lose that in the ocean for all I care."

"Hey," said Gunther, "don't you start up with the heritage, you mutt, even if it is just the top half. All right, my turn. Okay. Lithium. Never worked on me. I could eat lithium by the fistful and not feel a thing. Somebody told me it doesn't work on the sociopathic personality. I don't know, maybe I should've taken that as an insult, you think?"

"I think you should've whacked the whole passel of 'em," the bartender said. "All right: Garth Brooks. I don't see the appeal. Now, George Jones, now *there's* you a great country singer, him and Hank Williams. Steve Earle, if I got to pick someone from today."

Gunther waved a dismissive hand. "You're talking Greek to me now, Kevin. What, I look like a guy spends his time listening to country-western?"

Gunther Manzetti expected no answer, nor got one. One look at him was enough to dispel the slightest notion that he understood anything of steel guitars and truck stops. Lowdown women possibly, and broken hearts, but no one had the market cornered on these.

A German mother and Italian father, they'd each left such an indelible imprint on him that it couldn't have been worse had they painted Gunther the colors of their respective flags. Madeline had once said he looked like an experiment gone wrong. Ten years after defeat, World War II's European losers get together and pool their eugenic resources to breed a hybrid soldier, the seed of some future revenge. Then when they see what it looks like, the way the chromosomes are apportioned, they abandon the entire project.

Gunther Manzetti stood Aryan-tall, with a blue-eyed, sharply chiseled skull, and his blond hair clipped in a stiff brush cut. And? And: olive skin, plus a dark, lush Mediterranean vineyard of body hair. His pubic hair began, Madeline teased, just above his Teutonically cruel upper lip.

No lover of country-western, Gunther suffered deafness to nearly every other tone across the musical spectrum, as well. Rock and roll grated on his nerves, and blues he could not relate to at all. Jazz confused him because it sounded as though no one could figure out what they really wanted to play, or *if.* And classical and opera just plain bored the ass off him.

About the only thing he liked on occasion was movie music, music that made him feel as though something interesting was about to happen: a punch about to be thrown, a bone about to shatter, a car about to crash. He loved "The Peter Gunn Theme"; heard that ominous rolling bass riff and thick nasty brass in his head nearly everywhere he went.

Just like now, drifting in the background, and nothing more going on than simple conversation. He and Kevin discussing the most highly overrated things they'd ever come across.

"Teflon-jacketed bullets," Gunther said. "Yeah, they'll punch through a Kevlar vest you hit it with a good clean shot—why they call them cop-killers. But whatever happened to skill, is what I want to know. Don't need Teflon with a good clean *head*shot."

"Right. Fresh body bag is all," Kevin agreed. "Tiramisù."

Gunther blanked, everything going Greek again.

"Ah, this chichi dessert, my wife hears about it, it's like her mission in life, you know, just has to *experience* it"—drawing the word out—"gotta *experience* it with me. I take one bite and it puts me in a diabetic coma, just about. Like there's something the matter with plain old pound cake?"

Gunther took a pull off his margarita, smacked salt from his lips, and then he had it, the winner, the single most overrated commodity in all the world.

"Teenage pussy," he said.

"Get the fuck out of here!" Kevin cried, drawing looks from the six other drinkers. Too early in the afternoon for this dive to be drawing better than skeletal clientele. It was the sort of place that repelled normal tourists. "Teenage pussy overrated! You ever think maybe that lithium made a dent after all?"

Gunther held his ground, asking when was the last time Kevin had had any—any since he was nineteen, twenty? Kevin turned quiet on him, shuffling behind the bar and cracking scarred knuckles.

"I'll tell you what you're doing," said Gunther. "You're working from memory, and how old's that memory now, how long's it been? Twenty-five years since that teenage pussy, is it?"

"Twenty-two," Kevin scowled.

"Teenage girls, nice tight bodies and everything, tits that defy gravity, but it's mostly all show and no seasoning yet. Once the clothes come off and it's time to get down to the serious grind, they don't know how to *move* with a man. Like they got this idea all they got to do's just lay there, about as much life in them as a rug, and somehow they're supposed to be God's gift."

"I don't know, Gunther. I can think of, like, three billion other guys who'd be happy to disagree with you."

"What it is you're all in love with isn't teenage pussy. It's the *idea* of teenage pussy. It's that *Star Trek* thing's giving all of you those hard-ons. Going boldly where no man has gone before."

"Or just one or two others. I wouldn't, myself, be that particular. Virgins, you know . . ."

"Overrated," Gunther declared.

"Well, it's that risk of crying, and I really hate it when a babe cries in bed. But still, that teenage thing? You'll have to go a long way to convince me and any other swinging dick comes through that door over there."

Gunther's mind worked the problem until inspiration clicked. "I know how to settle this. Really prove it. Blind test, like the Pepsi challenge. They blindfold you, say, 'Here, drink this—now, which is better?' Like that, except with pussy." He could feel every neuron firing with brilliance. "Promote something like that, you could make a fortune. Vegas'd be out, but in Nye County, say, nice and legal? Get, maybe, a sixteen-year-old side by side with a forty-year-old. Guy antes up for the test, puts on the blindfold, then gets to hop in each saddle. Then he votes, which was better, one or two? *Then* we'll see who gives the better ride. Ten to one the majority vote comes back for the experienced woman."

Gunther's head swam with possibilities. Tapping his glass on the bar, he listened to the sound of dollars racking up as clearly as the dead thud of slot machine rollers behind him, some guy feeding it his paycheck a dollar at a time. Pulling the bandit's arm, settled into a rhythm that even Jehovah couldn't interrupt.

"Shit, I really should be checking into this. This could be the next big thing to hit Nevada."

Kevin nodded. "It's an inventive concept, all right."

"I need a new line of work anyway. Those Guidos'll have me thumping heads and lugging bags forever. Just can't get ahead." Gunther feeling itchy; better still, lucky. He slapped a hundred-dollar bill onto the bar. "Shot of tequila. My special deluxe."

"Aw, shit, Gunther," Kevin moaned. "When'll you ever give up on this? You never nail it, every time you miss I lose one more bottle back there—sometimes two—and I have to patch another hole in the wall. Not to mention cleaning up the mess."

Gunther blinked at him. "Yeah, so?"

"*And* someday you're gonna fucking kill somebody in here, and then the only pussy we'll be arguing about's the kind we're buying down in the prison laundry with a carton of smokes."

Gunther slapped another hundred atop the first.

"Well, okay," Kevin said. "But just this once more."

He racked open the register to cover his action, four hundred on the bar, while he set things up. First the shot of José Cuervo, looking like an ounce and a half of yellow bile. Then the saltshaker and a wedge of freshly cut lime.

Gunther flexed his shoulders, cracked his neck to one side, then the other; twisted his spine with a satisfying pop. Then he chambered a round in his Glock 9mm and tucked the muzzle in his waistband, loose, for an easy draw. "Peter Gunn" tearing through his head, all macho-heavy bass and brass.

Gunther licked the back of his hand, the thick triangular web inside the left thumb; tapped a sprinkle of salt on the wet spot.

"Take cover!" Kevin shouted, and from the perimeter came the sounds of clinking glass, scrambling feet—and that same cretin on the slot machine, refusing to break his mechanical stride.

Gunther licked away the salt, then tossed back the shot of Cuervo. He was lightning, he was thunder. With a sharp clack he slammed the shot glass back to scarred wood, an instant away from giving it a hard flick down the length of the bar, when the door banged open, and a harsh flood of desert light seared his eyes—

And everything was lost. He slumped where he stood.

"Fate intervenes," Kevin said with glee and no little relief. Gunther lowered his head to the bar, his prime moment dissolving into anticlimax while footsteps clicked toward him and Kevin swept away the shot glass and ate the lime himself.

"The money stays," Gunther said, but Kevin would have none of it, so Gunther had to raise his head and give him the look, *the* look he had long ago cultivated for deadbeats who didn't pay their debts. The look that promised pain and disfigurement, all those troubles that could be avoided if one was reasonable enough to see things the way they really were: Gunther's way.

Men like Kevin forgot sometimes—men who remembered what it was like to hurt another man, but just barely. For them it was all in the past, the only blood they saw now from the scraped knees of their kids. Families softened a man, but all it took to remind them of primordial reality was one annihilating glare.

"Interference," Kevin said, quieter now. "Nobody's fault."

Gunther nodded. "Play over."

"Not *this* routine again. Oh, would you just grow up one day." Madeline limped over and slid onto the next barstool. Limping? *This* should be good. "Honestly—cut you open and a five-year-old would crawl out."

He scowled. "Your timing's for shit today. I was on a roll."

"Oh yeah? If that were the worst of our problems right now, well then, this world would be such a happy place I don't think I could stand it."

"Something's wrong?"

Madeline gazed at the pack of Virginia Slims pulled from her purse. "Something's wrong, he asks." She gave him a sideways look, reeking of low tolerance. "Once again that keen brain of yours has grasped the obvious."

She lit her own cigarette. Only once had he made the mistake of trying to light one for her, ten minutes after they'd first met when she had dropped by Two-Eyed Jacks to scout table talent.

The downtown grind joint had been built more than twenty years ago on a loan from the Teamsters Central States Pension Fund and had been laundering money ever since for the two generations of loan-sharking Guidos who were its silent partners: Toby Costas and his father before him. Gunther worked collections, employed above-board by Two-Eyed Jacks as security, meaning he came in whenever he pleased and sat around watching the dancers while waiting to eject a rowdy, or to be unleashed to terrify a suspected card counter away from the blackjack tables.

The day Madeline walked in, she couldn't help but catch his eye. After three numb hours of staring at shimmying silicone and saline implants, he had found her the most real and finely seasoned thing in the room.

He had earnestly believed lighting her cigarette to be the gentlemanly thing to do. Instead she'd tried to burn his hand with her lighter, and he'd drawn his fist back to his chest, crinkling his nose at the stink of flash-fried hair. Nothing was worse than that smell. His hormones made an instant leap from lust to love.

"Shouldn't you be at the Coast now?" he asked.

"Yep." Plumes of smoke went gusting up through the sprig of coppery bangs that brushed her forehead. "He blew town today."

"Who did?" Gunther realized then that there was only one *he* in the world at this point that mattered. "Not Boyd, don't you go telling me it's that numbnuts Boyd . . ."

"Looks like the big jackpot for *you,* Gunther."

He tried to see the bright side. "So you stop skimming his table now, we're still seven hundred grand ahead."

"It gets worse. I didn't find it until today, but yesterday when he was at my place, he trashed my hard copies of the deposit records, all the statements. He closed out the local account that we were routing through into the Caymans. You and I, we can't get to that money. Only he can now."

Gunther gawped with dull horror. For a day that had begun with as much promise as any day, it really was turning to guano, one thing after another before he'd even left this barstool.

"Any particular reason he left?" Gunther asked. "Or you think maybe you just drove him away all by your own charming self?"

"What are you implying by that?"

Head in hand, leaning heavily on the bar, Gunther motioned to Kevin—two glasses of anything, just make them strong. "I mean maybe Boyd starts getting the idea he hangs around you much longer, he'll wind up with a crotch like a Ken doll, watching you barbecue whatever you managed to cut away."

Madeline jabbed the cigarette at him. "Don't you start with me, Gunther, don't you *dare.* As far as Boyd Dobbins is concerned, I was the frigging geisha girl he'd always wanted."

Gunther snorted. "Not that you see too many geisha girls with stretch marks."

"I'm closing my eyes now. And I'm counting to ten. If you

say one word before I'm finished—one word—then I swear I will find the sharpest thing in my purse and stick it through your hand."

Kevin brought two whiskeys, neat, a welcome diversion. While Madeline counted, Gunther drank and thought how remarkable his forbearance with her had been these past months. It was the rare man who could step aside and let his woman make time with another man. Madeline had opened both her home and legs to Boyd Dobbins, a purely mercenary act, knowing that his rogue dingus was the key to controlling the rest of him. But mercenary motives made them no less naked on those afternoons when Boyd dropped by before their shifts at the Ivory Coast, dealer and pit boss in bed together in more ways than one.

Gunther had insisted on hiding in the bedroom closet one day, the acid test—could he handle this infidelity for the duration? He found that he could. Amazingly pragmatic about the situation. That Madeline most workday afternoons wrapped her erstwhile showgirl's legs around Boyd's frantically bobbing ass and begged for mercy was just a cost of doing business. Still, Gunther *did* look forward to the day when he would put a bullet through Boyd's head. Call it Boyd's cost of doing business.

And Boyd Dobbins had hoodwinked them both? Somebody at this bar had committed a serious judgmental error.

Madeline made it to ten, then tipped back her whiskey. "His girlfriend found out about us. I don't know how—maybe Boyd talks in his sleep. Like I'd know what he does in his sleep? She showed up at my place yesterday afternoon five minutes after he got there and went on a rampage. Corn-fed-looking bitch, you know what she did? She destroyed that big fern out on the deck. Started throwing cactus all over, even tried to hit me with one. I was picking spines out of my foot all day."

When Madeline sighed, he could tell the drink was working a calming magic on her.

"Last night Boyd and I went on like usual. Honestly, Gunther, I didn't have any idea he was planning on running out. We've only skimmed a little over seven hundred thousand—who quits there? State lotteries, nobody even much notices anymore until they get into eight figures."

"So let me guess." Gunther was ready for the bottom line. "Everything's just peachy, you think, until you get to work this afternoon and there's a vacancy at Boyd's table."

"I stayed awhile, then told the shift boss I was getting sick—blamed it on oysters from the bar. He bought it. Six people got sick last week from the slimy things."

"Boyd go by himself, you think, or you think maybe he took your little cactus-tosser with him?"

"No, she's still around, I just came from there. She thinks it was just the sex, she doesn't have a clue."

"Maybe that was an act. Maybe Boyd left her behind to wrap up some business and she'll meet him later."

"My ass. He's left her as high and dry as he left me. And she didn't see it coming. Any woman knows that look when she sees it. You wouldn't understand."

Gunther sighed. A man could get tired of hearing that. To hear Madeline tell it, when a mood was upon her, if he was covered with poison ivy he wouldn't understand scratching.

"I'll tell you what I *do* understand." He killed off the whiskey and motioned to Kevin for a replay on the shot of tequila. "Boyd Dobbins has planted himself on the receiving end of some serious truculence."

Madeline's glass froze halfway to her lips. She looked at him sideways, almost a frown, nearly a laugh, close to worry. Just the oddest expression.

"Truculence?"

"Yeah." He nodded grimly. Skimmed a hand through his hair so that it stood on electric end, watching Kevin fill the shot glass. "Means terror, pain . . . you know . . . horrible things."

"Yeah, but *truculence?*" Madeline was scrunching up her face. "That's a stupid-sounding word. Especially coming from you."

"You got some problem with it?" His itchy feeling returned when he saw Kevin's knife split the green peel of the lime. "Let me tell you something. You don't know this, but last week, when you called me a maladroit humanoid, I went out and bought myself a dictionary. Yeah, I looked it up. And what I been doing since is, every day I learn a new word. So: truculence! I like that word a lot, so maybe you should just get used to hearing it."

"Oh, Gunther." She leaned in closer to him, curling one slim hand around his croquet-ball biceps and giving it a squeeze. "You're so cute when you try to prove you have an intellect."

He grinned and looped an arm around her shoulders, then waved her back away from the bar, as Kevin once again set before him the accoutrements of wager. Rituals were repeated, from the cracking of knuckles to the tapping of salt, to Kevin's bark of warning to all who watched:

"Take cover!"

Gunther licked the salt away, dropped the shot of Cuervo down his throat in one gulp. Smacked the glass to the bar and gave it a smooth flick to his left, down the runway like a draft beer in a western movie. He slid backward off his stool, pivoting clockwise on one heel and drawing his Glock while on the spin. His right arm was whipped up and out by the time he braked at a three-quarters turn and snapped a bead on the skittering glass. He squeezed the trigger, nothing to rely on but instinct. Chips of wood flew from a gouge across the bar, and a bottle against the wall burst with a thick nut-brown splatter.

Then the final insult: the sound of the shot glass clattering onto the floor.

"Shit!" he screamed.

"Nice going, Gunther," said Kevin. "You nailed the Bailey's Irish this time. That's a first."

"That was mine!" came a voice from across the room. Some guy crawling from beneath a table with a forty-watt grin. "*I* had the Bailey's. I'll take that in twenties, if you please."

Gunther went chasing after the obstinate glass as it bounced across the floor. He trapped it against the wall and kicked at it until it cracked apart, and he was still trying to stomp it into a fine powder when Madeline slipped both hands around his arm and drew him away, told him to stop, that he looked like a psychotic groom at a Jewish wedding.

He put the gun away, took a few deep breaths of smoky air to calm his nerves, and only then did it register what was going on at the bar: Kevin paying off someone else.

"What am I seeing here, brief me on this," said Gunther. "You got a betting pool going on whatever I might hit *instead*?"

"I thought you knew." Kevin shrugged. "You want to play Quick Draw McGraw, fine, but I'm the one incurring the expenses. Forget the Bailey's—you been pricing spackle and paint lately?"

Gunther sighed, let Madeline guide him out the door and onto the parking lot, a dusty slab of baked asphalt with a low-rent strip club and an X-rated-video outlet for neighbors. Daylight was on the wane now and shadows were long; neon pulsed, and the heat of late summer wrapped around them like a suffocating cocoon.

"I think I'm drunk, Maddy." Then everything made sense. "Know what the problem is? Fucking Kevin, I let him pour me those drinks and trick me into spending too much time yakking before I take that shot."

"Sure," she said.

"Next time I ought to just go ahead, let him get me good and hammered, and then I 'accidentally' shoot him instead. Let's see how smart he thinks he is then."

"Sure, Gunther."

"Worst day of my life."

"Yours too?" Madeline gave him a chummy slap on the shoulder. "But that's the beauty of Vegas, Gunther. Your luck can turn around any minute in the day."

She had a point. It was exactly why he had come here in the first place. That, and those miserable winters back east.

Madeline looked at him with a feral grin, her rouged cheeks stretching taut and her eyes aglow with mayhem and maybe thoughts of the redress of wounds old and new. Her whisper in his ear was seduction itself:

"Gunther . . . ? Say *truculence* again."

chapter three

Allison Willoughby had the universe figured out by the time she was twenty-five, the last six years serving only to reinforce her understanding.

Physicists had for decades been seeking an equation to unify the laws of space and time, the clockwork of planets and atoms, and she felt pity for them. All their numbers, just so much chalk dust. If only they'd come to her in the first place, she would have been happy to fill them in on how it really was.

There was a playwright somewhere, making everything up as he went along. Perversely cruel at times, at others possessed of an equally perverse sense of humor. Scientists and atheists alike would scoff, but she knew that he was real; knew that he labored overtime on her script because some nights she could hear him up there somewhere, chuckling.

But perhaps he, in his zeal to keep the surprises coming, had done her a favor for once. She'd not had the courage to leave Boyd on her own? The playwright had shown her the worst sides of him, then written him out of her life. Free again, to go anywhere and do whatever she wished.

Allison's decision to leave Vegas was made as soon as she'd turned Madeline DeCarlo away from her door. An odd choice even for

Boyd, whose penis had proved to be as indiscriminate as a garden hose. Then there was Madeline's allusion to some seven-hundred-thousand-dollar windfall that he had failed to mention.

Which sounded ominous. She supposed she'd known, deep down, that Boyd would one day pull some too-clever stunt that would come boomeranging back at him. She wasn't about to stay put and see what he'd done and what its fallout would be.

Allison packed that night, the silent living room split down the middle. One side held all the belongings she thought she would need while traveling, the other was strewn with those that could be safely boxed away until they might reemerge into the light of some better place, some other life.

That everything could fit in one room was itself a shock, but after an honest appraisal of the way she'd been living, Allison understood where it all had gone. Clothes, once they no longer seemed to fit whoever she felt she'd become, were left in closets she would never open again, or were given to charity. Most books, once read, had been left on shelves that she'd never thought of as her own in the first place. Across Mississippi and Texas, Montana and California, Arizona and Washington and now Nevada, she had scattered bits of herself, shed skins left behind with friends and lovers whom she'd outgrown, or grown to fear, or even to loathe.

Appliances? Few, and small. Furniture? None. She had always preferred her homes prefurnished. Buy a sofa, drop an anchor.

Looking at the meager piles, Allison realized that she had always kept it easy to leave, and quickly. A seventeen-year-old runaway still hiding deep within, laying out her escape routes.

The next morning Allison was at her bank minutes after the doors were unlocked. Leaning against the fake-marble counter, she asked the teller to close out her checking account; cash would be fine. She gave the pert and fresh-faced teller an unused check, for the account number, then signed the forms slid before her. The two of them went over the recent stubs in her checkbook, and their amounts, to leave a reserve for anything outstanding.

Allison frowned when they got to the end and saw a blank stub preceding the check she'd just torn free. That couldn't be right. She kept impeccable records. Nevertheless, check number 331 was missing in action. She supposed it could've stuck to the back of 330—they did that sometimes.

"Here you go, Ms. Willoughby," said the teller, then began counting it out. "Thirty-three dollars and fifty-eight cents."

"No," Allison said. "Oh, no. No no no no no. I don't know what your computer's telling you, but even after deducting for the outstanding checks, I've still got over fifteen hundred dollars in my account."

The teller peered again at the computer screen, pecking away at the keyboard. Perfect little fingers with their perfect little nails, not so much as a single crinkle on her perfect little face. What was she, three months out of high school? Something was terribly wrong here; this candy striper was not qualified to sit on the other side of the counter, in charge of Allison's life.

"Well, you *did,* until yesterday. Then that big check you wrote came through, and that about cleaned out the account."

"*What* big check?"

"Check number three-thirty-one. For fourteen hundred and forty-two dollars, even. Both dated and cashed yesterday."

Allison gripped the counter, the floor trying to throw her off balance. "I didn't write any checks at all yesterday."

The teller's eyes flicked back to her computer. Her perfect little mouth constricted into a circle of surprise. "Uh-oh."

At which point bank officers became involved, drawing her away from the lobby and behind closed doors. Taking her by the arm, gently. The loved ones of accident victims would be treated this way, ushered into some cold chamber to view the carnage while thinking, *This isn't happening, there must be some mistake.*

They didn't let her handle the processed check, offering her instead a pair of photocopies, front and back. They feared she was going to lose control, rip the original into confetti? She would prefer to reserve that treatment for the one who'd forged it.

"Oh, that son of a bitch," she whispered.

"And you deny having written any checks to a Boyd Dobbins yesterday?"

"You're damn right I deny it. The only thing I would've written for Boyd Dobbins yesterday was a death certificate."

She pieced together what she could, imagining Boyd yesterday morning after his night on the couch—his shoulder a giant festering sore, she hoped—pilfering her purse as she slept off her Southern Comfort in the bedroom. Imagining him at the table where they'd shared so many breakfasts, glancing at the bedroom door, hoping she wouldn't walk in on him and his practiced pen.

As a forgery it was impressive—another talent she'd had no idea he possessed. Both his name and her signature appeared at a glance to have been penned by her own hand, although under the scrutiny of a trained eye discrepancies would surely be apparent.

But motive? With a seven-hundred-thousand-dollar windfall, Boyd obviously hadn't needed emergency cash. Which meant he had done this to her out of pure mean-spirited vindictiveness. He'd even left a message, so there would be no mistaking it.

In the check's lower left corner, where it said MEMO, he had written all she needed to know:

Damage to car.

Fifty minutes later she was home again, thirty-three dollars plus change extra in the pocketbook, which wasn't going to get her very far at all.

Allison clung to the phone, an iced tea sweating in her free hand as she listened to the ringing. *Answer.* How easy it was to get religion down in the trenches. *Please, make her answer. Make her answer and I'll never ask for anything again, until the next catastrophe. That ought to square us until day after tomorrow.*

For a moment, all of heaven and earth seemed to smile.

"Constance?" she said. "It's me."

"Allie!" Her cousin's voice still embraced the drawl that Allison had worked hard to leave behind on Mississippi soil. "Hey, Allie Cat, how's life treating you?"

"Like a winepress treats grapes."

Allison covered the highlights and pictured Constance moving through the house in Yazoo City, cordless phone clamped between ear and shoulder, left arm slung around a toddler that rode her hip and clutched at her breast with tiny hands.

"I'd been thinking that maybe I'd be able to find a cheap car today," Allison said, "with a few good miles left in it, and have enough left over to get me down the road a little. But now? Boyd didn't even leave me enough behind for a bus ticket."

"Why, you poor thing." The sixth time Constance had said this. Enough. "Allie? A bus ticket to *where,* exactly?"

The question stopped her cold. In the chaos, she'd not even been thinking of a destination. Las Vegas was such a blight that direction scarcely seemed to matter.

"I don't know," she said. "I just want to *go.* I want to get out of this apartment because it smells like Boyd, and out of this city because it eats souls."

"And that bank of yours? They're not planning on making good on that check when you didn't even write the thing?"

Allison felt her blood pressure surge. "Not their policy, they tell me. Don't you love it? They give my money to that human plankton, they nearly bankrupt me, and it's not their policy. It's a criminal matter now. For all they care, I could've put Boyd up to it myself, so we could try to double my money."

"They didn't *accuse* you of that, did they?"

"Not in so many words." Remembering the looks she'd gotten, though: emotionless sympathy with a gilding of suspicion. Perhaps she had spoken wrong, moved wrong, looked and smelled and breathed wrong. Never quite good enough for them. Perhaps she'd shown them flaws, that if they would scrape a few years away they could find devious white trash beneath. Scrape away a few more and they would find some tainted girl who used to lie awake in her room, awaiting and hating the tread of the visitors who came in the dark to lie with her, upon her, until their weight grew too heavy to bear, and she would push herself far away, into green meadows beneath brighter suns than morning could ever bring.

Riding horses—now that was a fine dream. Gallant horses with stout backs and wild, flowing manes, they had never grown tired of carrying her through those nights.

She almost found herself in tears, and forced them back. She would not let Constance hear that from her.

"Okay, Allie, let's break this mess down. How much money *do* you have left?"

"About fifty-six dollars."

"And suppose you wanted to get yourself a one-way bus ticket to Yazoo City if you knew you had a clean bed to sleep in once you got here. Do you know how much that'd set you back?"

"It'd be in the hundred-and-sixty-dollar range, around there. I priced them a couple of months ago when Boyd and I had a fight."

Constance began suggesting options, things she might not have considered. Was anything due from the day care center? No; she'd just been paid, and had been calling in sick ever since. Did she have a credit card? No; first you need an actual credit rating. Anything she could pawn? Maybe her bicycle, but it wouldn't bring much. How about a damage deposit from the apartment? Worth a try, but no guarantee.

"How about . . ." Allison said, faltering. "Is there any chance you could wire me the rest?"

She'd not wanted to ask so bluntly, but they had skirted the issue long enough. She supposed she'd been hoping the offer would be the first thing out of Connie's mouth. Something was wrong; the long silence confirmed it before Constance broke the news.

"I would if I had it to send you. You know I would." Allison could hear a small voice, and Constance took a moment to mollify the little boy saddled on her hip. "Sorry. Got a thirsty kid here. Randy saw the neighbor's dog drink out of the toilet last week and now it's his life's ambition. But, Allie? A couple months back,

Jefferson lost his job, and he's not found another one yet. We've got us a little bit coming in on unemployment, but Jeff's about to gulp down the last of his pride and apply for food stamps to tide us over. We'll find a way to put you up. We just can't pay your way here."

Allison apologized, wouldn't have asked if she'd had any idea.

"Oh, you hush. These things happen. Jeff, you know Jeff, God bless him, his idea of an advanced degree is on a thermometer, so something like this was bound to hit us sooner or later."

But of course it had hit now. Someday she was going to have to tell Constance about the playwright.

"Listen, Allie, maybe . . ." Constance stopped, Allison knowing what she was about to suggest. "I mean, seeing as how you *are* in a bind and all, have you considered your father?"

"That's out of the question. Absolutely not." Hearing that voice again after all these years, forcing herself to beg for his help—how he would relish that. Had probably been waiting fourteen years to hear it. She remembered him as a man with coarse hands and the scheming patience of a coiled snake. There was no reason to believe he would have changed, or even could.

"Just a suggestion, and a lousy one," said Constance. "But Allie? Maybe someday you could see him again, and if you don't want to see him at that house you could do it on neutral ground. I wasn't planning on telling you this, but I think maybe you should know it after all: My daddy told me that yours had bowel cancer last year. Says they got it all, but you know how cancer is."

Constance's father and Allison's late mother had been brother and sister. Uncle Conroy's infrequent checkups on the old man had been, ever since Allison had left, her sole source of news about him. Bowel cancer—so the old man had a weakness after all.

"What I mean to say is," Constance went on, "if he should up and die one of these days, and you get to thinking *then* you wish you'd seen him once more . . . well, you know what I'm saying?"

"He'll never die. He won't, Connie. Men like him, the devil just keeps on giving them more and more years. Why should they go on to hell when they do the devil so much prouder right here with the rest of us?"

"It really hurts me to hear you still talking this way."

Hurt. Hurt by talk alone. There was worse.

After they rang off, Allison went down to the manager's apartment to check with Doug Powell about a damage deposit refund. He met her in the same clothes he'd worn the other day when she'd borrowed his car; different comic book.

The smaller of two bedrooms served as an office, beneath the grubby residue of Doug's life. He had the housekeeping skills of a sloth but the file cabinet was in order. He looked over the lease.

"No can do," he said. His round face was soft and helpless as a baby's. Even his hair was infant-fuzzy, the drab color of cold dishwater. "It's a year's lease and you've only been here eight months. The rules are very specific about this. My hands are tied."

"Doug, if you'd haul yourself up the stairs and take a look, you'd see that apartment is in better shape now than when we moved in. We painted it. We wallpapered the kitchen. We paid to have the carpets cleaned." All this we-talk left a strange taste in her mouth. There was no *we* anymore. "Isn't that worth something?"

"This isn't my decision!" he squealed. "I don't decide these things! They don't *let* me! I don't even write the checks when they're authorized. They're mailed straight from the property owners' offices."

Silent, she glared. Behind round glasses, Doug's baby blues began to widen. Nervous around aggressive women, oh, was he ever.

"And . . . and besides . . . the lease isn't in your name, it's in Boyd's." He cast a hopeful look past her toward the door. "Where *is* Boyd, anyway? Is he coming down? I like Boyd."

"There is no more Boyd. Boyd's over the hills and far away, and you know what I say? If he makes it as far as the ocean, I hope his brakes go out."

Doug swabbed his forehead, and Allison pressed forward with sweat and steam, swaying wheat hair and seething menace.

"I know how we can work this out," she told him.

"Stay back. You stay right there."

"Change the lease to read eight months."

Doug looked horrified. "Alter the base terms of the lease? I can't do that!"

"You see that little bottle of Liquid Paper over there on the desk? Open it up and get to work. It'll take you maybe a minute."

He argued, he shuffled his feet and tugged absently at his T-shirt. Doug Powell reminded her of a recalcitrant child, any of dozens she'd dealt with at day care centers, except she couldn't threaten to phone his mother to come get him early.

Allison stormed out of the office and began a search of the rest of his apartment. Comics were everywhere, in cardboard crates and scattered across tabletops. She rummaged through stacks and tossed aside strays; they spilled to the floor as Doug begged her to stop. She settled on one most likely to be ransomed—the gray cover drawn to look like a tombstone, big "S" insignia chiseled into the rock, and the epitaph HERE LIES EARTH'S GREATEST HERO. Doug froze as she held it poised for ripping.

"If you can't write the check yourself, okay, you can't write the check. But I want that damage deposit back, or I'll use this *Superman* here for confetti to celebrate my way out of town."

"That—that's the Superman Death issue." Doug held his hands out before him. "Do you have any idea how much those are going for now, with some dealers?"

"You'd better hope it's a lot less than my two-hundred-and-fifty-dollar deposit, or you might not see it again."

Doug tottered over to a chair and sat. Men were such children sometimes. The trick to manipulating them was to simply figure out which toys were their favorites, then get your hands on them.

"Suppose I change the lease. Do I get the book back then?"

"I'll mail it to you the day the check clears."

He grabbed a pen, sighing, surrendering with everything but a white flag. "I'll need a forwarding address."

. . .

She borrowed Doug's car again—at this point he would accede to anything to get her out of his hair. With her belongings out of the apartment, Allison went first to the police and filed theft charges against Boyd, then pawned her bicycle to inflate her bankroll by another fifty-five dollars. Cash outflow was immediate and painful, two boxes of belongings stamped for a fourth-class crawl to Constance's door.

In early afternoon she stopped by the day care center to give her resignation in person. To make her goodbyes to coworkers, the months of days and laughs starting to weigh on her heart; she had fit in here. But telling the children was worse. She knelt on the floor to give slow, squeezing hugs to those with whom she'd especially bonded . . . they having seen something in her that they wanted to love or be loved by, she having seen something in them that she felt a need to protect. They looked at her now, not understanding, smooth faces marred by hurt.

I'm teaching you an awful lesson, she wanted to explain, but they wouldn't understand this, either. *People leave you, or turn their backs on you, and even though that's what life is and you have to learn that . . . I'm sorry I'm the one you're learning it from today.*

She returned to the apartment building in midafternoon, life once again winnowed down to its mobile essence, everything in one large battered suitcase and a shoulder-slung duffel. She knocked on Doug's door, had to knock again before bringing movement from the other side. At a dimming of light in the peephole, she held his car keys in view, jingling them. He unlocked the door.

Such a difference a few hours made. Doug was holding a damp, bloodstained washcloth to his nose. Looking at her with two puffy eyes, rimmed underneath with purple crescents.

"I thought you told me Boyd was gone," he said.

That name. That terrible name. "He was here? *Boyd* did that?"

"You missed him by about half an hour. I don't know what it is he's so pissed off about, but he sure is, and he's looking for you." Doug's voice had the stuffy sound of a bad cold. "All I told him was that you'd moved out, you were gone already. I didn't say you'd be back later with the car. I didn't tell him anything else, honest I didn't."

She could not fathom this. Boyd—thief, forger, two-timer—had abandoned her, then had the nerve to come back angry? Drawing blood? Just more proof that Boyd's brain had been dropping screws all over the desert.

"File an assault complaint," she told Doug. "Call the police and swear out another warrant against him. That'll make two in one day, maybe they'll look a little harder for him."

Doug said he would, sure, get right on that—but there was no heart to it. She knew he had no intention of following through, that the last thing he would want now was to provide chuckles for a couple of cops who could find the lighter side of a beheading.

Allison touched his cheek with gentle fingertips. What shame he had to be feeling, buried in that sad and doughy physique. No Man of Steel was Doug Powell.

"I'm sorry. I really am sorry he did that to you."

Doug sniffed, dabbing at his swollen nose. "I thought I liked Boyd. Well, I don't like him much anymore."

"You and me both. We're a growth industry." She leaned in on tiptoe to kiss Doug's other cheek. "I'll print up the membership cards, you write the club charter."

This brought a lopsided grin and half a laugh. Allison handed him his car keys, and he wished her all the best of luck, whatever she was planning on doing next. She turned to go, then dug into the duffel bag.

"This is yours," she said, and gave him the purloined comic. "Just . . . do what you can."

And the way he held it to his chest, as if it were the most precious thing he'd ever owned, sent her off wondering what would become of him. If he would ever truly live, or remain content to do it vicariously through the exploits of tall heroes in bright underwear.

She walked several blocks, where she could catch a bus that would carry her south, to the fringe of the city, where highways beckoned and dreams could rekindle, and where she might once more cast her fate to the winds, and in with the kindness of strangers.

chapter four

Some days it just didn't pay to use your head.

Yesterday morning Boyd Dobbins had left Vegas feeling like the king of the world. He was Midas, his touch was golden. He was seven hundred thousand dollars wealthier and invincible. Transfuse his blood into the infirm and the old and they'd be up dancing. A man with his prospects needn't sweat the small stuff, either. Sore shoulder? He laughed it off; would have the stiffness worked out in a few more days. Dented roof and cracked windshield? As long as Allison had reimbursed him for the damage, with no insurance claim to risk jacking up his premiums, certainly he was adult enough to bear her no grudges.

He didn't even mind the scorching drive from Vegas to Los Angeles—I-15, south of Death Valley, all ugly brown desert, steep hills, and withered scrub too stubborn to die. These sterile miles Boyd enlivened with rocking stereo wattage, the soulful wail of his voice, and steering-wheel drum solos.

Los Angeles lay before him, spread open wide, as inviting and ripe as a mango. With a new name and new fortune, swimming pools and movie stars, a man could shed his past here and find his true destiny, in this twisted Shangri-La.

And then he got there, and in less than a day that glorious Midas touch had to go all hinky on him.

Truly, this was a malign universe.

His first stop was Pasadena and his brother Derek, who no one ever believed could be his brother. Stand them side by side and skeptics shook their heads. Brothers three, the Dobbins boys, and each had stepped away from the genetic roulette wheel with the lion's share of something.

Youngest brother Malcolm had gotten the voice, was working FM radio in Boston. Boyd, in the middle, saw no reason for false modesty, knowing that he'd come away with the looks. Dark-haired, dark-eyed, with long lashes and an easy crooked grin that made him appear more shy than he'd ever truly been, he was an irresistible choirboy that women wanted to take home and corrupt.

Good looks, velvet voice . . . he and Malcolm had been far, far luckier than elder brother Derek.

Derek had gotten the bones.

Maybe their mom had overdosed on calcium supplements during that first pregnancy. Derek's arms and legs had grown and grown—long, massive, clublike. His spine was a birch trunk, his rib cage the size of a whiskey barrel; his skull looked as big and hard as an iron kettle, seeming to stretch the skin painfully tight. For the past eight years he'd owned a discount stereo outlet on East Colorado Boulevard in Pasadena, Boyd wondering if his success was less a factor of price than sheer physical presence. Some poor music lover walks in to browse, sees Derek ambling over like a shaved lowland gorilla, and fears that if he tries to walk out without buying anything, his arms will be torn from their sockets.

So Derek was tall. So Derek's shadow could cause bladders to spontaneously void. Boyd looked over the whole package deal, what could have befallen him in the facial department, and felt none too bad about standing a mere five foot seven. One consolation—he fit into his Daytona more comfortably than Derek.

"What happened to your car?" Derek pointed at the spiderweb of cracks down the windshield.

"Suitcase blew off somebody's luggage rack on the highway. I guess they didn't have it tied down tight enough. I see that thing coming, bam." He shook his head. "I was so cool under fire. Didn't even swerve half a lane's width. I should be a stuntman out here."

"Uh-huh," said Derek. Just sitting there with that gigantic head of his, staring through the damage. "Boyd? Do I look like I'm suffering from a bullshit deficiency?"

Boyd rolled his eyes. Just no slipping one past big brother. Derek had watched him grow up from a five-year age advantage, and learned all Boyd's tricks when they were boys lucky enough to have parents who'd believe black was white, if the point was argued persuasively enough.

"Allison," he confessed. "Allison and a big-ass flowerpot. So listen, while we're at it? Don't go punching my right shoulder, whatever you do."

Derek laughed, the taunting and delighted laugh that only an older brother could deliver. "Allison, still?"

"And a big-ass cactus."

Derek laughed again, relishing his miseries. "And she sounded so even-tempered and sweet, the way you described her. Me, I'd've guessed it'd been that real ballbreaker you told me about. Your pit boss from the casino, what was her name again?"

"Madeline. Madeline DeCarlo." A shudder. Los Angeles in early September, sidewalks that could fry eggs, but with one mention of Madeline the temperature plunged forty degrees. "I deserve combat pay. And medals. *And* an Academy Award. God have mercy, that woman could make Rambo cry."

No wonder she was all alone. Most men probably took one look at her and foresaw imminent castration. Divorced four years ago—this much he knew about her, and she had a teenage daughter who'd opted to live with her father up in Lake Tahoe. The only thing Boyd wondered was what had kept them from fleeing any sooner.

He still found himself puzzled by that initial desire he had felt for Madeline when she'd lured him from Cactus Dirk's to the Ivory Coast. Dozens of other dealers and change girls and waitresses had been more his type: younger, cuter, less traveled. Maybe it was the way she'd moved—legs whose stride hinted at some ripened potency that years and mileage could not erode.

Admittedly, he'd not been free of self-interest. Madeline was, after all, casino brass, and her favor would do his career no harm. Then she'd put forth the suggestion that they skim the take from his table. It was a win-win situation, really.

As Boyd drove, Derek directed him along freeways and local mains, down into the heart of East Hollywood, where Derek said he could purchase the raw ore of a new identity. Big business down here, catering primarily to the illegals up from Mexico, in need of documentation for work and benefits and phony citizenship.

Boyd eyeballed the lay of the land—bodegas and liquor stores with barred windows, shabby storefronts and skeletal remnants that had been burned out years ago in the riots, and cars that didn't appear to have been running for at least that long. Music thudded, each bass note pounding hard as a railroad spike, while lowriders banged up and down along the streets on hydraulic chassis. And everywhere, on every wall, graffiti demarcated asphalt into boundaries. He looked at all the brown faces, began to feel pale and obvious, positively Scandinavian.

"Just let me do the talking," said Derek. "And you *listen* to me, I *know* you—you want to poke some guy's sister, you keep it to yourself, hear?" Derek motioned him toward a curbside roost, went on as Boyd wheeled over: "Long as everybody respects each other, it's cool down here, these guys'll give you no grief. The cholos, the marielitos . . . basically honorable guys, I've found. A lot more chilled out than most of the blacks, and nobody's holding you personally responsible for four hundred years of slavery."

"What are you saying, you've done some sort of business with these guys before?"

"These barrios down here, everybody went riot-crazy after the Simi Valley verdict, but how many do you think really gave a shit those cops got off for playing stickball with Rodney King? It was just an excuse to loot." Derek shrugged. "Some stereos got looted, some looters needed a place to move them, I sell stereos . . . you do the math, little brother."

Boyd nodded with admiration. Urban wartime profits were to be made, and where had he been? Up in Seattle trying to sell swimming pools and spas to people who'd just as soon finger him as one more multimillion-dollar defendant should their clumsy kids drown.

The new ID process couldn't have gone more smoothly, and offered curbside service. An entrepreneurial teenage gang-banger in Air Jordans served as a runner between the car window and one of the scabby buildings. Twenty-five minutes and $120 later, Boyd had a new Social Security card and birth certificate. The kid said he could throw in a green card, too, for that base price, although Boyd declined. With the two new documents, the kid explained, he now had all he needed to obtain a new driver's license, sign up for government benefits . . . all the same advantages of life he had enjoyed as Boyd Dobbins, but with none of the entangling legal baggage, should any come back to haunt.

"Well worth it, of course," Boyd said minutes later, back on the freeway, "but this new name, I don't know. Look at me, I don't look like a Peter Wackermann. Do you think I look like a Peter Wackermann?"

"What's a Peter Wackermann supposed to look like, anyhow?"

"Wears glasses. Was a fat kid who got beat up a lot. Probably Jewish. A chronic masturbator for sure, but he feels guilty about it. Not one of these things applies to me."

Scowling, Boyd began stabbing a finger at the radio presets; sombrero music, that's all he could find all of a sudden. A cosmic joke had just been played, he was sure of it. It made him think of something Allison had once told him, about this playwright who scripted people's lives as comedies, as tragedies. He'd not quite grasped the concept then, had needed more time for it to sink in; thought he finally understood now.

"Peter Wackermann . . . this is really starting to feel hinky. Those beaners, they're having me off, I *know* they are! Back me up on this, Derek, I'm turning this car around and making them give me a real name."

Derek reached over to seize the steering wheel with one giant monkey's paw.

"No. No, you're not. We're gonna go get you your new driver's license now, and you'll sit there marveling at what a wonderful Caucasian name Peter Wackermann is." When Boyd reluctantly nodded, Derek released the wheel. "You go back there, assuming your mouth doesn't get you killed, you know what'll happen? They'll send you on your way, and from then on you'll be spending the rest of your life trying to explain to people why Pop named you Juan Valdez."

He had a point. Huge ugly head like that, and Derek could score points on a wide variety of subjects.

"Besides, I'll tell you what Peter Wackermann is like," Derek went on. "Peter Wackermann's a guy who's got over seven hundred thousand dollars coming to him, and he's got a very patient big brother who's only requesting a token thousand-dollar finder's fee for connecting him with the guy who'll help him get his hands on it. Now, does Peter Wackermann sound like such a bad guy to be?"

Boyd smiled. He was centered again, calm, seeing the big picture. "Okay, now who's this guy you're taking me to tomorrow?"

"His name's Wayne Chang. Except people call him Wang Chung. You know . . . that band? Everybody have fun tonight . . . ?"

"Everybody Wang Chung tonight, yeah! I love that song."

"Guy's a top-shelf hacker. Just sits in front of his computer day and night, exploring, tinkering, covering his tracks. What he's really living for is the day some neural interface system comes along so he can jack directly into his brain, never have to leave the chair again. Just fall right into the whole Internet."

"Sounds like the model of mental health. How much does he want for doing this job?"

"A five percent commission on the gross."

"*Five percent?* That's over thirty-six thousand dollars!" Boyd moaned, profit margins being cannibalized before his eyes. "I thought he'd just charge a flat fee, a few grand at most. It's only one afternoon's work."

Derek was laughing again. "Listen, you're just lucky he's not your agent. Then he'd be skimming ten to fifteen off the top."

Boyd relented. Sacrificing five percent of something was better than retaining a full hundred of nothing. A complicated business was embezzlement in this befuddling age of computers and international banking. Gone were the simpler days of the classic after-hours raid on the boss's safe, then heading for the border.

"Speaking of skimming," said Derek, "you've got to tell me how you pulled this thing off. I'm dying to know."

"Well, to understand that," Boyd began, "you have to first understand that the beauty of the casino business is that nobody knows what the exact cash flow at a table is at any given time. I start my shift with an empty drop box and a rackful of chips, and this is the simplest it ever gets, because of the different kinds of exchange mediums we deal with. And how fast it all changes. I get cash whenever somebody buys into the game, but I also get foreign chips from other casinos, credit slips whenever I send any chips back to the vault, plus markers from gamblers playing on credit, and, the best part for *our* purposes, the fill slips that report the chips coming in from the cashier's cage all night."

Derek nodded. "I can see how this system begs for abuse."

"And I answered the call. Accounting scrutinizes everything to make sure it balances out, and it damn well better, but that's after the fact. While the table's active there's no way in hell of knowing how much of what is supposed to be there."

He went on to explain the importance of the fill slips, made out in triplicate by four signatories as a control measure so the amount of the chip fill was verified. Boyd himself was required to sign them, as dealer, as was Madeline, the pit boss; and they were also signed by the cage cashier and a security runner. The system was employed to keep everyone honest, and generally it did, except when all four participating signatories conspired to tinker with the numbers: say, signing for large amounts, but delivering small ones, and clandestinely pocketing the difference.

"So you had four people in on this instead of just you and Madeline?" Derek asked.

"Wouldn't have worked, otherwise. But the other two weren't in on the take. They only went along with it because Madeline had made a video of these two guys going at it during some employees' party. This was before I ever started working there. I'm not even clear on what was on the tape. Myself, I have no problem with two guys with the hots for each other. Whatever two or more people feel like doing in the privacy of a toilet stall, that's their business. But apparently this was some pretty kinko stuff."

"You weren't even curious enough to watch the tape?"

"I gathered it involved a copious exchange of bodily fluids. But the kicker was, the cashier's a Mormon. Really uptight group. Loads of Mormons in the casino industry, but the church won't let them work at the actual games, just the management and credit end of things. I don't understand the logic myself, but who am I to judge? So Madeline, she threatens to not only send a copy of this tape to the guy's family, but his church, too. That first night when she called us all together to tell those two how it was going to be? They cried, Derek. They broke down and cried."

"Ugly scene. That's cold, man. That is *cold*."

Boyd explained that when their shift was over, with the chips converted back to cash, he and Madeline would take the skim to the night depository of a bank, where they had an account in the name of a dummy company they'd set up on paper.

"Back up a minute," Derek said. "Who was converting it back for you? Because for sure none of you four could walk up to the cash-out windows."

"Yeah, you definitely need an outsider for that. I'm not sure who it was, though. Madeline told me I didn't need to know, it'd be safer that way. She just let him keep a little of the take each night. Easy money for him. So I never met him, just saw him from behind in the casino a time or two. Big blond guy."

"Uh-huh." Derek was sounding less impressed all the time.

On most afternoons, Boyd went on, he ran by Madeline's condo for carnal jubilee, then with his laptop computer and its built-in modem, they would access their bank's PC services and have the money deposited the previous night or two wired offshore into an account at another bank in the Cayman Islands. He kept electronic records in the laptop, and Madeline received the bank statements in a post office box she had rented for the dummy business.

"Why the Caymans?" Derek wanted to know.

"Hey, if it's good enough for drug lords."

Derek shook his head. "This is sounding like a hell of a lot of trouble. Why didn't you two just keep the cash liquid while you had it? What's wrong with a locker at the airport, or a shoebox?"

"That was our safety net in case we got caught. Look, the way a casino works isn't theftproof, but they do give it their best shot. What we were doing was extremely high-risk, and if we were going to get caught, they wouldn't have nabbed us first thing—the Gaming Control Board would've had us under surveillance awhile. So if I'm making trips to a locker, they know where the money is. If it's in my apartment, their goon squad tears the place apart. If I keep it in a U.S. bank, the account can be frozen just like that." Boyd snapped his fingers. "And I can't get to it. This way, it may be inconvenient, but at least it's *accessible* in the end."

"Assuming you aren't rotting in jail."

"Well, I took precautions there, too. Some nights I'd skim a few hundred directly off the drunkest players. You can tell when they're having too good a time to count their chips. You have to be careful of the eye-in-the-sky cameras in the ceiling, but I'm good enough with my hands. Palm one, or skip it back into the chip rack and block the view with my arm. So if I was ever caught, what I was hoping might happen would be, okay, I lose my job and they take away my sheriff's card to deal and maybe I get blacklisted by the entire industry, but they're reluctant to prosecute because I've been doing the public, too. Skimming off the casino, that's one thing, but the players . . . ? I go to court over it, then it's public information, and they've got a public relations nightmare on their hands. I mean, we're talking about people who went ballistic when the stuffed elephant lost a tusk and made some kids cry. How many changes of underwear you think they'll go through if it gets out one of their dealers has been skimming the gamblers? Fruit of the Loom doesn't even make enough."

Derek congratulated him on how well he had thought it through and immediately asked how he planned on keeping Madeline from accessing the money. Boyd told him how he'd closed out the local dummy account before leaving Vegas—Madeline's signature being one of the easier to forge he had come across, unlike Allison's, with all her loopy letters—and he'd destroyed her bank statements the previous afternoon following the fit Allison had thrown.

"I grabbed them while Madeline was picking cactus spines out of her foot. She had a load of laundry going and I stuck them down in the wash." Boyd shrugged. "It was an impulse thing."

"And you're counting on her not raising a fuss at the bank?"

"It might look awfully suspicious on her part, wouldn't you think? Drawing attention to herself like that?"

"Could be, but I'm thinking you shouldn't underestimate this woman." Derek tapped his anvil of a chin. "Clear something up for me. Madeline scouts you away from Cactus Dirk's and gets you on at the Ivory Coast. Okay, now: How long before she hits you with this idea to skim your table?"

"A couple of weeks."

"And she's got these two water sport enthusiasts on video already, before you ever got there. Right?"

"Right."

"How long before you first shtupped her?"

"One week," Boyd grumbled, disliking this what-have-you-done-now tone of voice from his bone-headed Goliath of a brother.

"And you don't see what she's up to the whole time? Guarantee you she was trolling the grind joints for just the right guy. You stupid weenie, she must've turned cartwheels the day she met you. When your pants drop, you turn into a pull-toy. Well, it's a good thing you're sticking it to her right now, because she'd've been sticking it to you one day, and probably with that big blond dude she never let you meet."

Boyd huffed with indignation. "I made the earth move for that woman. She wouldn't dare."

"No? Nothing I've heard about this woman reminds me of sainthood yet. You're better off rid of her."

Derek had a point again. Not knowing the vindictive lengths to which Madeline might—or even could—go to sour his life and recovery of the money, Boyd had thought the safest route to take would be to disappear altogether, not even go near that seven hundred thousand by conventional means.

All he needed was for this Wang Chung character to hack his way down to the Cayman Islands bank and bring that money back up in such a way that it was accessible to Peter Wackermann. But it would have to be sprinkled into different accounts, lots of them, in relatively small sums, as federal law required all transactions in excess of ten thousand dollars to be reported to the IRS. He most definitely wanted to avoid notice by them.

"Would you trust this Wang Chung if it was your money?" Boyd asked. "Say once he has everything set up for me, as soon as we step out the door, what's to keep him from going right back and transferring my money into his own accounts? It's not like I'd have any legal recourse, is it?"

"Relax. He's not so much a thief as he's an anarchist. So by doing this job for you, he gets to stick it to the system. Don't ask me what system, he's never that specific. Just as long as some corporation suffers a loss, he's happy, and he won't have any interest in sticking it to you."

"Yeah? If that's how he gets his chuckles, why doesn't he do this for me for free?"

"Scratch an anarchist, find an entrepreneur," Derek said. "I never met one yet who'd rather burn money instead of a flag."

. . .

By late evening, at Derek's Altadena condo, Boyd was tucked away for the night in the spare bedroom with most of a celebratory bottle of champagne fizzing in his belly. He looked over his new driver's license, trying to ramrod a mental connection between his handsome, mustachioed face and the name Peter Wackermann. *Height: 5'7"*. Damn. Should've thought to fudge an extra inch or two.

It occurred to him that his car was still registered to Boyd Dobbins. A small incongruity like that could trip him up badly down the road. Tomorrow he'd have to remember to ask Wang Chung about hacking into the Nevada Department of Motor Vehicles, to do some rechristening—if his five percent included that perk, as well. Dinky state bureaucracy, how hard could it be?

Boyd decided against trusting this to memory. Better to word-process a note to himself, something they would see as soon as he switched on the laptop tomorrow.

Boyd set the computer on his bed, thumbed the twin releases of the lid lock, tilted up the screen. Couldn't remember having left a slip of paper in there last night, resting atop the keys.

It looked like Allison's handwriting, if sloppier, as though she had written the note while drunk. Last night the sweet reek of Southern Comfort was obvious as soon as he'd opened the door after coming home from the casino. Allison had roused herself after he'd decided to catch a few winks on the couch before hitting the road?

Dear asshole, it read. He couldn't figure this out at all. *So maybe we never loved each other, but you at least owed me some basic respect, and that redhead harridan wasn't it.* Then a furious cloud where she'd begun to write something, then scratched it out. *You can have your toy put back in shape whenever you're ready to apologize. On your KNEES. If I feel like it.* Then another scratch-out—her signature?—followed by some new terrorist's moniker: *The bitch you shouldn't have betrayed.*

"What are you talking about?" Boyd cried to the note. He switched on the computer, to see what she'd done. "I loved you!"

Truly, he had, loving nearly everything about her and trying daily to remind her what those things were. A veritable goddess, she was, if a little crazy in the head now and again. She had to realize he wouldn't have invited just any woman to move to Vegas with him. And with Allison there'd even been the possibility of a future. Had she never learned of Madeline, he would have wanted it to be the two of them heading for L.A., together. But no, she'd had to force the situation prematurely, turn it vicious and ugly.

It was a sorely punishing loss. Allison was everything he'd ever wanted in a woman, except other women.

The laptop's liquid crystal display began to coalesce, warming up—

And when he saw what she had done, Boyd began to scream. What a knife she'd thrust between his ribs.

"This is a bitch!" he cried. "This is a bitch!"

With pounding footsteps, Derek burst into the bedroom like a parent who'd heard his child awaken from nightmares. If only. Boyd pointed a trembling finger at the computer, told Derek what she'd done: dumped everything from the hard drive. *Everything.*

"So let me get this straight," said Derek. "You never made backups of any of the data?"

Boyd crumpled Allison's note and hurled it at him. "You're so fucking smart, what do *you* think?"

Derek hadn't laughed this hard all day.

A poor night's sleep, a toxic champagne headache, and one more trip across the godforsaken Vegas–L.A. conduit later, Boyd found himself reduced to pounding on his former landlord's door, hope's last refuge. Without question, this had to be the worst day in anyone's life since the Crucifixion.

Doug Powell answered, frumpy and quizzical in his doorway. No recognition whatsoever behind those little round glasses. He was a complete cipher.

"It's me, it's Boyd Dobbins. From 2-C."

He realized the obvious when Doug pointed it out: the missing mustache. He'd rinsed it down the bathroom drain this morning, all the disguise he'd been able to muster, but effective. Clean-shaven, Boyd looked five or six years younger, his face more innocent and boyish than he'd seen since his mid-twenties, still blessed by smooth contours and that clear-eyed devil's twinkle.

After Doug let him in, Boyd explained the situation: He and Allison had had a minor little spat. Gone overnight to cool off, and now he comes back and lets himself in upstairs, to fix a nice apology dinner to surprise her when she gets home from day care, but the whole place is devoid of life.

Doug's eyebrows peaked into innocent arches; he hunched his shoulders. "What can I tell you, I don't know anything."

Boyd took a step closer. "Allison wouldn't move out without letting you know, without turning her keys back in. She *wouldn't.* She works with kids, she's responsible. So where'd she go?"

"I told you already, I don't *know* anything! I didn't even . . . didn't even know she was gone until you, until you told me."

Boyd sighed. Doug clearly had a freakish career ahead as the worst actor on the planet. Boyd slipped from his pocket a deck of cards and began to shuffle them into his palm.

"Doug, Doug, you tell me this but you're about as convincing as a drag queen with five-o'clock shadow. Come on, it's me. It's Boyd. No mustache, but I'm the same guy. Help me out here."

Plea after plea did virtually no good, the little butterball admitting finally that maybe Allison *had* moved out, very spur-of-the-moment-like, very mysterious, but he didn't know anything more than that. Believe him? Not really. Crack him in one lie and there were probably others.

"Make you a wager," Boyd offered. "I do this magic trick. You pick a card, but don't let me see it, whatever you do, and if I guess what it is, you tell me everything Allison told you about where she's going. I guess wrong and I'm out of here. Doesn't this sound like a fair way to resolve our dispute?"

"Oh, right." Doug planted dimpled fists on his hips, playing the seasoned skeptic. Total putty. "And the check's in the mail."

"Doug Powell, you are one tough nut to crack," said Boyd. He shuffled the cards with a flourish, fanned them elegantly, offered them facedown. Doug tweezed one free and held it cupped in both hands.

"And now," Boyd said, "we invoke the mystical powers of the third eye."

He coaxed Doug into holding the card by a lower corner and along his nose, so that its top edge lay against the spot centered just above his eyes. The third eye, Boyd explained, was the locus of inner vision, seeing all, intuiting all.

"Eyes closed?" said Boyd. "It's starting to come to me. . . ."

Doug huffed. "Can we get this over with?"

"You bet," and then Boyd drew back and punched the card dead center. Doug's nose gave with a pop and his glasses backflipped over his head. He tottered sideways, then his legs buckled beneath him and he dumped butt-first onto the floor, where he sat goggle-eyed, clutching at a fistful of blood.

The bent card had fluttered to the carpet, landing faceup.

"King of clubs, I almost said that!" Boyd exclaimed. "Now . . . can we talk?"

Failure always seemed worse after sundown, and once the cold, remote eye of the moon had risen, the only thing that would make him feel better was walking the Strip. Breaking a tacky sheen of sweat in the warmth of night, burning under neon, exiling himself to the carnival midway atmosphere.

A surgeon's hands, when it came to the cards, and he'd risked one for nothing. Doug Powell had been worthless, maintaining that he knew nothing about where Allison had gone. The only thing he'd added, finally, was that she acted as if she never wanted to see Boyd again—not alive, anyway—and that now he could understand why. It had just gotten too sad, watching Doug blubber and bleed into his hand. Finally Boyd had found a washcloth, filled it with ice cubes and wet it with cold water, and given it to him with a pat on the shoulder.

He was fresh out of ideas as to how to locate her. Allison was at heart a vagabond, a beautiful windblown nomad, with no place on earth to which she would automatically retreat. Maybe that had been part of what he'd found so appealing about her—knowing that should he gamble wrong one day, he could lose her completely. She would disappear like a shadow on a cloudy day.

Throw in nearly three-quarters of a million, though, and it became an entirely unacceptable loss.

If only she hadn't done so thorough a job on his computer. If he correctly interpreted her note, Allison had copied everything onto disks, to maneuver him into some sort of demeaning apology. He *was* missing several floppies from his stash, just hadn't noticed at first in his haste to pack yesterday morning. Had she merely trashed his hard drive and left it at that, he could've minimized the damage. Erasure didn't mean the files were gone, only that the system would overwrite what was there with new data. Wang Chung might have retrieved everything, although this was hypothetical now. Allison had seen to that too.

She'd taken one of his games, then copied it and recopied it until it had gobbled up every last megabyte of storage. All traces of that seven hundred grand were gone, but he could play Duke Nukem all he wanted.

Mingling with the tourists and Vegas flotsam, Boyd stopped at a cluster of newspaper vending machines. To one side stood a wire rack bristling with magazinelike flyers, most printed on cheap pulp stock. He had seen them plenty of times, flipped through them as well, if only to admire the displayed skin. Advertising for the regional sex industry—only in Nevada. Nothing but ads and maps showing the way out of Clark County and up to the legal brothels between Vegas and Reno. For local action, here where prostitution was still a theoretical crime, there were endless pictures and phone numbers, laced with innuendo—performers, dancers, live nude shows direct to your room, experience your wildest fantasies. All one big wink and a nudge.

By page seven, Boyd knew that if he did not get laid tonight, he was going to spontaneously combust. Must have been the idea of all that money. Money *was* an aphrodisiac, he believed, and having it just out of reach was an unconscionable tease.

He sprinted back to his motel, a couple of discreet blocks off the Strip, befitting his fugitive status. Up in his room he flopped on the bed and paged through this catalog of goddesses on demand.

Great lips; I'll come to you anytime. Leann. He kept going, found a picture of three girls with their pert bottoms thrust out. *How about OUR assets? We also do parties.* Three at once? Tempting, but as long as he was footing his own bill, there was a fine line between extravagance and overkill. *Hot blonde, 40-DD. Will climax!* Sure. Just like Jane Fonda in *Klute,* probably. *Call Jennifer—I can get so nasty I'll make you blush.* Not likely, unless she showed up with Grandma Dobbins in tow.

Boyd knew the moment he saw her that Krystal was the one. He liked her name, and sure as poker tables were green did he love her picture. A glorious and petite sprite of a young woman, no stranger to the gym, on one knee with her other leg exquisitely pointed toe-down like a ballerina. A cascade of raven hair fell halfway down her back. Her smile was charming, sweet, inviting; her eyes full of both enthusiasm and unsullied innocence.

I may live in Nevada, read her ad's clinch line, *but nudity is my natural state.* Clever, understated . . . this could well be the woman he'd waited for all his life. Boyd scrambled for the phone before some undeserving loser out there could beat him to her.

She was tapping at his door in forty-eight minutes, stripped in forty-nine. She stood five-one after kicking off her heels, as comfortable in her skin as Eve in Eden.

"You like what you see?" Krystal asked, refreshingly free of come-hither posturing, but why bother to ask in the first place? The answer was written all over him, from face to trousers.

"Obviously," he said, dry-throated, "you believe in truth in advertising."

She took him by the hand, steered him toward the bed. "Lies

just come back to haunt. Bad karma, you know. That's why the only lies I ever tell are to spare someone's feelings. So . . . ! How would you like it tonight, Brad?"

Krystal ran down the menu in tandem with his buttons and his zipper, and he wanted it all. By the time she'd stretched him out along the bed, the only fault he could possibly find with her was that she wasn't twins.

"You're just the sweetest guy!" she said, and took delighted pity on his indecision. "I hardly ever suggest this to a first-time client, because I'm afraid they might think I'm really weird, but, like, you seem really special, like you might be up for something, you know . . . different?"

"Connoisseur of the sexual smorgasbord," he blurted. "Lay it on me."

She pitched, he listened. She claimed—and rightly so, he imagined—to be the only call girl in Las Vegas who practiced techniques of the eastern sex masters. She told him that she could stimulate his chakras to give him an orgasm like none he had ever experienced. Which in itself sounded righteous . . . but chakras? Her terminology was spawned from some other planet than his own.

The chakras, she explained, were seven centers of energy, in a straight line down the center of the body. First discovered in the east, they had been known to esoterically wise men and women for thousands of years, long before western doctors were able to correlate them precisely with specific nerve centers. The more she explained, the more animated she grew. *This is no act,* he realized. *She really believes in this.*

From her purse she produced a drawstring pouch and opened it, spilled onto the bed seven rosy pink gemstones. "Rhodochrosite," she said. "It enhances blood circulation, and I think we both know how important that is for what we're about to do." She ran her velvet tongue along his body, planting kisses upon each strategic hot spot, then depositing a crystal. The first she nestled just under his scrotum, wedged between both cheeks.

"Hey. *Hey!*" he cried sharply.

"Relax," she said. And that smile—how could he ever deny the magic of that smile? "Trust me, you silly."

The next crystal went in his navel, the next she rested upon his solar plexus; another over his heart, one in the hollow of his throat. She handed him the last two. Told him, for the time being, to hold one just over the bridge of his nose and the other against the crown of his head. He obeyed, then scowled, not just because he had the feeling that this was some elaborate joke, that hidden cameras were rolling and somebody was watching through a two-way mirror, convulsed with hilarity.

"Do you wash these?" he asked. "Regularly?"

"Oh, sure. The energies have to be purified. Why?"

"Because on my face I'm holding a rock that at one time or another has probably been up some other guy's ass, is why."

"Oh, would you relax? It's not like it's the Blarney Stone," she said, then dipped her head into his lap. She took him in her mouth, swallowed him whole, and with each bob of her head, Boyd's misgivings and muscles loosened further. Solid to gel to liquid to particle vapor—this was his metamorphosis beneath her touch and her kiss, and she, bringer of miracles and stealer of breath.

Krystal knew the optimum moment to withdraw, then unfurl a condom onto him, then hop up to straddle his surging hips. She plunged him inside of her, all wet fire, her body like silk and steel as she rode him and rode him. Krystal leaned forward, small pomegranate breasts jiggling before his gaze as she reached out to hold the last two crystals in place, on forehead and crown, and freed his hands. She lay down atop him, pressing body to body, crystals trapped between as she set the rhythm, undulating like a dolphin through the sea. Maybe it was only the power of suggestion but he felt something astonishing about to happen, a delicious humming frequency that shot through him like golden lightning, as she rode him, rode him, until he felt himself explode, groin and belly, rib cage and skull, and she threw herself back off him and onto her knees with a delighted wail, and chunks of rhodochrosite went flying, to patter around them like hailstones.

All except the one up his ass.

For the first time in his life, orgasm hit Boyd so hard that he blacked out. Consciousness swam back in moments later—or maybe hours—counter to the slow spin of the room. He shook his head, blinked, saw her sitting on the side of the bed and smiling brightly at him. Her eyes were big and round, gray as sea foam, and under their spell he was lost, utterly lost.

"I could be wrong," said Krystal, "but I think I see a brand-new convert lying here."

"Sorceress!" Boyd cried. He sucked wind, rejuvenated and pure. "You're a sorceress and I'm in love."

Again, she told him he was sweet, and he lay there waiting for his land legs to return, watching as she gathered up her far-flung crystals. He told her this must be how the phrase "get your rocks off" originated, and she laughed, told him maybe, maybe so, that she'd never heard that one before. But from the look on her face he could tell that this was one of her diplomatic lies.

He struggled upright in desperation. Business and pleasure had both been transacted; after another couple of minutes she would be gone. How to keep her in this room, in his life? The blind date of all time, there had to be more left. When she opened her purse to drop the drawstring bag back in, he saw his chance.

"Hey. Cards," he said, and pointed. "Can I see them?"

"It's not the kind of deck you'd be used to seeing in this town." She handed them over. "It's a tarot deck. Sometimes I, you know, need a little extra help to figure things out."

Boyd nodded sagely. "Don't we all."

He flipped through them, noting the different suits, nothing with which he was familiar. Cups and wands, swords and coins. Plus others that didn't belong to any suit: the Hanged Man, Death, the Empress, others. The mother of his children, and she was immersed in the deeply goofy. A fine thing it was that love was so blind.

"I was a blackjack dealer, at the Ivory Coast," he told her while shuffling. "There seven months, only, and already I was the top-requested dealer for private parties up in the luxury suites. You have any idea the kind of tips you can make then?"

Krystal, half dressed and fully captivated, watched the flash and dazzle of his hands. "What made you number one so quick?"

With the bed a mess and the dresser top too slick, he dropped naked to the carpet and had her kneel down with him.

"Most blackjack games are dealt out of a shoe," he explained. "That's what they call that boxy thing that holds four, five, six decks at once to give card counters a rougher time. And keeps the dealer from peeking at the hit cards, or dealing off the bottom. But places do still offer games from hand-held decks. That's what they had me doing, *and* at a two-thousand-dollar-limit table, too. Because I was bringing to the table a little something different.

"Pretend you're Catholic," Boyd said, then whipped out five cards in a well-aligned row before her; whipped out five more, and there sat a quintet of crosses. "Hail Mary, full of grace."

"That's *so* cool! Except those are more like Eastern Orthodox crosses than Catholic."

He shrugged. "Hey, if I was really good, I could've made this old comedian named Teitelbaum happy. He was always coming to my table telling me to make a Star of David."

"Have you got any more?"

"Oh yeah, for sure, I'd do all kinds of tricks. Got the idea from Japanese chefs—you know, those guys behind the grills, they sling your food around, chop it up in midair? As long as you're cooking, why not make it entertaining?" Boyd flipped another card aloft so that it spun perpendicular to the floor; fired another at it, and knocked down the first card as if shooting skeet. "Most of your hard-core gamblers, they couldn't care less, they don't want to see all this, they just want to get down to business. But your garden-variety gamblers and tourists, they eat it up. They'll stay at the table twice as long because they're getting a show. That's the only reason the casino would let me do it in the first place, because otherwise, well, the security watchers pee their pants when they see anything deviating from the norm. But as long as it draws more money . . ."

"That was so amazingly cool! How do you do that?"

"Zen," he said. "*Be* the card."

Krystal gasped, awe spreading across her face like the break of dawn. Whispering, "I *knew* there was something special about you. I knew it the second I walked in here and saw your aura."

He gave the cards back and asked her to draw one for him—a quick reading to tell his fortune, his future. Krystal shuffled, intent and focused, like no hooker he'd ever seen trolling the casinos, her small hands nearly as skilled as his own. She drew the top card and turned it over to reveal some long-haired cretin sniffing a flower as he blundered off a cliff.

" 'The Fool'?" he read, scowling. He knew there couldn't be anything to this. "Somehow I'd expected better."

"No, oh no, Brad, no! This is *wonderful*! The Fool is, like, *the* most profound card you could get!"

He wondered how profound that tree-hugging moron would look at the bottom of the cliff. Skull fractures were *very* profound.

"It represents the beginning of a journey," she said. "You're on your quest for wisdom and perfection."

Boyd was greatly cheered. "How about riches?"

She considered this. "Gee, I don't see why not."

"Bitchin' good news!" He took the deck from her and began to shuffle. "Here, I'll draw one for the two of us, you *and* me. That I called you, that you're here? Maybe this was no accident. Maybe there's a . . . I don't know . . . a bigger picture to it, maybe."

Krystal was holding her breath, lower lip nipped between her teeth. He turned the card to reveal a nude man and woman, kneeling beside a red rose as they gazed into each other's doelike eyes.

"The Lovers," Krystal breathed. "Wow. Oh, wow."

"That's so amazingly cool," he said, smiling to welcome her to his life, that clear-eyed devil's twinkle never brighter.

Good thing these cards were no bigger than they were. He'd had to keep this one palmed for nearly three minutes.

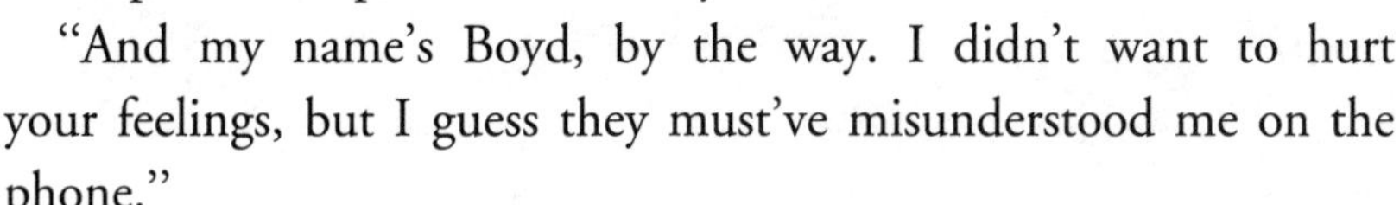

"And my name's Boyd, by the way. I didn't want to hurt your feelings, but I guess they must've misunderstood me on the phone."

chapter five

As Gunther tapped the puny knocker against the door, Madeline took his arm. For appearance's sake only—something about the pose felt ridiculous, as though the two of them belonged atop a wedding cake. She had always thought of Gunther Manzetti as the type who'd prefer to skip the nuptials, skip the honeymoon, and jump straight to the bitter recriminations and the adultery.

MANAGER, read an adhesive placard on the door; below, in piecemeal letters, DOUG POWELL. Gunther knocked again.

When it opened she found herself face-to-face with a dumpy raccoon of a young man wearing a grubby T-shirt and clutching the door for support. Both bruised eyes were swollen half shut behind crooked wire-rim glasses; his nose looked like a cherry tomato.

"Can I help you?" he asked, but his heart wasn't in it. With a face that sad, she wouldn't be running to answer any doors either.

"We're here to look at apartments," Madeline said.

"It's after nine. Not exactly office hours, you know."

"Sorry. Our schedules wouldn't let us get by any earlier."

Doug nodded. "What, you work funny hours or something?"

"Not unless days are funny," said Gunther. About time he spoke up. Standing there like a stone-eyed, blond-headed, olive-skinned golem, saying not a word, he tended to set off alarms in most people.

"You're in luck," Doug Powell told them. "We had one open up this afternoon, kind of sudden-like, if you don't mind seeing it before it's cleaned."

They said they didn't. Passkeys dangling from his belt, Doug led them down the hall and upstairs, dutifully taking them through the charade of inspecting apartment 2-C. Madeline tried to fake interest in this mundane tour.

She had seen the place already, not ten minutes ago—seen the vacant closets, gone through each emptied drawer. Gunther's idea; maybe they should pay a visit to Boyd's former squeeze and see if she still maintained that he'd left her behind and clueless. Gunther had knocked, and when he'd tired of waiting, popped the cheap doorknob with a credit card. There was a deadbolt and a chain inside, neither in use. Fifteen seconds in, the conclusion was inescapable: Allison doesn't live here anymore.

"So, the previous tenants, you say they cleared out in a big hurry?" Gunther asked.

"Yeah. Considering the town, though, that's not so strange."

"Where'd they rush off to, I wonder?"

"Oh, right, like most of the people in this building tell me anything about themselves. I don't know. They packed up and moved on like gypsies, that's all I know." He began to shuffle to the door. "So what do you think? Are you interested?"

"Are we interested, he asks," Gunther said to her. *"Are we interested."* Back to Doug: "Can't you tell by our beatific faces that we realize we're home?"

Beatific? Gunther's word of the day, probably, after rooting around in his Webster's. She suspected most of these words would end up with the life expectancy of mayflies.

Doug looked uncertain. "Well, you *are* a little hard to read."

"How's this for clarity, then: Let's go sign that lease."

Doug Powell locked up again, and halfway back down the stairs Gunther surrendered to curiosity.

"You don't mind me asking, how'd you get those Lone Ranger–looking bruises around your eyes?"

"Oh. You know how it goes. I accidentally stepped into a kick in my, um, my tae kwon do class this evening."

"Hear that, honey?" Gunther beamed at her from behind this lumpen troll's back. "We'll be safe here, got Bruce Lee to protect us from the ne'er-do-wells." When he clapped a firm hand across Doug's back, Doug flinched. "I don't guess there's many late rent checks in *this* building, is there?"

Watching Gunther, absorbing the way he worked . . . there was something about it that made him new to her all over again. She knew what he did but had never seen him do it, had only listened as he relayed the occasional story of a memorable collection, or reminisced about the dead, the dying, the broken. How they got that way.

Watching him become best buddies with Doug Powell plunged her back in time. Nine or ten years old, childhood in New Mexico spent in tract housing, days spent idolizing the boy next door. His name now forgotten but she still remembered *him,* sixteen years old and something terrifyingly appealing about his stride, his sneer, his cigarette. She would watch him while crouched below windowsills or from behind her father's Chrysler. Watch with delirium, desperate to be worthy of being noticed by him. He would charm neighborhood dogs and cats over to him, rub their coats until they squirmed against his hand. Then he would take his cigarette and blow on the tip until it became a glowing orange coal, and crush it into the animal's body while holding fast to its collar. He would slap the pet's kicking flank then, like a cowboy slapping a newly branded calf, and release it, send it squalling back down the street.

Strays received worse.

She recalled talking to him only once, asking why he did it; recalled his arrogant shrug and the smoke ring that wafted from his lips as he told her that you could get away with anything you wanted in the world, as long as you remembered that dumb animals would never tell on you.

Doug let them into his apartment downstairs, apologizing for the mess. His slovenliness was twofold: If it wasn't comic books, it was food. Once the door was shut, Gunther cracked his knuckles and called out to Doug's back while he ducked into his office.

"You do the repairs around the building?"

"Small stuff, whatever's not too specialized. Heavy-duty plumbing and like that, forget it, I reach for the phone."

"So if I were to ask you for some duct tape, say, you could let me borrow it?"

Doug reappeared in the office doorway, copies of a blank lease in hand. "I suppose. Why . . . do you need duct tape?"

"My car seat's got this split in it. Gets much bigger, it'll be like I'm trying to crawl back into the womb."

Doug went trotting over to a closet to fetch, and she stepped close alongside Gunther, tiptoeing up to put her lips at his ear. If he *really* wanted to impress her, she whispered, someday he was going to have to talk someone into digging his own grave. When Doug came back with the roll of silvery tape and handed it over, Gunther calmly drew the Glock from beneath his jacket and centered the muzzle on Doug's forehead.

"Okay, Mr. Tae Kwon Do," he said, "let's see how fast and furious you can whip those arms behind your back."

The bruised face looked more crushed than frightened. Gunther had her do the honors, binding Doug's pretzeled forearms, and as she wound the tape around, she could feel the animal trembling in his soft, rubbery skin. Gunther gave him a shove toward his bedroom, sent Doug sprawling across the unmade bed, and sat beside him, like a parent ready to tell a bedtime story.

"My guess is," Gunther said, "you're already getting the idea we're not here to talk real estate. And that once we get started, if we don't believe what we hear, you got problems. So you just chew that over for a minute, then we'll get down to business."

"Would you just get down to business *now*?" Madeline said. "Look at him, he wants to talk already. Why does everything have to be such a big production number for you?"

"So who made *you* the truculence expert all of a sudden? Do I come to the casino and tell you how to do your job? You want to speed things along, go look under the sinks and in that utility closet and bring me some drain cleaner."

She heard Doug moan and went stomping out of the bedroom, flinging doors open, looking at labels, banging doors closed. Ordering her around like this—they would definitely have words later on. She found what he wanted, and Gunther set the can on the night table by the bed, where Doug could see it.

"Crystal Drano. Let me compliment your taste in corrosives," Gunther said. "I knew this guy back east, in Philadelphia, liked to use Drano whenever an important conversation got clogged up. A little Drano and that flow of information'd open right up again. I always thought he should do a TV commercial, because this guy, he *believed* in the product. The people we worked for, they used to call him the Sandman, so . . . I don't guess I need to explain where exactly he'd put the Drano, do I?"

Doug whimpered, Doug squirmed, and the questions and answers began. Boyd Dobbins? Gone, gone a couple of days by now—but still around town. Here this afternoon, you just missed him by a few hours. See? See what he did to my face?

"What? What's this you're telling me? No tae kwon do?"

"What do *you* think, just look at me," Doug bawled. "He sucker-punched me, Boyd did."

"Now that's an interesting turn of events." Gunther stroked his chin. "Boyd schemes enough over his own business to pull a Houdini on everybody. But he comes back here today to blacken your eye sockets. Now why would he do a thing like that?"

Doug began to hyperventilate, tears squeezing from slitted eyes as he said he didn't know, *didn't know,* Boyd wasn't making any sense, so Gunther picked up the can of Drano and gaily danced it before the bruised face.

"Mister Sandman," Gunther sang, "bring me a dream . . ."

Doug wailed that Boyd had been looking for his girlfriend, but she'd moved out already and Boyd had come here asking where she'd gone. Madeline knew this was no case of Boyd's being crazy in love. Allison had to have had something he wanted, needed.

Doug swore he didn't know what any of it was about. Swore on Bibles and comic books that he didn't know where she'd gone.

Gunther sighed. "Maddy? Would it be too terrible a hardship on you if I asked you to go get me a spoon?"

Madeline brought him the one clean teaspoon she found in the silverware drawer, then saw him open the Drano, thrust the spoon inside, give the crystals a lazy stir. Wanting to watch, and not, then she took the initiative to move into the makeshift office. She knelt before the two-drawer file cabinet, the voices from the bedroom filtering softly in as she tried to comprehend the logic behind Doug Powell's filing system.

"So you've actually read all these comic books?" Gunther was asking. Still stirring that Drano.

Doug's hoarse voice: "Uh . . . uh-huh . . ."

"How many you got stashed around here, anyway?"

"About . . . f-fourteen thousand."

"Fourteen thousand! That's some serious hobby you got, then. There's actually some money in funny books, isn't there?"

"Well, there can be. For big collectors, speculators, like that." Doug's voice strengthened a little. "My real valuable ones, they're in that heavier box in the corner over there. I've got an original *Detective Comics* number twenty-seven from 1939 in there. Know what that was?"

"I give up."

"The very first ever appearance of Batman."

"Get the fuck out of here! *Really?*"

And she'd heard enough, slammed the first file drawer closed. "Gunther? Gunther!" she called out. "Does your brain need a leash to keep it from wandering? Forget the comic books, would you?"

"Excuse the hell out of me for trying to expand my horizons a little!" he shouted back.

Madeline yanked open the second drawer, cursing beneath her breath as she ran a fingernail along the file tabs.

"You know what the weirdest thing I ever heard about a comic book was?" Gunther said. "It was back in the seventies, had to be, and that rock band Kiss—those guys with all the freaky makeup?—they starred in this comic book, and before it went to press, they each poured a pint of their own blood into the red ink vats."

"Oh sure, I've got one of those. But there's one that tops that," said Doug. "A while back, this one publisher started doing comics about porno stars, and so this one girl, this actress from England, when she comes, it's really wet, and a lot of it, like a guy almost? Well, she poured a vial of that into the ink."

"No way!" said Gunther. "No. Fucking. Way. *Really?*"

Madeline found the file on apartment 2-C and slipped it out.

"Hey! Maddy!" Gunther called. "Is this true? That women can come like guys, some of them?"

Receipts, original lease, furniture inventory—she shuffled through white and pink and yellow papers. "Why are you asking *me* this? In more than a year, have you ever once seen me spray the headboard?"

"I'm asking because you're a woman. You should know these things, shouldn't you?"

"Except I'm not a lesbian. If you've been doing it right the last twenty-five years or so, you should've seen a lot more women having orgasms than I have."

"Something like this, I thought it might've at least come up in conversation, is all."

Madeline brought the file with her from the office into the hallway. Sighing, "Well, yes, if you must know. I've heard of it."

"I've heard everything now," Gunther told Doug. "Nothing can surprise me anymore."

"Yeah, well, stop the presses," Madeline said, and waved the slip of paper she'd pulled from the file folder. Doug craned his neck to see what she had, and there were no secrets between them now. Lost hope had a look all its own. You could see it at any hour in any casino.

" 'Damage deposit, forward to: Allison Willoughby, in care of Constance Wainright,' " she read from the paper, then the address. "I don't suppose you know anybody in Yazoo City, Mississippi."

Gunther shook his head. "Never even been in the state."

In silence, then, their knowing glances held across the room. Doug began to squirm on the bed, T-shirt drenched in sweat and his taped arms contorted behind him as he tried to push away with legs gone boneless. Gunther's hand hooked onto his shoulder.

"Better find a rag," he told her, "start wiping down whatever you touched."

She was swabbing the file cabinet when she heard the shot—a muffled pop—and a moment later a ragged choking wheeze. A cold hard knot gathered in her stomach, then broke in a gushing flood of warmth. This was the initiation, baptism of blood and fire. The suddenness and the irrevocability of it stopped her for a moment—was it what she really wanted? *Yes, if this is what it takes.* It had been a remarkably easy threshold to cross.

Gunther was cursing. She heard a steady thumping sound, like a leg in spasms; and the choking. "Hold still, hold *still,* for—" Then another quick pair of muffled shots, and silence.

They were out of the building two minutes later, and Gunther was balancing across one shoulder the three-foot-long reinforced cardboard box from the corner of Doug Powell's room. With his hair in that stiff brush cut, he looked like a soldier carrying a crate of artillery shells.

"Stealing comic books, that's low, even for you," she said.

"You heard him. There's money in these things. World's first look at Batman. Sell these, we got plenty of operating capital to work from."

They crossed the alley, into the parking lot two buildings away. She keyed the trunk lid of Gunther's white land yacht of a Cadillac, and he dumped the box inside.

"What happened in that bedroom?"

He looked down at the asphalt and gravel, hands in pockets, shrugging his broad shoulders. Gunther by moonlight, evasive and—could it be?—even a bit embarrassed.

"You were right on top of him, how could you screw it up?"

"It's not like he was sitting still for it, you know. I pushed a pillow over his face, shoved the gun into the pillow. Cuts the sound, cuts the splatter. He was kicking around, I guess is how it happened. Got the angle wrong and blew out the side of his throat." Gunther walked in a tight circle as she began to laugh, then halted, flailing his arms. "Well *you* do it next time, then, it's not as easy as it sounds, hitting dead center. Like trying to thread a moving needle."

She tossed him the keys and he unlocked his door, unlocked hers by remote. He started the car and boosted the cold air.

"The pillow bit, I got that one from *The Good, the Bad and the Ugly.* Lee Van Cleef squashes a pillow over this old Mexican's face and unloads right into him. I saw that when I was a kid and thought it was just the toughest thing."

Madeline watched his face as Gunther steered down the alley, toward a psychedelic blur of neon and flash. Saw in his eyes the rapture of adrenaline surge, and her heart ached to realize that their wild and reckless youth was gone, gone long before they'd ever met, and there was no one to go to for justice.

"*The Good, the Bad and the Ugly*?" he said. "Some great music in that movie. Now there's something I could listen to for miles."

She nodded, let him think she approved. Another cultural void between them, Gunther's whole life patterned after some old movie where all they did was spit, swear, and shoot each other.

And when she checked her face in the visor mirror, tugging it back toward her ears to pull the lines out of it, she wondered if, as for vampires, the blood of the young might not renew them both somehow.

chapter six

As Allison hitchhiked her way out of Las Vegas that Friday night, she turned to see it receding behind her like a patch of glitter strewn across the desert. Lot's wife, she remembered from hellfire Mississippi sermons, had looked at a burning Sodom and Gomorrah this way and been turned to salt. It made less sense to Allison now than ever. The sight of a disappearing Vegas filled her with such exhilaration that for now it did not matter she was just days from total financial destitution. She'd never felt more free—the fly that had chipped itself out of amber.

"You know what that place was like for me?" she said to the older woman who'd offered her the ride. The car hummed beneath them, southeast, over the Boulder Highway. To the west the rims of distant hills sawed into the blue-black night, spilling stars. "It was like trying to wear the wrong set of clothes. They fit my ex-boyfriend perfectly, but they didn't fit me."

"Then you have better taste in clothes than he does, dear," the woman said. Her gray hair was smartly trimmed and layered, and in the dashboard's glow looked the color of mercury. "It doesn't matter how hard you try to pretend otherwise, it still feels wrong, doesn't it?"

Allison nodded. "I guess I'm lucky, though. Sometimes things can feel wrong for so long you start thinking they're what's right after all." Remembering the feel of her father's hands, charged with new expectations that she had never dreamed were a daughter's obligation to fulfill. Mothers thought they prepared you for everything, but they didn't.

Where the tip of Nevada stabbed down like the point of a dagger, they crossed the river into Arizona, south of the curving wall of Hoover Dam. They drove southeast into desolation's dusty heart, while night deepened and the moon crested overhead, full and round and bright as a silver dollar.

They parted company at Kingman, her ride's path now veering southwest toward Yucca. The older woman offered her a room for the night, breakfast in the morning for a fresh start. Tempting, but Allison declined; sleep in Yucca, and tomorrow she would have to backtrack. As well, she'd been gone but a few hours, the urge to keep moving like the deep marrow itch of a healing bone. The woman smiled sadly, with a final wish of good luck, then continued on her solitary way.

Allison set up temporary camp in the booth of a truck stop, the suitcase and duffel forming a protective wall as she drank her coffee and listened to the night. Outside, travelers rolled up to the gas pumps, stood blearily as they fed their machines, then paid and journeyed on with replenished junk food stashes. Beyond, highways met in confluence as white lights drew closer, and red lights vanished into the distance. She pulled her attention back inside, to the table of the empty booth ahead of her. Plump flies buzzed in from other tables, other windows, circled, lighted, left again. Same story, smaller scale.

The waitress who filled and refilled her mug was a bedraggled-looking teenager, hair pulled and clipped to one side to shield an angry cluster of acne on her forehead. Allison put in a word with her that she could use a ride—anybody here continuing on toward Phoenix? The girl said she'd check while on her rounds, reporting back in as though taking bids, something more alive about her now than ten minutes ago. Flattered, perhaps, to be entrusted with something more than coffee, omelettes, pie.

Barstow and Flagstaff, somebody else going on *to* Vegas—the destinations were pushpins on a map, and all wrong. She got a refill of coffee and settled in to wait awhile longer.

The waitress had her linked up after another half hour, and Allison had already noticed the man pulling in, four big doors and Utah plates. Sandy-haired, with glasses. Maybe a Mormon—he had that suited, well-scrubbed look that she associated with the door-to-door Brigham Young brigade. The waitress pointed him out as he sat at the counter, finishing a tuna melt that he ate with knife and fork instead of fingers. When the waitress relayed he was going to Phoenix, he turned on his stool and nodded their way.

"He's not been giving out tracts, has he?" Allison asked.

"Not yet. But whenever they do that it's in place of a tip, usually. Like, thanks a lot."

The man offered to carry her bags but she declined, lugging them herself to his wide backseat. He was only a few years older than she, yet seemed older still, by choice, reservedly polite and stiff in the spine. As they stood in the cool desert night, neon buzzed and names were swapped, Allison for Marshall J. Dillon, and she couldn't help but grin. He wanted to know if it was really that amusing.

"Were your parents big fans of *Gunsmoke*?" she asked.

"My parents never watched TV." She felt chastised by the way he said it, like a reproachful parent himself. "Marshall was my uncle's name. Most people are tactful enough not to bring this up when we're introduced."

I can see why now, she thought, and apologized as he unlocked her door. "I met a John Wayne once, and he didn't seem to mind the inevitable. He seemed flattered."

Dillon was quiet as he drove, preferring to listen to some talk radio show. It sounded very conservative, callers and host frothing at the mouth about the enemies of decency. All the usual suspects. Their cure for everything was so simple: Both father and mother in the home equated with stability, crucial to the balance that the callers sought to restore across a land gone wrong.

Allison's gaze lingered on the car phone, and she felt like making her own plea over the airwaves: *Tell me what it was* I *did wrong, to make him come up those creaking stairs so many nights.* They could have peeled back the shingles, the polite Mississippi veneer, and looked inside that house, and they'd have seen all the right pieces to their puzzle. *So you tell me whose fault that was. Mine? And mine again when he decided that the way it began wasn't enough anymore, and he had to start bringing—*

She heard the radio show abruptly cut off, and there came the click of the tape deck as it automatically reversed from one side to the other, then the show resumed after a few dead moments. On tape. Dillon was listening to this on tape.

He opened up after a while, growing friendlier with neutral small talk. She learned that he was a sporting goods salesman with a four-state territory. He spoke of how team sports built strong character in young men. Dillon asked what she did.

"I've worked mostly in day care centers the past few years."

"Is that right." He seemed intrigued. "Then we're in the same business, really. Developing young minds and bodies. Although it's my opinion that day care's no substitute for a stable home."

"Hey," she said flatly, "what is?"

"I'd never turn my three over to day care. No offense."

"None taken." Allison biting back the urge to ask why, if his children's home life was really that important, he'd taken a job that sent him out on the road.

Route 93 unfurled beneath them, mile after desolate mile, past moonlit boulders the size of mountains. Their path had been cut through by wind and rain and dynamite. In the shadow of these hulks and spires, civilization was sparse. She could count the towns on one hand so far, sprouting in the flat clefts where the earth leveled out enough for a few streets, some foundations, a church, a saloon.

Another lay just ahead, heralded by a sign: Coyote Ridge, population 423. Another blink-and-you-miss-it small town, one exit and a dusting of lights in the near distance, and then it was all behind them in another five heartbeats.

"Do you always dress like that?" Dillon asked.

Allison frowned, startled. She'd changed back in the truck stop bathroom, today's earlier sundress too cool for the desert night. Jeans now, and a midriff top, both comfortably snug; the faded old denim jacket lay across her lap. She held it tighter.

"No," she said, as if this were any of his business, "but the petticoats and bonnet don't travel as well."

"It sends a message. You should be careful of a thing like that." She could feel his hard stare in the night.

"Then let me make *this* message clear: You're making me very uncomfortable. Could you stop it, please."

"I'm responsible for you now," he went on. "What's it been, an hour and a half, more or less? All this time and responsibility and I've been wondering what's going to happen to you, if you keep telegraphing yourself this way, this way you—" His breath sounded ragged. "You could be hurt. You could be very seriously hurt, and, and . . . no one would know, no one would, would . . . *come.*"

"Stop the car and let me out. Now. Right now."

"Don't be ridiculous, you don't have anybody to protect you."

"The ones who were in charge of that did a pretty lousy job of it, so I've done fine on my own." She tensed, glancing at the speedometer, saw they were doing seventy. She could never jump, not at this speed. Besides, the remaining core of her life was in the backseat. "Now stop this fucking car so I can get out."

"Watch your language." With a sigh of disgust he stabbed one finger at the tape player to shut it off. By dashboard light the rigid curves of his face gleamed with moist heat; a glow reflected from his glasses, turning the lenses to molten disks. "My children ride in this car. I will not have it profaned."

One silent mile, most of another. Allison had pressed herself against the passenger door. Couldn't read him, couldn't decide on his intentions. He'd made no attempt to touch her. Couldn't tell if he viewed himself as her guardian, her assailant, her—

(father?)

At the roadside leaned a sign announcing a scenic stop a few hundred yards ahead. She pointed.

"Could you stop here?" No reply. "I have to use the bathroom. If you want me peeing all over your seat, okay, but you might have a hard time explaining that one to your kids. And we haven't even discussed your wife, have we?"

Dillon veered off the highway and into the darkened site with a violent spray of gravel. It was little more than a widening in the road, deserted, a few picnic tables and a trash barrel pocked with bullet holes, the expected rustic outhouses. Red sandstone crags zigzagged upward, and beyond a railinged lookout yawned the chasm of night.

As soon as the car slewed to a halt, Allison yanked at the door handle, found that Dillon had locked it from a panel on the driver's door. She felt his fingers entwine in her hair, then curl into a fist, and her head was snapped painfully back. When she scratched at his wrist, his other hand punched her sharply behind the ear, and her vision burst with sparks of white.

"I'm sorry, I'm so sorry," he was saying, "you just . . . you remind me of someone . . ."

Allison twisted her head around, and if she'd thought she could reason with him still, that feeble hope was scuttled when her gaze fell on his lap. He'd undone his slacks, the fly gaping, the pale curve of his erection greenish in the dashlight.

"I—I have a gun," and he dropped his free hand into the gap between seat and door. There it lingered as he jerked her head across and down, twisting the fistful of hair and forcing her head toward his lap.

She clamped her mouth shut, averting her face. Flailed with her arms, clawed at his leg, and for this he punched her again, banged her head against the steering wheel. When her elbow struck the dash she felt a small stem of hardware give beneath it, as her crazy bone jumped with nerve twinges.

Dillon was somewhere above her, apologizing in the night, so

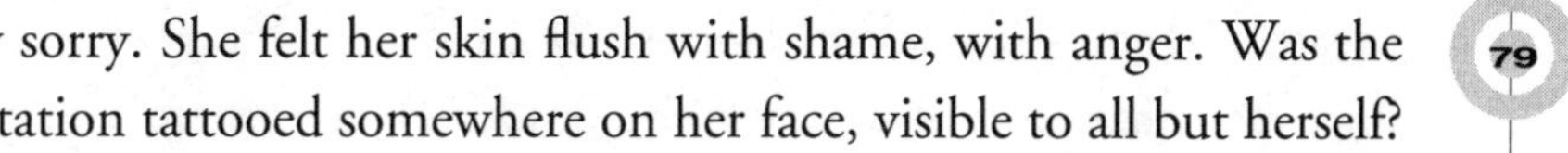

very sorry. She felt her skin flush with shame, with anger. Was the invitation tattooed somewhere on her face, visible to all but herself? A smell that drew any nearby predator? They took it for granted she was theirs, was this it, the license given as though by some scarlet letter?

Her nose was crushed against Dillon's thigh as he squirmed, and she kept her face averted. Realizing that her mouth was not what he wanted after all, she felt the hot, dry length of him rub against the side of her cheek, her ear, in her hair. Above her, Dillon panted, while deep within, Allison gagged.

Deeper yet there rode all the wild horses, still waiting after so many years to carry her away, until her body had served its purpose to whoever had commandeered it. Until she could return to it, sore and bruised. *Ride away, ride away free from it all—*

On the dashboard something popped, a metallic click where she'd banged her elbow. Allison turned from the horses when she realized what the sound was. Gun or not, she didn't care. Dillon was bluffing, and if he wasn't, maybe he would shoot through her and into his own leg and the last postmortem laugh would be hers.

Blindly, she fumbled at the dash, pulled free the warm stem of the cigarette lighter in the same instant she bit down on his thigh. He cried out, relaxed his hold long enough for her to stab her hand into his crotch, to press the glowing orange coils into the glans of his penis like a branding iron. Dillon screamed, and she caught a scorched whiff of bitter stink.

His hold on her broken, Allison surged upright and bailed over the front seat and into the back, cracking him along the jaw with her dusty brown boot. She righted herself on the backseat, then grabbed her Levi's jacket from the front and whipped a sleeve around his throat. Tightened the noose with both hands, dragging her weight into it, shouting in his ear as his fingers clawed at the denim. He bent backward over the headrest, face bloating and darkening in the netherlight. She held the garrote with one hand, balling the other into a fist, to pound it down onto his face the way hungry men will pound upon a tabletop. Once, twice, seven times, eleven, breath and spittle exploding from between clenched teeth, pounding until her hand throbbed, then she unlocked the nearest door and dragged her jacket, her luggage, herself out into the clean chill of night.

She stood in the rocks and dust, beneath moon and stars, and tensed a moment, waiting for the gunshot that never came. Hearing only the faint sob of someone else's tears.

Backtracking north, Allison got a hundred yards up the road before hearing the car start again. She looked back to see it returning to the highway, red taillights weaving away in the dark like the receding eyes of a banished devil. But this was no victory—the same devil would come again when she expected it even less.

North, she guided herself along the center line, keeping a watch on the road for snakes, and other things that bit.

Life was so good to him sometimes, Boyd was almost tempted to believe he didn't deserve such a rich bounty of beauty and reward. While dealing blackjack he had seen no few tourists learning that they could not beat the house edge, and turning in desperation to patron saints. If ever there was a tipoff to incompetence, a full-blown novena was it. Saint Expedite was popular, the bringer of money, and evidently on vacation much of the time. But somebody up there was always on duty for Boyd, it seemed, and he supposed he should just accept it. Clearly, his was a charmed life.

Take his luck. Down for a day, Allison ransoming his computer files, but he'd decided this was Los Angeles' fault. L.A. was just plain evil, a smog-filled trench where his big brother would always be waiting to laugh at him. He never should have planned on living there in the first place. Krystal would say that the very intent had injected bad karma into his life. Within a few scant hours of returning to Vegas, he was back on top of the world again. Love had returned to his life. Of all the call girls in all the flyers along the Strip, he had to call Krystal Lyte.

After seeing him turn up the Lovers card from her tarot deck,

Krystal made him pack and they'd left the motel together. She led him back to her apartment as though it were the most logical next step in the world. That he was moving in seemed implicit—she'd told him that the motel was beneath him, that she wouldn't be able to stand the thought of him languishing there. Boyd prided himself on being astute enough to realize that most men would by now begin questioning this turn of events, and thereby spoil everything. Not him. He had once again been patted on the head by grinning angels, and surely it would only be a matter of time before they clued him in on how to get his money.

"Interesting decor," he told Krystal as he surveyed her apartment. Suns and moons and stars, rising and setting in each room. Every flat surface held a candle or an incense burner. And then there were the rocks. Oh yes, rocks aplenty. Crystals lay everywhere, in every size imaginable. Scatterings like jeweled gravel, jagged chunks the size of his fist, massive geodes like meteorites whose hollow shells had split open to reveal miniature galaxies. As for walls and fabrics, she had a definite affair going with peach and rose pastels.

"I thought you'd like it. What I've tried to do is create an environment for myself that's both energizing *and* harmonious."

"That's *so* apparent. It's very tranquil. Like a Zen garden." Boyd noted with approval the sunken, kidney-shaped bathtub. "Are those Thermajet Model 1200 airflows I spy down there?"

"Wow, you don't miss a thing, do you?" Krystal bit lightly down on her lower lip while tossing her head back, the raven spill of her hair glimmering. She was the pinnacle of human evolution. "Are you wanting to take a bath now?"

"Krystal Lyte, you read my mind. Let's fire up this little bit of paradise, why don't we." She cranked handles, and faucets gushed. "You wouldn't happen to have any champagne chilled, would you?"

She did. As water thundered, from the kitchen there came a clink of glasses and the pop of a cork, while Boyd raided the linen closet for towels. Carrying a plush armful, he lingered before a hallway bookcase he'd passed over when she'd first shown him around. Most of the titles on her shelves struck him as about what he would expect to find in this well-appointed fairy palace. *Crystal Magic. Crystals: Pebbles from God's Driveway. Tracing Your Ancestors to Atlantis. Blame It on Your Past Lives.*

"I could make a reading list for you." Krystal had rounded the corner from the kitchen, carrying a tray laden with a black bottle, stemmed glassware, fruit. "Some of those you wouldn't want to read right off. They're a little too advanced for beginners."

"Ah," Boyd said. Most he wouldn't want to read, period. Then a matched pair of book spines caught his eye.

"Hey. *Hey.* Wait a minute." The titles alone filled him with dread. "*The Complete Marquis de Sade,* volumes one and two? What are these doing here?"

She shook her head. "It's not what it looks like."

"I'm not into pain, Krystal, really I'm not. I can't stress this to you enough: Boyd Dobbins is not into pain."

"Then hush up about it, you silly, neither am I. And if you'd just get in that tub, I can *show* you how much I'm not either."

Boyd lit candles while she sowed a handful of bath salts into the water. When she pressed a switch to activate the airjets, the entire tub metamorphosed into a steaming cauldron. She was out of her dress in moments, and stepped down into the bubbles, stood in the center smiling at him, arm extended. Her hair began to dampen with sweat and cling to the contours of her shoulders, her breasts, and for a moment Boyd could only stare with the awe of a boy opening one of his father's secret magazines, to see for the first time the mystery of the unconcealed other.

"You really are Venus on the half shell, you know that?"

"And you're just the sweetest guy. Now pour the champagne."

They soaked and wallowed, fed each other grapes and slices of mango and papaya, tipped their glasses to each other's lips to let the champagne tickle from within, while the surging water tickled everywhere else. They leaned against opposite ends with their legs twining together in the center, and she would lift her feet to diddle his chest with her small, nimble toes.

"I didn't think this was, like, any of my business back at the motel," she said, "but now that, well, things have turned out the way they have . . . what happened to your shoulder?"

Boyd touched the skin, still tender and red, speckled with a dozen tiny scabs. "I went through a very upsetting breakup the other day. It just . . . came out of nowhere, but it was for the best. Obviously. She wasn't a well woman, in a lot of ways. Would you believe she did this to me with a cactus?"

"Ow! Ow! Ow!" Krystal recoiled with empathy. "After we dry off, maybe I can help you with that. I've got crystals to promote healing and reduce pain." Of course. Of course she would. "You aren't married, are you? This wasn't your wife?"

He wiggled his fingers. "You don't see any evidence of old rings, do you? No, she was just the final stop on the path to your door. We broke up, I was dealing with the loneliness, then I found you. See how it all fits together? Would the cards lie?"

Krystal squealed and lifted both legs to drum her feet onto the roiling water. "So you're not planning on seeing this woman again, ever?"

"Well, I need to talk to you about that. . . ."

And then he felt awful, because her sweet little face seemed to crack right in two, so he hastened to explain that while his heart belonged to her, access to a substantial amount of his money belonged for now to Allison. Seeing Allison again would just be business, about which Krystal, he was dismayed to learn, had no room to complain. When her pager went off, he sat in the bubbles with growing dejection as she put their conversation on hold, grabbing her cordless phone and checking in with what he assumed was her escort agency.

"At the Flamingo Hilton," she was saying. "Wait, I didn't catch that—what was that room number again?"

"Hey. Hey!" he cried. "What is—"

Krystal grinned at him, slid down in the tub a fraction. Her leg shot out of the water, instep clamping over his mouth. Boyd sputtered and she giggled, splashed water at him with her hand.

"No, no, I'm not still entertaining now," she said.

Boyd yanked her pruny foot from his mouth. "Like hell she's not!" he shouted toward the phone. He struggled free of her leg and lunged for the phone in a great tidal surge. "You tell that degenerate at the Flamingo he's got two good hands, and if he's so horny, put them both to use!"

Krystal was swatting at him with one fist, twisting the phone from his reach. "Look, maybe it's not such a good time right now, maybe you should send somebody else. Tia sort of looks like me. If he's drunk maybe he won't know the difference." Boyd could hear a faint male voice, yammering from the other end. "Look, some things have come up, I sort of need some time— What? No, no, you silly, that was my brother, his wife's just left him. . . . I do so have a brother! Don't be so paranoid!"

She talked her way out of it, then tossed the phone onto the heap of towels. Glared at him. "That was a dumb thing to do, Boyd, yelling at him like that."

"Well, hell—" He squirmed, sloshing in the turbulence. Gazed down at the water, his nipples. His hairless chest looked boiled. "This call-girl thing, I don't know about this in the long term."

"It's how we met in the first place, Boyd. How can you have such a problem with this?"

"You don't think it's going to take some adjustment on my part, that you're planning on continuing in this line of work?"

"I don't see why this should come between us. I'm sure you met lots of women in the casinos—you *had* to. Now did your last girlfriend hold that against you? Did she ask you to quit?"

"Blackjack doesn't require condoms! Blackjack has no risk of venereal disease! And I would never leave you sitting alone in this tub to go deal a game of blackjack!"

"I have a job to do, and I have my reasons for doing it. And I have bills to pay, Boyd. You have bills, I have bills, everybody has bills. If we don't pay our bills, they take our toys away. That's how it works."

He sighed. She had so much to learn. "If it's bills you're worried about, how many bills you think the two of us'd be able to pay with three-quarters of a million dollars?"

"*That's* how much your ex took you for?" Krystal swung a hand into her forehead with a soft, wet slap. "Wow. Oh wow. I must be living right, finally, because this level of karma . . ." Then her widened eyes went narrow. "You're not, like, planning on killing her or anything, are you? Because I can't go along with that—"

"Would you relax? I don't plan on killing anybody."

Even if he were so inclined in the first place, there was no need. Most things that could be had by killing could just as easily be had for a well-told lie.

"But while I'm thinking about it," he went on, "there's one thing I need to warn you about. We get stopped by the police, or anyplace else I might have to flash ID, you have to remember to pretend my name is Peter Wackermann."

chapter seven

Allison's first true look at Coyote Ridge came when Saturday was still virginal, the sun just high enough to glare over the red rocks that would forever prevent the town from expanding east. It was one main street and a handful of intersections, the grid-work layout falling apart at the edges, with half-conceived roads skewing off into odd angles and dead ends. A desert town scattered with sun-baked buildings, low on opportunity and high on dust. A sweaty tableau of red and brown, white and gray, beneath a sky lightening into cloudless blue. Green, however washed out, was striking, and limited to a few pines mangled by sun and wind.

For the first time in her life she'd slept on a public bench, a duffel bag for a pillow, awakening before most of the town. She sat for a while in the quiet dawn, watched Coyote Ridge come alive around her. Rubbed out the stiffness and found the diner that she knew had to be around here somewhere—just look for the cluster of pickup trucks with the gun racks.

She did not realize how hungry she was until setting foot in the diner, assaulted by the cruel aroma of two dozen breakfasts. Mostly working men at the tables, all eyes up and lingering just a moment too long—a stranger in town and no idea who she was, their glances at each other full of subtle small-town telepathy.

You don't want to know, she almost said.

Allison ordered, washed up in the rest room, cleaned off the dust and a film of sweat that still carried the taint of Las Vegas; came back out and ate possibly the best breakfast of her life. She waited until the check came to grill the waitress.

"You wouldn't happen to need any help here, would you?"

"Full up. Sorry, hon." The waitress shook a head of peroxide hair, obviously guarding this job as a long-term investment. "You could check down at Dickory Doc's. That's a bar. There was some trouble the other night, I hear there may be an entry-level position for a bright young career woman."

"And Dickory Doc's, where's this?"

The waitress aimed a chipped pink fingernail at the bank of windows overlooking the main drag. "Well, right here we're at one end of the beautiful Sunset Strip. Doc's is at the other."

A decrepit truck then passed before the windows, swerving and farting clouds of exhaust. Allison could have sworn that in the pickup's bed she had seen a man wrestling with a frantic and mad-eyed goat.

The waitress grinned, pointing after the truck. "That way," she said. "Just follow the high rollers."

Making up the posters was Krystal's idea. Everyone looks at posters that lead off with HAVE YOU SEEN, she told Boyd, because they always think they might've. Telling him then how she could never pass by one for a lost dog or cat without wanting to cry, because she imagined the owners making their hopeful rounds, thinking this might be the one to reunite them with their lost pet. She would focus on the animal's picture, trying to get a sense of where it might have gotten to, like a psychic aiding the police, but it never worked.

"It's the thought that counts," Boyd said, trying to cheer her up, for she had worked herself into such a state of sorrow.

He went through his luggage until he found a photo of Allison that would reproduce well, a close-up shot when he'd surprised her with the camera one morning. Allison, deep in thought the instant before, now turned to the lens, composed despite his interruption. Disheveled blond hair pushed back from her forehead, and her eyes as green as moss, staring clear and defiant, and maybe a trifle disappointed, as though she'd just awakened from a splendid dream and knew she could never find her way back. Tip of her thumb at her pensive lower lip. He wondered what she'd been thinking about; and why, when he met her gaze from that picture, a worm of hurt nibbled below his heart.

Boyd mocked up the layout on Krystal's Macintosh computer, leaving a block of white space for the photo, and filling the rest with the promise of a reward for any information leading to his finding Allison Willoughby, last seen leaving Las Vegas on Friday, September 8. He added her height, her hair and eye colors, other vitals. Across the bottom he pasted a number for the answering service to which Krystal subscribed for the benefit of her regular clients. This allowed them to bypass the escort service, which she could in turn avoid dealing in for a cut of her private liaisons.

As he proofed it, Krystal read the mock-up over his shoulder. "Is all that true?"

"Not exactly," he said. Obviously she was referring to the part about Allison having vanished without her medication, and how if she was off it for too many days, she would be at risk for seizures, delirium, worse. "I'm just trying to up the sympathy factor. How's it work for you?"

"Strike that bit about spinal deterioration," she said, "and put down miscarriage, instead."

"Oooo, good idea! That *really* turns her into a ticking bomb, doesn't it?" Boyd hopped from the chair and squeezed her around the waist. "You're getting the hang of this."

He printed a laser copy of the layout, trimmed the excess from the photo, double-checked the dimensions, then ran everything to a Kinko's copy shop. He sprang for full color, leaving orders for the photo to be enlarged, then inset, with a rush-job request for a thousand copies.

"You really want to find this poor girl, don't you?" said the clerk, a pudgy woman with tiny cross-shaped earrings and matching necklace.

He bowed his head, biting on one knuckle. "I'm all the hope she has left in the world."

"And a much better world this would be if there were more out there just like you. God bless you, Mr. Wackermann."

"No, God bless us, every one," he told her.

Dickory Doc's didn't open until noon, every last grim thing Allison had expected and steeled herself to tolerate, from Wyatt Earp–era wooden floors, to the bison and cougar and coyote heads mounted on the walls, to the stuffy air whose molecules seemed to rub across the skin. The sign in the window read *Waitress Needed,* Magic Marker on cardboard. Allison grabbed it on her way in and walked it over to the bar, where a big-boned, leathery man with a gray ponytail and red bandanna stood alone, toweling off mugs.

"Can I tear this sign up now," she asked, "or do you want to interview for a few days first?"

He looked her over, flat-eyed and deadpan, with the grizzled beginnings of a beard, or the advanced stages of a binge. "No, just leave it in one piece," he said, amiable enough. "What if you get shot too, then I got to make up another one."

"Shot," she echoed. "The waitress I'd be replacing was shot. Here? In this bar?"

"The sheriff ruled it an accident." The man watched her for a moment, then, taking pity, smiled through the graying stubble, dry lips like rawhide. "She's not dead, if that's what you're worried about, and it wasn't me. If it's any encouragement, I got another one works here, been here six years and hasn't been shot once."

"Knifed?"

"Not to my knowledge."

"I'll take it," said Allison. Vagrants couldn't be choosers. "I feel lucky."

"Good attitude. I like that."

He drew her a beer to seal the hiring, drew one for himself, and they sat at the dim bar, dust motes swimming all around. They watched the day grow hotter outside, coughing up as much of their lives as it took to keep the silence from becoming ominous. His name was Clarence, he told her, and he discouraged people from calling him Doc, let alone Dickory. He had given the bar its name because when he'd bought the building twelve years ago, it had been full of mice, like the clock in the nursery rhyme.

"Yeah, Punjab ate well *then,*" he grinned, and took her back in the stockroom to show her an enormous cat holding down stacked cases of Budweiser, curled into a surly wrecking ball of yellow fur, tattered ears, and attitude. "Of course, that was when you could still *move* your lean, mean self," he said to the cat, then scruffed the back of its neck. Punjab blinked and rumbled like a wheezing panther.

"That's the biggest cat I've ever seen," she said.

Clarence nodded. "Nineteen pounds, last time I weighed him, and he waddles like two ducks sewed together. Don't you?"

Punjab hissed with malcontention.

"Oh yeah, you're the devil, all right. Hung around this bar long enough, he's learned to understand English, I swear he has."

Clarence ushered her back out to the bar, where they finished the last of their drafts. He pointed, finally, at her luggage on the floor. "Most people don't bring along their bags to look for work. You just get into town this morning?"

"Just."

"Know anybody?"

"You mean besides you and Punjab?" She shook her head.

"So what do you think of the place so far?"

She took a breath; looked out the window, where a strong wind swirled up a dust devil in the street. "I think if I'd gotten here a day or two sooner, I might've met up with Thelma and Louise."

. . .

That afternoon, Clarence put her in touch with a local real estate agent who had two rentals available. Price was the sole determining factor, Allison opting for the considerably cheaper, silver-skinned and rounded trailer on an unshaded lot of cracked earth. It came with a few mismatched pieces of furniture, at the end of a three-quarter-mile walk from Dickory Doc's.

She used the bar's phone to call the sheriff in Prescott and report last night's assault, wincing at the suspicious pause on the line after she gave Marshall Dillon's name. "Look, I met a John Wayne once. It does happen," she said. A deputy would be over to take a formal complaint later, she was told, and then she hung up feeling certain that nothing would come of it, that she would be bottom-of-the-pile priority. Even if Dillon was picked up, even if extradited from Utah, she'd have to come back in a few months to testify in court, word against word, hers against that of a fine community pillar who refused to send his kids to day care.

Allison worked her first shift that evening, Saturday night in Coyote Ridge, Dickory Doc's packed elbow to elbow, and thumping with country-western and blues-rock. Excluding that fateful Casino Night in Seattle, she'd not waitressed in seven years, but fell readily back into the routine, arms and legs and hands remembering how—the balance of a tray, the clinking weight of four longneck bottles dangling from each handful of splayed fingers. Drinks were simple, mostly beers and shots, and demand was high.

She learned faces, a few names, most reacting neutrally to her presence—beneath notice, or yet to prove her worth. She found herself soon involved in a case of mutual dislike with a fortyish woman named Loretta, all hips and swagger and ratted red hair. Of course she liked whiskey sours; of course Allison didn't make them properly. It wasn't until Loretta lit a Marlboro and groped some cowboy's thigh that Allison realized why she had disliked her on sight: Loretta was chipped from the same mold as Boyd's atrocious and slack-tummied playmate from the casino.

Allison slept late the next day, then walked around Coyote Ridge to see what little else there was to see, strolling up and down the main drag peering into shop windows. The one surprise was the presence of a motorcycle dealership on the edge of town, near the diner . . . Coyote's Paw Harley-Davidson. She gazed in at the showroom gleam of lacquer and chrome, wanting suddenly the feel of wind through her hair, just her and an iron horse. Red lettering stenciled across one plate-glass window read WE CARRY ST. JOHN'S APOCALYPSE, and she wondered what that meant.

In the center of town she found what she later supposed was destiny, the pen of the playwright in this from the beginning. A mere day and a half after attempted sodomy, it was no accident that she encountered the hunting gear shop. Wall racks bristled with the long barrels of rifles and shotguns.

Under the watch of the bald, sunburned proprietor, Allison perused the four glass cases full of revolvers and semiautomatic pistols. Lethal and invested with dire potential, they gleamed, they invited the fit of her hand.

"Can I see that one there?" she asked, and pointed, wondering how long it would take her to save enough to match the price tag.

Knowing suddenly that it was something she would have to do, that, wild horses or not, you could never ride far enough away as long as the worst wrongs remained unrighted. Because there was abuse, and there was therapy, and, finally, there was justice.

Boyd and Krystal packed for the road Sunday morning, picked up the posters from Kinko's, and traded Vegas for the desert. As he'd not yet gotten around to repairing his windshield, they took Krystal's car, a snazzy little Mazda the color of coral, with a five-CD changer in the stereo.

The idea was to cover, to a radius of a couple hundred miles, all the routes that Allison could have taken away from the city. Fortunately, these were few. The highway grid in and out of Las Vegas was a simple X, with a couple of secondary roads branching off the east half after several miles. The city's isolation was, Boyd had heard, a major factor in discouraging armed heists of casinos. While it could be done, theoretically, overcoming the small army of casino security would still be the easy part. The true ordeal would be getting away from a city whose conduits could be shut down with a minimum of roadblocks.

They began with U.S. 95 to the northwest, on his guess that Allison might have intended to head back up to Seattle. Out here in the broiling wastelands, they would stop at small clusters of businesses that scratched out their livings catering to travelers, or at the true rogues who went at it alone, their gas stations or their cafés occupying a patch of ground like lonely homesteaders. Up the posters went, with staples or tape, and sometimes a crusty owner would demand to know what they thought they were doing, always softening when they saw Allison's picture, and her fate. "She could die if we don't find her," Boyd would tell them, and they would relent and nod him toward some high-visibility area, wishing him luck, and by the time they got to Beatty, Krystal had become Allison's dear hand-wringing sister.

"Some good job we did on this poster," he said while they pulled back onto the highway. "It's really getting to them, when they take the time to read it."

"It's not what it says, it's the picture." Krystal drove with one hand, waved a copy at him with the other. "It's the picture that's selling it to them. They like her on sight, most of these people—can't you tell?"

Boyd shrugged, miffed. "Well, don't forget who took the damn picture."

"She *is* pretty," said Krystal, "but there's something else going on there. In her eyes, I mean, like something that goes way back." Krystal nibbled at her lower lip, steered around the sun-dried remains of a dead dog. "Oh, that's so sad." Back to the photo. "Was she abused when she was young?"

"Say what?"

"When she was young, was she sexually abused?"

"No," he said, almost defensively. "She would've told me something like that."

"Don't be so sure." Krystal handed the poster back, staring at the road, the vanishing point on the horizon. "There's a look sometimes, when that's happened. It's nothing you could, you know, measure, but it's there. I have a client, a psychologist, he comes to Vegas on junkets with a bunch of other psychologists, and he once told me he could tell within the first two minutes of meeting a woman whether she'd been molested as a child or not."

"That's creepy." Boyd put the poster back in the box, where he wouldn't have to look at those staring eyes. Allison would have told him—wouldn't she? "That shrink, did he say . . . I mean, what was his, um, impression of . . . of you?"

"A clean slate. Dad and my uncles and the neighbors, they all kept their hands to themselves." Behind big dark sunglasses, she broke into a wide and beautiful grin. "He said I was goofy enough as it was, without that adding any more baggage."

"You'd tell me, wouldn't you? If he was wrong, if he missed something, you'd tell me?"

"Of course, you silly. We're soulmates, it was in the cards. We can't have any secrets."

No secrets. She really believed this was the best policy, as surely as he believed he'd not yet heard the weirdest from her. They had decided the other night to impose a moratorium on further revelations, let the rest keep while they got to know each other better over the next few days, after which the riskier admissions could dribble free whenever the moment felt right. A good plan: It would allow him time to devise the proper spin on where this money they were chasing had come from. He wasn't sure how Krystal was going to react, karmically speaking, although surely she could live with it if he was expected to overlook the call-girl thing.

And when he watched her sleep each night, he wondered if there wasn't some miracle unique to Krystal. Her body and, while he had never given much thought to these things before, her soul. *Whore.*

Say it—she was a whore. He could mouth the word above her in the moonlight but could not feel it connect, as though the word and all that it implied rinsed off her like rain. None of it could touch her, because she would not let it.

After blanketing U.S. 95 with posters, they took a couple of days for the south and southeast roads out of Vegas. Next they dropped down to southwest-bound I-15, the sterile pan of Southern California desert that he was really beginning to despise. Wicked L.A. karma shimmered on the horizon, and he knew he was going to have to fess up about skimming the casino eventually.

Laying preliminary groundwork. That was the trick.

"You do much gambling back there?" he asked her, Boyd driving now and finding that he could think better behind the wheel.

"A little." She toyed with a pewter pendant shaped like a crescent moon and inset with fuchsia sugilite. "I'm in and out of hotels a lot, kind of, and I've got the cash right there, so . . ."

"You win, or lose, mostly?"

"Oh, lose. I know I'd do better if they'd just, like, quiet things down some. Everything's so *noisy,* all those slot machine buzzers and bells, I can't focus, my vibes get all screwy."

"Yeah, they tend to count on that. How much do you lose?"

"Not much. Usually I'll drop one or two hundred combined on the slots and the wheel of fortune, sometimes craps, before I come to my senses."

"Stay away from the wheel, that one's a sucker trap. Highest house advantage there is. Gambling for people without a frontal lobe. No offense." He wagged a finger like a lecturer. "I'll let you in on a hard reality not a lot of people even recognize. The reason the house always comes out ahead is because, with very few exceptions, even when you win they don't pay off on the true odds you're risking on your bet. When you lose they make money, and when you win, they still make money off you."

He had her now. Krystal tucked her slim muscled legs beneath her on the seat, turning toward him as if learning she'd just been fleeced. "Like how?"

"Take the roulette wheel. That's an easy one to explain. The American version has slots numbered one through thirty-six, plus zero and double-zero. Thirty-eight in all, right? Now suppose you and I are there at the table placing our bets. Forget the red and black, forget split bets, line bets, all that. Just a straight-up bet on one number. How old are you again?"

"Twenty-five. Come on, sweetie, get with the program. I've told you once already, you can't remember it? For me?"

"I'm sorry, babe. Too many numbers in my head. I forget again and I'll suck all ten of your toes in public." She giggled; damage control was complete. "Let's say we slap down an even ten dollars, straight up on twenty-five, one chance in thirty-eight of hitting. And we win, because your vibes are so strong the ball can't help but drop right where it's supposed to. So how much should we be getting back then?"

"Three hundred and eighty dollars."

He shook his head. "Three-fifty. Roulette only pays off at thirty-five to one, and they keep the rest for themselves. So in the long run, if we play all night, they'll still come out ahead."

"That sucks! And they build this kind of advantage into every game?"

"Damn near. Only it's not always so obvious, sometimes it's hidden deeper in the game." He glanced over to see her frowning at the injustice of it all. "So this is why, when people hear about a casino, any casino, taking a big loss, a hard hit in the wallet, this is why it makes their day. This is why the people that stick it to them are seen as, well . . . as heroes."

"You can bet I'll cheer louder for the next winners I see." Krystal was turning this over, he could tell, seeking cause and effect. "The people that defy the odds, they're like walking karma that comes back at the casinos to settle the score."

"Krystal my love, you are *so* wise," and he smiled because the world was so good to him it was almost embarrassing. "I couldn't have said it better myself."

. . .

Beginning their second day on the road, Krystal would, every few hours, use her cellular phone to check her answering service. Since her cellular had Automatic Call Following, a roaming feature that would link it with whatever satellite happened to be nearest overhead, they could make calls from practically anywhere.

Messages left about Allison were steady, and the follow-up procedure simple: Boyd would return the calls, question whoever had left them, and decide these people were insane. One of them had just seen Allison doing table-dances in Reno. A trucker had gotten a blow job from her at an I-80 rest stop. One caller offered to find her for five hundred dollars a day plus expenses, while yet another had seen her doing local newscasts on TV in Idaho.

"Idaho has TV?" he said, and hung up. How discouraging. He'd not expected anyone to serve Allison up on a platter, but if they could at least get a handle on the direction she had gone, entire sections of the country could be eliminated.

"It was her, I'm quite sure of it," another man guaranteed. Boyd rolled his eyes, almost telling him to stand in line with the other sure things, who wouldn't have known Allison if she'd spat on them. "I won't soon forget her."

It was the end of the week now, and they were on their final stretch, papering I-15 from Vegas northeast across the tip of Arizona, into the high country of southwestern Utah. At midmorning they were taking a break at a rest stop, and Krystal had strayed off by herself. He could see her meditating in the lotus position atop a small hillock, against a backdrop of pines and wind-sculpted rock, everything dwarfed beneath wide blue sky. Sometimes he expected her to float right up into the clouds.

"She said her name was Allison, I remember that distinctly." The man sounded as though he was using a cellular as well. The connection fuzzed and waned, came back again. "This medication she's supposed to be taking—is it in part to curb violent mood swings?"

Boyd almost said no, then remembered the havoc Allison had wreaked on his car, his shoulder, Madeline's cactus patch. "She needs a little help with that sometimes."

"The last I saw of her was in Arizona, near a little town by the name of Coyote Ridge," said the man, and the way he described her, how she looked, how she talked, left little doubt in Boyd that he finally had a genuine sighting. "If you find her again, it may be worth a sum of money to you for me to see her again, if we could arrange that. She's caused me some . . . problems recently. Of course, this is something I'd want kept confidential between us."

And something about the man's voice began to touch Boyd like a chilly finger. He'd periodically heard voices like this in the casinos, and they would unnerve him with the prospect of whatever activities their owners might have in mind for the rest of the night. They sounded like people who placed a lot of importance on freezers and shallow graves. When he hung up, he didn't know which he was more grateful for: the lead, or to be rid of that voice.

"Looks like we finally got a possibility," he told Krystal as she returned from her meditations. "But I think the nutjob who gave it to me must've had a rough time growing up. I mean, what kind of parents would've named their kid Marshall Dillon, anyway?"

chapter eight

The air conditioner in Dickory Doc's wheezed like a horse ready for a bullet in the head. The place was beginning to smell as though its patrons were sweating out their drinks as quickly as they could pour them down, a smoky distillation of stale beer and tequila and sour gin. Close-walled, the bar felt charged with reckless passions and volatility, the wrong night to be stroking hair-trigger tempers.

This afternoon, at Coyote's Paw Harley, they had told Thomas St. John that he'd picked a bad day to roll into the Ridge, some freakish weather pattern folding the heat in upon itself to stew the town in its own gritty juices. Even the normally cool desert nights offered little relief, just more of the same.

For nine days on the road out of Panama City, Thomas St. John had been drinking down the miles the way others here drank their whiskey: hard, fast, and relentlessly. His van filled with new leathers to be delivered in a great southwestern loop—Florida up to Oklahoma, across the Texas panhandle, to New Mexico and now Arizona—he had left home with a sense of ghosts at his back and a burning need for open road. During yesterday's journey down a two-lane highway between magnificent red buttes that scraped the sky like the humps of stone bison, he knew there to be something therapeutic about traveling in their shadows, and in the smells of gasoline and bad coffee.

Ordinarily, he was surrounded by the smell of leather, soft and malleable. Leather, his stock in trade—cycle jackets and longrider dusters, chaps and vests, hats and caps, belts and slacks and skirts. He alone designed, with two dozen employees to cut and stitch the patterns into life. Not quite mass production, but he'd never been keen on the idea of upgrading himself into facelessness.

It was this craving for human faces that compelled him to schedule road trips twice a year, personally delivering samples of new leathers. Northern states every spring, southern and southwestern states in early autumn. Pointless, strictly from the accounting ledger's perspective—wholesalers and UPS delivered more efficiently than he could manage in his van. But nothing could replace the benefits derived from seeing where his labors would hang, from talking with those who stocked them, from meeting the people who looked them over, tried them on, paid their money, and wore them home. Isolate yourself from this, Tom was convinced, and you make yourself lesser for it.

The label, ST. JOHN'S APOCALYPSE. The motto, *Clothing for the End of the Road.*

"See those two?"

Tom felt a nudge at his elbow. Teddy Serafino owned the cycle shop, had insisted they come to Dickory Doc's before Tom turned in back at the bed-and-breakfast. Teddy was the son of a mixed-race couple, one parent white, the other black, and on the barstool at Tom's right he sat as hard and compact as a stone wall. A wiry goatee darkened a face the color of caramel; loose black spirals of hair brushed his shoulders, strayed onto one of the new leather vests Tom had brought to town.

"Those two, down at the end," Teddy pointing at a blond barmaid and a redheaded customer who squabbled across the bar. The subject of their mounting aggravation was lost to the general din. Tom tried to read their lips for a sense of what it was all about, but couldn't. Just didn't like breathing each other's air, maybe.

Teddy waggled his finger at the bar in front of himself and Tom. "Next round says those two'll be scratching eyes out inside of five minutes."

"You're on," Tom said, mostly to prove to himself that faith in a total stranger could still go rewarded.

Teddy activated the stopwatch feature of his wristwatch and they settled in for the duration. They mopped sweat with napkins already soggy from the bottles and their foreheads, the tension like a loaded gun at the other end of the bar. The others paid it no attention—desert rats and cowboys and bikers, and the women who attracted them, or were attracted by them. They converged like the symbiotic breeds that frequent a watering hole on the African savannah, obeying a universal law: Drink, for drink you must, but drink knowing you run the risk of turning into another's meal.

As much a charm school dropout as the redhead already looked, she grew meaner still over some new insult volleyed across the bar. She tried to get in the last word once the blonde's back was turned by flinging a pickled cherry at her.

"Maybe I should've told you before we bet that this has been building up awhile," Teddy said. "That blonde's new around here, been here about a week. Me, I wouldn't've minded knowing a little more about her, you understand, see if she'd like to straddle the hawg someday, but she got this definite 'Do not disturb' sign hung on her, you know what I'm saying? Thing with the redhead, I don't know *what's* up with that."

"Just the heat, is all," Tom said. Ever the optimist. "Now if we were in Canada, say, this wouldn't be happening."

"If we were in Canada, that redhead, she'd be throwing a moose pie instead of a cherry."

"I beg to differ. Cool climates lead to cool heads. Eskimos? In their native language, they don't even have a word for war."

"Yeah? How 'bout bashing the brains out a baby seal's head, they got a word for that?"

"Capitalism, I think." Tom rubbed the edge of Teddy's new vest between thumb and forefinger. "I should talk." Then he paused with his bottle before his mouth. "I still say another ice age might go a long way towards world peace."

Teddy shook his head. "Vikings. You forgot about Vikings. There goes your whole theory right there."

"Well, I tried," he said. It was no easy thing, figuring out how to save the world.

"Vikings fascinate the hell out of me," said Teddy. "I read up on those bad motherfuckers all the time. Sailing around in those wicked-ass longboats? Very first one-percenter-breed bikers, far as I'm concerned. And fearless? I read about this one, got captured in battle, about to get beheaded with an ax. Well, my man wasn't about to go out on his knees, bent over no block of wood, so he told them take that ax and hack him straight across the face instead, so everybody could see he didn't go pale in the face of death. They obliged . . . and so did he."

"That's one tough Viking!" Tom marveled. "Four years in the Marines and I never saw anything to compare with that."

"Yeah. Bygone age, though." Teddy shook his head sadly, then sat upright on the stool, pointing at the other end of the bar. "Looks like we got us a winner!" He clicked off the stopwatch.

"Time?"

"Three minutes, twelve seconds. You never had a chance. No one ever went broke betting on human meanness."

Tom nodded, truly sorry as he watched the stewpot of bad blood come to its inevitable boiling head. Harsh words led to a shove, the shove to a slap, and the slap was the pin on the grenade. The redhead decided to try using the blonde to wipe down the bar, and glass went crashing while drinkers grabbed whatever they could salvage, then cleared aside to give them room. Dickory Doc's roused with a mighty roar by the time the blonde landed a solid clout to the redhead's jaw and scrambled across the bar.

Tom glanced up at the big, grizzled man at their own end of the bar, a gray ponytail tied back with a red bandanna. Given the air of deferment to him, obviously whatever he said was law.

"You're not going to stop this?" Tom asked.

The man shook his head. "Nah. When a storm's been blowing up for this many days, you just got to let her blow herself out."

Tom had never yet seen a catfight that was not a spectacle of awe and horror and hilarity. There wasn't the brute strength of men out to break a head, and there was often even less finesse, and so they were almost comical, with uncontrollable roundhouse swings and the faces that can only be made by enraged women. But then there was the pure animal viciousness of tooth and claw; a dark, red-eyed bloodlust that few men ever achieved.

They kicked and they gouged, tore loose flaps in each other's clothes, bit when they could. When they weren't grunting in fury, they called each other names. In time they flung each other out the door to land beneath the stars above this desert town where dreams and old dogs came to die.

"I don't guess anybody calls the sheriff, do they," Tom said.

Teddy lifted one eyebrow. "Friday night, no high school football, now what do you think?"

Cheers met every move as the four mean little fists pummeled away, or yanked out a dangling lock of hair and whipped it aside like a puny scalp. Locked in a deathgrip, the sweaty women went rolling across the gravel lot, through an oil slick left by some drizzling engine.

When the blonde gave her rival's head a good knock against the lot, Tom thought she might be able to snatch victory from what was looking like defeat. But then the redhead reached up to bum a lit cigarette from some burly truck jockey, and went to work on the blonde's shoulder. She burned in one hole after another, through the tattered T-shirt, then skin, and the blonde began to yelp. For the redhead it was as good as scenting fresh blood. Her fingers jabbed forward, going for one wide green eye but missing, grinding out the cigarette on the blonde's cheekbone.

The lot erupted with roars of admiration, while Tom's gaze lowered, downcast. There was no comedy left now, only tragedy. He remembered when he used to try to intervene at such times as this, playing the peacemaker, before being taught the real value of a smile and an empty hand.

It didn't take long for the redhead to finish, with open-handed slaps and bitter bloody grins. Two final kicks in the ribs, and the blonde curled up like a question mark at the end of her life's sentence. She lay in the gravel and the dust and the oil, not moving except for the labor of ribs as she tried to breathe. The redhead was up and swaggering back into the bar to nurse her own wounds, drink her just rewards, celebrate victory. Something to tell her grandchildren about someday.

The sated crowd was swift to break, following its champion, like chickens with their pecking order, strutting away to leave a bird-sized heap of feathers and blood. To the rest, she didn't exist anymore, barmaid or not, and Tom found that peculiar.

"Hey, you coming?" Teddy asked. He glanced through the open door that he held.

"I don't think so. I'm rolling early tomorrow." He peeled two dollars from his wallet to pay off. "Spoils of war. Cheers."

Teddy tucked it into one of the new vest's slash pockets. He slapped his hand into Tom's for a soul-shake, slipped back into interlocked fingertips, then fired his index finger like a pistol. "Next year, then." He rubbed an admiring hand down the vest. "Got a real *Road Warrior* feel happening with these, should be moving like a cheetah on crystal meth, so keep my racks full, jah?"

The door shut on the voices and music, the lot empty now. Tom stared with a moment's trepidation toward where the blonde lay in her pain and defeat, deciding that if no one else cared to, then it fell to him to see if she needed help, or was even conscious.

A week before his first day on the road had been the 31st of August and the hottest day of the year, summer in the Florida panhandle saving up for a final blistering hurrah of sweat and tears. On that day Thomas St. John buried his mother.

The passing of Lorelei St. John had left him all but bereft of family, none remaining now save for Aunt Jess, down from South Carolina to mourn her sister's passing. Thin and arrow-straight, white hair knotted into a wispy bun, Aunt Jess poked along with a cane she did not need. Whenever he looked at it, Tom wished that he'd known more of his forebears. The cane had been handed down from some great-grandfather of Tom's who'd distinguished himself by bootlegging whiskey during Prohibition, and by bribing and conniving his way clear of any threats from the law.

Both Aunt Jess and his mother had, for as long as Tom could remember, claimed the man with a scandalous pride, defying the rest of the family who'd just as soon have locked his memory away in some musty closet. These two women had understood the grand old man even if no one else had: There was the law, and there was you, and, through no fault of anyone, sometimes the two of you just could not live with each other.

Cemeteries made fine places to nurture regrets, and certainly his family had their share. Here it was too easy to recall his mother under stage lights, pretending to be someone else, from the mind of Tennessee Williams, Eugene O'Neill. Dreaming, perhaps, of bigger, brighter stages onto which she had never walked, films she had never had a chance to star in. She pretended it didn't bother her, that Broadway's and Hollywood's loss was community theater's gain, but Tom had always known otherwise. While she'd been a fine actress, she couldn't carry off such a charade twenty-four hours a day. And it was for this that Thomas St. John grieved, as much as her death. The world had never been a particularly kind place to most mothers, especially those who had to try their best in spite of all they were inside, before their children, and all they ever wanted to be.

In the final stages of her cancer, Lorelei St. John had for weeks vacillated between burial and cremation, finally opting for the tradition of earth and roots. While he could not bring himself to ask, Tom wondered if she hadn't also chosen the cemetery as a devious ploy to bring him up here more often. A man could visit two graves as easily as one, and maybe he needed to. Mom, even in death, nudging him a few rows over, to stand before that headstone dated five years back and carved with the name HOLLY ST. JOHN, and to someday make his peace with it. To forgive the young woman who lay below it, forgive the husband he once had been to her.

But some things could not be rushed.

How they nagged at him, these persistent and unquiet dead.

He'd told no one, but for the past five years Tom had visited the grave of a stranger more often than that of his wife, one of a dozen surrounded by their own wrought-iron fence, a final family gathering from over a century ago. The thin dark wafer of tilted headstone was still surprisingly readable: DEBORAH SWEETWATER. She'd been born February 24, 1858; died November 16, 1877. *Walking with Jesus now,* the concluding sentiment to mark her passage.

He had no idea who she'd been, nor the life she'd led, only that she'd died at the age of nineteen, and this seemed as cruel an injustice as he'd ever really thought about. For some reason, five years ago, Holly's grave a new blot on the landscape, he'd adopted Deborah Sweetwater, or she him, as a kind of guardian saint.

Her name, those tender dates—they prompted in him a hundred questions, and when he'd imagined their answers, along came a hundred more. What had Deborah looked like? Sounded like? He wondered if she'd died a virgin; liked to think she had not. Wondered if she might have come here alone on summer days, to linger over the grave of a young man who'd perished long before she was born, and wonder if, time being no obstacle, they might not have made perfect lovers for each other.

They talked, in their fashion, Deborah Sweetwater listening to those things that professionals charged eighty dollars an hour to listen to, offering her advice for free. Some days, when the breezes fell still, he really thought he could hear her voice over that gulf of more than a century.

Oh, I do believe Holly'd like to hear from you, Deborah would say. *She's got her some places to go, Tom, and she can't get there from here, not so long as you're hanging on her like an anchor on a balloon. And I've a suspicion maybe it's the same for you too. . . .*

I think she's *sorry. So how 'bout* you, *for once?*

It always came down to this, and always the temptation was strong: to stand over Holly's grave and tell the woman, the body, whatever soul that lingered, to go to hell. But what would be the point? He'd told her as much already, five years ago. And look how well things had turned out then.

After his mother's burial, Aunt Jess elected to stay at Tom's beachfront house until Lorelei's headstone was erected. He took her up to see it, the granite slab anchored and leveled, the ruptured earth tamped smooth around the base. The cemetery was theirs alone, the earth seeming to breathe with rhythms that refused to be hurried. Oaks grew vast, green as Eden, and the elder headstones were slowly turning to pebbles—seasons of hot, wet air kind to one, cruel to the other.

Jess stood for a time without moving, hands laced together atop the cane, then lifted it to point at the polished gray face of Lorelei's stone.

"You made a fine choice, Tommy," she said. Thirty-six years old, premature gray streaking his hair, and still he was Tommy. "She'd've liked that. She'd've liked that very much."

Certainly he hoped so. Names and dates told nothing about who they marked, and while he'd still conceded to them, chiseled above was what he hoped would speak loudest to any stranger who might pause here. Cut into the rock was a pair of stringed masks, tilted side by side, that even Aristotle would have recognized. One mask smiling and the other crying, all the laughter and all the tragedy in the world reflected in their immutable faces.

Aunt Jess looked into the sky, starting to blacken with the threat of rain. "Coming up a cloud," she said, then shrugged it off. "What pains me most is that this plot here's a plot for one. And that's not right, that's not as it should've been." Aunt Jess looked him in the eye. "That was a wicked and hurtful act your father committed, running off the way he did. Leaving her alone with a four-year-old. It did something to her, more than she'd let on. There was no reason for her spending the rest of her life alone. But for better or probably for worse, that was her choice."

Jess dropped her hand to his, gave it a squeeze. "You've your own choice to make. What she most wanted you to hear from her own heart, she left to me to tell, because she didn't think she could get it out and still look you in the eye. So I told her even if it took this cane against your tail to make you listen you'd hear it.

"You buried a woman five years ago, and I know you still hold this notion it was your fault. But you didn't put the razor to her wrists. She did that all of her own choice. People who do such a thing do it no matter who it is they have in their lives. They do it because they choose to, not because someone drives them to it."

He nodded, having heard it before, from more than one mouth.

"Whether or not you remain alone is your choice," Jess went on. "But the last thing our Lorelei would want is for you to favor her in one regard: *Don't let your fear make that choice for you.*"

Both her hands folded back together atop the cane, and as he watched her, he heard the distant rumble of thunder. Jess looked at the new stone as if it could be reasoned with, or set at peace.

"Well," she said to it, "I told him, so that's that. Didn't even have to wallop him none, either, so maybe he listened."

And he had. But listening was the easiest thing in the world.

"Look at it this way, Tommy," Jess said, lighter now that she was freed of obligation. "There's someone out there for you. There sure is. She's breathing right this instant. In, out . . . in, and out again. The same as you. You just have to try hard to hear her." A smile now, and above it, the same bright eyes he recognized from family pictures of long ago. "I wonder what else she's doing right this instant. Ever think of that? Where she is, what she's doing?"

He looked at the headstone, at the simple faces carved there. The comedy and the tragedy. All the world a stage and all upon it merely players.

"Yeah," he admitted, finally. "I wonder that a lot."

. . .

Tom crunched over to where the fallen barmaid lay in blood and gravel and dust, went down on one knee beside her.

"Do you need any help?" he asked.

She lay in shadows and her eyes did not open. After a moment, her backhand flashed and a big chip of gravel ricocheted off Tom's forehead.

"A little lower, and maybe you can put my eye out next time." He fumed for a moment, even if this woman's pride was the last thing she had left to guard. "Anybody I can call for you, then?"

She struggled to rise onto one elbow, began to snicker when she saw him shield his face with crossed arms. The little bit of laughter did her face some good, battered as it was, all tangled hair and dirty scrapes, trickles of blood and swelling, and that crusty hole on her cheek like a wound from a .22-caliber bullet.

"No. Not one soul." She looked as though she wished she'd never gotten up that morning, maybe all year. "Pretty sad, huh?"

He'd lowered his arms by now, pulled a black kerchief from his pocket that he sometimes used as a bandanna. "It's clean," he said. She went scooting backward to lean against a dusty fender and dab away at the damage.

"You know, what I can't figure out is, how come nobody moved in to stop it, you coming from behind the bar." In any bar he'd ever lifted a bottle in, it was the Eleventh Commandment: Thou shalt not mess with the barmaid. Break it and unshaven angels would be dancing on your head in seconds, if only to save themselves from thirst.

The woman gave a spiteful look at the closed door. "Loretta? She's local. I'm not." This said it all. "You must not be either, if you didn't know."

Tom shook his head. "Just passing through."

She huffed with a low whiskey laugh. "Looks like your IQ just shot up forty points."

He grinned. "You're sure there's nothing you need?"

Her hand dropped to her side, came up with another big pebble that she held as if deciding whether or not to throw it. No fire behind it this time, just a stubborn pride and a smile too painful to let loose.

He nodded, started across the lot against a backbeat of bass, thumping like a sick heart inside the bar. With one last look back he saw that some enormous yellow cat was lumbering toward her. It stopped, looked at Tom and seemed to scowl in a terribly wise and intolerant way, then sauntered into the woman's arms. She hugged it like a lost child.

He got into his van, backed out, angling for escape, and when he stopped to gear it into drive there came a frantic thumping up along the side. Then her splayed hand slapped glass, and there she was in his window, more life in her than he'd thought was left. He cranked the window down.

"I just saw your license plate."

Florida tag, picture of a manatee in the center. "And?"

"You wouldn't happen to be going back there, would you?" The hope in her voice, her eyes, lit her up and put the damage into dim perspective. *"Would you?"*

"Eventually. I've got a lot of stops along the way, though."

"Can I ride along?" The fingers of both hands went curling over the edge of his door, fierce as eagle claws. "Only as far as Mississippi. I'll go halves on gas."

The last thing he wanted was an argument, her on one side and his conscience on the other, both of them telling him the very same thing. At least his conscience would never throw rocks.

"Mississippi?" he said, then what must have sounded to both of them like yes. Probably not the best decision he had ever made.

But the heat made people crazy, and crazy never ran out of ways to show its face.

chapter nine

Boyd could feel his chest loosening, thought he sensed it in Krystal as well, both of them breathing with relief now that the fight was over and Allison was moving without crutches. For more than two hours they'd been sitting fifty yards from Dickory Doc's, parked within the shadows alongside an adobe building whose front windows were filled with saddles and boots and hats.

"I don't mind telling you, that hurt to watch," he said.

"You don't think we should've gone over there and tried to stop it, maybe?"

"And end up part of tonight's hit parade too? What would that accomplish?" He patted Krystal's thigh. The bruises and the blood had visibly bothered her. "Hey, she'll be okay, Allie's strong. She's got good bone structure."

They watched as she finished speaking with some rangy fellow who then drove off in a van. While the plates said ST JOHN, he didn't look like any Bible-thumper, with those black clothes and that coiled wariness in his step. Boyd couldn't figure out the relationship; their body language didn't belie real acquaintance. Allison remained on the parking lot, alone, hugging a cat the size of a sandbag. After a few minutes she carried the cat inside.

"She's going back to work after all that?" Krystal sounded astonished. "Wow, that takes some moxie."

"Yeah, but if I know Allison, she'll be spitting in drinks."

"Are you sure this wasn't a wasted trip, that you've got your facts straight? I mean, look at this place, Boyd. Do you think anyone with the kind of money you say she took from you would choose to stay in a place like this?"

"I didn't say she had the money. What I said was she took my *access* to it. I don't think she even realizes what she's got." He sighed, fanning himself, the two of them sweating like a pair of hormonal teenagers. He pointed toward the stereo, where for maybe the sixth time today the same five CDs were playing, all mellow keyboards and Gaelic lyrics, the woman's voice overdubbed until it sounded as though the Mazda was surrounded by a choir of clones. "Could we listen to somebody else besides Enya for a change?"

Krystal looked wounded. "Don't you find her soothing?"

"Yeah, she's soothing. I'm about soothed into a coma, is the problem." He ejected the discs and replaced them with a few he'd brought along. Texas rockabilly, the Reverend Horton Heat. Guitars jangled and smoked, and Boyd was good for a few hours more.

This had been their longest day yet, and most productive. They'd followed this morning's lead down from Utah and come into town hoping only to find someone who might recognize Allison's picture, perhaps recall anything she had said about a destination. Never dreaming she'd still be here after a week. The chromosomal wreckage staffing the gas station had been no help. On the hunch that Allison might've been more interested in food than fuel, they had shown her picture at the town diner, to be told that she was working down the road. Dickory Doc's was already teeming with evening life when they got there, and Krystal popped in long enough to make sure that it was indeed Allison.

By the look of things in that parking lot just now, Allison hadn't wasted any time charming the pants off the entire town.

"I don't see why we can't walk right in and reason with her, now that we've found her," Krystal said.

"We didn't exactly part under the best of terms, and for sure after that fight she's not gonna be all that mondo jovial seeing me now." He shook his head. "Good karma stretches only so far."

"So what are we doing here, then?"

"I figure we bide our time. Find out where she's staying and maybe take a peek through her things first chance we get. There's no need for any unnecessary ugliness."

"So we won't be getting back to Vegas for another whole day?"

"At least."

Krystal flipped open her cellular phone and telescoped the aerial out the window. He could tell by the tones where she was calling, their tune ingrained after days of repetition. At this point it seemed a waste of money.

"We've found her already. Why keep checking for messages?"

"I've still got a career, you silly." She leaned over to peck him on the cheek. To think where those divine lips would be were they in Vegas right now was agonizing. "It's the weekend, I might have some regulars wondering what's happened to me. I can't just stand them up without any explanation."

It never ended. Of all the call girls he could've fallen for, he had to pick the one possessing a conscientious work ethic.

"I can't listen to this," he said, and left the car, toting one of the bottles of water they'd been relying on to stave off dehydration out here in Eastwood country. Boyd strolled quickly at first, then slowing after her voice had drifted away to nothing, quickstepping again when her flighty peal of laughter reached him.

What a godforsaken little dump this place was, suffocating beneath a blanket of low, dark clouds. They turned the sky bleak, claustrophobically devoid of stars, with barely a hint of the moon seeping through. No wonder people beat on each other here—the town itself drove them to it.

He looked back at Dickory Doc's, at the glow of neon in the windows, remembering a concept he'd heard another dealer at the Ivory Coast expound on during a break. Theory had it that there existed parallel universes, an infinite number, and each time you made a major decision you created another one where still lived the path your life would've taken had you decided the other way.

Odd as it was, he couldn't help wondering what he and Allison were doing tonight in the parallel universe where he'd said no to Madeline's scheme to skim from his table. Or in the universe where Allison had never become suspicious and gone snooping after him.

Of course, in those universes he'd never have met Krystal, which hardly seemed fair, so he wondered if there shouldn't be one where you got to have it all—one measly parallel universe in the cosmic crapshoot where you broke the house bank. Surely there had to be a way of tapping into this system. By the time he got back to the car to find Krystal off the phone, he could imagine zapping between universes as easily as channel-surfing by remote control.

"Hey sweet thing," Krystal said, "what'd you get up to out there?"

"I've just been thinking about probability theory and quantum mechanics." Boyd realized then that there had to be a universe in which Krystal hadn't become a hooker at all. "I have some exciting new ideas to share with you."

"Oh, cool." She waved a scrap of paper with a number written on it. "But listen, first, something weird has come up from that poster. Someone really wants to talk to us, he's called four times since I checked this morning. The last couple times, he told the service to be sure and tell us Allison left a package with him."

"Package?" His heart skipped a beat. "What kind of package?"

"It's just an answering service, they don't go into that much detail."

Boyd looked at the paper, saw that there was no name. "This is a Vegas number. Oh man, if we've come all the way down to the pimple of the universe for nothing . . ."

When he returned the call, it was answered on the fifth ring by some cautious, neutral voice. Boyd explained who he was.

"Right, right! Howdy! Thought you'd never call. Howdy!" The guy sounded suddenly overjoyed, although his accent was definitely no howdy accent. East Coast, more like. Las Vegas again—it could rewire a person from the gender out. "So I ran into your runaway girl, the one on the poster, and . . . you still there?"

Boyd could feel a heat headache coming on, exacerbated by the threat of idiocy. "Still here."

"Howdy! Right! Like I'm saying, she comes into my place of business and checks this package behind the counter, and tells me she'll be by for it sometime later, or send someone else for it. Says she's heard I sometimes store items in transit, for a small fee, if you catch my drift. Now, never mind I'm thinking I don't know this girl. I see your flyer, and I'm thinking if she dies, maybe I'm in the middle of something and don't know exactly what I'm in the middle of, and that's not such a good place to be in this town. So are you the next of kin, or what?"

"The next pea in the pod. Have you opened up that package?"

"What are you saying? Are you *accusing* me of something?"

"No no no no no!" cried Boyd. "I'm just asking. For all I know right now, we could be talking about two different women."

"What are you saying about my eyesight? Are you accusing me of blindness? Are you saying I got no memory for faces?"

"Would you calm down? Just chill out a minute." Fifty to one this was a hustler on the scam. "When did she bring this in?"

"Two, three days ago, maybe, like that?"

Which did not sync with the timetable that put her here. "No, that doesn't fit with the other information I've got. It had to be somebody else you saw."

"Hey, pisspot, if my help in this isn't appreciated, I don't need this disrespect. I got two good eyes, and I'm telling you I talked to this girl two, three days ago."

"Good for you, asswipe." Scam artist for sure. Krystal was looking quizzically at him, and he winked—everything's under control. "I just saw her myself, less than an hour ago, not fifty yards from where I'm sitting right this instant."

"Oh yeah? Just where is that, cock-knocker?"

"Coyote Ridge, Arizona. You're not even in the right state anymore, shithead. She hasn't been in Nevada for a week."

The man seemed to relent. "Well? Hmmm. Maybe you're right." He started to laugh. "One thing, though. I don't know if it means anything to you, but when she was checking this package with me, she starts tee-heeing, says whatever I do, if he should come in after her, don't give the thing to some short numbnuts with a stiff shoulder, because she'd whacked him with a cactus."

Boyd moaned and went weak, letting his head fall against the steering wheel. The horn bleated once.

"Umm . . . about some of those things I just said . . ."

"Oh, so that meant something after all. I guess that'd make you numbnuts, then. Who's the shithead now, smart guy?"

"You're talking to him." Boyd laughed anemically. Clearly, he was going to have to get a handle on this diplomacy thing. "Look, some angles on this end just aren't squaring. Let me get them figured out first, and I'll get back to you tomorrow. I'll make it worth your time, I promise."

"You do that." He began to turn more sympathetic. "Seemed like a nice girl, this runaway of yours. I don't know what she's into, but me, I'd hate to see her run into any truculence, you know. Well! Tomorrow! Let's count on it."

The line went dead, and Boyd stared at the phone.

"What was that all about?" Krystal asked.

"I don't have a clue." Truer words he'd never spoken. "But I think maybe the parallel universes are starting to converge."

chapter ten

Gunther hung up his phone a moment before he heard Madeline hang up the other extension, then met her in the hallway. His grin broadened, Gunther waiting for her to admit who exactly had put them back in the running for the seven-hundred-thousand-dollar sweepstakes.

"Okay," she finally said. "You played that fairly well."

"Fairly well. You *loved* it, you're not fooling me one bit." He grabbed her wrist as she jabbed his chest with rigid fingers, the nails like maroon daggers dimpling his shirt and the skin beneath. "Only thing you do worse than take a compliment is give one, anybody ever tell you that?"

She was laughing in his face then, but not cruelly. He could smell the last few cigarettes on her breath, felt her fingers curve into sickles as she dragged the points down his chest.

"You're a savant in your own way, I'll admit that," she said. "If you need a pat on that hairy back of yours, then I *did* enjoy the way you got Boyd so agitated he blurted out where he is."

"Yeah. You make a man think he's arguing with an idiot, he'll tell you anything."

Gunther went on sudden attack, seizing a double handful of Madeline's breasts and burying his face in the smoky copper of her hair. She whooped and thumped a fist against his back, and he grabbed her around the waist, twirled and dipped her, both of them laughing as he spun her upright again.

"Come on, let's go get you packed, we're back on the road tonight." He started to pull away, but she drew him up short with one hand clamped around his arm. In his face a second later, her kisses like bites—carnivorous, more teeth than lips.

Departures would have to wait, it looked like.

They dragged one another to his bedroom, tearing off clothes along the way. On the bed they grappled for supremacy, and when his touch glided from her ribs to the looser skin sagging from her belly, Madeline slapped his hand away, slapped his face, and he had to grab both wrists and flip her over, then bite the back of her neck until she stopped kicking. After she promised not to slap anymore, she lunged for the bedside table, the tube of lubricant that sat there curled halfway up from the bottom like toothpaste.

Madeline preferred it anally half the time, and tonight was no exception, starting out on knees and elbows and gradually letting him drive her farther and farther down, until she lay flat out, at one with the mattress. Her right arm would begin to flail, lashing back with a fist that she battered into the side of his hip. Mornings, he would be black and blue beneath the pale olive of his skin. Pain for her was give as well as take, and essential. Sometimes Gunther wondered what it would be like to look her in the face during sex, but the closest he ever got was catching her profile in a death's-head snarl as she wrenched out her climactic feral grunts. They were eerily low, like a man's, and sometimes the connection was made: This is what it would be like in prison.

After it was over they lay atop tangled sheets, and Madeline was all drying sweat and curling cigarette smoke and willful calm in the night. She always caught her breath before he did.

"So are we off to get you packed, or what?" he said.

"Yeah, in a minute." Dragging on her cigarette, a dim outline in the darkness. "You know as well as I do there's not a lot we can do before it's daylight and places start opening up again."

Gunther watched as she crushed out her half-smoked cigarette in an ashtray, its Two-Eyed Jacks logo clotted over with ash. In the gloom her hand trailed slowly from her mouth, down between her breasts, lingering over her stomach before she tucked her entire arm across it in such a way as to cover as much as possible. Her hand curled into a secret fist, clenching, unclenching.

"When we catch up with him, after we get whatever we need, I want you to promise me something," Madeline said. "If anybody else gets in the way, fine, you do what you need to do. But I want you to let *me* be the one to kill Boyd. I want that for myself."

"Sure," he said, but did not know why she was even bothering to ask. "It's all brains on the wall to me, anyway."

For the past week they'd had to confine the hunt for Boyd Dobbins to their free hours, still having to maintain normal appearances with their regular gigs. Back at the Ivory Coast after a feigned pair of sick days, Madeline went through the motions of firing Boyd in absentia for failing to report for his shifts.

Gunther continued to work out of Two-Eyed Jacks, as though he had nothing better to do than collecting that weekly ten-percent vig for Toby Costas. On his own time he circulated from one no-tell motel to the next, guessing that if Boyd was still in town, he'd be keeping as low a profile as possible, which eliminated the high-visibility glitz of the hotels along the Strip and downtown. For days Gunther flashed a picture of Boyd that Maddy had pulled from a casino file, greasing the occasional desk clerk's palm, finally running across a fellow who recognized the photo: Lose the mustache and that's him, a one-nighter who'd not been back. After further prompting, the Iranian clerk remembered Boyd leaving with what appeared to be a fine-looking working girl.

It was the closest Gunther could get. After two more days of dead ends, Madeline claimed some vacation time, and they had set out for Mississippi yesterday afternoon to see if they couldn't shake things up from the other end. Boyd had shown up at his old apartment looking for Allison, which had to be significant, but he apparently didn't have their advantage of her forwarding address.

Approaching Kingman, on U.S. 93 in Arizona, Madeline had him wheel the Cadillac over to a convenience store so she could stock up on cigarettes and Tab. At first, Gunther had thought she was standing there daydreaming in front of the plate-glass windows.

"Would you look at this." Madeline peeled it, tape and all, from the inside of the window. She began to laugh while reading the poster. "This is her. This is the bitch who killed my fern."

"Maybe she was off her medication that day." He continued to read over her shoulder. "I wonder if she's sick, for real."

"Oh, go look up today's word in the dictionary, Gunther, if that's all the sense you have. Look up *ruse,* why don't you. Whatever the truth is, do you really think he'd put *that* down?"

" 'Call for Krystal or Mr. Wackermann with information,' " he read from the bottom. "Mr. Wackermann—what the fuck?"

"Sounds about like the kind of alias Boyd would come up with."

"That sand nigger at the motel was right on the money, then. Krystal . . . doesn't that sound like a hooker name to you?"

The trip to Mississippi aborted, they returned to Las Vegas. Gunther called as soon as he walked in the door, found it was an answering service that would not budge an inch on the identity of its client. Bureaucratic civilians—there were ways around *them.*

This morning Gunther had gone down to Two-Eyed Jacks, to its sanctum of private offices. In accounting toiled a slight man with allergies to nearly everything that grew, and a hairline that receded more each fiscal quarter. Joseph Farraday was employed by Two-Eyed Jacks the same way Gunther was—little more than surface only, to legitimize his income. For sixteen years he had worked as a skip tracer for credit and collection agencies, electronically running down deadbeats across the country, sometimes even across international borders. Then he smartened up, found he could do the same job for Toby Costas and make better money. Joseph Farraday had gone to work for Costas three years ago, bringing along thousands of dollars' worth of pirated software, and earning the inevitable nickname "Joey Ferret."

Gunther shut the door and slid the flyer onto Joey Ferret's desk. "This is an answering service. Can you dig me up anything else on this number, who it might be answering for?"

The Ferret went to work, pecking two-fingered at the keyboard of one of his computers. Took no time at all.

"Here we go. Sundowners Answering Service," he said. "I know that name. They do a lot of business with call girls."

"What about this Krystal name on here? Can you find out who that is?"

Joey Ferret said he'd give it a whirl, that it would take a bit longer, for Gunther to have a seat. He peered into the screen with fingers flying, trying one thing, then cocking his head for a moment of analysis, then attempting another.

"You still banging that pit boss from the Ivory Coast?" the Ferret asked during a lull, and Gunther said he was. "I just don't get you. Out those doors and on those stages are girls got asses that squeak, they're so compact, and you barely even look at them anymore."

Gunther brushed it off. "Maddy's seasoned. I like seasoned."

"You don't think there's such a thing as being *too* seasoned? I mean, I like salt on my eggs, but I don't go dumping the entire shakerful on them." The Ferret pecked out another few keystrokes, then shook his head. "I can keep trying later if you want, but it's looking like Sundowners keeps its phones and its local area network totally separate, so I couldn't even begin to crack its database from outside and see who's who. Which is smart of them, really. You consider some of the clients they're taking messages for, and the business that's about to be transacted, what you have there is prime blackmail material for someone like me."

Gunther thanked the Ferret for his help and decided he'd just have to concoct a story that would both intrigue and mystify Boyd Dobbins, then dangle that bait until the numbnuts hooked himself.

On the way back out into the glare of day, Gunther lingered before one of the stages, let the dancers lick their lips and grind for him, hustling him for a tip. He shook his head and went on, unable to fathom the appeal of all that silicone.

After they'd run to Maddy's condo so she could pack, Gunther said he had one more stop to make. He backtracked up the Strip, then took Flamingo Road to Maryland Parkway, pulled into a strip mall, and glided to a stop before a broad storefront whose windows were papered half over with bright posters and die-cut placards of masked men in skintight costumes. DISGUISE THE LIMIT was spelled out in red letters across the storefront's overhang.

"A comic book shop?" Madeline said.

"You know I've been wanting to sell that boxful from a week ago." They walked back to the trunk so he could lug out the cardboard crate. "Well, I want to get this done before we leave again. Plenty of cash in hand if we hit any snags. Get the lid, would you?"

Madeline slammed it shut. "I just thought you would've taken care of this before now."

"I can look for Boyd, or I can sell comic books. Unless he's gotten into the comic business, I can't do both at the same time, can I?"

Madeline grinned. "You were reading them, weren't you?"

"Just no putting one over on you, is there, Maddy? Listen, I tried taking care of this once already, but the guy I need to see wasn't in." She kept staring at him every step of the way. Finally Gunther sighed, giving up. "Bet you didn't know that Batman had a lot bigger ears in 1939 than he does today."

She opened the door for him and in they walked. Heads turned. Granted, they didn't exactly blend. Browsers and buyers slouched before racks along the walls, scurried between rows of cardboard crates atop tables in the middle. Most of them looked like kids he had picked on in school while growing up in Philadelphia.

"Well, *here's* a hot place to be on a Friday night," Madeline said. "How*ever* did you come across this place, anyway?"

"It had the biggest ad in the Yellow Pages."

"Most of these guys couldn't get laid in a women's prison."

"Don't you go scaring anybody. I want to get a good price."

He set the crate on a counter that bracketed part of a wall. Behind it, holding court with some skateboard-toting kids, the man Gunther presumed to be the owner sat like Buddha, with physique to match, his T-shirt barely capable of containing its vast burden. When he deigned to suffer Gunther's interruption, he turned his head, turtle-slow, great with body odor, knowledge most trivial, and self-appointed superiority.

"You've just got to be Calvin," said Gunther.

"Well I'm not Hobbes," he said, and his acolytes tittered. His clipped voice was haughty, adenoidal.

Gunther slapped the side of the crate. "Brought these by yesterday morning but I missed you. Guy I talked to said you're the only one authorized to make big buys."

"A thousand pardons, I like to sleep days." Calvin stretched in his reinforced chair and blinked his tiny pig eyes. "Let's see what you have, my friend."

As Gunther pulled the top from the crate, Calvin rose like a colossus and fished his hand inside where the comics stood lined up, each in its individual plastic bag with cardboard backing.

"These feel warm, my friend. These feel *very* warm. Where have these books been?"

"In the trunk of my car."

"In the trunk of his car, he says," Calvin declaimed to the toadies. They shook their heads, aghast, and Gunther wished he could dunk each unwashed scalp into the nearest toilet, just like the old days. "Would you stick the Declaration of Independence in the trunk of your car, my friend? Or the *Mona Lisa*? How about the Dead Sea

Scrolls? Would you stick the Dead Sea Scrolls in the trunk of your car?"

"No," said Gunther, "but right now I'm getting a real urge to stick *you* back there."

Calvin blinked and began to flip from one cover to the next, more attentive with each one, like a man who'd brushed aside silt to discover gold. When he spied the greatest prize, he slowly pulled it free, held it to the light as one might hold a diamond to the sun. From the hangers-on came gasps of awe.

"*Detective Comics* issue twenty-seven," Calvin breathed, and clutched his chest. Beneath his T-shirt, flabby man-tits jounced and jiggled. He slid the comic from its plastic bag onto the counter, then began turning pages with tweezers, meticulous as a jeweler. Calvin begged for a moment to compose himself, and sat, stealing glances at Gunther that alternated between unease and greed. He guzzled from a sweaty bottle of Yoo-Hoo until his hands steadied. "I'll give you two thousand dollars cash for this box, right now."

Two grand sounded positively phenomenal for a box of funny books. He looked at Maddy, smirking at this turn of fortune. She rolled her eyes—never wanted to credit him with one damn thing.

"That one in your hand alone's worth a lot more than two thousand, and you know it, Calvin!" said a teenager with chopped, orange-streaked blond hair. One of the few females in sight.

"You hush yourself, Amy!" Calvin glared at her. "Your presence here is detrimental to my business, so kindly take yours elsewhere." To Gunther: "My offer still stands, my friend. Pay no attention to the delusional child."

Amy came muscling her way through to Gunther's side. "Maybe next time you'll think twice before trying to pass me off a *Reid Fleming, World's Toughest Milkman* number one reissue as a first edition." She stuck her tongue out at Calvin, then tugged on Gunther's sleeve. "Just make him show you a price guide."

"Children should be seen and not heard." Calvin tried to shoo her away, but she wouldn't be deterred. "I'm a busy man, my friend.

Now I think you'll find my offer more than fair, but if you choose to listen to the immature rantings of—"

Anybody working this hard to prove how anxious he *wasn't* to make a deal was up to no good. Gunther reached across the counter, making a clamp of his curled index and middle fingers and trapping one of Calvin's thick nipples between the knuckles. He twisted.

"I got your attention now, gutbucket? Good. Reach wherever you got to reach, and let's take a look at that price guide before I decide to go two-for-one on titty-twisters."

Calvin proved cooperative, and Gunther continued to apply pressure as pages were flipped. Calvin then held the volume open while Gunther skimmed listings until he found the right line.

"Ninety-two thousand dollars?" Gunther cried. "You fat fuck!"

"That's only for near-mint condition. Which yours is *not.*"

Gunther shook his head. He'd been in some weird places all across Vegas, but this one was the outer limits. He looked at Amy, who stood beaming and so vindictively triumphant that he thought if he ever had a daughter, he'd want her to be like this. Have to do something about that hair, though.

"Hey, you. Amy, right?" Gunther said. "What condition would you say this is in?"

"Better than good. But very fine might be pushing it—see all those dog-ears? I'd settle for fine, if I were you."

Gunther checked book value. "That's still thirty-four and a half thousand. How 'bout it, Jabba? You got that kind of money?"

Calvin paused from rubbing his sore teat. "Oh, I'm *sure.*"

Gunther repossessed the comic, slipping it back inside its sleeve. Calvin grumbled his way through the rest of the box to see what he could afford, while Gunther had Amy keep tabs with the price guide. Final bid on everything for which the shop had sufficient cash, better than half the crate, rose to $2,280.

"Okay, that," said Gunther, pointing at Amy, "plus whatever she wants in the shop. That's the deal, chunky boy."

Calvin buried his face in his hands and nodded. Amy whooped and sprinted for the racks. And for a moment, Gunther felt exactly like some mysterious avenger in a western town, who'd stepped in off a dusty street to right the wrongs of the corpulent and greedy land baron. All eyes gazed on him with awe; he was their champion.

Never did get his name, he imagined the geeks would whisper for days to come, *but he sure cleaned up* this *store.*

chapter eleven

The dream was old but had come on its own this time, instead of having to be forced while awake—horses thundering over prairie grasslands, with flaring nostrils and manes that snapped in the wind. Allison riding in the lead, bareback—no one needed a saddle in dreams—and knowing that she could ride without stopping, ride to the edge of forever, where even memories could be left behind. She clung to the reins even as the alarm clock ripped them from her hands, turned them to filaments, mist, nothing.

But she'd held them before; could always find them again.

All the aches and pains from last night's wiping across the parking lot were waiting in ambush. She faced the bathroom mirror fearing the worst, and it was bad—bruises mostly, a few scrapes and scratches, her left eye blackened. The cigarette burn over her cheekbone was in a class of its own. She told herself she'd better get used to it, for it would probably leave a dimpled little scar, a lasting souvenir of the Coyote Ridge experience.

Soon to end, at least. Another hour and a half, and this town would be behind her. Her ride had said he would be here at eight-fifteen.

She showered, then camouflaged the damage as best she could with makeup and the length of her hair, brushed forward to fall across the worst side. Finally, she broke into a giddy smile at the steamy reflection, the prospect of escape sinking in at last.

Her suitcase and duffel were packed already, late last night after work just before she collapsed for a few hours. Her stubborn refusal to slink away in total disgrace had been worth additional tips. Better still, it had seemed to unnerve Loretta, take some starch out of her swagger.

Outside, the day was bright and already plenty warm. The low quilt of clouds had blown over, and with them the suffocation in the air. Forty-five minutes until the van would be by, just enough time for her last bit of business in town.

Her boots kicked up dust along the half-formed road, as she passed a few other trailers and the patches of scrub that grew snarled beneath the withering sun. Gazing toward the khaki hills and red rocks, as imperious as ruined castles, she admitted that the land did possess an austere beauty that would have been so much more apparent to her were it not for the ugliness that the squatters had brought with them.

At the final bend of the road, before it hooked to the main street, was another patch of blight, given over to the remains of machines that had been used up and cast aside. A few old trucks sat burned or rusted down to their skeletal frames. With them lay the insectile pieces of an oil pumping rig, slathered in grease. Broken washers and dryers. Hardy weeds. She took note of it this time only because of what *didn't* seem to belong.

The car was some sporty Japanese model, coral paint pristine beneath a layer of dust, so unlike the faded, blistering surfaces Allison was used to seeing here. Its windows were down. A gorgeous young woman was sitting in the passenger seat, her dark hair limp with heat and sweat. It looked as if someone else might be in there as well, asleep, the driver's head in her lap.

What's her *story?* Allison wondered as their eyes locked across the dustbowl of the road. She looked so young, so fresh and unspoiled, like a little china doll but with a tan and a hundred-dollar haircut.

Ornate bracelets rattling on one wrist. Another hapless life sucked in by the peculiar gravity of Coyote Ridge. She smiled at the woman, got a shy, even embarrassed, smile in return.

"You might want to get inside somewhere before long," Allison told her. "Or at least find some shade. It won't matter if your windows are down or not, this sun'll turn your car into a kiln before the middle of the morning."

"Thanks, I know, I'll have to do that," she said, then stared at Allison for a beat too long, as if thinking they should know each other from somewhere but unable to place it. Then she turned her head away to yawn, as a large crow descended to perch on a scrapped wooden door and pick at the carcass of a lizard.

Allison walked on, recognizing this stranger for what she so obviously was: younger by a few years, less mauled by time, with vital decisions yet to make that she might still make wisely. *She doesn't look like she belongs here,* Allison thought. *And I do.*

A few minutes later she stepped inside the gun shop.

Officially it wasn't open yet, but she'd heard talk enough, and there they were: eight or nine aging cronies who gathered on Saturday mornings as regularly as their wives went to church come tomorrow's sunrise, to sit around and chew the fat of today and all their yesterdays. Slim-legged and potbellied, faces and hands as tough as pemmican, they drank coffee by the gallon and squinted through the window at the problems of the world.

She banged the door shut and all conversation ceased, their kingdom violated. Allison reminded the owner that she'd been in last Sunday, had looked at a nickel-plated .38 revolver and put down a ten-dollar deposit to hold it.

"Yes ma'am," he said, and strolled behind the counter. "Are we putting down another ten today, or are we going whole hog?"

Allison pulled the cash balance from the pocket of her cutoff shorts and held it under his nose. The conversations resumed behind her, quiet and sporadic, the old men watching now with a bemused tolerance.

"Not planning to up and shoot Loretta, are you?" one asked.

"No," said Allison. "I think I'll just let her poison herself from the scalp in with red dye number five."

They guffawed at this, slapping thighs. A couple dredged up tin cans from beside their chair legs; hawked and spat into them.

"If you don't mind me saying so, young lady," said another, "you surely do take a mean punch."

Allison smiled faintly toward the floor, suspecting it was the closest thing to approval she could expect in this town. She busied herself with the paperwork that the owner brought out. Had to show him a valid Arizona ID, and had brought along a driver's license with a few months left on it, from the year she'd lived in Tucson before moving to Seattle.

Revolver and a box of bullets totaled $242. After rent and meals, it was nearly everything she had. She still wouldn't have made the total if not for last night, cleaning up at closing time. Not proud of it, she'd stolen a trio of twenties peeking from the wallet of a man passed out face-first on his table. The theft went down easier after she imagined he'd been one of those laughing hardest while she bled.

The dealer started to hem and haw when he realized that she expected to walk out with the gun this morning.

"Seven-day waiting period after purchase," he said, and a few of the old men grumbled petulantly. "You can thank the Brady Bill for that."

"I started paying you a week ago. Are you saying that doesn't count for anything?"

"Sorry. Layaway, that was, not purchase."

"Oh, hell, Farley, just backdate the damn slip and sell the girl her gun." This from one of the hardier old gents in their circle. "Cash sale, who's to know? You never sent a one of *us* out your door empty-handed for a week. She's not off to kill nobody."

No, Allison almost said. *Not in Arizona, anyway.*

Halfway back to the trailer, she took the gun from its paper sack. It felt heavier when held properly, by the grip; more real than it had moments before, an anonymous weight in a bag. She scuffed along the road, saw that the young woman and the coral car had vanished from the junklot. Thought of firing a few test shots at the wreckage, then decided against taking the time.

The bullets felt like smooth, cool pebbles in her palm. She opened the cylinder and slid six of them home; put the gun in the sack again and felt no different than if she were coming home from the market.

She did not notice the door to her trailer standing open an inch until she was reaching for the handle. The thin metal frame was bent where it had been pried open. Damn this town—they knew she had next to nothing, yet they would pilfer even that?

From inside the trailer came the sound of something sliding, then a thump; a muffled voice, evidently unhappy. Good. His day was about to get worse. Allison held the gun, let the sack with the rest of the bullets slip to the dirt as she walked in. Through the window she saw that the coral car was parked just behind the trailer, out of sight from the road.

The small, sweaty young woman noticed her first, saucer-eyed and frozen in guilty surprise in the kitchen, where she'd been going through cabinets. In front of the sofa, Allison's duffel bag and suitcase lay spilled open, contents strewn out. She came up behind the man who hunched over them, urgently rooting through it all, shaking his head, and there was something dreadfully familiar about him, even from this angle.

"Uh," said the girl. "Um. Oh wow. Sweetie?"

Allison thumbed back the hammer on the revolver as she aimed down at the back of the familiar head. *It couldn't be.* The click of ratcheting metal got his attention in a heartbeat. He froze, hands raising in slow surrender.

"What do you think *you're* looking for?" she asked.

"Oh, this is a bitch," the burglar groaned.

"Boyd?" she cried, and looked incredulously at the shamefaced woman in the kitchen. "You're with him? *Him?*"

"We're . . . we're soulmates," she offered weakly.

"Oh yeah?" Allison could not suppress a laugh. "Who told you that? Did he?"

"It was a mutual revelation," Boyd said from the floor. When he turned around, she was taken aback to see that his mustache was gone. A Boyd she'd never seen, a smooth Boyd who looked as though he should be doing pouty cologne ads in magazines written for the terminally vapid.

"Allie, listen," he said, "can we be honest with each other?"

"You shut up a minute." She waved the revolver, and rather enjoyed the sight of him retreating against the sofa. She turned to the hand-wringing young woman in the kitchen. "The thing about Boyd is, he'd lie to see if he could get away with it when the truth would save his life."

"Don't listen to her, Krystal," Boyd said, then glared up at Allison with halfhearted defiance. "Obviously, you underestimate my self-preservation skills."

"They don't seem to be working very well today, do they? You break in here like this, you seem pretty *un*skilled to me." Allison sighed, imagined the playwright somewhere up above, how he must be chortling by now. "*Damn* you, Boyd! You're just lucky you didn't find me a week ago, I'd've shot you on sight."

"So you," he said hopefully, "so you're over that now, huh?"

"I'm not over a damned thing!" For a vivid moment she thought it really might feel good to shoot him—not fatally, maybe just a flesh wound to make him think awhile. "Do you have any idea what you did to me? It's all your fault I'm even here!"

"Come on, Allie, let's not get all caught up in blame. We both said and did some things I'm sure we regret—"

"Shut up. Just *shut up.* I don't want to hear anything you have to say." She lowered the gun, eased the hammer down. "You're sitting on my panties. Get off my panties and start repacking this mess you've made." She flicked the revolver at Krystal. "You too, airhead, as long as you're such soulmates."

Nine minutes past eight. Allison glanced out the door for any sign of a van coming down the road, asking for a few more minutes, a prayer to the playwright. As she watched her belongings being jammed back together, curiosity got the better of her.

"How'd you find me, anyway?"

"We made posters," Boyd said. "Your face is in windows in a two-hundred-mile or so radius around Las Vegas. So . . . if you run into anyone who looks at you kind of funny, like they're wondering if you're off your medication . . . that might be why."

"Medication? No, that's enough already. I don't want to know any more."

"People really were sympathetic to you," said Krystal, as if to cheer her up. "Weren't they, Boyd?"

He nodded, said they sure were, as he folded a pair of jeans and patted the back pockets. She asked what he was looking for, what they were doing here in the first place, and Boyd smiled that annoying so-glad-you-asked-that smile he'd perfected selling pools in Seattle. Started asking if she remembered the night before they split up, trashing the hard drive of his computer and leaving a ransom note behind. Ha ha, nice joke, Allie, good one, but could she please give him the backup disks, because some of the files contained crucial family genealogical trees that would mean the world to his poor grandmother, if she could just see what he'd found out from the Mormon archives in Salt Lake City.

"I don't have the faintest idea what you're talking about," she said.

"Come on, don't you remember? You were drinking pretty heavy that night? Even the note you left me looked slurred. You signed it 'The bitch you shouldn't have betrayed.' "

A small facet of memory began to clear. That's right, she *had* wiped it all clean. It was starting to come back, barely, through the Southern Comfort mist—

"So are the disks here," he went on, "or are they inside that package you left back in Vegas three or four days ago?"

—then she lost the strand of thought, for now she really had no clue what he was talking about. More lies. They'd finally begun tripping him up regardless of which way he turned.

Eight-twelve. Whatever Boyd was trying to chisel out of her would have to keep, and if it had to keep forever, that served him right.

Allison stepped to one corner, where a lamp wobbled atop a rickety table. The day after moving in she'd told the landlady how frayed its cord was, down to bare wire in places; she'd been given a roll of electrician's tape to take care of it herself. Tape in hand, she ordered Boyd and Krystal into the kitchen. Pulled a chair away from the table and tossed the sticky roll to Krystal.

"You," she said to Boyd, and jabbed with the gun. "Sit down. And you"—to Krystal—"tape him to the chair."

"Hey," Boyd said. "Aren't we getting a little carried away?"

"I've got a ride coming, and I *don't* want you following me. I don't ever want to see you again, period. Don't want to hear your name. I don't want to know you exist."

He shook his head. "You're not taping me to this chair. I've been more than patient, but I'm drawing a line with this. What, you're going to shoot me? I know you better than that."

So sure of himself—she couldn't stand it. Couldn't hold her arm still. Allison swung the pistol and cracked its short barrel against the side of his forehead. His knees buckled but her arm kept swinging, out of control. She whipped him as he fell, another split opening on his head; struck him on the forearms as he lifted them to shield himself. On the shoulder as he sagged into the chair, then Krystal swooped in, throwing both arms around him, begging her to stop, please, *stop*. And so Allison did.

"You don't know anything about me," she told Boyd, with quickened breath. "Not one damn thing that ever counted."

As Krystal began taping, Allison tossed a paring knife onto the table so she could cut the stretchy black vinyl. Boyd watched them with dazed eyes, cuts trickling blood along his hairline. He voiced no objection when Allison went through his pockets. A deck of cards—typical Boyd. She dropped it onto the table beside him. A comb. His wallet. She counted more than $140, took all but a twenty.

"I'm leaving you enough for gas. You'll owe me the rest, but if I never see you again, it'll be worth it." Allison stuffed the cash into her pocket. "I swore out a warrant for your arrest the day I left Vegas, so you might watch out for that. But even if they pick you up, you'll get away with it. I don't plan on going back there for anything, ever again. Not even to see you tried."

"How long do I have to stay like this?" he mumbled. Strips of tape manacled his wrists behind the chair's back, lashed each ankle to a metal leg, and coiled around his torso, chair and all.

"I'll have my ride drop Krystal off in town, and she can walk back here to cut you loose. *Don't* come looking for me."

"Would you at least turn the air conditioner back on?"

"Sweat it out, Boyd. Maybe it'll purify you."

He asked for a drink, so she had Krystal oblige. Allison watched her kneel beside him, holding the jelly jar to his lips, and wondered what peculiar devotion had grafted her to him.

"I'll get the rose quartz and amethyst out of the car just as soon as I get back," she was telling him, "and we'll go right to work on those cuts. Okay, sweetie? Just think cool thoughts while I'm gone."

Allison scowled at their kiss, and the twist in her stomach made no sense at all. Boyd neither wanted nor needed her anymore, and she was better for it. So *why* did it still seem to matter that he so plainly demonstrated it in front of her?

Life after Allison—she supposed she'd always hoped that such a thing did not really exist for a man, and here was proof it did.

She had Krystal leave the trailer first, then dropped the gun into her oversize purse and slung it from her shoulder. Looped the duffel's strap over the other and hoisted the suitcase. Looked at Boyd sitting captive in the kitchen and peering glumly out the window.

"Don't stab this one in the back like you did me," she told him, so Krystal would not overhear. "Why she adores you, God only knows, but I think she's a lot better than what you deserve."

He looked down at the floor a moment. "She's a hooker."

At one time Allison might have laughed; could find no reason to right now. "So?" was all she said, and walked out into the harsh light of day.

Eight-nineteen. They stood in front of the trailer, her bags on the ground, both of them staring in silent expectation until she heard the rewarding sound of an engine rounding the far bend.

"Was it your father?" Krystal asked, without looking at her.

"What?"

"Your father. Was he the one?"

Allison stared at the toe of her boot, grinding in the dirt. How had she known? Not that it mattered.

"My father. Yeah." She followed the van in, as if taking her eyes off it would make it disappear. "He was the main one."

"With me it was my grandfather." And then Krystal laughed, as if she just couldn't believe it all, that life was too strange for anything but laughter. "What gets into them, what do they think?"

Allison shook her head. "Too many pricks, not enough brains. What happens to their hearts is anybody's guess."

It wasn't until after he'd already left the barmaid in the parking lot last night that Thomas St. John realized he hadn't gotten her name, nor given his. Introductions would be in order this morning, as well as an apology for running late. Hardly his fault, though; some bickering couple in the diner had monopolized the waitress with questions while he cooled his heels at the cash register.

Unlikely-looking couple. Tall, both of them, and older than Tom by a few years, although the woman carried it worse, with a nasty air about her, and a natural sneer, as if each passing year left her angrier. The man appeared impressively fit but had a bizarre combination of blond hair and olive skin, and a Germanic-looking face that lacked only a dueling scar. He would spear each bite of his pancakes as though killing them.

"Getting like a message center, this place," the waitress apologized when she hurried to work the register. "People all the time losing track of each other, this town's not *that* big."

Tom followed the directions the barmaid had given him. Her trailer sat at the end of the road on a baked slab of desert browns and scruffy chaparral, a tin can that had been kicked from one edge of Coyote Ridge to the other.

She stood waiting outside for him, moving toward the van with her entire life in a suitcase, a duffel, and a purse as big as a saddlebag. She was not alone; a friend come to say goodbye, maybe.

"Don't worry, I'm not trying to sneak in another one on you," she said. "Can you just drop her off in town on the way out?"

"Sure," he said, and helped toss the luggage into the back of the van, in a spot he'd cleared. Names were exchanged, finally, and they got in. For friends, the two women seemed awfully quiet.

He turned the van around, backtracked up the road. No one said a word until Allison Willoughby pointed toward the last few stores along the edge of town, near the motorcycle shop.

"This okay, Krystal?" she asked, and it was.

He slowed, idling as Allison let Krystal out, and maybe there was some closeness there after all. He could not hear what was said, just watched them, curious. Some mystery shared that wasn't his to know as each touched the other's arm, tentatively, and nodded. They did not hug goodbye.

Allison returned to the van. The moment he wheeled onto U.S. 93, her middle fingers popped up like a pair of switchblades, and with jubilation she jammed both arms out the window. He honestly believed that had they known each other, she might've skinned down her cutoffs and jammed her bare bottom out instead.

"Worst week of my life," she told him, before one last lunge out the window as Coyote Ridge began to slide out of sight: "Fuck you all and the inbred horses you fell off of!"

She laughed then, laughed like a woman freed of weights, now ready to spread wings and soar. She tumbled back into the seat, radiant with relief, propping her feet against the dashboard in their dusty brown boots, and bare-legged up to faded cutoffs and a purple shirt. Last night's blood and oil and grime were washed away, leaving only the black eye, the bruises, the burn. She'd tried her best to hide it with the thick sweep of her hair, but it made for poor camouflage. Pretty enough, under it all, her face as oval as a cameo locket, but the wary set of her eyes and the tiny lines around them hinted of other nights just as bad.

"All that hatred in one week," he said.

"Yeah, well, I didn't sleep much, so it felt like two."

"I'm guessing you weren't there by choice?"

"Real Rhodes scholar, aren't you?" She glanced at him, her clear green eye widening, softening with apology. "Sorry. We can, um . . . we can talk later if you want, but right now, if you wouldn't mind . . ."

He nodded, said sure, there would be plenty of time, then she turned her back on him to stare out her window at the roadside gliding past—every view different and every view the same, and he thought for a moment that that was an awful lot like life.

chapter twelve

The temperature in the trailer was climbing past cruel and unusual. The door stood wide open, but that didn't help matters. The place was a prison farm sweatbox. For a while Boyd had to blink as though his eye had a twitch, to keep it clear of stinging blood, but now the flow had dried and his forehead felt stiff. Strain as he might, he could do nothing to loosen the tape. Krystal and that work ethic of hers again. Do a good job, even if it meant trussing up her sweetie like a frayed toaster cord.

Pistol-whipped by an old girlfriend, taped to a chair by the new one. Today wasn't going down as one of his better karma days.

Boyd had thumped himself, chair and all, over to the kitchen window so he could keep watch, spot Krystal the moment she came into view up the road. He heard the car before he saw it, sailing around the far bend and emerging from behind a miserable screen of shacks and other trailers: a big white Cadillac. Bless her kind heart—she'd flagged a ride so he wouldn't have to suffer as long.

The Cadillac coasted to a stop in a churning brown cloud, and the driver stepped out first, a stranger to Boyd. Nevada plates, so he was no local. He looked the trailer over, his blond, brush-cut hair stiff against the breeze, eyes concealed behind a pair of Ray-

Bans. Boyd drew back from the window, starting to sour on this turn of fortune. When the passenger door opened, his last hopes fled on a sigh of resignation. Madeline? Here? Now?

He recalled his one glimpse of the back of the blond Titan that Madeline had employed for their skim's chip exchange, and Derek's insistence that Boyd was their disposable patsy. Damn that brother of his, and his gigantic brain.

Heavy footfalls on the wrought-iron steps, then the doorway filled with the Titan's angular frame. He stood casing the empty living room, slipping off his shades before looking to his right, into the kitchen. He bent forward at the waist, as if mistrusting a mirage.

"Howdy!" the guy said, and broke into a laugh, this one word all he needed to say: the guy on the phone last night.

I, Boyd thought, *am one dead blackjack dealer.*

"Maddy. Come here. Have a look at something," he called out. "I got a surprise for you."

She joined him in the doorway, a fresh Virginia Slim dangling from the corner of her mouth. The both of them bubbled with slow, welling laughter.

"Hey, Madeline." Trying to muster up a little of the Dobbins charm. "You're looking good."

They sauntered into the kitchen like two old friends invited for coffee. Madeline's thug leaned against the refrigerator.

"Where's my money, Boyd?" she asked.

"Right where we left it." He saw no harm in the truth, for all the good it would do her. "It's the getting to it that's the bugaboo right now."

She picked up the depleted roll of tape, then dropped it back to the table beside his comb and wallet and deck of cards. "Your former honey do this to you and leave you like this for us?"

"Who, Allison? She was in a mood again."

"I'm almost starting to like her." Madeline took a luxuriant drag on her cigarette, fuming like a chimney and looking him over as she might inspect a cut of veal. "So where is she now?"

Boyd tried shrugging. "Take a peek around—does it look like anyone lives here now?"

She reached forward with the cigarette, tapped ash onto the crown of his head. He shuddered and shook like a wet dog. Madeline laughed, but stopped when she saw her dead-eyed thug hunkering down to examine the cabinet beneath the sink.

"Gunther? Gunther. What are you looking for down there?"

"What am I always looking for? It's not here anyway." He rose, pulled a pistol from beneath his jacket, and drew a bead on Boyd's head, and Boyd ducked and weaved as though trying to slip a punch. Gunther followed, watching him dance, then turned the gun over to Madeline. "That's only if you need it. Don't get carried away." To Boyd, then, hitching his thumb down the length of the trailer as he began to walk: "Bathroom back this way?"

"You tell me, I never made it that far." To Madeline, then: "You know, this is the second gun I've had on me and it's not even nine in the morning? Yours has lost a little impact that way."

"Yeah? *Wait.*" She teased the muzzle down one cheek, then the other, as he stiffened, waiting for the worst. "The difference is, the first one wasn't fired."

With Gunther gone, banging mysteriously around the other end of the trailer, Madeline straddled him in the chair, gun in one hand and cigarette in the other. She held the glowing coal near his eye while dry-humping him as he squirmed.

"So Allison's gone, you were telling me," Madeline said. "Did she go alone? Or with somebody else?"

His eyes were squinted shut, his neck craned and head twisted back to tendons' limits. He could feel the small circle of heat millimeters from his eyelid, the muscled grind of her hips.

"She caught a ride, some intense-looking guy in a black van," he said through clenched teeth. "I don't know who it was."

"Not good enough," she crooned, and he began to feel the crisp sizzle of eyelashes withering to ash.

"Florida plates, vanity plates, I saw them earlier, said 'St. John.' " He spelled it.

Her eyebrows knitted. "I think I saw that van earlier."

Like a malign force of nature, Gunther returned, waving both arms in frustration. "What kind of domicile is this anyway, got no fucking cleaning products around? How's a man supposed to work under these conditions?" He stopped. "Hey. Get off him, you skank. That phase of your relationship is over."

Madeline laughed, and the weight slid from his lap. Gunther dangled his keyring out to her. "How about you run back into town, get me some drain cleaner? Crystal Drano's best."

Krystal. Boyd glanced out the window, saw with relief that the road was still empty. He hated to contemplate what they would do to her if she walked in on this.

"Tell me something, Gunther," said Madeline. "Why is it *I'm* always the one being sent out of the room for drain cleaner?"

Boyd felt himself going pale, as it registered what they were talking about. What it would probably be used for.

Gunther pointed at him. "*He's* for sure not going anywhere. You see anybody else around here that that leaves?"

"I'm *not* your slave, and I'm *not* your errand girl. I'm your partner in this, and I was making progress without any help from you. I don't see why you can't make do with whatever's here."

"What am I supposed to do, spray him with Windex?" Gunther stomped over to the refrigerator, flung the door open. "Hey, this is good. Half a burrito. Here, see how far this gets you." He threw it at her, and she swatted it to the floor. "Maybe it's just me, but burritos don't rank very high on the truculence scale."

"Always with the truculence!" she shouted. "You know what I need to buy you instead of drain cleaner? A thesaurus. I'm getting sick of hearing the same idiotic words coming out of your mouth. Find some synonyms, Gunther. Variety is the spice of life."

"Oh, that's original right there. You make up that proverb yourself?" He slammed the fridge door. "Fucking ballbuster, you want variety, how 'bout tonight we throw that tube of K-Y jelly out the window, and see what a hard-ass bitch you *really* are."

Boyd watched in horror, trying to melt into the chair. This was like witnessing two dinosaurs in combat, knocking down palm trees and churning up tons of earth.

Madeline gave in, trading the pistol for the keys and roaring off in a cloud of dust and fury. Gunther watched her go, mopping sweat from his forehead. Took off his sport coat and draped it over the other kitchen chair, rolled up his shirtsleeves.

"I don't know how it is you plan on using this drain cleaner exactly," said Boyd, "but whoa, I'm here to tell you it isn't one bit necessary. You want to have a talk, we'll have a talk, let's just leave the drain cleaner out of it."

"No, you don't understand. Necessary, unnecessary—that's got nothing to do with it. I *like* drain cleaner."

Boyd tried not to shudder, to keep a clear head.

"It's like my personal signature."

Boyd nodded as if he understood this mentality. Shot a glance out the window, behind Gunther, and had to stifle a groan. How much worse could this get? Plenty. Krystal was two hundred yards up the road, walking swiftly back and blissfully unaware.

Think. Gunther was big, Gunther's veins were filled with freon . . . but he did seem possessed of the sort of single-mindedness that often meant, beneath it all, squatted an Achilles' brain.

"Drain cleaner, what kind of signature is that?" Boyd said. "That's no good."

"Like you'd know?" Gunther snorted. "Believe me, it makes an impression."

"No no no no no. That's not what I mean. I'm talking personal style as a function of location. Something that doesn't just say who you are, but makes a statement about where you're from."

Boyd breathed deeply, flying by the seat of his pants. He'd started to sweat profusely, could feel watery, reconstituted blood trickling down his cheek.

"Drain cleaner's very reliable."

Boyd rolled his eyes. "Sure, so's a collie, but it's got no style unless you're killing shepherds. You're from Vegas?"

Gunther nodded, seemed interested in hearing him out.

"See, that's where your image comes apart. Drain cleaner, now that'd be fine if we were in Detroit, some industrial city like that." A glance out the window at Krystal, adjusting her sandal in the middle of the road. "You being from Vegas, what you need is a signature that *says* Vegas. Something to do with gambling."

"Gambling." Gunther frowned in concentration for a moment. "Like Russian roulette, for instance."

"That's one possibility."

Gunther considered this. "Yeah. I like the tie-in. Be even better if I had special bullets, painted red and black, you know. I knew a guy back when I worked Philadelphia, was a big fan of Russian roulette." He lifted his pistol, showed it to Boyd. "So instead of getting close up and personal with drain cleaner, what you'd rather do is play Russian roulette with a semiautomatic."

Boyd flinched. He'd walked into that one.

"Because those one-in-one odds," Gunther said, "that tends to take the element of chance out of things."

"That's why it's not for you, then." The sweat was really rolling now. Get out of this alive, and Krystal was going to have to submerge him in Gatorade. "I look at you, and you know what I see working for you? Cards. Cutting cards."

Gunther looked skeptical. "Get the fuck out of here. Cards. No, I got a good thing going with this drain cleaner. I'll stick with that." Slowly, though, inevitably, he began to reconsider. Boyd watched the possibilities crawl across that dark Germanic face. "Cards—you really think so? Okay, maybe I can see this after all. Get kind of a riverboat gambler image working for me, you think?"

"Absolutely!" Boyd nodded with enthusiasm. "The thing is, the cards aren't intimidating by themselves—it's what's at stake when you cut them. So you can see, well, the possibilities are . . ."

"Limited only by my imagination," Gunther finished. "You know, you make a real solid case for this."

Boyd nodded down at the deck on the table. "Come on, open 'em up. Let's try a dry run."

Another glance out the window, Krystal less than a hundred yards away. *Don't hurry, babe, don't walk so fast—*

Gunther shuffled. "I draw high card, I put drain cleaner in your eye. Low card, all I get to do is break a finger. How's that sound?"

Boyd's stomach lurched. "Doesn't give *me* much incentive."

"First one, this is my card," Gunther said, and turned up the nine of spades. "Okay, now yours." The king of hearts; fine karma abounded. Gunther nodded with satisfaction, regardless. "You know what the beauty of this system is? Really, I can't lose."

"Except you'd draw it out *much* worse, really make your guy sweat over it," Boyd said. "One big mistake on your part, though: I don't even get to cut for my own card?"

"Why should you?"

"Because letting a guy cut for his own card gives him the illusion he's in control of his own fate. That way, he draws low, it's not something *you've* done for him—he's let *himself* down. He draws high, so what? You're still in charge, you're holding the gun. It's like you're the house, and you've still got the house advantage." Boyd nodded toward the deck again. "Let's try this one more time, but come *on,* let me at least cut for my own card."

Gunther balked, said he liked Boyd packaged in the chair just the way he was. Boyd looked down at himself—what, two free hands were going to do any good when his legs were taped to the chair? Gunther relented, got the paring knife, and held the pistol to his head as a precaution while slicing through the tape at his wrists. Boyd loosened up his shoulders while Gunther shuffled.

"I draw high card"—Gunther began to laugh—"and I cut off your balls!"

Boyd laughed along with him. "And *I* draw high card, I get to pork Madeline while you watch!"

Both of them roared, until Gunther waved him down—too much, much too funny. "You already did that! *Months* ago! I was in the closet. I almost put a bullet in your head that afternoon!"

Boyd abruptly stopped laughing, face draining of blood, as Gunther cut, held up the card. "Uh-oh, king of diamonds. Looking bad for the family jewels."

Krystal was seventy feet away. No way could Gunther miss her if he turned around. Boyd's heart was trying to climb his throat, and he steadied his hand, reached for his cut.

"Two of clubs," Gunther announced. "I *love* this game."

Boyd slipped his portion of the deck from right hand to left, all but the top card. He flicked his wrist and let the card fly, just as he'd done that night in Seattle at the groping senator.

The edge of the spinning card caught Gunther squarely in the right eye. His head snapped back and he staggered, screaming with the pain and the surprise and, Boyd supposed, the indignity. Boyd lurched to his feet, bringing his chair up with him while grabbing for the other, scuttling forward as Gunther brought the gun around and fired wildly. Once, twice—the kitchen filled with a gritty cordite reek. Boyd felt the third bullet whiz past his ear, and swung the chair as hard as he could, to smash it across Gunther's head and shoulders. And still, the man tried to aim. Boyd swung again, off balance and flinching at the loud pop of gunfire. He dented the refrigerator door with a devastating blow. Felt the impact as the next bullet punched into the chair seat, then solidly swatted Gunther again to send him reeling toward the wall.

Boyd pressed the advantage, still conformed into the shape of one chair as he battled with the other. He shuffled forward like a very old and arthritic lion tamer. The chair legs caught Gunther by the chest and shoulders, to drive him crashing back through the kitchen window. He teetered on the sill a moment, then plummeted from sight with a heavy thud.

Boyd bellowed like a Viking but forgot to cut himself loose; held his four-legged bludgeon aloft and, hunchbacked, shuffled furiously for the door. Gunther's sport coat slipped from the back of the chair to drape over his face, and the legs smacked into the doorframe above his head, and he went tumbling out the door, down the wrought-iron steps, to land out in the dirt and glare. He felt nothing, infused with adrenaline. Grabbed the dropped chair with one hand and, with the other, began dragging himself, both chairs, and sport coat across the ground, toward his fallen foe, ready to pound the psychopath into wiseguy hash.

Then he saw that Gunther was out cold, lying where he had fallen in a crooked sprawl. Each elbow and each knee was splayed in the same angle from his body. He had landed in the shape of a swastika.

Krystal fell beside Boyd, had covered the last of her trek in a sprint. She hugged him, kissed him.

"Who's *he*?" she asked.

"Some homeless guy! Now could you get the knife out of the kitchen and cut me loose?"

As Krystal ran into the trailer, Boyd squirmed the final few feet to Gunther's side, to pull the gun from his grasp. Then he disentangled the sport coat and plunged his hand into its pockets. Found an ink pen, a box of Chiclets, a straight razor, then came out with Gunther's wallet.

A new sound up the road, the whine of an overdriven engine—what fresh hell was this? He shouted for Krystal to hurry. Sliding around the bend came the huge white Cadillac, trailing a dustcloud as thick and virulent as a plague of locusts.

Madeline.

Krystal ran from the doorway, dropped to her knees, and began to saw the paring knife through the tape.

"I brought your wallet and your comb, too," she said, "but your cards were all over the—"

"See that car coming? We *really* want to get away from her."

Gunther began to groan, and one arm to twitch.

When he was loose enough to manage the rest, Boyd told her to get the car. He hacked at the final bonds, watching the Cadillac's grille come barreling down the road, then sprang from the ground, filthy tape trailing from his limbs and sides like buckskin fringe. He grabbed Gunther's wallet and gun, kicked him in the head, and lurched around the side of the trailer.

The Cadillac slewed to a halt, Madeline trying to block the path of their Mazda, but with all this flat ground she might as well have tried blocking a driveway with a toy. She flung the door open to bolt from the car. He lifted the gun, peppering away at the Cadillac's tires, and Madeline jumped back inside for cover. The front tire went flat in a burst of air, and he began plinking at the rear, missing until the pistol emptied.

Krystal swung the Mazda around, pushing the door open from inside, and Boyd fell into the passenger seat. She took off again, while out the window he saw Madeline rushing at them through the wind and dust, howling with fury. Her arm flashed, and something hurtled through the air to thunk against the hood. It bounced back at them, hung on the wipers for a moment, then rolled up the windshield in a shower of pale blue crystals, and was gone.

"Was that what I think it was?" Krystal asked.

"Yeah," he said, breathless. "Those two back there? They have some really unique uses for it."

All they needed for the moment was a little distance between themselves and the trailer. Krystal careened south on U.S. 93, then pulled into the scenic stop two miles from town. While a picnicking family watched with alarm, they washed away dirt and blood at the outside spigot and plucked the electrician's tape from him. He drank directly from the faucet's gush until his stomach sloshed and his head spun, then staggered back to the car.

"Did you *know* those people back there?" Krystal asked.

"Her I did. She used to be my pit boss at the Ivory Coast. Pit *bull* is more like it."

"What about him?"

"He was planning on cutting my balls off and putting Drano in my eyes, if that clues you in on his personality." Boyd began to inspect the purloined wallet, the driver's license. "Gunther Angelo Manzetti? What kind of name is that?"

"Why would they want to kill you, Boyd? I'm getting the idea you haven't told me everything that's going on."

"No. No, I haven't," he sighed. "And one of these days we'll just have to sit down and get all this hoo-ha sorted out."

He continued to see what Gunther's wallet had to offer, found a slip of paper tucked behind the currency. He showed Krystal the note with Allison's forwarding address in Mississippi. Constance—okay, he recalled hearing that name before. Allie's . . . cousin?

"I don't think she's getting away from this place as clean as she thinks she is," he said.

"You mean those people would follow her all that way?"

"For over seven hundred thousand dollars? Wouldn't you?" He glanced at the note again with fresh insight. "Doug Powell, that butterball! He was holding out on me about her! And half of that damage deposit is *mine.* How'd *they* end up with this, anyway?" He considered Gunther's methods of persuasion. "Uh-oh . . ."

At least he and Krystal were back in business. Warning Allie who was coming might go a long way toward forgiveness—worth, at the very least, the reward of his own property.

chapter thirteen

At least Madeline waited until he was fully conscious before giving him grief. Gunther ruled out consideration for his feelings right away. Probably just wanted to be sure he didn't miss any.

"Did it ever cross your mind that maybe you're not cut out for this line of work after all?" she asked.

"So I had an off day," he grumbled.

"How hard did that have to be?" Just had to keep twisting the knife, didn't she? "*You* had the gun, *he* couldn't move, but *you* let yourself get taken out by the seven of spades. That's not an off day, Gunther. What that is is a terminal case of the stupids."

He sat on the trailer's wrought-iron steps, holding his head in both hands. Madeline had uprighted one of the kitchen chairs to sit beside him and nag. Nobody would be sitting on the other chair again, ever. At least some of those bent legs, Gunther assumed, he was responsible for. Broken glass glittered in the dirt, and past the end of the trailer, the Cadillac canted toward its left front fender, the tire buckled down onto the rim. He'd already gathered up his sport coat, with its pilfered pockets, and realized his wallet was missing, along with that beautiful Glock Model 17.

"How do I look?" he asked.

"If I didn't know you, I would run the other way." Then the creases in Maddy's forehead smoothed out, and she seemed to soften for a moment. "Don't worry. A little soap and water, maybe some disinfectant, I'm sure it'll clean up better than it looks."

Better than it felt, too, he hoped. He had tried probing with careful fingers, touching cuts and lumps and scrapes in abundance.

"Do you have to squint like that? It looks perverse."

"I can't help it, Maddy. My eye hurts like hell. The Drano couldn't be much worse than this."

She dragged the chair closer and thumbed up his right eyelid to peer at the damage, pursing her sun-seamed mouth and leaning into his face with smoky breath.

"Is it . . . oozing? Feels like that card sliced my eyeball open like a grape."

"Oh, quit whining, you big baby." Her fingers felt cool and surprisingly soothing. "You're not going to lose it, but you've got a bad scratch on the cornea. We'll have to get you a gauze bandage to cover it, because for sure we can't have you going around squinting like this all the time. You look like Popeye."

Satisfied that he wasn't going blind, they took stock of the situation. Boyd was secondary now, reserved for when a convenient opportunity arose. For now, Allison was number one—whatever it was she'd taken from Boyd, they could figure it out after they caught up to her. And it wouldn't be a bad idea to find out what they could on the guy she'd ridden off with. Her new address in Mississippi was gone with Gunther's wallet, but Madeline remembered the Wainright name, was sure she'd recognize the rest when she saw it in a Yazoo City phone book. At least he'd had smarts enough to keep most of that comic book cash in his luggage.

"What we need to do ASAFP," Madeline said, "is get that tire changed and get ourselves out of here. There's not much moving on this end of town, but that doesn't mean one of these desert rats up the road didn't call the sheriff."

Gunther shrugged it off. "Hey, we're the victims here. Some tumbleweed cop drops by, *we're* the ones with the shot-out tire. We tell him we came down here to square some things with a couple old friends, and one of them started going aggro on us. Say we think he was hitting the crack pipe all morning. Outback cop like that, he hears crack, he'll drop a load in his shorts."

After changing the tire, Gunther slung the dead one into the Cadillac's trunk, leaving the lug wrench and jack for Madeline to stow as he trudged into the trailer. Breakfast not two hours ago and already he was starving, all this truculence amping up his metabolism. He took a look through the wrecked kitchen, found nothing but famine and disappointment, and finally had to pick up the squashed half-burrito from the floor, brush it off, and decide that, no, it was not beneath him.

Back in the bathroom, he finally saw the ugly truth of what Boyd's trickery had done. Blood, dirt, and sweat had marbled into a reddish-brown paste caked across his face. He forced open his right eye, a pink mass with a dense red line of broken capillaries just left of center. All in all, he was a frightshow.

He took off his ruined shirt and shook out the worst of the dust, then washed up; was patting himself dry with a damp hand towel that Allison must have left behind when he heard the arrival of another car. Gunther slipped out of the bathroom and down the short hallway, easing along the trailer wall to the living room's window. He peeked out from its corner.

A white sedan sat outside, a flashbar on its roof and the gold star of the Yavapai County Sheriff's Department on its door. Not exactly lightning response time, but Gunther had checked the atlas last night and found Yavapai to be a desolate jurisdiction with a huge expanse of ground to cover. Five minutes more and he and Madeline could have been out of here.

She was speaking with a lone deputy, their voices inaudible, but she seemed to be telling quite the vivid tale. She pointed wildly up the road, back toward town; threw both hands in the air, all outrage and victimization. She led the deputy to the Caddy's trunk to show him the perforated tire. What she *wasn't* doing was paying one bit of attention to the trailer. Good girl.

From here, the deputy looked young, polite, officious—a kid, really, lean as a whippet, with broomstick posture and dark green aviator sunglasses. He returned to his car to check back in on his radio, waiting for what seemed far too long.

Whatever abruptly pulled his trigger, Gunther couldn't guess. The deputy rushed from the car with gun drawn and voice raised, and now every word was clear as he shouted for Madeline to hit the ground. The kid dropped beside her, knee in her back as he clapped a pair of cuffs on her wrists, then hauled her up and hustled her toward his cruiser.

Gunther did a quick fade down the hallway, ducking back into the bathroom, seeing what he could improvise with. All told, there had been better times to lose both his Glock and depth perception. He stuck the hand towel in his waistband, then wrenched the towel bar from the flimsy wall. It felt too light in his hand, nothing more than cast aluminum. The lug wrench would have been better.

Gunther made a smooth transition into combat mode, heard the fierce grind of "The Peter Gunn Theme." He'd just retreated into the stuffy bedroom when he caught the deputy's first step onto wrought iron, then decided the bedroom was wrong. Conceal himself this far back and the element of chance was gone—the kid would *know* he was there. Better to move up, keep the boy guessing.

He was in the bathroom again when he heard the deputy cross the threshold. Gunther climbed onto the vanity, straddling the sink and ducking beneath the ceiling. Just inside the doorway, he pressed flat against the wall and waited.

"Mr. Manzetti? I know you're back there. If you got a weapon, throw it on out now, and you follow next. You can save yourself a world of hurt that way. You hear me, Mr. Manzetti?"

The voice sounded brittle, the kid nothing but a bundle of nerves trying to convey authority. Ten to one he'd never done this outside of training simulations. Gunther imagined him in a Weaver stance, sweating every step, pistol leading the way in a two-handed grip as he pretended that Gunther was no worse than an automated plywood target that might pop up along a track.

"I already got your lady friend locked up tight. I don't bat five hundred, Mr. Manzetti, I bat a thousand. Up to you, easy or hard."

What Gunther could not figure was *why* this tumbleweed was after them at all. He couldn't fault Maddy; she'd looked to have played her part like a pro. Odder still, the deputy had called him by name, information he couldn't have gotten from the Cadillac's license plates. The registration wasn't even under his own name.

Gunther let it go for now, quashing everything but instinct and awareness as the deputy took careful steps up the hall. He sensed a pause, then heard a sudden flurry as the deputy yanked open a closet door, found nothing, and continued.

Gunther held his breath. Stooped already, he reached down to grab the scummy bar of soap, rose again.

A tiny creak in the hall, four feet away. Three. Two. Gunther tossed the bar of soap across the bathroom and into the shower; it landed with a thud on molded plastic.

When Gunther saw the pistol and two forearms swing through the doorway, he kicked out from atop the vanity, knocking them against the bathroom door. He swooped down to club the deputy's wrist with the towel bar, and the pistol went clattering to the linoleum.

The deputy's babyface went raw with panic, and he fumbled at his Sam Browne belt—pepper spray, probably. Gunther tagged him across the chin with a hastily thrown elbow, doing little harm but spinning him as the kid rolled with the punch. From behind him, Gunther snapped the hand towel around his face and caught the free end, drew both taut, skinning the fabric tighter than a mask. Gunther could feel the hard shell of a Kevlar vest beneath the beige uniform shirt. He dragged the blind and struggling deputy into the bedroom, where he would have more elbow room.

Gunther kept up the pressure as he shifted both ends of the towel to one hand, then swung the aluminum bar, battering into the contoured terry cloth until it began to stain red, and the towel went heavy in his hand.

Gunther laid the deputy on the floor, the towel stuck onto his face, and cuffed his wrists behind his back with a second pair looping off his belt. He whipped the bloodied towel into a thick gag and tied it in place; ripped the beige uniform shirt away and unfastened the vest and worked it off over the deputy's head.

After snatching the handcuff key, he hurried outside to let Madeline out of the car and turn her loose before she blew up at anything in sight, him included. Too late. Her fuse was gone. He chilled her out with a no-nonsense, one-eyed glare, had her swing the Cadillac around the trailer. She parked beside the bedroom window, through which he chucked the deputy so they could load him into the trunk, out of sight from the distant neighbors.

"Get those comic books out of there first," he told Madeline. "I don't want him bleeding on the box. Put his shirt under his head."

Gunther made a quick pass through the trailer, using his own shirt to wipe down whatever he'd touched. Not that it was likely to make much difference, but still, there was principle involved. No sense making it any easier to tie him here than it had to be.

If nothing else, at least he was now armed again, even better than before. He collected the pistol, a Browning 9mm. With another key from the deputy's Sam Browne, Gunther raided the cruiser and freed the pump shotgun from its rack. Plus the vest made a nice bonus. As an afterthought, he grabbed the flat-brimmed sheriff's hat from the seat before running to the Cadillac.

Madeline pointed to the hat. "You're not going to fool anyone with that thing."

"Who am I trying to fool? This is our proof-of-purchase." He slammed the trunk lid on the deputy and waved Madeline toward the driver's seat. "What I'll do is ride in back. We meet anybody else on the road, what I'll do is wave this hat and point to the trunk, make like if they don't back off, I start blasting through the backseat. See if that doesn't get them thinking twice."

The road back into the heart of Coyote Ridge was clear, and Madeline gunned for it. He saw something lying off to one side, had her brake immediately. Opened the door and snatched it up as she rolled past. Fortune had smiled again. He held the opened can of Drano across the front seat and shook it like a rattle.

"Still feels about half full!" He grinned. "I got to start remembering to carry this with me, that's all there is to it."

After leaving Coyote Ridge on U.S. 93, they cut over onto secondary roads as soon as they could. Unfamiliar territory, all of it, and too insignificant for the maps. The best they could do was navigate southeast to Phoenix, losing whatever pursuers they might have earned. For sure, backup had been on its way to Coyote Ridge even before that deputy had set foot in the trailer, but apparently he'd been too much of a hot dog to wait.

Gunther figured they had less than twenty miles before the county line into a new jurisdiction. If the state police from the DPS hadn't already been called in, they soon would be, although he was counting on the deputy's disappearance to sow enough seeds of confusion to buy them sufficient time to make it to Phoenix. Had they left a dead deputy at the trailer, they could've counted on a helicopter or two being scrambled almost immediately.

They kept zigzagging southeast after crossing into Maricopa County, twice having to turn off onto private property when they thought they'd spotted, far ahead, an oncoming car with a flashbar on the roof. Once it was a luggage rack; once the real thing.

Twenty miles or so outside of Phoenix, Gunther decided they should cut due east awhile, toward the interstate; maybe come into the city from the north, or even loop around and enter from the east, through Scottsdale.

The Cadillac streaked toward the vanishing point on an arid horizon, the endless flatlands punctuated by clusters of saguaro cactus. With the interstate a few miles ahead, Gunther spotted a dirt road branching off to the left, leading into a low climb to a red rock formation jutting from and crumbling back to the ground.

"Pull up in there a few minutes."

"What for?"

"Time to dump the garbage."

He had been weighing the diminishing odds of being stopped this close to Phoenix with the mounting liability of carrying in a hostage. The middle of the city wasn't the place to go yanking people from the trunk when you were trying to blend. If worse came to worst later on, he could always bluff with the deputy's hat.

Madeline stopped the car beside a pair of tall, narrow boulders that looked like the fossilized fins of ancient sharks. Smaller rocks lay heaped around their bases, and from the shadows of a tiny cave they were watched by the impassive eyes of a horned toad.

In the trunk, the deputy was conscious by now, but sapped by heat and tomato-red. His brown uniform slacks and white T-shirt were soaked through with sweat. He tried and failed to focus his eyes as Gunther pulled him from the trunk and set him upright.

"You think you got problems?" Gunther said. "I got a thirty-four-thousand-dollar comic book and no place to sell it."

The deputy grunted past the whip of bloody towel stretched across his mouth. Gunther relented—who was he going to call out here?—and untied the gag, tossed it aside. The kid stretched his mouth, working his tongue around like a scrap of leather.

With the pistol, Gunther prodded him over to the rocks, felt Maddy's eyes on their backs. Felt, in some small way, that he was performing for her, a redemption for the day's blunders.

He found that he wasn't hating Boyd quite as much now that he had somebody else to take it out on. Found he could even admire Boyd's guile. Ninety-nine guys out of a hundred couldn't even begin to think of talking themselves out of a situation like that. Could never have put a plan together. All they could do was beg.

"Don't kill me," the deputy rasped.

Gunther patted his shoulder. "You think *that's* what we're here for?"

He laid the kid out on a slab of rock, back on his pinioned arms. As Gunther squatted by him, the deputy looked up, pleading with his eyes, the right swollen half shut. Gunther empathized.

"Don't. I have a family. I have . . . have a little boy."

"Family, that's important to you. Being with them."

A slow nod.

"Over time," said Gunther, "you got more dead relatives than live ones, is the way I look at it."

Tears began to squeeze from the deputy's eyes. Not so badly dehydrated after all. This was good. Moisture was good right now.

"I'll give you a chance. More chance than you were planning on giving me back there. I like playing the odds. I'm giving you every chance to walk out of this desert." He took the can of Drano from behind his back, where he had been holding it out of sight, and set it on a rock beside the deputy's head. "There's just one catch. This one thing. I just got to get this out of my system."

He'd already changed clothes in the desert so he wouldn't come into Phoenix looking as though he'd fallen down a cliff. They pulled into a strip mall with a pharmacy and bought medicated eyedrops and circular gauze bandages and white tape, then ducked into a four-shots-for-a-dollar photo booth so Madeline could treat him and secure a bandage in place. Outside the booth, he looked into the primping mirror with approval, then decided what the hell, as long as they were here. He fed a dollar into the slot and dragged Maddy back inside, onto his lap, as the camera flashed at five-second intervals. As soon as he saw the strip of pictures, they seemed a waste of money—Maddy hadn't kept her mouth shut for a single one.

Next stop was a florist shop, to browse their Yellow Pages for a cut-rate body shop where he could drop the Cadillac for an overnight budget paint job. Get that white Caddy off the road, and return to it tomorrow in one that wouldn't flag attention.

"What color you think we should go with?" he asked.

"Painting the car? Why not just steal one?"

"Because stolen cars get reported. Makes no sense to go from one car they're looking for to another they're looking for."

"Gray," Madeline said. "We should go with gray."

Back outside at a telephone carrel, he called a body shop to clear an appointment for later in the afternoon, then made a mental checklist. Paint the car, lay low in a motel until tomorrow. He would have to retire the license plates, but it shouldn't be any problem to find a car down from Nevada and make a switch that was likely to go unnoticed. The average traveler paid about as much attention to his plates as he did to speed limits.

Next, he called Joey Ferret at Two-Eyed Jacks.

"I need you to run a license number for me."

"Do you have any idea what you're asking right now?" said the Ferret. "Right now you are skating on extremely thin ice out there on your own and you have somebody we both know very pissed off over this. Am I getting through to you?"

The tone of his voice came as a shock. Joey Ferret had never talked to him this way; had never had any reason to do so. Another sudden mystery, something rumbling beneath the surface. Outback deputies who knew his name, and now this.

"What's going on?" Gunther asked.

"I shouldn't even be talking to you."

"Then let's make it easy for you. You run me this plate, dig up the particulars on the guy, and what I do is drop out of sight and all our problems are solved. You, me, and any interested third parties. How's that sound?"

The Ferret gave a weary sigh. "As far as I know, this is a secured line, but I'm not taking any chances. You find yourself a fax machine and send it to me that way, and sit tight for a reply. Think you can do that without leaving a mess behind?"

Gunther said he could manage fine, took down the number for the fax line, and turned to Madeline for advice. They sought out a photocopy center in the strip mall, full of college kids who fed papers into rows of whirring machines. Madeline took care of it, paying two dollars to fax a single sheet to the Ferret's office, with the license number that Boyd had spotted through the window when Allison's ride had picked her up.

Florida tag, the note read. *ST JOHN.*

Twenty minutes, and the information came. They took the reply fax outside, drinking Snapples that Maddy had picked up at a juice bar two doors down, reading as the sun's heat bounced at them off the asphalt.

The black van that Boyd had seen belonged to Thomas St. John, of Panama City, Florida. Five feet eleven, 165 pounds, thirty-six years old, black hair, brown eyes . . . the standard driver's license trivia. The Ferret had done some supplemental digging to provide them with not only St. John's home address and phone number, but those of his business, a custom leatherwear firm called St. John's Apocalypse.

Below this was a more personal message from the Ferret: *Your favors here are used up. Call if interested in knowing why.*

"Not a bad day's work, Gunther," said Madeline. "You got yourself worked over by someone who couldn't move, and it looks like you've managed to alienate opposite sides of the law."

There was no pleasing this woman. He returned to the phone and fed in more coins.

"Just keep your mouth shut and listen to this story," the Ferret told him. "Story about a guy we both know. What this guy did last night was take a boxful of comic books to a place to try selling them. You know the thick-headed guy I'm talking about?"

"Yes," Gunther said quietly.

"Fabulous. We're communicating. The guy that owns the shop, soon as he saw the contents of the box, he started to get nervous, see, because he recognized them. Some of those comics in that box were so old and rare that not just anybody'd have them lying around. And grouped together like that, the collection's about as individual as a fingerprint to a guy like that comic shop owner. He'd never in a thousand years expect somebody to walk in off the street with it, acting like he doesn't even realize what he's got. But then, along comes Thickhead. Are you following this so far?"

"Yes," Gunther whispered.

"It wasn't the first time the comic shop guy had seen this collection. He'd appraised it already, last year, for one of his regulars. And what made him so nervous when he saw these comics again was because he knew from the newspaper that his old customer had been found capped in the head a week ago, in his own bedroom. So, guess who he figures is standing right there in front of him."

"Sure," said Gunther. "Who wouldn't."

"My point exactly. So after stone cold Thickhead leaves, what the shop guy does is have one of his customers run out and catch the license on the car that's driving away. Now, here's the part where it gets really weird. The shop guy closes up and immediately starts trying to cut a deal with the Vegas PD and DA's office, so he can get a reward for turning in the killer. But he doesn't want money. What he wants is the rest of the comic books Thickhead brought in, after they're no longer required as evidence. He's got a big hard-on for this book from the late thirties—Batman's first appearance. There's only fifty or so of them left in the world. He's wanted the thing ever since he first appraised the dead guy's collection, found out the dead guy got it from his grandfather, who'd bought it new for one thin dime because he liked detective stories. So. Do you see where this is heading?"

"Hey," said Gunther, "I'm not blind."

"The shop guy picks Thickhead out of a mug book, and by this morning the cops are most seriously interested in finding out what he knows about the dead guy. Some brain in that Thickhead, huh?"

Gunther was slowly banging his frontal lobe against the edge of the phone carrel. "Any word on Thickhead having any accomplices or traveling companions, like that?"

"Unidentified redheaded female. You want the exact wording from the comic shop guy's statement? This is from a friendly source in the department. You want to hear it?"

"Go ahead."

" 'Attila the Hun, with cleavage.' "

Gunther straightened up, bristling. "Now *that's* out of line." If and when he got back to Vegas, he was definitely going to have to take that Calvin geek from the comic shop and tie him down for a long, long demonstration of various industrial solvents.

"So if you see Thickhead," said the Ferret, "you might want to tell him to come on back into the fold, under some protection, until this blows over."

"Yeah, I'll do that," Gunther said, and hung up, knowing that as soon as he tried any such thing, that would be the last anyone heard of Thickhead, ever again.

Get picked up on this murder charge, and he would be a huge liability to Toby Costas. Liabilities were dealt with under a zero-tolerance policy, by people you thought you could trust. Blame the police, the FBI. They just loved to get a man in this position and start squeezing nuts. Then they'd dangle before him a chance to wipe the slate clean by turning state's evidence on however many of his former associates whose names they could properly spell on the indictments. The feds might even have enough clout to keep him from standing local charges on that situation with the deputy.

Not that he really wanted to see it come to that.

Madeline had strayed over to a bench during the phone call, sipping her fruit juice while glaring at the fax paper. Someday, sitting pretty with all that cash, they would look back on this day and laugh.

"I got something to tell you," Gunther began, and she gave him a look that could have split atoms. "But there's one thing I need to know first: What are your feelings on Mexico?"

chapter fourteen

By Phoenix, Thomas St. John had grown accustomed to Allison's watchful silence. Strangers they may have been, but it felt as though they'd settled into a comfortable respect for one another's distances, the isolated corners in each of them around which the other had no right to look.

He made two stops in Phoenix—one a motorcycle dealership, the other a leather store. Out of the way, she watched him unload boxes as he bypassed his wholesalers. She came in out of the heat to browse while he renewed acquaintance with those who worked here, who came through the doors. Those made itchy by thoughts of an open road, any road. Most of them pursuer as well as pursued, whether they realized it or not, chased by demons of varied breeds as they rushed toward some confrontation that waited around the next bend, or the next.

He watched Allison from the back as she lost herself in racks and daydreams—the boots, the faded shorts, the tied-off blouse, the wheat-blond hair blown about her shoulders. And the lingering way she sidestepped along those racks . . . one step firm to anchor her to some new spot, the other long leg gliding in more slowly, with an ethereal grace. How unbruised she appeared from behind.

They left Phoenix and were dropping down to Tucson before she seemed to unlock herself, tucking one leg beneath her and turning toward him rather than the window. The van was still too warm from sitting locked, its air thick with the soft rich smell of leather.

"After I met you on the parking lot last night," she said, "I got to feeling almost afraid of whatever could've brought you all the way from Florida to that godforsaken urinal of a town."

"Now you know."

"You wouldn't think a place like Coyote Ridge would be able to support a Harley dealership like that."

"Local support doesn't always have everything to do with it. It's how far away you can draw your buyers in from, and keep them. A place like Coyote Ridge, you've definitely got lower overhead in your favor. Teddy Serafino—he owns Coyote's Paw Harley—he tells me he's had repeat buyers from as far away as Denver."

"And you stock the leather racks. I never would've figured you for something like that."

He grinned. "Yeah? What *were* you figuring?"

"Well, look at you. Black jeans, leather vest, extremely watchful eyes, van all loaded down . . . maybe a drug runner."

"But you came along for the ride anyway."

"That's how much I wanted out of Coyote Ridge." A cockeyed smile worked around the puffier spots on her mouth. "An actual craftsman. You don't see many of those around anymore."

Sad but true. Sometimes he felt he belonged to a species no longer heralded and going quietly extinct. More and more the world resisted those whose hands were made to shape livings from its fruits and fibers. This newer world would shear away their rough excess in its prefab molds, turn them into cogs to fit machines, make them easy to replace when they wore out.

Money could get tight at times, but freedom was compensation enough—in charge of his day, lackey to no boss. He found reward in taking a swatch of leather and shaping it to fit an ideal, or better yet, discovering the notion sunk into the leather already, like Michelangelo, who claimed he never carved statues, only freed them from the blocks of marble. Leather was alive—it breathed and aged, it flexed under pressure, it took on the unique stamp of its owner. Seeing what he could make from it felt as though he'd taken something dormant and made it vital again.

Poor consolation, however, for the sad-eyed noble cows.

Tom groped on the floor behind his seat. He came up with a folder and gave it to Allison, and she flipped through the pages, sketches made over the past few months—new designs, variations on old. He'd usually show them wherever he stopped with a delivery, seeing what met with the best reception.

"Any of those do anything for you?" he asked Allison.

Some did, some didn't. She slid one from the stack and held it up, her eyebrow cocked. The sketched vest had been born of dual inspiration—half biker, half bondage. "Seriously?" she said.

He shrugged. "Some people like a lot of straps."

"Some people *need* a lot of straps."

After their late-afternoon stop in Tucson he turned due east, and grew bold enough to ask how she'd come to be stuck in Coyote Ridge. It took a few more miles of desert and carrion, greasewood and sage, before the story began to emerge. The name Boyd came up several times, spoken as if synonymous with siring by jackals. Tom nodded, getting the idea that Allison knew how to nurse a grudge.

"So I started hitching out of Vegas, got as far as the Ridge before I decided I didn't want to chance some of the risks. So my priority became saving up for a bus ticket home to Mississippi."

"Your family couldn't have sent you ticket money?"

"I only said it was home. Who said anything about a family?"

You did. It's written all over your face, he thought, but pressed no further. Blood or not, family wasn't always necessarily something to be proud of.

They weren't far into New Mexico when he pulled off to pass the night. Tom got a motel room with twin beds. Allison had made no move to rent her own, and doubtless could not afford it anyway, so surely twin beds would suit both their needs. He didn't learn how wrong he was until after they had gone out for a platter of fajitas for dinner. Back at the motel, Allison informed him she would sleep in the van.

"There's no reason for that. Look, it's not a handout. I'd've had to get a room whether you came along or not."

She planted herself on the parking lot, those bare, booted legs steady as pillars, arms folded across her chest. "I've slept in worse places. The van should be plenty comfy."

Tom argued, but she held her ground, so stubborn he felt sure that if thrown from an airplane, she'd fall up out of spite. He gave up.

He went inside, then stepped back out to bring her a pillow and blanket, and caught a completely different look in her eyes. Gone was the woman of moments before, with whom no bargain could be struck. Allison was staring beyond him with a basic mistrust of four walls and a door that she'd been unable to conceal quickly enough. Fourteen hours, two states, and 350 miles hadn't quite done the trick: He'd not yet proved himself.

"If you change your mind," he told her, "just knock."

But the knock never came, as he knew it wouldn't, and while he waited to fall asleep Tom wondered if she'd refused to come in because she smelled death on him and didn't consciously recognize it. Or maybe she had, but was too polite to say so.

Holly St. John—a name on a tombstone now, but not always. A face in pictures stored in the bottom of a trunk, at the back of a closet, but a face that could never be evicted from dreams.

The marriage seemed even more fragile and fleeting than it already was when he considered that it lasted 843 days. The number looked too finite, the span too easy to grasp: a beginning, a long middle, a bloody and unanticipated end. He could conceive of it as a whole, almost hold it in cupped hands.

Auburn-haired and obsidian-eyed, Holly had a look about her that Tom never failed to find arresting, graceful and imposing and streamlined all at once. She was like a falcon that could never be

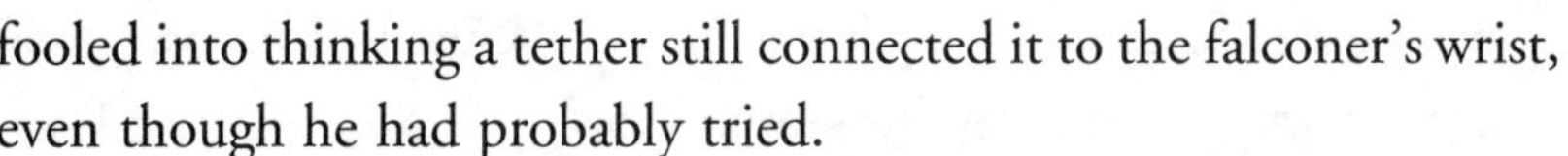

fooled into thinking a tether still connected it to the falconer's wrist, even though he had probably tried.

Most of his first year out of the Marine Corps had been spent astride a motorcycle. He'd not had a haircut since his discharge, and his thirtieth birthday was far enough ahead that it merited no thought. Responsibilities were for those who'd already mapped out their lives. After four years of discipline, he now preferred whim and chance.

One day's detour to a crafts festival outside Estes Park, Colorado, and there she was. A potter. She had been a potter. Tom found himself drawn again and again to her hourly demonstrations, as each time she treadled the wheel with one foot and shaped an inanimate gray lump into something that looked as though it had existed since the dawn of time. The contradictions of her hands fascinated him, their power and finesse and control. After the fifth pot he'd watched her make, in as many hours, Holly made it easy on him—told him to either talk to her or she would call security. He showed her the jacket he had made, nearly a year before, although the weathering it'd seen since had aged it. She told him he should be behind a worktable in his own booth, but by now he was beginning to feel it was finally time to go home again.

He'd wondered ever since if it had been the shift in climate that had wreaked subtle havoc on her, on hormones and neurons. The wet heat of the Gulf Coast was not for everyone; its contrast with mountain air would be doubly harsh. But whenever he looked to the climate for blame, Tom knew he was hunting for simplicity in a pattern where there was none. You could live with someone for a lifetime and still never know the innermost workings of her mind.

Holly smelled women on him when there had been none. Stayed up for days on end, while on others she could scarcely budge from bed. More than once he'd heard one-sided conversations held behind closed doors in otherwise empty rooms, and these frightened him the most, even more than her talk of suicide. These threats, while unsettling, were made without conviction and in a lackluster daze. The conversations, though, had never been intended for him to hear in the first place, which made them all the worse. Just Holly and an empty room, her low, erratic voice like something from another world.

They'd told him later it would wear anyone down—the coping, trying to talk sanity when in fact he had begun to doubt his own. Family and friends told him it was not his fault. As if family and friends could know everything that had been said, done, thought.

On the 843rd day, Tom found her huddling in the bathtub after he'd spent an hour at his workbench, using a razored utility knife to slice strips of leather.

"I'm going to do it," she told him from the bath. "Tonight's the night. I know that now."

It was the same thing he'd been hearing every few weeks for at least a year, more tiresome than alarming by now. Trying to reason with her, tell her how much she was loved and needed—these never seemed to work. Maybe she needed instead to be shocked.

He still remembered the sound of his voice, a cold disgusted ricochet off blue tiles. Even now he sometimes dreamed of pulling his hand back before he set the utility knife on the rim of the tub, beside the dry bar of soap.

"So what the hell are you waiting for?" he said, and left her alone, shutting the door on her dementia and listening, waiting for the voices to begin. Fooling himself for a time into thinking that the silence was good for a change.

He rose in the middle of the night to check on Allison, a task neither asked for nor required, so perhaps it was curiosity more than anything. He stepped to the rear-door windows of the van and peered between the gap in the curtains.

This made the second night in a row he'd seen her curled on her side, and while this time Allison appeared serene, it did not come free. In her makeshift nest of pillow and blanket, surrounded by a protective rampart of luggage and cargo, she slept with her hand upon a snub-nosed revolver. Its nickel plating shone with a gleam of moonlight, and she touched it the way she might've touched a teddy bear twenty-five years ago.

He wondered about the peace it brought her, why that was what it took. No one started out this way; people were hounded to it, all the trust gnawed out of their bones after they were brought down struggling and in shock.

And it was much too late at night for something like this, for all the conflicting aches and confusing impulses. The core of Allison's story might be true, but he was certain that many of its nuances had been pruned away. He tried telling himself that the sooner she was out of his life, the better for them both.

Then he went back inside to sleep through as much of the night as would have him.

After his shower Tom offered to go for breakfast in a bag while Allison took her own shower. As she agreed, their eyes held, unspoken understanding that they both knew he was making himself scarce for her benefit.

"I'll just leave the key on the table," he said.

Her revolver was nowhere to be seen this morning, although he suspected she kept it close at hand, maybe in that giant purse. Walking along the frontage road, breathing new morn air and diesel exhaust, he wondered if she'd owned it awhile or had bought it in Coyote Ridge. The latter might, at least, explain why after a week she hadn't even managed to scrape up enough for bus fare.

Allison looked refreshed when they returned to the road, exuding that fine clean smell of a woman with the worst of the world washed away. She wore her bruises less self-consciously than yesterday, seemed unconcerned with hiding them; holding her head higher, and to hell with what anyone thought. Her hair blew free about her face and shoulders, and he indulged himself, imagining what it must feel like between stroking fingers.

Try it once, though, and he'd likely lose a hand.

"Where to today?" she asked.

"We'll head on into Las Cruces, be there in a couple hours. Then we turn south a little, into Texas, go to El Paso. We should be heading east across Texas for most of the afternoon, come back north into New Mexico to hit Carlsbad."

Allison nodded, then fixed him with bright, enigmatic eyes. A bruised Mona Lisa, with her smile of secrets and privilege.

"What?" he said.

"Guess what *I* found around dawn this morning."

"I don't know, you tell me."

But as soon as she went digging through his belongings on the floor, he knew what it had to be. A blush began at the soles of his feet as she rested the small flat box on her lap.

"I saw this box, and I'm sorry, but I just couldn't help myself. I was wondering, Now what could he make from leather that would be small enough to fit in there? Because of the size of the box, well, I was thinking it could only be for one part of the body, so whatever it was, I just had to see it. . . ."

She opened it and began to pull out the tiny books. Flipping through them, Allison read the titles aloud: "*Bobby Meets the Dinosaurs. The Jolly Barnyard. Little Bear Goes to the Moon. Mr. Putter and Tabby Pour the Tea. The Ever-Living Tree.* So, are these what you curl up with when you're on the road?"

"What, I give the impression of having a first-grade reading level?"

"I'm just kidding. These belong to your kids, right?"

Tom shrugged uneasily behind the wheel.

"Either they do or they don't, that's simple enough."

"I don't *have* any kids." It came out more snappy than he had intended. "But someday, if I do . . . then these books, well . . . they'll belong to them then. Is that simple enough for you?"

She was looking more closely at him, but it went deeper than that this time. Past the scar that creased the corner of one eye, past the weathered skin and the black hair that was showing gray even in his mid-thirties. She saw these things as though they were somehow new.

"You buy these," she said softly, "and you hang on to them? You just . . . hang on to them?"

He wished she would go ahead and laugh, get it over with. Couldn't she see from his face that he picked them up all across the country? That he really *did* read them when it felt as if the next day was taking too long to arrive? That it was starting to hurt, for there was no one he was reading them to, and he was beginning to fear there never would be?

With unexpected reverence, she aligned the books in her hands and returned them to their box. "I think that must be," she said in a hush, "the single sweetest act of faith I've ever heard of."

"Maybe the most futile, too," he admitted. "I'd probably make a lousy father anyway."

"Think so? You don't *know* about lousy fathers."

"Don't I? Any law says you get to have a monopoly?"

Allison lowered her eyes. "No. No law." Then she turned the spotlight back on him like an accusation. "What's your problem, then? You don't have enough faith in yourself to try and get past the shitty example he set for you?"

"Maybe I could answer that better if he'd stuck around long enough to set one in the first place."

He sometimes wondered if somewhere out there his father was still alive, wondering what had become of his son. But this was a trail thirty-two years cold, no more and no less real than a small boy's dream of being swung from a giant's arms.

That's all he was now, that elder St. John—dream vapor, a featureless phantom who lurked on the edge of memory, in most ways more powerful in his vagueness than if he'd remained in the flesh all these years. Phantoms never stooped, never withered.

And Tom did *not* want to talk about this. Surely his name on the van's registration granted him right of refusal.

They rode in silence awhile, during which Tom refused to look her way—except from the corner of his eye, and that didn't count. Allison merely stared out the window, head on hand and elbow on upraised knee. Losing herself out in that passing desert, austere and mottled as with the ochers of a spilled paint pot, and in her seeming reverie, haunted, perhaps, by old ghosts.

That was the trouble with ghosts: One place was always as good as another whenever they were of a mind to follow.

"I wish *my* father hadn't stuck around" was all she said, and no more until Las Cruces.

chapter fifteen

If good things came to those who waited, they were overdue for a bounty. Even Gunther seemed bored, and she'd not thought this possible. Had always thought of Gunther as the type who could shut down his nominal higher brain functions and outstare a lizard until it crawled away in defeat.

High noon on Monday, as they simmered behind the wheel of a Cadillac going nowhere. The town of Brady simmered along with them. Somewhere here in mid-Texas they had exchanged the dry heat of the southwest for something heavier, wetter.

"Give me that fan," she said. "Your turn's up."

"Five more minutes," Gunther pleaded. "Come on, we got to keep me cooled down. I get too hot and infection might set in."

"The heat's not going to infect your eye. You're just being selfish. Now give me that fan."

With a huff, he offered it. A silly-looking thing, all white plastic, not even the size of a coffee mug, but it put out a solid breeze. An adapter cord plugged it into the Cadillac's cigarette lighter. With the clothespin-like swivel on the bottom, Madeline clamped it to the steering wheel and turned it on herself.

"I've been thinking about you and this new Drano shtick of

yours," she said. "I think you've got a really sick eye fetish. I'm just wondering where that comes from."

He seemed to take this seriously as he stared across and down the street at a business called Hawg Heaven. A brick building on a wide lot filled with rows of gleaming chrome, virgin tires, and streamlined frames. And nothing going on at midday. All the action was here on their side of the street, at the walk-up ice cream hut where they were parked.

"Never really crossed my mind before," Gunther said, "but you could be right. When we were kids I used to take my sister's dolls and gouge out their eyes. Or if they were too small—Barbie dolls, like that, tiny-eyed things—I'd black them out with an ink pen."

"Why did you do that?"

"I don't know. Hear her scream about it when she found them, I guess. She had this funny way of crying, like she was about to suffocate."

"I mean why the eyes. That's weird, Gunther, don't you know how weird that is? Most big brothers would just steal the dolls or hide them or rip up the clothes. They wouldn't go for the eyes."

"I don't know why I did anything. I just saw the eyes and I thought it'd be funny to put them out. All those blind dolls, it'd crack me up to look at them." He scowled. "She was always watching me, my sister was. Always waiting to tell on me for something. It was like she'd leave those dolls of hers around on purpose, like they were her spies. Maybe I just wanted to send her a message."

Madeline couldn't help but laugh—picturing Gunther as a boy, mutilating dolls with his vindictive resolve. A junior wiseguy in training. "Did you leave them in toy cars after you did the hits? Or scattered around their little tea party tables?"

"Fuck you," he said. "See if I ever tell you anything again."

"And now look at you, Gunther, you and your bandage. There's a *bizarre* kind of justice in that, you have to admit." A chuckle threatened to overtake her. "There's got to be a word for it, this eye business boomeranging back to haunt you. There's just got to be a word for something that perfect."

He looked annoyed and embarrassed by it all. "Yeah, well, if there is, *I* never ran across it, so let's drop the whole thing."

"Testy?" she cooed. "Are we getting testy now?" She poked at his ribs, at his flat, muscled stomach. Loved to watch him squirm, on the verge of taking a swing at her but never letting himself slip over that edge. Not with her. Another woman maybe. Never her.

This often seemed the glue that kept them together. Where else could he find such symbiosis? Madeline suspected that he was the rarest of the rare among his criminal kind, in that he gave no indication whatsoever of having cheated on her. Not because the opportunities weren't there—in Vegas, opportunity practically crawled onto the nearest tabletop and spread its legs—but because the notion simply didn't seem to occur to him. His needs were few, focused, uncomplicated. He was the only man she had ever known who passed by other women and not only didn't stare, but appeared to take almost no notice of them at all.

Why she spent so much time dreading the moment that he would, Madeline did not know.

She found a peculiar benefit in his being half blind these days. One eye bandaged was one eye that couldn't betray her, show him the truth of her that the mirror had noticed but that Gunther, so far, had not. One eye bandaged improved the odds, gave her a little more time to sustain the illusion, whatever he saw when he looked at her.

Beyond Mexico, they hadn't discussed plans for the money. She wasn't sure she would tell Gunther the truth. Even before scouting Boyd for the skim, the intention had been there: take part of the money and disappear for a few weeks, into the finest clinic for cosmetic surgery that she could find. What years had taken away, the knife could give back. Get everything done in one long ordeal of cutting, lifting, and tightening: breasts, eyes, neck, face, jawline, stomach—especially her stomach—and bring them all back up to the standards still defined by her legs.

She had even rehearsed her temporary departure, replaying it in her mind until every word was just right.

I'm going to be gone for a few weeks, she would tell Gunther when the time came, *and I don't want you asking me where. But I'll call you every day, and when I come back, it'll all make sense to you then, and you'll be glad I went. We can't really start over until I do this one thing.*

Madeline looked over at the line for ice cream—high school girls on lunch break, wrinkles and sag the farthest things from their minds. Tiffany would look like them in a few more years.

It never felt as if she should have a daughter, not even an absentee living with her dad, but there Tiffany was, back in Lake Tahoe. Residue from another life. Growing up without Madeline, perhaps without need of her, maybe even better off for it. Quite possibly she would never see Tiffany again, and she had no trouble accepting this. Maybe her ex-husband had been right: If she'd ever had one maternal bone in her body, it had long since been broken.

All told, by going to Mexico, Gunther might be giving up more than she would.

"You're handling this a lot better than I thought you would," she told him.

"Handling what?"

"You know. That you can't go back to Vegas, that you're out. That they'll probably kill you if they find you back there."

"Aah. So what. It's not like I hadn't already gone as far there as I was ever gonna. Toby Costas, he had his way, I'd still be doing collections when I'm eighty, trying to drag some asshole behind my wheelchair. Half full of German blood, you know, I could never be a made man with those guys anyway."

He'd told her before of how they demanded racial purity for their innermost circles. How you could work for them, but never be one of them. She had immediately known the feeling, working as pit boss where most others were not only men, but men who thought that women belonged onstage or serving drinks. All the education she would ever need on the subject of exclusion.

"The Guidos made that real clear to me early on. That's the one thing that really frosted my balls back in Philadelphia. That ethnic thing. Halfway there wasn't good enough, and there was nothing I could do to change it. I was never gonna be one of those guys, not really. The Guidos got a lock on things like that."

"I thought Costas was a Greek name."

"Hey, they're all Guidos to me. So I say get on to Mexico, and the Guidos can go to hell. I don't need all that made man shit. All those vows and their secret ceremonies, I might as well go join the fucking Masons."

Undoubtedly he would be better off. The feudal appeal of mob life notwithstanding, Madeline knew that most of its members were hardly the intellectual cream of society. Routine stupidity cost them plenty. More than a decade ago, in one of the few brilliant things he'd ever done, Gunther had left Philadelphia after a tipoff, not thirty-six hours ahead of a dragnet of indictments and raids that swept through the Philly mob, which among gangs and lawmen alike had the reputation of being the stupidest criminal organization in history. Casualties of turf wars lay bloody in the streets instead of disappearing without a trace. Grunt-level soldiers who'd grown up on one side of the city had no idea how to navigate on the other. They couldn't run the city, said an FBI informant, because they couldn't find it.

The roundup that Gunther narrowly escaped had begun shortly after an entire carload of them agreed to turn state's evidence. They had smartened up only enough to realize that dead rivals were better off vanishing, so after a hit one night, they'd stuffed the body in the trunk of a car, intending to bury it in New Jersey, except none of them had noticed the bloody Armani jacket hanging out onto the bumper. They nearly made it as far as the state line, but entrapped themselves at their first toll booth on the Penn Turnpike when among the lot of them they could not come up with enough change.

Madeline recalled a book titled *The Gang That Couldn't Shoot Straight.* But poor Gunther. He had fit right in with something far worse: the gang that couldn't *think* straight.

So by now both of them had nothing left to lose, and Madeline supposed this would give them the will to do whatever it took to make things right for once.

And it all began here, beside this ice cream hut.

"What's this, coming up?" Gunther pointed down the street, a block and a half away. "That look like a black van to you?"

They'd gotten out of Arizona yesterday through subterfuge and guile. Local and state jurisdictions would be watching for a man and a redheaded woman in a white Cadillac, so they had instead shown them a blond woman alone driving a gray one. Gunther had ridden on the rear floor until they were deep into New Mexico. The Dolly Parton wig she'd worn since Phoenix was the most hideous accessory she'd ever touched.

Gunther opined that they would be better off intercepting Allison Willoughby on the road rather than waiting until she got to Mississippi. The sooner they recovered whatever she had taken from Boyd, the sooner they could get after the money and head for Mexico. Plus they had no idea what kind of circumstances they'd find Allison in once she got off the road. Conceivably she could be staying with family or friends who spent all their free time oiling a houseful of guns.

They'd spent last night in Abilene, Texas, and first thing this morning Gunther had her call the Panama City business line for Thomas St. John. They'd already tried it Saturday, after Joey Ferret had supplied the goods on Allison's ride, but had been turned away by a recording that suggested they call back during weekday business hours.

When she got through from their motel this morning, Madeline asked to speak with Thomas St. John about doing some custom work—price being no object—and was told that he was out on a delivery trip and not expected back until the end of the week.

"If that guy's making deliveries," Gunther mused, "chances are he was in that pisspot Arizona town on business."

The only place either of them could imagine moving leather

goods was the motorcycle dealership near the diner where they had eaten breakfast. Neither of them could recall the name of the place, although Gunther still had his receipt in his sport coat pocket. He got the diner's number from information, then called.

"There's a motorcycle place, catty-corner across the road from you," Gunther said. "Right?"

"Coyote's Paw Harley, you mean?" said a waitress.

"That's the one," he said, and hung up.

He got their number as well, then called the dealership for the owner's name: Teddy Serafino. Madeline kicked back with her coffee and cigarette and watched him go. A gleam of cunning lit Gunther's eye as the hunt overtook him, this one thing at which he excelled. It was not unarousing. She felt a heat apart from the rising Texas sun as he phoned Panama City again, and now it made sense, why he'd had her place the first call. You can't have the same voice calling twice with different stories.

"Hey, who's this?" he asked. Then: "Lianna, how you doing, it's Teddy Serafino, from Coyote's Paw Harley. Arizona, right." Gunther tried to wink, just couldn't manage the same effect with the gauze bandage. "Say, Tom was by the other day, you know, and when he got out of here, he left behind a big envelope of papers—invoices, like that, looks like stuff he might be needing. I'm guessing he hasn't missed it yet, since he hasn't called, see if he left it here. But, say, you got an itinerary on him, where he's planning on being today? Maybe I can catch him someplace, see if he's needing this stuff. Overnight it to him someplace else tomorrow if he does."

The woman put him on hold for a couple of minutes, came back with the list of stops that her boss had mapped out. Four of them, they slashed southeast through the middle of Texas. He would be starting out from Odessa, then making stops in San Angelo, Brady, and finally San Antonio, where he would spend the night. She gave him the numbers of each place Tom would be stopping.

After Gunther hung up, they spread the road atlas across the bed and began to triangulate distances and intercept points.

"Okay, here's us, and here's them." Gunther's finger picked out

Abilene and Odessa. "Looks like we overshot them yesterday by about a hundred and eighty miles. That's not bad, really, considering."

Without a firm idea of when St. John would be leaving Odessa, trying to beat him to San Angelo would be risky. Brady, almost due south of Abilene, would be the better place.

"Look at this, we got barely over a hundred miles between us and Brady," Gunther said. "They got over two hundred from Odessa, plus however long they lay over in San Angelo. We can be there way ahead of them."

"Hawg Heaven?" Madeline read it off the list.

"That's the way she spelled it for me." And Gunther looked so cute all of a sudden, the one good eye wide and blameless, as if he sensed another pending attack on his education. "That's *exactly* the way she spelled it." Shaking his head. "Hawg. These motorcycle and leather freaks, I don't understand them one bit. They got no respect for the English language."

A black van it was, and just maybe the one they were waiting for. It slowed, pulled into Hawg Heaven's asphalt lot. Stopped.

"Okay, Cyclops," said Madeline. "What's the next move?"

"If he's making deliveries, they'll be here awhile, so what I'm thinking about is another ice cream, as long as you're hogging that fan."

"Bring me another chocolate-dip cone, while you're at it."

Gunther left the car as soon as they made sure it was Allison who emerged from the black van. He appeared unconcerned, loose and easy and content. Saturday's fiasco with Boyd was forgotten, the bruises and injured eye something he no longer acknowledged.

Seeing Allison again, even at a distance, was enough to bring back their confrontation from two and a half weeks ago: Allison's furious arrival that afternoon, catching her with Boyd, ruining everything. Madeline decided that she could not hate Allison for that part of it, at least—there was no way she could've known.

Moreover, you had to respect anyone willing to unleash that much anger against her man.

Allison's voice, though, above the clamor of the car alarm: *What's your problem?* she had said. *You can't hear yourself age?*

Another woman was worse as an enemy, more cruel than most men, because she instinctively knew where to find the jugular and how best to open it. Another woman could leave you dying inside before most men were even able to sense a weakness.

She could hate Allison all right, but for the proper reasons. Madeline could hate her for seeing so much so quickly, and for knowing how to exploit it. She could hate Allison for her smoother skin and her rounder eyes, for the hair that she knew would look great even after a night's sleep. Most of all she could hate her for the years that Allison had not yet lived.

Gunther was back, bearing ice cream cones, licking at the creamy rivulets the sun sent trickling down both fists. She bit into the chocolate-dipped bulb of her cone, the thin shell crunching between her teeth like a tiny skull.

"Nothing happening yet, huh," he said.

"They carried in some boxes. Now they're inside. What do we do about that, Gunther?"

"Here and now, nothing. Big-ass van like that, sticks up over most everything else on the road, it won't be hard to follow. All we do is hang back this afternoon, till they stop someplace that's running low on one thing."

"And what would that be?"

Gunther looked at the roof, disappointed, as if expecting her to know better by now.

"Witnesses," he said. "What else?"

chapter sixteen

Southeast across Texas, the contrasts in the land ahead and the land behind became more manifest. The deserts had been left for good, tended as they had always been by their red stone spires and arches, like the remnants of a vast cathedral prevailing from some aloof and pitiless antiquity. East and west Texas were two different states, even if the map said otherwise. It was green here in the east, full of bristling pines, with lush hills and shaded bowers that owed more to the south than to the west.

The more the land began to thicken around them, the deeper Allison withdrew inside herself. An hour out of Brady, Tom made the connection: They were getting closer to her home, its nearness more inescapable every time she looked out the window.

Allison broke her silence once they started listening to the blues, tapes that she dug from her bag, well-played cassettes that must have seen a hundred rooms, a thousand bottles. Old music, as primitive and powerful as the elements, those hounded voices made tinny by the funnel of decades. Her favorite was a collection of historic recordings made on the old southern state pen work farms and plantations. Unknown black men who sang not for fame or money, but because it was the last true freedom left to them.

"Listen to this line," Allison commanded, and he tuned in.

It ain't but the one thing I done wrong,
I stayed in Mississippi just a day too long. . . .

"I have an idea how he might've felt," she said. "Did you ever wonder how come it's the innocent that usually get locked up in the worst prisons? And I don't mean the kind with bars. I mean the kind of prisons that people carry around inside themselves."

"It's crossed my mind." Tom saw, in a culvert ahead, the armored shell of an armadillo as it trundled through the weeds. Rounded and happy in its prison, because it knew no other way.

"A lot of them down here believe in original sin. No one's innocent, they'll preach at you. But I think that's just something they've convinced themselves of so they won't go crazy. It's a lot easier to hang on to your mind when you think you're getting what you deserve. A lot easier to turn your back on someone else when you're sure they are too."

"And they've still got the gall to call it love," Tom said.

"But then you have to wonder what kind of prisons those good neighbors believe eight-, ten-, twelve-year-old girls deserve. Especially when their fathers are holding the keys. In their cold hands." Her jaw tightened, words squeezing past clenched teeth. "What do you want to bet they don't spend much time trying to fit *that* into this system they've worked so hard to get a handle on?"

He wasn't going to argue with her there.

For he'd noticed that the more they stopped, the more people everywhere were intent on proving her right. At gas stations and truck stops and diners, they'd walk in and gazes would flicker their way. Newcomers were always checked out, over coffee or an ice-cold drink, with a lazy eye and feigned disinterest, surface details taken in while idle minds filled in the rest. Tom and Allison were one thing but most people saw another.

Her bruises had deepened into more vivid colors, as bruises will do. Royal purple, sunrise yellow. At stop after stop, Tom had caught similar reactions on too many of those assessing faces. An admission to a brutal brotherhood in the eyes of too many men; a grim recognition in those of too many women.

It happened again south of Brady when they stopped for a late lunch. The café was all flyspecks and sizzle, squeaking hinges and faces that glistened with sweat, mostly oilfield roustabouts and salesmen. The only one with no attention to spare was a young mother, trying to shepherd her three little ones around the table.

The looks from the rest were not lost on Allison. "Maybe I should wear a sign around my neck," she said. " 'He didn't do it.' "

She laughed softly and nudged his shoulder. It was the first time that they had touched. A warm circle on his arm felt as if it were glowing, and he realized how badly he wanted her to touch him again. And this time, to linger.

"Can you read lips?" she said. "You know what they're saying, don't you? What they've been saying in most of these places?"

"Oh sure." Although he didn't need any special talent. " 'The bitch must've had it coming.' "

As they ate, she wondered if she wasn't talking too much. If she'd told more about herself than she should have, dropped her guard too low. In three days she had given Thomas St. John more hints about her distant past than she'd given Boyd in nine months. Although hints to Boyd were like acorns dropped in sand—no depth there to take root in the first place.

She hadn't wanted to admit it at first, but there really was something deserving about Tom; some decency worthy of more than lies of convenience, sins of omission. Any man who collected books for children he only hoped to have someday should be met halfway in trust. And he liked her, too; she could tell from the way he watched when he thought she wouldn't notice. From anyone else this would be something only to discourage, but he was so obviously fighting it himself that he needed no help from her. All the same, ego demanded that she regard this as something of an affront. What was so wrong with her, from where *he* was sitting, that he had to battle his feelings? Admittedly, though, the gun and her habit of sleeping with it in the van extended little welcome.

She'd done some watching of her own, and was better at doing it on the sly. He had an artisan's hands, Tom did, strong and precise in their movements, heavily veined and nicked by mishaps in the shop, a few short, thin scars pale against the darker skin. Another scar, not as easily explained away, made a small comma out from the corner of one eye, but seemed at home on a face that had seen a lot of sunshine, and lots of rain, and had not turned from either.

Why couldn't their paths have crossed last year instead of now? The playwright again, nothing ever coming easy, or at the right time. A year ago she might not have turned him away as she'd have to now, having no right to make him into the same kind of murderer that she was probably going to be after a few more days.

"What is it?" she asked, noticing his face. He seemed to have forgotten about his last bites of barbecue.

"That guy over by the counter. I know I've seen him before. Just can't remember where."

With a subtle turn of head she spotted him, something almost Aryan about him were it not for the darker shade of his skin. His right eye was masked by a white gauze bandage. He was receiving a handful of change after buying a bag of chips off a rack by the register, and idly glancing in their direction.

"Not with me you didn't see him. Definitely I'd remember the eye patch." She fought an urge to stare. "That hair. I wonder if he dyes it. Does that look like a bleach job to you?"

Tom grinned toward his plate. "What do you say we give him the benefit of the doubt. He doesn't look much like the dyeing kind to begin with, does he?"

"You'd be surprised. I never met anyone yet who didn't want to change *some* God-given thing about themselves."

"God." Tom seemed to muse the word over as if he had never heard it before. "Is that big g, or little g?"

"It's just figure-of-speech g. Don't go changing the subject like that." When she saw that he was about to proclaim innocence,

Allison wagged a finger. "Yes, you were. Because you knew I'd have to ask what you'd change about yourself."

What a bashful thing he could be. If there was anything more endearing than a grown man who could still blush, she didn't know what it might be.

"As long as you're talking about dye jobs," he said, "you can't not have noticed I'm a little . . . um . . . prematurely gray."

"And you don't think that adds character?"

"Character I have no problem with. I was just hoping it might work itself out along a little different timetable, is all." He challenged her with a direct look. "Your turn."

"I always thought I could do with a smaller derrière. Mine's always looked a few degrees too wide to me."

"And you don't think *that* adds character?"

She fished an ice cube from her water glass and flicked it across the table. "You're more devious than you let on, throwing my words back at me like that."

"Like you left me any choice?" He shook his head. "That hind-end talk, Allison, that's dangerous ground. Why do women do that? Put a man in a position where he'll hang himself no matter what he says? I've always wondered that."

"I'm not allowed to tell."

He pushed back from the table. "In that case, I'm excusing myself for a few minutes. See if you can keep from coming up with any more flaming hoops for me to jump through while I'm gone."

Allison watched him bow out, toward the rear of the diner, where a faded arrow promised rest rooms and neutral ground.

Alone with an empty plate, she realized that she'd lost track of the man with the bandaged eye and maybe-bleached hair. But his purpose had been served already. That was the worth of strangers—they gave you something to talk about, compare yourself to.

A moment later Allison heard a baby begin to cry, and looked instinctively for the sound, toward the doorway.

. . .

The bulb in the ceiling belonged in an interrogation room, blasting the toilet with a wretched glare. Tom washed his hands while someone grunted over in the stall. Its wooden partition was thick with white paint, full of gouges and graffiti—crude boasts, pleas for company, the occasional agnostic prayer.

In Magic Marker, black and bold: *This fucking life had better be worth it.*

Wet-handed, Tom looked into a mirror turned cruel by the light. Flaws were exaggerated and assets nullified. Still, it only worked with what it was given. Squint lines when there was nothing to squint at. So would he do away with them if he could? Shed a few years, smooth out that character? Some mornings, why, he had so much character he hardly even recognized himself.

She was drawing him in, even if she hadn't meant to. That which could hurt was always more appealing than that which could not. Three days, and everything Allison had brought with her into his van on the first was still there, only more of it: Her smile was warmer, her laughter louder, her silences sadder, and her curiosity sharper. And somewhere in that purse was her gun.

Final rustlings from the stall—hoisted pants and shuffling shoes, a loud flush. The wooden door banged open and there stood the man from the counter, one eye bandaged and the other staring as if startled. He clutched a bag of Doritos.

Tom nodded, took a step away from the sink to give him room, plucking brown paper towels while the man wet his hands under the faucet. Every move looking too forced, too mannered.

"Have we met before?" Tom couldn't help asking. "Because I know I've seen you someplace before."

The man was coaxing a palmful of pink soap from the crusty dispenser. "That your usual pickup line?" He tilted his head toward the graffiti. "Write an ad on the wall next time, why don't you. It'll weed out the straights."

"My mistake."

"Course, it might bring out the fag-bashers instead. But that's the chance you people take."

"My mistake, I said. I don't know you."

"Fucking-A right you don't know me."

But he did. From somewhere, he did, and this guy knew it. Tom was getting a strange read on the situation, something off balance here. He could either walk away and keep wondering, or stir the pot to see what churned up. And walking away was no good—too many uncertainties in life already.

Tom wadded his damp towels and tossed them into the trash. "Maybe you can settle a bet I got going out there."

Now the guy looked confused, on unsure ground. "A bet."

"A bet, yeah. The woman I'm with, she's dying to know." Tom pointed at the blond brush cut jutting from the man's head. "Is that color natural, or is that a bleach job?"

The cyclopean eye blinked rapidly. "Is this for real? What kind of question is that, you ask another guy that in a toilet?" He was shaking his head now, indignant. "You're worse than some fudge-packer, man, you are *rude*. But you wanna know so bad? Yeah, it *is* my color!" He stopped, face pinched and inquisitive. "Which were you betting on?"

"Me? Bleach."

Then Tom had it, memory connecting the man with another café not very different from this one. No eye patch and with a woman whose own red hair had looked equally improbable. Only a few days ago. What were the odds of this?

"Arizona," Tom said. "Coyote Ridge."

"Shit," the man said, rolling his head about in disgust. When he thrust one hand beneath his sport coat, Tom began to wonder if he hadn't stirred the pot a little too hard this time.

chapter seventeen

The crying baby was slumped to one side of his stroller as if beset by all the miseries that ever were. His mother was trying to maneuver the stroller through the café's door with one arm while supporting a sluggish toddler upon her hip with the other. As her third child, a boy a year older, strayed ahead outside, oblivious, the stubborn door jammed against one of the stroller's wheels.

"Jacob!" his mother called. "You get your little bottom back here and—" But he was gone. Allison could see him through the window, prancing across the parking lot.

She was farthest from the door but first to move, the others in the café pretending not to notice, or saving face with false starts now that it was taken care of.

"Thanks," the woman said after Allison freed the stroller and took over pushing it for her. The baby might have been no happier for it but his mother certainly was. "I keep telling God he should have us grow another arm for every one of these critters we carry to term, but so far all I'm getting's a big fat no."

"It'd just be more hands to wring," said Allison.

"So how old are yours, then?"

"Three and five," she said, the words so smooth and natural they did not even feel like a lie.

This woman appeared younger than Allison by several years, and already three children under age four. It agreed with her, though, and if she looked tired, it was not with regret. Her sandy hair was functionally short, her clothes durable. Allison wondered what her days were like. What her last thought was before sleep and her first upon awakening; what dreams she dreamed in between. And if, when she prayed, she said thanks.

Will I ever—? Allison wondered, and did not finish.

The sleepy middle child was belted into the car, the stroller folded while Allison held the baby. He wiggled against her arms, squirmed against her stranger's breast, then began to relax as she gently rocked and twirled. Tears dwindled to snuffles, and she kissed his porcelain forehead, smooth and moist and sweet.

His mother smiled back over her shoulder while leaning half into the car. "You've not lost the touch, that's for sure."

"No," said Allison. "Nothing's ever lost."

Jacob had been circling them, arms extended like the wings of a plane, and his mother got him to land in the backseat. Oklahoma plates hung on the car, its fenders creased with old scrapes. One headlight held in place with duct tape. Allison handed over the baby boy and said goodbye and watched the car roll off the lot, too aware of the sudden emptiness in her arms.

She turned to rejoin Tom back inside, and caught sight of a familiar face peeking at her from another car several yards away. Its owner tried to duck from sight again, not quite fast enough, and if she wasn't the last person in the world Allison expected to see right now, Madeline DeCarlo ran at least a very close second.

Gunther couldn't understand why it was coming down this way. In the rest room of a cruddy diner in some flyspeck Texas town? It wasn't supposed to happen like this. All he'd wanted was a closer look at this St. John guy, some chips, and a chance to peacefully unload breakfast. These were not extravagant wishes. So Thomas St. John and Allison Willoughby wanted to eat? Gunther praised their timing—he could take care of all his humble needs in one stop.

Except now the leather freak had somehow recognized him.

It went deeper than the face. He'd recognized intent, knowing in the same instant as Gunther that they wouldn't be walking out of here like two civilized strangers. Thomas St. John was fast on the uptake, you had to give him that.

Gunther went for steel, yanking the Arizona deputy's gun from his waistband, remembering too late he hadn't finished washing his soapy hands. The pistol squirted from his grip, slick as a melon seed, and smashed against the mirror. It fell toward the sink, to bounce amid a brittle shower of glass and the crunch of Doritos.

They both lunged for it, Gunther throwing a rough shoulder to slam St. John against the rest room door, St. John thrusting with a piledriver blow using the heel of his hand. No street brawler's move—it looked to have been delivered with all the authority of the U.S. military, and caught Gunther along the side of the jaw with a jolt verging on dislocation.

He punched short and hard into the center of St. John's black shirt, just below his breastbone. If a man can't breathe, he can't do much else. Somebody must've taught St. John this, too, although to go for the throat. Gunther averted his head barely in time to absorb on the side of the neck a glancing chop from the knife edge of St. John's hand. A solid hit might have caved in his entire voicebox. Suddenly this was a bit more truculence than he really cared to handle.

He swept the sleeve of his jacket across the top of the sink, to fling a small glittering storm of glass. As St. John recoiled, Gunther took the chance to wipe his hands on his shirt and get one on the pistol. A low blur—the edge of St. John's boot hacked into Gunther's knee. Unhinged and off balance, he went crashing against the stall wall. Wood cracked. Paint chips flew. A roll of toilet paper unspooled across the floor.

Gunther racked the pistol slide to chamber a bullet. He grinned, despite the awful throbbing of his jaw, then peripherally saw what was coming for him next. Round, the color of a brick, it slapped onto the side of his face like a wet, rubbery mouth.

A plunger.

Gasping for wind, St. John drove him back, leaning one-handed on the plunger, his free hand seizing Gunther's wrist to keep him from aiming. Gunther felt himself wedged into the corner of the rest room and stall walls, neck bulging with veins as he strained against the press of slimy rubber.

Gunther squinted over the lip of the plunger and glared. Saw the unblinking fury in St. John's eyes. Couldn't breathe, running on fumes, and still the man meant grim business. St. John gave his gun hand a knock against the wall. Gunther's finger twitched; a gunshot cracked. Plaster dust sifted down the wall.

Another inch to the right, and the plunger would have cut off Gunther's wind entirely. It squashed his nose to one side, sealing it off, but he managed to suck a breath through the corner of his mouth, stretched just beyond the red rubber bell. The fresh-drawn air tasted of bowl deodorizer, and a sour tang he had always associated with subways.

St. John was good, but even he couldn't outlast his oxygen-starved muscles. Gunther felt him start to give, and cracked his knee up into St. John's face as he buckled; his head snapped back with a cut cheek.

Gunther ripped the plunger from his face and lurched forward, his knee painfully mushy beneath him as he backhanded St. John, got behind him in a choke hold. He raised the Browning's muzzle to the bleeding cheekbone and swung around to face a fractured arc of mirror still clinging to the wall. It reflected the two of them sectioned into a mismatched jumble of pieces, but St. John saw, thought better of struggling in the crook of Gunther's locked arm.

Gunther took a deep breath, then bulldozed St. John toward the rest room door. "Get that, would you," he said. "Me, I'm fresh out of hands."

. . .

"What do you think *you're* hiding from?" Allison called across the gravel and settling dust.

Madeline DeCarlo drew haughtily upright behind the wheel of a boatlike gray Cadillac. Its paint job was a shoddy one, leprous blisters starting to bubble across the hood and roof and trunk.

"Nobody's trying to hide." Madeline now stared boldly at her, across the width of the front seat and out the passenger window. "I just knew if you saw me here, you couldn't resist coming over and exaggerating your own self-importance." A barbed pause. "I see you've proved my point already."

"What are you doing here, anyway? Shouldn't you be back in Las Vegas trying to remember how to count to twenty-one?"

One corner of Madeline's mouth ticked. "You're the whiz kid, let's hear *you* get close without taking off both boots and your bra."

"I'm not wearing one today," Allison told her. "Mine still stand up on their own."

"I guess there's not much there for gravity to grab hold of, is there? Now, that big ass of yours, that's another story."

"Better watch the sun, Madeline. Tan a few more layers, and nobody'll know you from an alligator bag."

Allison held her ground, still smarting. *That* one had hurt. Madeline hadn't picked up on her bottom all on her own, had she? Boyd. Boyd must have let it slip at some point.

"You never answered the question." Allison stepped toward the Cadillac. "What are you doing here?"

Madeline cocked an elbow on the steering wheel as she fished a cigarette from her pack, lit it at her leisure. Blew a plume of smoke. Her sneer held contempt for everything in its range.

She's everything I never wanted to be, Allison thought, *and almost everything I might, if I'm not careful.* Some people knew no better than to spend years swallowing every bitter drop that life forced on them, until their souls were boiled alive. To look at Madeline was to look into one possible future, and be galvanized by the knowledge that she had to avoid it.

"What the hell are you *doing* here, Madeline?"

"Not that you'll ever know what it's like, but back in Vegas, I've got a fifty-four-thousand-dollar-a-year career. People with fifty-four-thousand-dollar-a-year careers get paid vacation time. We get to use it however we want, and I have a sister in Louisiana I'm wanting to see. Any more bright questions?"

Allison smelled lies. There was no reason for this woman to suddenly begin explaining herself. And why would anyone with her salary *drive* such a trip? They weren't even on a main route.

First, Boyd turning up in Coyote Ridge after having screwed Madeline out of hundreds of thousands of dollars. Now Madeline herself. These were too many coincidences.

They want something from me, Allison thought, *and whatever it is, I'll be damned if I let anyone just take it.*

Dangling from one shoulder, her purse seemed to gain weight. How had she managed to live this long without the solemn promises of the gun?

"I don't know what scheme you're working, or what you had cooking with Boyd," Allison said. "I don't want to know. But if you show up in my life again, ever, you—"

She was denied her finish by the soft pop of a gunshot from the café. Madeline showed little surprise, road-bleary blue eyes too immediately knowing.

Tom, thought Allison, her fear for him surprisingly strong.

Madeline began twisting toward the backseat. Whatever was there, Allison could not see, drawing the revolver from her purse regardless. She rushed the last steps to the Cadillac, thrust her arm through the open passenger window, and fired a warning into the seat. The loud report was contained by the interior, like a firecracker in a can, and Madeline jumped with the shock of it.

This was the first time Allison had fired the revolver. Her hand felt warm, tingling pleasantly with the recoil, some luscious new intimacy developing between palm and grip, finger and trigger.

"Get out," she ordered. "Get out on my side, not yours."

Madeline gawped at her. She rubbed both ears with her middle fingertips, then stretched her mouth wide, as though fighting the air pressure of a descending jet.

"Get out of the car!" Like trying to communicate with an elderly aunt. *"Get . . . out of . . . the car!"*

She motioned until Madeline, disoriented, got the idea and scooted across the front seat to the passenger side. When she put her hand on the door handle, Allison smacked the revolver against the windshield.

"No. Through the window!" said Allison. It earned her a look of confusion. She jabbed a finger at Madeline, then circled the windowframe and jerked her thumb to say "Get moving." Incensed, Madeline responded with a middle finger.

Allison waited until she had squirmed halfway out the window before whipping the revolver down behind Madeline's ear. One arm gave a halfhearted swipe at her, then thumped against blistered sheet metal. She hung across the door, fingertips brushing gravel.

When she looked at the café Allison realized how calm she was, supposing she could thank her father for that. For teaching her long ago that no pain was so great it couldn't be switched off like a light, and that sudden death wasn't anywhere near as bad as lying back and taking it slow.

Tom's vision wasn't fully clear until the gunman had stumbled them both out of the rest room. Whatever he'd said just before shoving them toward the door, Tom hadn't understood, the guy's jaw apparently numb after nearly being popped out of joint.

Tom had no choice but to move with him. Physically, the man was in excellent condition; the bulge of his biceps pressed into Tom's throat hard as a rock. Much more pressure on his carotid arteries and likely he would black out.

A steady forearm and pistol thrust into Tom's field of view, sweeping over everyone in the café. Meals interrupted, they held silverware halfway to their mouths, or set it back onto their plates with a quiet clink.

"I *told* you that was a shot back there," the waitress said to the gnarled old cook behind the counter and grill.

They halted beside the table where Tom and Allison had eaten, deserted now except for dirty dishes. Tom could feel the gunman shifting behind him, just as surprised to find Allison missing.

"Bear tuh helltit zhee ko?" the guy muttered in his ear. Tom translated, most likely: *Where the hell did she go?*

"How am I supposed to know?" Tom rasped. "I was back there with *you.*"

The gunman barked a command evidently intended for the entire café, but it emerged as an incomprehensible garble of mush. No one moved, until a nervous few dared to glance at each other with confusion. He squealed with frustration.

"Pots a batter?" he cried. "Hugh atolls tone peek inklidge?" Tom made sense of this one: *What's the matter? You assholes don't speak English?*

Spatula in hand, the aproned grillmaster stepped up to the counter, a hairnet webbed over his grizzled skull.

"Son, I'm sorry, but nobody can understand a damn word you're saying," he explained. "Now, if you was to write it down—"

The gunman's patience snapped. The pistol crossed in front of Tom's face, inches away, the thick trigger finger curling. Tom squeezed his eyes shut, face on fire with the first shot, peppered with hot cordite dust and blasts of burning gas. His eardrums felt as though they were folding in on themselves, muffling the crash of the old cook into his kitchenware, then the jangle of what might have been the telephone being blown apart on the wall. Five shots, six. The gun went silent again, and Tom's lungs felt seared by the reeking cloud lingering about his face.

Coughing, he cracked open powder-burned eyelids; they felt scalded and grainy, as did both cheeks. The waitress and remaining diners were cowering beneath the line of fire, a couple begging, or praying. The waitress began to cry, and the gunman swung around to sight in on her next. Tom clenched both hands on the encircling arm, dug his bootheels into the floor, and twisted. Weak-kneed, the

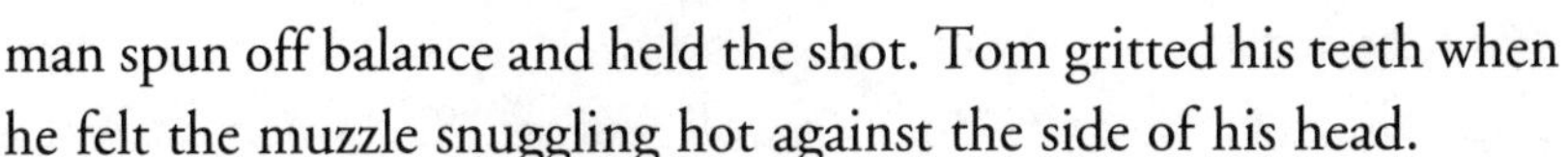

man spun off balance and held the shot. Tom gritted his teeth when he felt the muzzle snuggling hot against the side of his head.

"Nobody else," Tom croaked. "Let's just take it outside."

"Tyut ub!" he shouted in Tom's ear. *Shut up.* "Dut tyut ub!"

Tom looked askance, extreme right, through the front windows, saw Allison coming toward the door. Surely she'd heard the shots, knew better than to walk in. Wait—her revolver hung from one hand and she was dragging a limp woman by the wrist, face obscured by a tangle of unnatural red hair. A weaving snake trail in the gravel and dust led back to a gray Cadillac.

All that kept the gunman from noticing was angle. With two eyes he couldn't have missed them, but his bandage plunged the entire front of the café into a blind spot. Tom strained against his arm, began a pivot to stop him from turning the wrong way.

"I won't give you any trouble," he said. Now Allison was nowhere to be seen. "Go on, drag me out of here, nobody'll try to stop you, and I'll be the biggest kiss-ass hostage you ever saw, just don't shoot anyone else."

Fused from hips to shoulders, they backed through the tables. Tom's eyes met those of a grimy roustabout who averted his own in shame. Tom smelled sweat; a moment later, urine.

That voice in his ear again. Either he was getting better at deciphering, or the feeling was returning to the gunman's jaw. And it was the first glimmer Tom had gotten that this was no case of wrong place, wrong time, wrong lunatic. For some reason, the man had already made an effort to find out who he was.

"You better have your keys, leather boy," it sounded like he said. "We're taking your van."

Allison hadn't gone back for Madeline until she'd heard more gunfire. No idea what was going on inside the café, sure only that this bitch was responsible.

Through the window, Allison saw him from the side: improbably blond and bandaged, backing toward the door with a gun that swept from the innocent to Tom's head and back again. She did not hate him, did not fear him. Bullets. Only bullets. She'd had far worse inside her, and lived to never tell the tale. Not all of it.

She planted herself to the right of the doorway, to keep on the man's blind side. Madeline was starting to rouse, drooping onto both knees in front of her, slung from the crook of Allison's arm. Allison tapped her on the side of the head with the .38's barrel, shook it before her focusing eyes.

"One word out of you, and this"—Allison shook the revolver again—"this finishes whatever it is you start to say."

The door began to open. She hoisted Madeline onto her feet, felt her begin to squirm with groggy resistance, nothing that was going to get out of control in the next moments.

At first Allison didn't know why she didn't shoot when the target was right there, four feet away and blind to her. He'd be dead before he knew it. But she could not.

The man kept his pistol trained on the diners until he pulled Tom clear of the door; bent his elbow so the door, as it swung shut, would not jar the gun. For a moment he was aiming into the sky, as vulnerable as he was likely to leave himself.

Allison announced herself with a warning shot over his head. He flinched, kept his hold on Tom while wheeling to confront her. She was shielded behind Madeline by the time he turned, jamming her own gun up under Madeline's chin. He froze, his aim lingering to her left in hesitation, as they squared off with hostages close enough that each could kick the other.

She thumbed back the .38's hammer, let Madeline feel the cylinder rotate against her throat.

"If one of us dies here," Allison said, "it'll be all four of us, I promise you that."

"Shoot her, Gunther." Madeline had found her voice. "*Do* it."

"You move that gun another inch toward me, or him"—a glance into Tom's eyes—"and I'll take the top of this bitch's head off."

Whatever he saw in Madeline to care about was beyond anything

Allison could perceive. But it was there—she recognized it in the indecisive fear burning in that single eye.

"Gunther? Gunther!" barked Madeline. "What are you waiting for? Don't you let her do this to me, not her. Now you make that shot and you make it count!"

"Shut your ugly face!" Allison screamed in her ear. "You can't wait for lung cancer to kill you?" To her unlikely beau: "What's it going to be, Gunther? Are you really that eager to see her brains? Because if you are, just let her talk you into trying, and I swear to God I'll splatter you with them."

Allison scarcely recognized the voice coming from her mouth, the menace and the absolute conviction. A practice run, perhaps, with the voice she'd expected to be using in another day or two.

See, Daddy? See what you've turned me into?

Gunther's gun arm wavered. Glaring, he uttered something that Allison couldn't make sense of. Madeline and a bad eye weren't enough? He had to have a speech impediment too?

"Try English," said Allison.

"I think he said he's not going to stand here and let himself get turned in to some sheriff," Tom told her. "That if that's what you got in mind he'd just as soon start shooting and get it over with." He paused. "That *was* it, wasn't it?"

Gunther nodded, satisfied.

"You need a *translator* now, Gunther?" Madeline said through clenched teeth. "It never ends with you! Never! Never!"

"I hurt his jaw," Tom explained.

Madeline gave her man no slack. "Why don't you let her try shooting *you* in the head, instead? It's all solid bone anyway!"

The scabbed, bandaged face lunged over Tom's shoulder as if Gunther had forgotten about having a hostage. Scowling, he raved, and Madeline began to crow that he might as well save his breath, as she couldn't make out a single word he was saying. He rolled his one horrifying eye in futility, then slapped Tom on the cheek.

Tom began, with reluctance, to explain how Gunther now felt

that a bullet to the head might not be so bad compared to the idea of spending his life in Mexico, if he had to spend it with her. Madeline began to quiver.

Allison watched, appalled, listening to it all slip out of control. She'd been about to suggest a truce, not wanting the law in on her business any more than he did on his. Now he looked anything but in the mood to bargain. Madeline and that damn mouth of hers. Spiteful, yes—but who would have guessed that she could carry on this way with a gun beneath her chin?

"You go in there half blind, now you come out *mute*?" she was screaming.

Gunther bellowed, beyond words. Whether Tom sensed a moment of vulnerability or got lucky, she couldn't tell. An obedient captive one instant, in the next he had wormed one arm up through Gunther's to slip the choke hold and jabbed back with his other elbow into Gunther's middle. Tom caught Gunther's gun arm, trapped it; spun on one heel to throw him off balance; pitched him over one hip into the dust. He stamped hard on the wrist of Gunther's kinked arm, breaking his grip on the pistol, and kicked it away with the other foot. Lunged to snatch it up, and aimed down at a stupefied Gunther, who lay blinking up at blue sky.

It seemed to have taken no time, like watching a movie that skipped frames of film. Even Madeline had nothing to say.

Allison withdrew the gun from beneath Madeline's chin, gave her a shove, and backed out of her reach, circling around to Tom's side.

"He shot the phone apart in there," Tom said, "but we passed a gas station about, what, a half mile up the road? I'll make sure they don't go anywhere if you'll take the van and call the sheriff and an ambulance."

"No," she said softly.

"No? He shot an old man inside, Allison. I don't know if he's alive or dead, but—"

"Then we'll go make the call together and be on our way, and it won't take any longer than if I go alone. But I'm *not* sticking around for the sheriff." She was already striding across the lot. "I'll leave the van at the station and keep going on foot, if I have to, and say thanks for the ride . . . but I'm not waiting around to explain myself to anyone in a uniform."

She paused by the van door, one leg hiked up onto the running board. Tom stared after her with the confiscated pistol dangling beside his thigh.

"Are you coming? Or do you want to throw me the keys?"

He cursed, waved at her, begging one moment's patience before rushing to the café door. Staring faces withdrew from the window. Through the doorway she saw him hand the pistol over to a man inside, speaking tersely to him.

And what did this mean, that Tom not only wasn't ready to say goodbye to her yet, but that this overruled whatever obligation he felt to stay behind? It meant plenty. Nothing was trivial now.

He jogged to the van. Pointed at the peeling gray Cadillac, asked if it was their car. When Allison said it was, he borrowed her revolver and flattened two tires.

"Every time I think I have you figured out a little better," he told Allison in the van, "you throw me another curve."

They screeched up the road to the gas station and made the call, then he asked to switch places so she could drive while he rested in the passenger seat. She didn't blame him; one cheek was cut and bloody, and his eyes were red and his skin blotchy from what he said had been pistol shots going off directly in front of his face.

She began to tremble, finally, and gripped the wheel tighter so she wouldn't weave all over the road. She focused on the power poles along the side of the road, and the birds settled upon them.

"You were great back there," Tom said after a time. "Most people, they wouldn't be able to handle themselves near as well in that kind of situation. So . . ." He bent forward at the waist and cradled his head in both hands. ". . . thank you."

Allison nodded. "We're going the wrong way if you're still planning on going to San Antonio."

Tom shook his head. "I got someplace else in mind now. Spend the night where I know it'll be safe so we can get this situation figured out. You knew those two back there, did you?"

"Her I did. Him I've never seen before."

"I'm guessing they must've been following us for a while. I don't know how they did it, but they had to have picked up on *my* schedule at some point. So my schedule gets scrapped."

"I'm sorry," she said. "I know it's my fault somehow, but I don't know what it was about."

"Don't take this wrong, but . . . are you wanted for something back west? Running from a warrant, something like that?"

"No. Nothing at *all* like that."

"Then why wouldn't you stay put for the sheriff?"

"I pulled a gun of my own, Tom. I don't have a permit for it. I'm not going to let them take me in for defending myself."

"That's it?" he said. "This is Texas, Allison. I don't think you had much to worry about, under the circumstances."

She shook her head. "I'm not taking any chances. Nobody's going to take that gun from me, and don't ask me to explain it. Please. I'm no fugitive, you're not harboring one or transporting one—just don't ask me to tell you anything you don't really want to hear."

Allison looked into the blood-threaded map of his eyes until he nodded, and then he curled into the seat with his head resting against the door.

"Tell me when we get to Route 290," he murmured. "I'll let you know where to go from there."

Again Allison thought about the gun; why she'd chosen not to shoot Gunther unaware and be done with it.

The gun was consecrated. Oh, she'd lived and slept with it in constant reach; had for three days drawn perverse comfort from it, a shaky invincibility. It was her secret armor, her retractable claw. She'd used it to leave her mark on Boyd—to bleed him, just a little. First him, then Madeline. She could use it to frighten, to bluff, to threaten; could fire a warning shot; could loan it out to flatten a tire, and none of these would rob the revolver of its anointing.

To take a life, though, would diminish it somehow, for it had been bought with another life in mind. And when she brought it to him, it must be virginal. That was only fitting. There would be more than justice in that. There would be poetry.

Madeline felt too worn out, too headachy, to say anything more. Besides, Gunther's translator had just left. It wasn't as much fun when he couldn't fight back. He just took it, scowling like a sullen adolescent.

The whine of van tires was fading as Gunther picked himself up out of the gravel and dusted himself off. Radiating grim purpose, he stalked, limping, back to the useless Cadillac. Two tires dead, it canted toward the passenger side. Any minute now, sirens. Any minute. Madeline caught up to him just as he popped the trunk lid.

"Hey! Shitheads!" The café door hung open, their appointed guardian waving Gunther's lost pistol. "You get back down and kiss that dirt 'fore I whang a couple by your skulls!"

Gunther ignored him, wincing as he held his jaw and waggled it experimentally. "Ow," he said. As long as she could watch his lips, maybe communication wouldn't be lost after all. Rimming one entire side of his face was an angry red semicircular arc, inches long, abraded into the skin. She didn't want to know.

"You hear me?" the roustabout yelled. "I'll kill you my own damn self, you don't shag ass back here! Get me a medal for it!"

"Get a dick first!" Madeline spat in his direction. Then, to Gunther: "His hands are shaking."

"That's what I figured." Blocked from view by the trunk lid, he shed his decimated sport coat long enough to slip on the vest of Kevlar body armor. Put the jacket back on to conceal the vest. Stepped out from behind the trunk. "He'll run out of bullets before I run out of shells."

Gunther leaned into the Cadillac's rear floorboard, brought out the twelve-gauge she'd tried to grab before Allison had fired the shot that had thunderclapped her eardrums. He pumped the slide to rack a shell into the chamber.

Madeline blew him a kiss, and all was forgiven.

"We need a car," he told her, enunciating very carefully. "We don't need witnesses. I'll take care of everything."

He headed for the diner's door.

And his hands were steady.

chapter eighteen

Allison drove until they ran out of daylight, kept driving until she wondered if they weren't going to run out of Texas. She'd put over 250 miles to the northeast between them and this afternoon when the end of the road turned rough and rutted, somewhere between Palestine and Nacogdoches.

Tom directed her off the road and up a long drive that wound past a thicket of trees, then opened into a gently rolling clearing. The quarter-moon showed her what the headlights didn't reach—a ramshackle clutter of outbuildings and corral fencing, the rusty stitchwork of barbed wire. The vehicles looked no more mobile than the darkened ranch house that sagged and sprawled as though worn out at the end of a long day.

"I don't think anybody's home." Allison was tempted to hope there never would be.

"Dwight said just be patient if things looked that way." Tom had called some old friend of his later in the afternoon. Called, and washed his cut and powder-burned face; put together a makeshift ice pack that they'd replenished at fast food stops. "He said he might be on a job tonight, hard to say when he'd be finished."

"What does he do?"

"As long as I've known him, a little bit of everything. This late, what he's usually up to is repo work."

"He's a repo man?" In the dark, she groaned. "I don't know about this, Tom. I had a friend once, he got his car repossessed by a couple of those guys, and they *really* seemed to enjoy their work a little too much. Like it just made their day to take this guy's car away from him."

"Dwight doesn't do cars." Tom went for his door handle. "I'm going to go look for a key now. Maybe he's left one under a mat or someplace."

He was halfway to the house when she decided he had the right idea—stretch the legs, breathe fresh air. Spend most of the day in the van and you stepped out smelling like a tannery. The night was starry and immense, filled with a buzz of insects, while from some unseen pond came the solemn drone of bullfrogs.

Movement, then, and the sound of paws thumping swiftly across the ground. She saw something streak out of the darkness ahead, flank Tom, and hit him from the side, but all he did was stagger. With eager yelps the dog began pogoing off its hind legs—a large German shepherd. It dropped back to the ground and turned its wary attention to her, deciding friend or foe.

"This is Dirtball," Tom said. "Give him a good long sniff off the back of your hand and let him make the first move after that."

"Hey there, Dirtball." The snuffling dog concluded that her hands could remain attached. "Why'd you ever stand for anybody sticking you with a name like that?"

Tom shushed her. "Don't hurt his feelings. Dwight told him it was the name of many warrior kings and Egyptian pharaohs."

"And a fine, noble name it is," Allison told the dog, and scruffed his large head between her hands.

"Dirtball'd be close to seventy now, as dog years go. Hasn't slowed him down any, though. He's like Dwight that way."

"You mean somewhere out there tonight there's a seventy-year-old repo man running around?"

"More like sixty-four, sixty-five, actually," Tom said. "Kind of inspiring, isn't it?"

While he searched the front porch for a key, Allison wandered the grounds, Dirtball trotting along as though deciding she needed supervision. Maybe to keep her from getting lost in all the junk. Stacks of tires sat beside dismantled farm equipment, harrow blades gleaming with moonlight. Lawn ornaments composed a small forest, from Romanesque birdbaths, to a tacky flock of plastic flamingos, to an assortment of ugly garden statuary, most of the peasant-and-burro variety. An old army field artillery gun.

Allison detoured beneath a flat roof extending from the back porch. Atop sawhorses, over a litter of wood shavings, lay what looked to be an unfinished coffin, four feet long; closer up, it better resembled a rounded sarcophagus, with engraved symbols.

Tom had found no key, so they settled in to wait. More than an hour passed, and Dirtball heard it first; jumped to his feet and raced barking toward the road. The night filled with a rumble of approaching engines; headlights swung up the drive and a pair of full-size pickups came barreling along. Dirtball paced beside the second so closely that Allison feared he would slip beneath its wheels, and then she realized that it was pulling a twin-size horse trailer. As it passed by on the way back to the pastures, she could see that the trailer was not empty, two wispy tails draped down the outside of the gate.

"*That* was his repo job?" she asked.

"Told you he doesn't do cars."

They followed around back as the trucks idled before the stable and outside lights winked on. The trailer gate was dropped with a clang and four men clustered behind it, the tallest giving orders with a passionate waving of his arms before he turned and came striding up the gentle slope toward the house. He whipped a broad-brimmed hat from his head and slapped it against his thigh.

"Oughta see the sides of those animals, looks like stretched shammy over a couple of whiskey barrels," he called out, furious.

"I can see as how a man might get behind in what he owes, no sin there, but if there's one thing I can't abide, it's some cheap son of a bitch thinking he'll save his last dollars letting a horse graze a meadow already been picked clean. No oats, no hay, no nothing, I'll be *damned* if I look on a thing like that one more time without putting somebody in the hospital."

"Good to see you too," said Tom.

If Dwight was sixty-four, he'd been blessed with either good genes or the will to turn away the years as sternly as he might a trespasser. He had the ropy build of a born ranch hand and moved with the loose stride of a man half his age. While he'd lost his head of hair, the remaining fringe along the sides combed back past his ears, his mustache grew thick and peppery. Around his waist he wore a gunbelt, the heavy revolver clunking against his thigh, nearly to his knee.

"Sorry, got ahead of myself." He shined a flashlight at them. "What happened to your face? Looks like you been in a tussle with a steam iron."

"That'll take some explaining."

Dwight nodded. "Hungry, then? I sure am." To Allison: "I hate to eat before I go out after a horse. All I wanna do's stretch out for a nap instead. Who are you, anyway?"

Tom introduced them and she shook Dwight's callused hand. He shooed them toward the house with promises of food and drink.

"You first," he told Allison. "Them horses ain't the only things too skinny back here," and she did not know what to say to that, but if he asked, she'd probably kill for him, too, now.

Dwight Lee Judson, she learned, was the father of one of Tom's best friends during his stint in the Marines. Tom would visit whenever passing through, even after Dwight's son had left for San Diego, and the friendship seemed to transfer naturally from the younger Judson to the elder.

From the dining-room table, Allison watched the rhythms of easy familiarity between them as Dwight sliced and fried bacon and Tom gathered eggs from the refrigerator, then chopped onion and green and red peppers. He moved around Dwight in ways so subtly deferential that she doubted he was even aware of it. She recalled him telling her how his own father had walked out on the family when he was barely old enough to remember. It did not take much insight to understand what he saw in Dwight.

They cooked enough for six, and were joined by the three men from the stable—two Mexicans and a skinny Vietnamese who worked for Dwight as all-around hired hands. While eating, they recounted for Tom and Allison tonight's repossession of the underfed horses.

"You take a man's horse, it tends to aggravate him," Dwight said. "So I like to get the sneaky part done with everybody asleep and in bed. Doesn't always work out that neat, though, so whenever we need a diversion, what I do is, I send Nguyen up to the front door with a bunch of legal papers. You get him talking faster than an auctioneer, in his native tongue, it tends to befuddle most people. They can't understand him *or* the papers."

"Then sometimes I get this guy like tonight," Nguyen said. "He look at me, and he say I look too damn familiar to him from the war, so I say, 'Hey, I nine years old when that war over, didn't shoot nobody, but you push me too far now, I give it a try, see what I missed, only difference, now this time I got your law on *my* side, deadbeat.' "

"That tends to befuddle them too," Dwight said.

"Does it ever come to that?" Allison asked. "That gunbelt . . ."

"Which I made for him after some not very subtle hints," Tom said.

"Don't interrupt the lady. What I do, I load the gun with two blanks and four live rounds, and in the event of belligerence, I hope like hell the sound of those two blanks discourages them from whatever else they got in mind. That's done the trick, so far."

"Of course," said Hector, one of the Mexicans, "he won't tell you about the time he fired that gun and spooked all eight horses we were supposed to be after. How long did it take us, three hours to get them all rounded up again?"

"Thereabouts." Dwight stared glumly at his bacon and eggs and black beans. "That *was* a mess."

" 'S'okay, Dwight," said Carlos. "You just forgot those horses hadn't seen as many John Wayne movies as you."

After supper, Hector and Carlos and Nguyen went home. Dwight piled the dirty dishes in the sink to soak, then Allison left him and Tom alone at the table with a bottle of sour mash and time to catch up on each other's days. She was by now getting the idea that there was no Mrs. Judson, not anymore.

As she ran a hot bath in a clawfoot porcelain tub and did some soaking of her own, their voices carried in to her, if not their words; light at first, with laughter, turning serious after a while—Tom, giving an account of their afternoon, she supposed. Accounting for her presence as well.

They were still at it long after the tub drained, and Allison wandered the house with wet hair and bare feet, intrigued by the peculiar collisions of decor. In the TV room, a wall with shelves full of Zane Grey and Louis L'Amour faced an opposite wall devoted to a sweet and unexpected fascination with ancient Egypt. Framed prints of the pyramids and Sphinx; bright paintings on papyrus of Egyptian gods. He owned no few trinkets, as well, often chipped or worn smooth of detail. A few fragmented jars, paint still visible. Small statues; amulets carved from crystal, ivory, stone.

Later, Dwight came out to explain sleeping arrangements, if she was ready to turn in. He had one guest room, and it would be hers. Tom would sleep out back, in the small bunkhouse that Hector and Carlos and Nguyen sometimes used, as well as the migrants hired on when the melon crops were in.

As she lay down, Allison listened to the murmur of voices and the clink of the bottle and glasses. Listened to the myriad sounds of their being alive and taking a comfort in them that peeled away years, decades. Like a child again, needing all those small sounds of a house that lived and laughed and protected those inside.

The way it was supposed to be.

The next morning, Tom left the bunkhouse and trudged up to the house, lured by the scent of coffee wafting from open windows. His face felt better, the cut cheek held together since last night with a butterfly bandage made from tape, the powder burns treated with a salve. The red blotches had faded, but it would be a few days before all the gray-black speckles worked themselves out.

With Florida time an hour ahead, and St. John's Apocalypse open for business, he found Dwight's phone and called in. When Lianna Murphy answered, Tom asked if anyone there had given out details of his itinerary. Silence, then a hesitant admission that, yes, she had given out yesterday's schedule, but only to Teddy Serafino, of Coyote's Paw Harley-Davidson, when he'd called about some papers that Tom had left behind.

Coyote Ridge again. It all kept pointing back there.

"I did something wrong, didn't I?" Lianna said. Tom told her to let it go, that everything was fine . . . but if anyone else should call trying to track him, please keep those details confidential.

It shouldn't be a problem. Those two from yesterday would be cooling their heels. It was no guarantee that they didn't have partners running loose, but if they were the brains of the outfit, he would take his chances with the rest.

Next, Tom called Coyote's Paw Harley and asked Teddy if, by chance, he'd left any papers behind on Friday. Teddy knew nothing about them, said he would keep his eyes open. That clinched it.

Gunther and Madeline had known enough about him to track him across three states, to impersonate one of his retailers, to lie to one of his employees. Tenacious work, but nothing that any competent skip tracer could not have managed. A little information and a knack for lying went a long way.

After breakfast, he went for a walk along the roads around Dwight's, ignoring the horizons of pines and power lines. Eyes downcast in thought, sun beating on his head and tender face as he tried to piece the rest together.

What had Gunther and Madeline wanted, anyway? Something they thought they could get from Allison. Something she claimed not to know about. He was inclined to believe her. When it wasn't done for love or revenge, the only other reason people like that killed was for money. And a woman in Allison's position had nothing worth killing for, much less crossing four states to do it.

Somebody else, then, must have put them onto her. Let her take the heat, a sacrificial lamb. But yesterday should have ended it, with Gunther and Madeline in jail and Allison's trail lost.

She was up and around when he got back, with Dwight at the stable. Area lenders paid Dwight to board some of the horses he repossessed, but it was one of his own that he was starting to saddle, smoothing a blanket over the back of a gentle roan gelding. It wasn't a horse Dwight ordinarily rode; rather, one whose mellow temperament made it ideal for his grandchildren.

Dwight had the girthstrap cinched and was fitting the bit and bridle into place by the time Tom finished digging for what he wanted in the van and brought it down to Allison. She was sitting on the top rail of the corral, enraptured by the proceedings, one boot tapping impatiently.

"As long as you're doing this," Tom called to her, "might as well do it right," and he sailed the hat to her like a Frisbee. She caught it, tried it on, and while it sat a little low on her forehead, she wore it well. Brown leather, aged and weathered in-shop; flat-brimmed and a little floppy, with a thin metallic band woven into slits circling the base of a boxy, flat-topped crown.

"I love it." She adjusted the angle, her wheat-colored hair spilling from beneath. "Know something? You do good work."

"Stole the design from a Clint Eastwood movie, though," he admitted. "*Two Mules for Sister Sarah.*"

Dwight peered over. "I thought that looked familiar."

Allison wore the hat with a tarnished radiance, earth angel finding her way again after some terrible fall. He'd not realized that the hat was a gift until he saw her smile, and knew he could not take it back.

Dwight helped her into the saddle, gave her a few pointers on the roan's habits, watched attentively as horse and rider crossed the corral, trotting at first, picking up into a canter. He called for her to shift more of her weight down to the stirrups, and she did so, leaning closer toward mane and muscular neck as the horse picked up speed, circling the inside of the corral. She shifted the reins to one hand long enough to jam the hat farther down onto her head, then leaned smoothly into the roan again, finding the rhythm and letting her body go with it, with the flex and stride and roll of all that power.

Tom and Dwight leaned against the corral, eyes following the circle; looking for different things, seeing them.

"Told her she had to prove to my satisfaction she wasn't gonna get her neck broke, I let her take that roan out past my sight," Dwight said.

"She looks like she's doing fine."

Dwight nodded. "Done some riding before, but not a lot, I'd wager. Not as natural to her as walking, but she's got the hang of it." He scratched with one boot tip at a cluster of weeds. "Told me she'd grown up around horses, rode all the time when she was a kid, but . . . that was so, I shouldn't've had to tell her to drop more weight down to them stirrups. I don't know. I just got the feeling that was mostly wishful thinking."

"I couldn't tell you," Tom said. "The subject never came up."

"Should've seen her asking me, could I saddle her one up and let her take it awhile." Dwight grinned. "Just like a kid, eyes all wide and lit up. I'd've told her no, her face would've cracked right in two. Told her okay, and thought she just might piddle her drawers right then."

"No kidding?" Tom laughed softly. "Then you've seen a side of her I haven't. She keeps that part of herself pretty bottled up."

"Well, then maybe this is just what the horse doctor ordered. Something about young girls and horses, anyway. You ever notice that? They go through this phase, most of them, where they just love their horses, can't get enough of them. Draw them, read books about them, watch shows about them. Put up pictures. Even if they never been within fifty miles of one. Funny, way that happens."

Tom tried to remember if Holly ever mentioned going through such a phase, thought she might have. She would've been the type.

Allison brought the roan around again, slowed it, then brought it clopping over to where he and Dwight stood. She looked down at them from beneath the brim of the leather hat, twirling one rein and slapping the end of it against the saddle horn.

"So . . . ?" she said. "Can I leave the kiddie pool now?"

Dwight opened the corral gate to let her loose into acres of tree-studded pasture. When she snapped the reins and kicked the horse into motion, Tom smiled after her, happy to watch and to be alive, and he thought she rode like a dream.

She kept the horse out longer than she'd thought she would, losing track of time—morning one minute, the next looking up at the sky and thinking the sun couldn't possibly have shifted so far to the west. Time passed differently up here. And if, in whatever direction she rode, she eventually reached a fence, it was still good enough, for the sun recognized no fences, shining on both sides, and the wind blew through them as if they were not there.

Hector stabled the roan when she brought it back, and the ground felt new and strange beneath her. A pleasing soreness had crept into her bottom and the inside of each thigh.

Dwight was busying himself in the open workspace beneath the porch's extended roof, hunched over the peculiar coffinlike thing she'd noticed last night. By day, details were more evident, and unmistakably Egyptian in nature. It was rounded, tapering toward squared-off feet, with a headdress that curved broadly around a smooth, staring face. A thin beard jutted down from the chin.

"Thought you'd be halfway to Looziana by now," said Dwight.

"One horse thief around here, that's enough," she said, and his eyes were amused over the top of his bifocals. "I saw this last night. Are you expecting a short mummy?"

Dwight shook his head, sandpapering away at the suggestion of hands fisted against the thing's side. "It's not for any mummy, it's for me."

"Funny—you look taller than this, close up."

"Well, it's not for burying in the first place. At least not with anything in it." He blew away the sawdust. "This's what the Egyptians called a ushabti. Only thing dead Egyptians really wanted to do was enjoy the afterworld. But they couldn't trust the gods. You know how gods are, always something else they need done, never satisfied. So what the Egyptians'd do was, they'd put these inside their tombs, so in case the gods wanted 'em to work, the ushabtis were there to do the work instead." Dwight straightened, patted it with affection. "Theirs weren't nowhere near as big, but I'm making up in size what I lack in numbers. Those gods can kiss my ass if they think I'll make one for every day of the year."

Allison looked at him with mild alarm. "Um . . . you're not . . ."

"Dying? Not as anyone's told me, no." He grinned, suddenly self-conscious. "It's just something to do."

"I saw all those pieces you have inside. Some collection. I wasn't expecting anything like that, first seeing you last night."

"Happy to exceed your expectations, then." He eyeballed the surface of the ushabti, began sandpapering again. "Been meaning for thirty years or more to get over there and see those pyramids, just haven't gotten around to it yet." Dwight shrugged. "I don't guess they're going anywhere."

Allison traced her fingers along the two vertical columns of hieroglyphs carved down the front.

"What does this say?"

"It's a rather impolite boast, and I'd just as soon not get into it, if you don't mind." Dwight sanded furiously for a moment, embarrassed. "I've never yet made up my mind on what some folks say about us living lifetimes before this one we're living now. But the way I've got it figured is, if that's so, what I must've been in one of those lives was one of Cleopatra's lovers. So maybe that explains something about me and Egypt."

Allison drew a cup of water from a five-gallon jug sitting on a table. She asked where Tom was, and Dwight said that the last he knew, Tom had gone off in search of a newspaper. Shortly after, he admitted that it had been Tom who'd given him the impulse to carve a ushabti, upon being told months ago that Tom's mother was dying and he'd begun to worry about how to mark her grave with something more meaningful than mere name and dates.

"He was right, you know," said Dwight. "Those stones, they don't say a whole hell of a lot about who's down below."

"What did he decide on?"

Dwight told her how Tom had had the headstone engraved with the masks of comedy and tragedy, for all the dreams that the woman had never gotten to live out. Allison's heart ached for him, and for her, too, even though she'd not known until now of the woman's life, death.

"He's not married, is he?" she asked.

Dwight huffed. "What is it you two do all day in that van? Sit there and each look out your own window?" He let her stew in that a moment. "He was. He's not anymore."

"What happened?"

"Shouldn't you be asking him this instead of me?"

"Probably. But I'm asking you anyway."

Dwight hadn't looked at her for a time, absorbed in his work, and would not look at her now, either. "She died too."

Allison stared at him, stared until he sensed the pressure of her eyes and her silence. In time he crumbled, telling her it had happened five years ago, in a bath, with a blade. Once it was out, Allison realized how aware she was of the birds, the clouds, of everything great and small about this moment. Whatever else was to happen, this would be a moment she'd remember forever, because it explained so much about Tom.

"Holly was three months pregnant at the time," Dwight added quietly. "If she knew it herself, she'd not told anyone else about it. It was . . . something he found out after."

Allison felt herself nodding, if only to let Dwight know that she'd heard, while she thought of those sad little books that rode with Tom in his van. All the miles and all the nights.

Why is he telling me this? she wondered, for it was far more than she'd asked. Now Dwight *was* looking at her, something in his throat keeping him from saying another word. He did not need to. It was all there in eyes as strong as the sun, in lines cut by weather and years: a warning, stern as a prophet's.

You be careful, she thought she read in it, *because you have touched him whether he admits to it or not, and maybe he's touched you too, so you decide whatever it is you want, and live with that choice, because I will not see him toyed with.*

It would've been presumptuous of him, of anyone, to have said it aloud. That he did not need to—seemed unable to—gave it more weight than words. She met his gaze until he hunched slowly back over and began his sanding again.

Not knowing what possessed her to do so, she walked over to him and placed her hand upon his until it halted, its wiry hair like bristles against her palm, then she leaned over to kiss him lightly, once, atop his smooth, sun-browned head. Allison was nearly to the porch door before she heard the scratching resume.

She found Tom at the kitchen table, surprised that Dwight hadn't known he was back. He said nothing even when she took off the hat and scruffed out her sweaty hair. She realized then with a plunge of heart that he looked absolutely crushed.

He heard us out there, was her first thought. *He heard us and it brought everything back too close again.*

She paid no attention to the newspaper until he splayed one hand over the front page and spun it around for her to read.

7 SLAIN IN DINER MASSACRE read a secondary headline beneath the main banner, while the picture of the building jolted her back a day. Only a shattered plate-glass window changed its face.

"I left those people with a loaded gun," Tom said, his voice hoarse. "I don't . . . understand how they . . ."

Allison collapsed into a chair to read the article, scarcely understanding any more by the time she was through. A shotgun was the weapon of choice used on six of the seven. They'd been found scattered throughout the building, shot from the front and shot in the back; found by sheriff's deputies summoned by an anonymous caller. No suspects yet; a number of leads being followed up on.

Where had a shotgun come from, anyway? Madeline and Gunther were plainly unarmed when Tom had turned over the pistol. *Somebody else,* she thought. Someone who'd come along afterward and . . .

And she knew it couldn't really have happened that way.

Tom didn't say it, but she knew he had to be thinking that she was the more culpable of them, because they'd never have left if she hadn't been so adamant. She wished he'd just say it, get it over with.

Her hand slid across the table, her fingers curling loosely over the back of his forearm. Before long, even thinking about it grew too much to bear, so she watched Dirtball as the dog slept in the center of the floor. His legs and paws twitched in sleep, and she wondered what dogs dreamed about—if they dreamed of rabbits, or of things no one would ever guess. If she could dream of flying, why couldn't they?

There would be no such dreams for her tonight, though. She knew she would remain rooted stubbornly to the earth, with those already in it, and those who belonged there.

Tom passed the darkest hours alone in the bunkhouse, never knowing the time, only that last night's comfortable mattress felt too hard tonight.

Hours earlier, he and Allison had taken the van back to the nearest crossroads of civilization to contact the Kendall County sheriff's office. They used a gas station pay phone so the call could not be connected to Dwight, giving as much information as they could on

Gunther and Madeline DeCarlo. It wasn't much, but at least the names—half of one, all of the other, and both from Las Vegas—were more than they'd seen in the paper. Tom hung up as soon as he'd given all he could.

For hours he lay in the dark, mired in one moment's decision and all the sorrow it caused. Horrifying how it would echo on and on. Today, spouses were devastated, parents heartbroken, children robbed. Next year, someone would wake in the middle of the night, feel the empty spot beside her, and cry. Years later, there would be no father to escort a bride down the aisle of a church. On and on, a hundred people, a thousand, thinking back to yesterday and wondering why it happened.

Why? *Because somebody left her feeling like she had to run. And somebody left me feeling like I couldn't let her do it alone.*

He'd wondered about her last night, up at the house. If her head rested atop a nickel-plated lump beneath her pillow. If, when she stirred in sleep, her hand strayed to touch its cold comfort, just in case. While Dwight inspired trust, Tom was sure she'd trusted her father, too, once upon a time.

But tonight was different.

The first soft knock he dismissed as his imagination. The second was bolder, not to be ignored. Allison came in and sat upon the end of the bed, giving no sign of wanting the lights on.

"This is . . . what it is," she said. "It can't be anything more. But it isn't anything less, either. It's what it is."

He took her outstretched hand in his own, palm to palm, their fingers interlocking.

He didn't suppose a man and a woman could spend nearly every waking hour of four days together without each entertaining the question of what the other must be like to love, if only for a night. The wounded and the wrongly imprisoned were no different, and maybe even needed that question answered more. Needed so badly to believe that the world wasn't one huge conspiracy; that there really could be a place of justice and grace for them after all. That two could find it more easily than one.

If only for a night.

They each trembled at the touch of the other, her skin hot and his own cool, fire and ice that clung together in urgency and desperation. They made of love all those things that were most needed in the dead of night—a hope for tomorrow, a bid to bury the ghosts of all the yesterdays. A month from now, or a week, would they recall each other's names? Would they even want to?

They made love and made of it what they could, as good as they knew how, the best parts still locked inside their bodies and their hearts. Because it was what it was.

If only for a night.

"Why is it," he asked later, "you talk like I'll never see you after tomorrow, or the day after?"

Allison seemed to mourn as she sat on the bed, ankles crossed and arms wrapped around her drawn-up legs. The healing cigarette burns on her bare shoulder looked dark as pitch, holes punched clear through to her soul.

"What I told you earlier," she said, "don't act like you didn't hear me say that. Live with the rules, Tom."

"To hell with the rules, there are no rules." She stared at him through the gloom, not budging, and he wanted so badly to know everything. "Who are you, Allison? Who are you really? What am I taking you back to?"

She dodged this, instead pointing to his middle, where a thick, knotty scar bisected muscle and curled around his left side, over the hipbone. Before tonight she would have had no way of knowing it was even there, and had taken it well. He had seen people looking a lot more appalled by it than Allison was.

"How'd you get that?" she asked. "It looks like someone tried to cut you in half."

"That? My Good Samaritan badge of honor?" Tom laughed without mirth. "A few years ago I got between two guys, trying to stop a fight. In a bar. Father and son. Carpenters, the both of them. I didn't even know them. I found out later that they'd come from a job, putting down new flooring. That's why the one still had his linoleum knife."

He remembered the blade, dull silver, its wicked curve like a stubby scimitar. Remembered the cold, searing tug at his side; the slippery loop of gut that slid free before he could get his hands over the gaping wound. How unreal it had looked. A rubber joke.

"If you didn't know them," she said, "why would you care in the first place?"

"It was just hard to watch. What they were doing to each other. Saying. Like if they kept at it, one of them was going to throw something away that he wouldn't be able to get back. Something I never had."

"That's just the way some families are, Tom. If they're both adults and it's their own business, why *should* you care?"

He thought this over a moment. Why indeed. "Do you know how the military trains you to kill? I don't mean the individual methods. I mean the psychology of it. You know how they do it?"

She shook her head no.

"Repetition. They ingrain it in you so deep that when the time comes, your body can just take over and do it automatically. It's in your muscles. In your bones. All the moves are programmed right there, because you've made them so many times in practice you don't have to think about it. You just do it. By then they've had you taking out dummies and people-shaped targets for so long you've got no problem reducing a live human being to just another shape. After I was discharged, I decided I really didn't want to be that guy. That wasn't how I wanted my eyes to see. So I tried to deprogram myself. Force myself to *look*. And that day? Those two guys? They weren't looking at each other like father and son, Allison. They were looking at each other like shapes. Maybe I was a fool but I couldn't stand there and just watch it happen."

Allison turned away. "Your life seems to have this habit of entwining itself with others that can only hurt you."

"Are you trying to tell me you're no different?"

She bowed her head, yellowed bruises veiled behind a curtain of blond. There was his answer right there.

"Tell me what I'm taking you back home to. I think you owe me that much."

"Why, because you did me the great favor of sleeping with me? Your magic sperm is a healing balm, is that the way you see it?"

"No, that's *not* the way I see it!" he said, too loudly. "It's because you didn't kick in dime one on gas all day yesterday, and I wasn't going to mention it!"

She blinked at him, then they sputtered with laughter, the kind of laughter that tolerates few secrets, fewer lies. And when the truth came, Tom was not surprised.

"I'm going to kill him. I'm going to put a bullet in him and see if that doesn't unlock this door I've been trying to rattle open for years. Because I just can't live anymore like I'm only half a human being."

"Your father," said Tom, and she nodded. "You figure that'll be the answer for you."

"I've tried everything, Tom. Good and bad. This is all that's left, the last thing I know to try. And the reason it feels right is because it's the one thing he most deserves."

His first impulse was to try talking her out of it, but the big problem was that it was night out, when ghosts are strongest. There could be no talking redemption into someone in the dark. You could only stay beside her, hoping the light was not too far away.

Allison found the small, flat box resting on a table; opened it and took out the books it contained. She ran her hand along covers that showed worlds where children rode dinosaurs, where gentle old men lived better lives blessed by old cats, where sweet-faced animals would never harm a soul.

"When I was a little girl," she told him, "I had a book like this that my aunt gave me. About a girl and her horse. I thought if I read the book enough, and said my prayers, then one day I'd wake up and the horse would be waiting for me outside. I must've run downstairs every morning for four solid months before . . ."

Allison stopped, pulling herself back to now; the awful now.

"It's never like the books say it is, is it? If only, just once . . ." She could not finish, or hadn't the words for it, but still he knew exactly what she meant. She held the books to her breast, tightly, while Tom held her to his own.

And although he knew that everyone had to grow up and learn the truth someday, he wondered why some were forced to learn so much sooner than the rest, and from the very ones who were supposed to protect them from it.

chapter nineteen

So this was where Allison had grown up. This was Yazoo City. The population sign on the edge of this drowsy, oak-choked little burg read in the very low five digits. Boyd gave it all an impartial going-over while he and Krystal rolled through downtown for a second pass, and concluded that if Allison had grown up here, she probably hadn't lacked for nap time. Clearly, Las Vegas had left him a spoiled man.

"Is it possible to yawn to death?" he wondered aloud.

"That's not very nice," said Krystal. She clung happily to the steering wheel, soaking in every sleepy nuance as Tuesday evening fell. "I think it's charming. I think we should come back someday for vacation. Maybe a nice little bed-and-breakfast?"

"Sure. Why not." When she hopped on another planet like this, he found it best simply to humor her. "Why don't we just move here permanently, parlay our respective trades, and open up a gambling parlor and whorehouse."

"Good idea, sweetie." Krystal patted his thigh. "I think we'd have trouble getting the loan, though."

He found this as depressing as it was true. Just too many laws on the books. "No victim, no crime"—as common sense, this had much to commend it. Maybe even "Petty victim, no crime," if one was left wiser by the experience; education wasn't free. But no, these days you couldn't swing a dead cat without hitting somebody whining about being a victim, and somebody else itching to sue you on behalf of the cat. Sadly, they were living in unnatural times.

"We're about a hundred and thirty years too late coming down here, I think," Boyd said. "We missed the golden age. I would've made an A-number-one carpetbagger."

"Maybe you were in another life."

"That would explain a lot."

"As soon as all this is over we really need to have that past life regression done on you, and see who you were before. I'm just dying to know when and where we were connected. Because for such an immediate bond to develop like it did, and the *way* it did, with that tarot card? Wow. Oh wow. I'm *this* close to being sure we've been lovers throughout history. Oh look—a phone booth."

Krystal wheeled the car over and he hopped out, grabbed the phone book chained inside. He flipped through until he found the local map and street index, tore them out, then went skimming the white pages. The forwarding address on Allison that he'd found in Gunther's wallet was in care of Constance Wainright; off to one edge of the note the word *cousin* had been jotted and circled. He saw no listings under her name, although a Jefferson Wainright was listed at the same address. Boyd ripped the page and jumped back in the Mazda, studying the map and orienting their position to it.

"Okay, we're in business," he said, and pointed. "Let's go see if we won the race or not."

It had taken them four days and nearly sixteen hundred miles to get here from Saturday's tumult in Coyote Ridge. All things considered—and ignoring the possibility of again meeting up with a dementoid who wanted to put drain cleaner in his eyes—Boyd was having the time of his life. There was no breath of freedom so fresh as that drawn on the open road, and Krystal sweetened the air wherever she was. The bottles of Dom Pérignon took care of themselves.

It was mind-boggling, her acceptance of him. Allison had on Saturday shown him in the worst possible light, yet it rolled off Krystal like water off a swan's back. She almost had him believing he really *had* drawn that Lovers card from the tarot deck. Nothing could alter her belief that they were karmically destined for one more lifetime together. All in all, a sweet deal for him.

He supposed he could learn to live with the call-girl thing, if she dug in her heels. She was bound to get it out of her system one day. As far as the rest of forever, he was wondering how he could lay his hands on a picture of her mother, see what kind of genetic window into the future it provided. If he'd still have his swan in the long term, or if he had a real ugly-duckling-reversion time bomb on his hands.

Late Sunday morning she'd begun to pester him again about why Madeline and Gunther had been gunning for him, where this money had come from. Krystal had already seen and heard too much for him to contrive any significant deviation from base facts that would hold together, and so, worn down and still sore-headed from the pistol-whipping, he'd told her the truth: He and Madeline had been falsifying the fill slips for the chip rack of his blackjack table and skimming the proceeds away for several months.

"You stole it," Krystal clarified. "You mean you stole it."

"We didn't *steal* a penny." Boyd firmly shook his head. "We, ourselves, *gambled* on our skills versus standard casino security procedures, and we happened to win. Remember what you and I talked about the other day? About the house advantage, the way a casino stacks the odds and the payoffs in its favor?"

She said she did, but—

"Remember the way we decided that anytime some casino loses big, it's karma coming back around to bite that casino in the ass? Remember the way you said you were going to cheer for the next big winners you saw?" He put his head to hers and tilted down the rearview mirror to catch their reflection. "Well . . . rah rah."

Krystal had to pull over to the side of the road and let him take the wheel, then made him suffer through nearly one hundred miles of silence while she got all the karma sorted out. Finally deciding that in a case such as this, perhaps his actions could be sanctioned. The money, after all, was coming from one corporation in a vast industry that existed only to suck dry the bank accounts of tourists, the idle rich, and obsessive-compulsives.

"You weren't planning on redistributing any of it, were you?"

"Like Robin Hood? That's a novel thought," he said, "but no."

"And Madeline's share? By rights, half of it *is* hers."

"Madeline wants me dead. If that's not forfeiture, I don't know what is."

"It's kind of a gray area," Krystal declared, "but I don't think what you've done is karmically punishable."

"Bitchin' good news!" he cried, overjoyed at the way she put it all together. This was real world philosophy, a thousand times more practical than guilt-drenched Catholic confession. By extending these principles, then, to the big picture, Krystal was not nearly so distressed yesterday when their cash reserves began to deplete and he appropriated a booklet of traveler's checks from a restaurant table while their owner administered the Heimlich maneuver to an elderly gentleman choking on filet mignon.

"It's a corporation, remember," he reminded her. "And they're fully insured."

After which came the process of converting checks to usable cash. Reserving one unsigned check, he demonstrated his forgery technique on the rest, after practicing until he had the signature down: You didn't try to copy the signature right side up; rather, you turned it upside down and drew a replica, thereby eliminating all traces of your own handwriting.

He enlisted her help when it came time to pass the checks. As cashiers were required to witness the transactional signature, and match it to the original, Boyd would display the single unsigned check and poise his pen. Krystal would then chime in with a diversionary question or action, during which he would substitute a presigned check and feign the rest. It was a good system.

"The neat thing is," she said later, as they made a hot, dry stretch of Texas blacktop go down smoother with a shared bottle of DP, "I don't feel like a criminal."

"That's an entirely healthy attitude."

"I mean, I know we broke the law, technically, but—"

"Law, what law? What you have to do is get yourself past that kind of puritanical thinking." Maybe it was the champagne talking, as he had never reasoned things out this clearly before. "There's the law of politicians and the interests of the rich, and then there's the law of the jungle. I don't need to tell you which came first, which one keeps a better balance."

He had her swerve close to the side of the road as he rolled down the window and whizzed an empty Dom Pérignon bottle at a no-passing sign. It nicked the top of the sign without breaking; spun out of sight, into the weeds.

"Boyd," she said sharply. "You shouldn't litter. Do you have any idea how long it takes glass to decompose? Like half a billion years or something."

"Sorry, babe. High spirits just got the best of me." Clearly, there were lines with her that he could not cross. "Later on I'll pick up some trash and reestablish the balance."

This mollified her, and they leaned together in the center of the car for a deep soul kiss of peace restored, straying across the center line until a blaring horn yanked her back to reality, or as much reality as she ordinarily dealt with. She careened back into the right lane, blew a kiss to her angels, and patted the Mazda's dashboard as though it were an obedient dog.

Boyd waited until his cardiac rate returned to normal, then told her how—getting back to this slippery concept of legal and moral relativism—she was already predisposed to making such bold distinctions for herself. This call-girl thing, for example. Now that wasn't strictly legal, was it? But obviously she had made her peace with that. And he respected this; truly he did.

"So maybe," he concluded, "since I've been laying so much on the line with you, you could return the favor . . . and tell me why it is you're so committed to this career choice you've made."

"You know, I think you're ready to hear it," she said. "I really think you are. Because you've come a long way in ten days."

Driving all day and still she looked so fresh; clean raven hair in a breezy torrent around her face, so smooth, so flawless. That face was a bit like unsculpted clay, no fixed set to it yet—by life and by years, by laughter and tears. Allison had her set. Krystal did not. For a moment Boyd found himself confused, because having it seemed better somehow. More real. More dependable.

"I'm making amends for a past life," she said. "More than one, actually . . . but mostly this particular one."

"Okaaay." He should have known. "And you were . . . ?"

"The Marquis de Sade."

"Well," said Boyd. "Well! I . . . I didn't see *that* one coming."

"Oh, Boyd, I had some real problems then, let me tell you."

"Problems," he echoed, nodding.

"I mean, my name from that life was the basis for the word 'sadism.' And have you read any of the books I wrote? *Justine*? Or *Juliette*? Or *120 Days of Sodom*?"

Frowning, Boyd said he had not. He calculated his chances of escaping injury were he to leap from a moving car, decided they weren't good, then dismissed the idea. Krystal was eccentric. That was all. He could compromise on eccentricity. For that body and what she could do with it, and unconditional love, he'd not yet settled on the depths beyond which he would *not* compromise.

"Well, don't, not a word of them," she warned. "They're just dreadful, the most appalling stories you could ever read in your whole life. I'm *so* ashamed. I'm pretty sure I intended them as indictments of the ruling class in late-eighteenth-century France, but hardly anybody took them that way, so what does it matter? The damage was done."

"Damage," he murmured. "I'm . . . still having trouble finding a link between this and the call-girl thing."

"Oh, sweetie, I'm just trying to do my little part to balance it all out. Like you picking up a bottle for the one you threw out the window? Except it's a little more involved. I mean, oh wow, I was personally responsible for so much pain being inflicted, that now I feel obligated to, well, you know . . ."

"Inflict pleasure," he concluded with a groan. "I notice you've decided not to do it for free."

"Well of course not. That would make me a slut. So as long as I've got to make a living somehow . . ."

Briefly, Boyd entertained the notion that he should become her agent, that plenty of TV talk shows would pay big money for delusions this deep. Napoleons were a dime a dozen . . . but *this*!

"So," he said, not knowing what else to say for now. "So. You were the Marquis de Sade."

"*And* Mary Todd Lincoln. That's another one where I could've done better. I was such a nag to poor Abe." Talk show gold mine and she didn't even realize it. "That's why I've been thinking we should get a past life regression done on you. We really should find out where we connected." Krystal looked suddenly stricken. "You *do* believe you've lived before, don't you? I was just taking for granted you did."

"Let's put me down as undecided." Ever the diplomat. "I guess I'd have an easier time of it if everybody wasn't running around with such grandiose histories. I would gladly shake the hand of the first guy who came up to me and admitted the best job he ever had was hauling buckets in a Roman vomitorium."

"Okay, so you're a little skeptical, I can accept that," she said. "I'm glad you told me. Because after some of the lines I've had run on me? It's, like, your honesty is so refreshing."

There. That was it. That was the big reason he knew he could not let this woman go. She said to him all those things that he'd never heard from any other woman.

. . .

When they got to the Wainrights' neighborhood, the thing that struck Boyd was how wide everything was. Wide houses, wide yards, the tops of trees so wide they sometimes shook branches with the trees across the wide street. Krystal parked along the curb, so he could gather something a little more substantial about the lay of this green and foreign land.

"I suppose it would've been too much to ask for to pull up and see that black van Allie rode off in," he said. "I really hate not knowing whether she's in there or not."

"If I were you, I'd be more concerned about that Gunther guy being inside already."

"And Madeline." He shuddered, recalling Saturday morning. "What a perfect waste of sperm and eggs, those two."

"Now, sweetie, there's a reason they act that way," Krystal said. "Inside, they're still just frightened little children."

"Frightened little *homicidal* children, maybe. Kind of puts the squeeze on us, doesn't it?" Although, realistically, how much did they have to worry about? Gunther had him taped into a chair, a gun on him the whole time, and still couldn't hold him. Either some of Krystal's radiant good vibes had rubbed off or Gunther Angelo Manzetti was the most colossally brainless human being on the face of the earth.

Just the same, he would happily keep Gunther's confiscated pistol handy. He'd studied it long enough to figure out which part did what, then bought two boxes of bullets. On Sunday morning, he and Krystal had detoured into a secluded stretch of New Mexico desert, where he'd gone through the first box of fifty rounds to familiarize himself with the weapon. Krystal opted to have nothing to do with it, personally, and insisted that he first approach the saguaro cactus he'd used as a target to ask its forgiveness. Boyd took its silence as a nod of approval.

Zen, he kept telling himself. *Be the gun.* Never forgetting that he was much happier just being the card. The cactus emerged from the experience little the worse, and the pistol had remained in the glove box ever since.

They watched the Wainright house for an hour, an occasional figure passing before the screen door or one of the windows. The most frequently glimpsed stood not yet four feet tall; a ponytail whisked at the back of her head. A younger child, with the full-tilt speed of a two-year-old, once went charging for the porch. He got halfway out the door, unencumbered by pants or underwear, before being snatched from behind by his T-shirt. That would be Constance in action. Boyd began to suspect that wide hips might be a family trait, augmented in her case by plumped thighs. The price of motherhood, maybe, among the women of this clan. He filed it away for future reference. You never knew what tomorrow could bring.

The last Wainright showed himself once, a silhouette that looked to be plump not only of thigh, but of everywhere else. He stood briefly before a window, or as close as his stomach would allow, after which the only thing Boyd could see was the erratic flickering of a nearby television.

"That had to be Jefferson," Boyd said. "And you can bet he's not in there watching *Buns of Steel.*"

At no time did he see a silhouette or shadow that looked like Allison—the way she stood, the way she moved. He let another half hour pass, then dug the cellular phone out of the backseat.

"You're calling them?" Krystal asked.

"Why not? I'd say she's had time to get that kid bathed by now, wouldn't you?"

He punched out the number. Constance caught it in the middle of the seventh ring, a little breathless.

"Hello!" Boyd said. "Have I reached the Wainright residence?"

"You sure have." Quite the accent this woman had. And she was one of Allison's people? His ex had gone to some lengths to strip herself of audible roots.

"This is Peter Wackermann, calling from Las Vegas. I *do* hope it's not too late." If it was, Constance was too polite to say so. "I'm the bookkeeper for Gingerbread House Day Care, where Allison used to be in our employ until about ten days ago. And this . . . this wouldn't be her cousin Constance, would it?"

"Why, yes, it sure would be."

"Constance! This *is* a delight! Forgive me, but I feel like I know you, Allison talked so much about you. Not a day went by, I don't believe. I can almost picture you now, and let me tell you, it was some lovely portrait she painted. And how are the kids?"

"They . . . they're fine." She sounded a bit mystified. "Lainie's still up, but I just got Randy tucked into bed, not five minutes ago."

"Randy—of course. I bet he still raises a fuss at bath time, doesn't he?"

"Allison said *that*?"

Boyd assured her she had. "Again, I'm sorry to be calling so late, but Allison left you with us as her forwarding address and phone, and . . . has she arrived there yet?"

"No, she hasn't, she called to say she's had some delays."

"I ask, because, like I said, I handle the payroll here, and Allison has one more small check coming. But! We suffered a virus in our computer, and portions of the master payroll files were lost, so I'm working late trying to rebuild. I was hoping I could find Allison in so we could get her Social Security number again."

"So she *does* have a check coming?" Constance asked, and he said yes. "You have no idea how happy that's gonna make her! And here you could've kept that money and she'd never have known the difference!"

"Well, hush my big mouth! It's too late now, isn't it?" Boyd laughed with her. "Has she given you any idea when to expect her?"

"I shouldn't think it'll be much longer. She sent a couple of boxes of her things, and they've beaten her already, just sitting here waiting. So I'd say any day now, and I'll be so tickled to see her, why, my eyes are just gonna fly right out of my head."

"And I wouldn't blame them one bit," Boyd said. "We all miss her around here. And the children? Inconsolable for days! Finally we had to start putting Prozac in their afternoon milk. I'm joking of course. Well, fine, I'll not keep you any longer."

He tried to get away and found she wouldn't let him, that he had made a friend. For life, apparently, which seemed to be the scope of the story she launched into, something about growing up a couple years behind Allison and wanting to be just like her, and how she wished Allison would get over her rambling and settle down one day, and something else about when they were girls, ambushing Jeff with crabapples, and had it not been for Allison she might not have met the future father of her children. Finally Boyd had to tell her about the urgent call on the other line.

"I get the feeling she doesn't get a chance to talk to adults much these days," Boyd said once the call was finished and they were a block away.

"So we get a motel for now?" Krystal sounded relieved.

"And the biggest bed they offer." He whooped and clapped his hands, drummed them on his knees. "Allison shipped boxes ahead of her. Bet you that's why we turned up one big goose egg back at her trailer. Those disks were never there in the first place. Our karma holds out, we won't have to wait for Allison and deal with her grudges at all."

"So tomorrow we . . . do what, exactly?"

"Who knows, we'll figure something out." His brain was taxed for one day. "Keep a close watch on your side, there's got to be a liquor store still open somewhere." One bottle of Dom left, and with this festive mood he was in, just one wasn't going to cut it.

"You don't really plan very far ahead, do you, sweetie?"

"It's basically an energy-saving tactic," he explained. "I don't like to clutter my thoughts with a lot of alternatives for situations that never come up. That way, I'm always open to the moment."

"Wow," said Krystal, with admiration. "So you apply Taoist philosophy to your life, too."

"I do?"

"Sure. Having no plan?" She sounded positively tutorial. " 'To know, and not be knowing. To do, and not be doing.' I really wish I had your discipline."

"Well," he admitted, very modest, "it's a way of life, and a state of mind." Then, as long as he was on a metaphysical roll: "And later on, when we hit the sheets? You think we could try doing it without the rocks for a change?"

chapter twenty

When the sun came up on Wednesday, it shone hot and searing, as it should on any day of reckoning, and burned the dew off the meadows in a haze of mist and birdsongs.

Breakfast was a grave and silent affair. If Dwight didn't know already that Allison had spent the night in the bunkhouse, Tom felt certain that nothing at the table was going to give it away. They might just as well have eaten in separate shifts.

"You're welcome to stay longer, you know that," Dwight told him later, "but I'm not so sure you don't need reminding. Might do you some good, one more day."

Too tempting, Dwight's invitation. Tom could've gone to the van and brought back his bag, done it with relief, because some grim inevitability had been postponed another day.

"Whenever I'm here, it shouldn't be for any other reason than I want to be. Not because I need you to hide me from something." And poor Dwight nodded, not even knowing everything there was to hide from. Patricide, wasn't it called?

Tom looked down toward the corral, where Allison was spending her last minutes with the roan. She was wearing the hat again.

"I don't completely know what I've gotten myself into. But right now I think the best thing for me to do is see it through."

"I'll be here," Dwight told him, "if you have any need to . . . pass through one more time. For any reason. For however long." He turned an unsettled look toward the corral. "That goes for either of you. I expect you'll make sure she gets the message."

Tom promised he would, making good on it as he and Allison rode away after a night that should have left everything new and different, but instead made it just that much more strained. Without last night, he'd never have known what she was planning.

"He's a good man, Dwight is," she said. "It wouldn't be fair to involve him in something like this. After it's done and can't be taken back. I couldn't do that to him. Or to the horses." Allison frowned. "Yeah, I know, Tom. I went and involved you. The only thing I can say in my defense is that I didn't intend to."

"It's worse for me now than it is you, at least where that pair from the diner are concerned. You, they've lost track of. Me . . . they won't have any trouble finding me at home or at work."

Allison shook her head. "You don't have anything they want."

"I've got blood, don't I?"

They *would* come, if they weren't caught along the way. He'd called his offices this morning and asked Lianna Murphy to put the word out among the other St. John's employees. Describing Gunther and Madeline, telling her if they saw anyone like that around the shop, to call the law immediately. He'd placed a second anonymous call to the Panama City police, tipping them off to Gunther and Madeline's possible arrival.

"Did you ever figure out what it was they wanted from you?"

"Yeah. I think so," she said. "Saturday morning when you came to pick me up? Boyd was inside. I'd just taped him to a chair so he'd stay put. He showed up looking for something—something I didn't even remember until he started to remind me. Even then it took some time, because . . ." Allison stopped for a moment, shifting gears. "I'd just wanted to hurt him. At least make him stop and think about the way he and Madeline had hurt me earlier that day."

She filled him in on the rest, as much as she knew or could deduce. Had there not been so much blood, he would have laughed at how ridiculous it was. Six of them, squabbling across the country over an embezzled prize that was rather paltry, as fortunes went, and not even tangible. Just binary code on a disk of magnetic oxide that could fit in the palm of his hand.

"Madeline and Gunther, you couldn't help involving me there, because you didn't know," he said. "But what about your father? You had to have a reason for telling me. Did you want me to run? Did you think it'd be the easiest way to scare me off? Or was it just your final test, to see how far I'm willing to go for you?"

"I never asked you for anything other than a ride. Anytime you want, you can decide when I've ridden far enough."

"You don't want that any more than I do."

"Maybe not, but I could live with it. I've lived with worse. Besides," she said, beginning to soften, "you left one out."

"What's that?"

"Maybe I told you because I want you to talk me out of it."

He wondered if, when Allison looked at him now, she saw a man so desperate to save lives in atonement for others he'd lost that he would let a stranger gut him in the smoke and the garish neon luster. How easily a man like that could be manipulated.

"I don't think you really want to be talked out of anything," he said, "because you know one day you'd never be able to forgive whoever did the talking."

"So drive," she murmured, and he did, wondering how many hours were left for him to give it a try, regardless.

They stopped for gas and the state of the world. Tom bought newspapers while she bought three candy bars, rationing them the way a convict might ration cigarettes: one for now, one for later, and one for hard times.

She watched over his shoulder as he spread the first paper for news of fugitives, followed his finger as it settled on a photograph and a drawing, side by side. The article filled in the rest of the swath they'd been cutting since Nevada.

Gunther was wanted in Arizona as a suspect in the Saturday kidnapping of a Yavapai County sheriff's deputy, who'd been found Monday in the desert just north of Phoenix, dead of exposure and scorched by the sun, his eyes burned out by some caustic chemical. Gunther was also suspected in the execution-style shooting of an unnamed Las Vegas apartment building manager.

Doug. She nearly began to cry, then swallowed it down like a sickness, and watched the miles accumulate in white line hypnosis, trying to goad her conscience into showing its useless little head so she could poke at it again, perhaps kill it once and for all.

Oh, my Daddy, she thought, sending it like a prayer into the eastern sky, to precede her, *you have so much to answer for, what a shame you have only one life.*

In Mississippi, they rode the last miles through shadows and valleys. The sun burned through leafy treetop lattices; kudzu vines choked the land below. Everywhere the eye turned was a rich green, but their mood was the gray of old barns fallen to rot, and the weathered signs in lawns hawking boiled peanuts by the pound. Little towns simmering in their own dark secrets watched them pass, for one never knows when another's secret may go public.

Allison was going through with it, and nothing he could say made any difference. She rode holding the gun in her lap as though it were the one telling both of them what to do, where to go.

Everything, he supposed, but how to live with it tomorrow.

Now and then they would roll past a bus station or a shady inviting curb, and he would wonder why he didn't save himself and what remained of all he held dear. Put her out to finish the trip on her own. Mississippi, after all; his promise had been kept. His answer to himself was pure fool's logic—that as the voice of reason, only his presence could dissuade her in the end.

They crossed over a ribbon of muddy brown river, where down on the banks, two thin black boys held fishing poles. Only when he saw the sign did he realize that this was the river for which her home was named, and how close they were. And that he should have asked himself long before now if his desire to see her get away afterward was worth being an accessory to murder.

He tried to see the justice. She'd provided no details, which made it easier for him to imagine what her father had done. Silent as a totem, staring from her bedroom doorway until she could sense him over her shoulder, or from the other side of sleep, feeling the force of his compelling hunger long before she felt the press of his hands. The closer the little river town grew, the deeper it ached. Men in love, or approaching love, must have a burning need to torture themselves with what they know of a woman's past. Even on the best days, love and pain were never very far apart.

They reached the house when shadows were beginning to stretch and good Baptist families would be sitting down to dinner. It was an unassuming place, two stories of clapboard and peeling white paint and loose shutters, behind disinterested elms. Allison had him circle the block once, rigid in her seat, assailed by the reek of memory.

"How long has it been?" he asked.

"Fourteen years. I ran away a couple months after I turned seventeen. And never been back since. Not even when Mama died."

"But you're sure he's still here?"

"My cousin would've told me if he'd left. He's there. By now he should have at least two bottles of Dixie emptied and the *TV Guide* folded back to tonight's shows."

Well, thought Tom, *sounds like a man who needs killing.*

So the van would not be seen in front of the house, he parked around the corner and another two blocks up, in the shadow of an outbuilding behind a vacant house. As they backtracked on foot, the first swollen thunderheads darkened the sky. A neighborhood at peace, it was scented with magnolia and eucalyptus and meals on stoves, and gardens thrived under a blanket of wet heat.

"You don't think it'll look suspicious to your cousin," Tom said, "the day you come back, your father turns up dead?"

"Sure it'll look suspicious. I never claimed to be planning a perfect crime." She hiked her purse strap higher on one shoulder. "But deep down inside I know she'll be glad. He did her once, too. Once that I know about—there could've been more. She pretends it never happened, so I quit bringing it up. But she remembers."

"Where was your mother while these things went on?"

"You mean when she wasn't cracking the backs of our hands for telling hateful lies?"

They came upon her old house from behind, along an overgrown path and through a wet smell of moss and old flagstones striped with glistening slug trails. Tom hoped that the years hadn't been kind to her father. That he would open his door, and just the sight of a withered man would be enough to appease her. That she would see what he'd become and realize that time would always be far more relentlessly vindictive than she.

Porch steps creaked like screaming souls, and she banged on the screen door as bold as Saint Paul could preach.

Tom heard the scrape of the knob and watched the heavy inner door swing open, heard the chatter of the TV before seeing the man standing there trying to make sense of them: two strangers, maybe, or one stranger standing beside Willoughby's own problematic and haunting ghost, returned to flesh after fourteen years.

"Hey Daddy," said Allison, flat and neutral.

He stared. "Well, girl. I always did expect you'd find your way back one day." Then he turned his head to one side and spat what might have been a fleck of tobacco. "But I'll give you this much: I always expected you'd be alone and crawling."

"That's two more things you got wrong, isn't it? Maybe you'd better give up on trying to figure me out."

Willoughby started to laugh, a liquid rumbling in his chest, and the seams of his face pulled back taut. They already drooped in such a way as to give him a look as sour as curdled milk. He must've been around Dwight's age, but in all the worst ways, with the latter-day bearing of a man who'd been as stout as hickory in his prime. He still had the arms, the shoulders, and if he carried himself now with a stoop, he would apologize to no one for it. His hair was a dirty white, thinned well back along his crown, and had not seen a comb since morning. When he stepped back from the door to let them in, Tom saw the plastic pouch hanging low from beneath his thread-worn shirt.

A mean old man holding his colostomy bag, Tom thought. *I'm going to hell for sure.*

Allison waited for the door to latch behind her and her father to back out of the entry hall, then drew the revolver from her purse. Tom shut his eyes until he realized she wasn't going to shoot first thing.

"Well Lord have mercy, what's *this*?" Willoughby stared at the gun pointed at his chest. He seemed more amused than anything, as if this were some game of bluff and bravado, love and hate, that only fathers and daughters could understand.

"One bullet for you," she said in a small voice, "and four more for each of those friends of yours you whored me out to."

He'd . . . *sold* her? Tom felt a sick plunge in his gut and heart and soul. No idea. He'd had no idea any man could slither so low as this.

"That's five," Willoughby said with fresh contempt. "Who's the last one for—you, or your witness here?"

Allison gave it a moment's thought. With smug satisfaction she spun at the hip and put a bullet through the center of the old man's television. His face went slack as noxious smoke leaked from the hole and drifted to the ceiling.

"Aw hell," he moaned, genuinely saddened. Then he turned for the dining room, through a double-width hardwood doorway. An aged oblong table stood there on carved gryphon's feet. "Well, I'm going to sit. You can shoot me in the back if you can't wait for me to properly situate myself."

He moved more slowly than he actually seemed to require. The air in the dining room felt warmer by ten degrees from the chill of the living room, where a Cool King window unit strained with all it had left. The faint underlying stink became more noticeable back here where it was warmer.

"Connie told me your insides had started to rot away," said Allison. "It does a lot for the air around here."

"Ever since I got my satchel here they've had me taking these chlorophyll tablets so my shit won't stink. But I guess you can only smell so fresh." As he settled into his chair, he peeled the colostomy bag from his side and slung it by its aperture from one of the chair-back's spindles. Willoughby gave Tom a once-over. "Now where are your manners, girl? Who's your fella?"

"His name's Thomas St. John," she said as they joined him at the table. "And he's almost restored my faith that men don't have to be made of what's leaking out of you into that little bag you drag around."

Willoughby snorted. "Leaves your face looking like that and still he's your own Sir Lancelot? Now that *is* a wonder."

"He's not the one who did this. Tom's never laid so much as an unkind finger on me in all the time we've known each other."

"Congratulations, sir." The old man winked and thrust his hand across the table for a shake. Tom let it pass, dwelling on the bag dangling beside Willoughby's shoulder like a trophy. "Ain't she something? Now most girls, they'd get a man stirred up to do their killing for them, but not this one, no sir. She'll dirty her own hands, won't you, princess?"

"You shut up, Daddy. You don't think I'll do it?"

He waved her down but kept his eye on Tom, a shrewd old poker player who refused to be bluffed. "How about *you,* Thomas St. John? Could you put a bullet through the chest of your poor old daddy? Right there at his own supper table?"

"I'd have to track him down first." He was trying his best to stand hard, not let Allison see pity and disgust get the better of him. He feared that if she saw that, she'd toughen up for the both of them, and there would be no turning her back. "Then? Who knows?"

"Ran rabbit on you, did he?" Willoughby mused. "Bet he took off on you when you were just a little bitty sprout, didn't he?"

"If he was anything like you," Allison said, "that was doing Tom a favor."

"Well now, maybe that could be true, but you still can't stop wondering about him . . . can you, son?" The old man smirked with his seamed face and his crinkled viper's eyes. "Maybe he just wasn't ready to be a father yet. Had a few wild oats yet to sow. Got that business took care of, then who knows, maybe he started over like young Tommy St. John never even drew breath at all."

Allison's whisper was a whipcrack: *"Shut up, Daddy."*

Willoughby scowled at her. "Now what'd I teach you, girl? You don't go interrupting a couple of gentlemen trying to get to the bottom of a matter." Another wink for Tom. "How about you, Tom St. John? Any young whelps wondering where you've got off to this fine evening?"

"I wouldn't be here looking at you if there were."

Willoughby reeled in his chair. "Not a single *one*? You don't say!" As he hunkered forward again, Tom could feel the man drawing him in, seeking someplace bare and raw to hook into. "Not any problem, is there? Lordy, I'd sure hate to think of that dogging you around for life, and the reason I ask, Tom, looks to be gray in your hair already, and it does make a man look some long in the tooth for not even being started in his family ways—"

He was actually glad when Allison pulled the trigger. The old man jumped as, behind him, a brown fan splattered across the faded wallpaper, ran in rivulets toward the baseboard. Willoughby gazed upon the dripping ruin of his colostomy bag.

"Now that hurt," he said. He wrinkled his nose. "See what I mean about them chlorophyll tablets? They don't work miracles."

Two shots so far—might the neighbors have heard? There were no sirens yet, drawn by the first. At least the windows were down, for the air conditioner. And these old houses were built solid, to hold their secrets. Maybe it could contain this one last one.

Willoughby had gone a shade paler, his wrinkles and wattles tightened up as he understood he might have misjudged his daughter. Tom suspected that he'd not taken her seriously until this moment.

"I expect I must appear quite the joke to you now," he said, newly humble. "Carrying 'round this sack of my own slops."

"Joke? A *joke*?" Allison steadied the gun in both hands, lean brown arms outstretched and her cascade of hair sweaty damp. "Do you see me laughing, Daddy? Did you *ever* see me laugh? I always thought I'd start laughing again once I could stand over your grave, but I can't wait anymore for you to die on your own."

"God's own time, princess."

She brandished the revolver. "This is all the god you need to concern yourself with now." Allison took a deep breath and gagged, choked it down. Glanced toward the front door. "Do you still do it? Are there any little neighborhood girls you coax in here?"

"No. It was . . . just you."

"Don't you lie to me, Daddy. I know what you did to Constance that day we went picking peaches."

"Just the one time, princess. Just the once. Because Connie wasn't you." His eyes grew misty, one hand creeping forward across the table, as though he were groping for some beautiful thing that lived now only in his mind, or in his dark and malignant heart. "There was never any other but for you."

Allison's head began shaking, tiny movements as she slumped in her chair. She still loved him, Tom realized, or a sliver of her did, some resilient ember burning inside her that Willoughby and his friends, for all their snuffling animal grunts, had never managed to extinguish.

Tom was past knowing whether this was good news or bad.

"Daddy," she groaned, and turned to Tom, forcing the gun into his hands. "Just hold it on him," she said, then fled her chair. Allison went scrambling down a hallway, to disappear behind a slammed door. He could barely hear her getting explosively sick.

"The girl often did have a tender stomach," Willoughby noted, "even as a little bitty thing. Carsick a lot." He stared at Tom with strange eyes, as if ready to burst with laughter at a joke that only he had understood all along. "Now as I recall, *you* were never that way. Good settled stomach on little Tom-Tom."

". . . what . . . ?"

"No need to play ignorant for my sake, son. Allison's busy, she can't hear us." He shook an admiring head. "Yes sir, I believe most men would surely let surprise get the best of them, walk in ready to blast an old man and who do they see but their *own* old man, more than thirty years gone. You have yourself some jim-dandy self-control, I'll give you that."

Tom couldn't believe what he was hearing. A ploy so desperate it was beyond pathetic. "I thought I'd heard some bullshit stories before, but you just took first prize."

"Oh, I'll admit maybe I didn't do so right by you either, Tom-Tom, but is that any way to talk to me now?" And the old man smiled, chuckling as Tom had often imagined his own father would: so superior, a callous man who'd take his family's love and flick it aside with no more thought than he would give a cigarette butt. "Look, a man can move to Mississippi and call himself Willoughby, as easy as he can call himself St. John. Though I don't believe he *ever* under any circumstances expects to see his young ones find each other purely by chance. What *are* the odds of that, I wonder?"

In challenge, Tom stared into his face, searching for any trace of flesh or bone that could be matched with some old picture he'd not seen for more years than he could remember. Or something that could be aligned with what he saw in the mirror . . . and there was nothing. Although he'd always tended to favor his mother, and if Allison did likewise—

No. No, this just could not be. To entertain for one moment this contemptible ploy was to play the old sadist's game.

Willoughby narrowed his rattler's eyes. "Don't know what your intentions are with the girl, but unless you've got her good and fooled as to what a fine man you are . . . why Tom, you might want to rethink them. Especially if you're having thoughts of family going through your head. How *do* you think it'd affect the poor girl, she finds out her own half brother's sired her a fat little mongoloid baby? Can't even sit up on its own, why, what a pitiful thing that would be." He ogled down the hall at a dim sound of retching. "I don't believe she'd bear up so well, myself."

It felt as if the house were contracting around him, like a vast stomach that digested the hopes and promise out of anyone who walked in. Astounding that Allison had made it out alive at all.

"I don't believe one word of this," Tom said. And a small whisper within: *But what if . . . ?*

Willoughby shrugged. "Face value, I wouldn't expect so. Hell no, these are some long odds. But if it's proof you're needing, well, son, see that Bible on that shelf over there? Hand it over and we'll get down to some proofing business."

It looked very old; an heirloom, maybe. A leather-bound Bible with a strap buckling it shut, fat enough to gag a crocodile.

"Swear on a Bible, you think that'll prove anything to me?"

Willoughby sneered. "What kind of idjit did you grow up into, boy? You're telling me you never heard of a Bible's got a family tree wrote up in the middle of it? Folded up in there between the Testaments? Why would I even bring it up at all if I couldn't show it to you right there in black and white?"

Tom looked at it again, dusty and waiting to be cracked open, its secrets of life and death and birth revealed. He could have left it there and always doubted. But always wondered. Yet what if he saw his own name, thirty-six-year-old ink scratched in by Willoughby's terrible hand? The old man would know that as long as they never checked, Tom could never truly rest.

He stepped over to the shelf, revolver in hand; brought the Bible back and slid it across the table. Willoughby's mouth curled into a simpering grin as his fingers worked at the leather strap.

"I'm calling your bluff."

Willoughby nodded, as with some diseased paternal pride. "I'd never expect any less a gamble from any son of mine."

He propped the Bible against the table's edge, canted at a preacher's angle, then cracked the thick cover back. He stroked one knotty hand down the pages, then brought it back up, and of all the surprises Tom never expected the book to yield, a pistol was at the top of the list.

He wasn't even thinking as he scuttled backward in the chair, wood scraping across wood, and swung Allison's gun up level. But Willoughby's quick-draw days, if ever he'd lived any at all, were behind him. Tom fired twice across the table into his chest, then clenched the revolver in both hands, shaking like a man with feverish chills . . .

Waiting for a dead man to make another move.

That quickly? It was over that quickly?

He stood, wobbly, and grabbed the Bible to stare down at its mutilated pages, cut with a pistol-shaped hollow. Flipping from Old Testament to New with his heart squeezing up the back of his throat, in case he still found that family tree.

"Tom? *Tom?* You . . ."

Hands on walls, Allison braced herself steady in the doorway.

"Oh, Tom. What have you done?"

"He . . . he wanted his Bible," Tom whispered. "I didn't know."

"What, no atheists in foxholes, at the end?" She walked over, very slowly, stepping around the blood and the shit, staring at the man she called her father. This creature of dreadful hunger who ruined lives, slumped now in a chair with his gray-whiskered chin drooping to his chest, calm malice dimming in his open eyes. "No. Not him. Never him."

Tom understood that he would never truly know what Allison was feeling as she brushed trembling fingertips over her father's stilled skull, his face, his hard wide shoulders. She looked relieved and she looked cheated, and not quite sure how she should feel about either.

Tom tossed her gun onto the table. It landed with a heavy clatter, spinning slowly, like the bottle in a more innocent game that even brothers and sisters had been known to play.

"Two bullets left. He won't feel them anymore." Tom chewed at the side of his lip. "But . . . maybe . . . you still might."

Allison took forever to wrap her hand around the wooden grip, then lifted the gun and cradled it to her breast, eyes closing as she seemed to dwell on something, thinking on it so fiercely that whenever she opened them again, those green eyes would demand nothing less than recompense for the compounded sins of twenty years and more. All in one shattering moment.

Tom turned his back, knowing that this should remain solely between her and her father. Hoping he would not jump like a scared rabbit when the trigger was squeezed, the cylinder rotated, and the hammer fell.

Waiting for Allison to tell him that he could turn around again.

chapter twenty-one

A high ball of hot white glare, the sun already had it in for him when Boyd came to Wednesday morning. He threw back the sheet and blinked groggily across at the other pillow and Krystal's tiny feet, neither of which so much as twitched until he finished coughing himself the rest of the way awake. One foot flexed, then the other, her toes beginning to spread experimentally. When she kicked him in the head, it wasn't hard enough to do any damage, although it did stir into life a dormant headache, and she came awake with a torrent of apologies.

"Don't worry about it," he said, then ran one hand beneath his back and crinkled his nose. "But I would like you to recognize how sexually democratic I am. Looks like we were both sleeping on wet spots."

Krystal attempted to sit up, propping herself back on both elbows. "I know how awful champagne hangovers can be—are you sure your head'll be okay? If you want, I can get out my snowflake obsidian and my hematite, and see if we can make it better."

"This is no job for the rocks, babe. I'm pretty sure I've got Tylenol and codeine packed away somewhere." Boyd flopped off the bed and let the motel room settle around him; rummaged in his suitcase until his grab bag of pills for all occasions surfaced. He washed down three Tylenols, then poked a hesitant finger into his crusted pubic hair. "Shower'll take care of the rest."

It made a new man of him, and while it was making a new woman of Krystal, he walked dripping over to the phone and called the Wainright house. When Constance answered, he stamped one foot in disappointment, pinched shut his nostrils to disguise his voice, and asked for Lars. She informed him he had the wrong number and that was that. He'd really blown it last night—as long as he'd had the woman in such a chatty mood, he should've thought to ask what she had scheduled for today. Ten to one she'd have given him an hourly itinerary.

He scouted the dresser-top wasteland of champagne bottles and ice buckets, but found nothing left. A crying shame, considering the significance of the day. As cool water pounded in the shower, Krystal sang a somnolent little tune that Boyd recognized from one of her CDs. She had apparently memorized the Gaelic lyrics. Maybe remembered the language from a former life.

At the very least they deserved a celebratory breakfast, so he called the manager and promised his high school dropout son a ten-dollar tip if he'd run down the street for fresh strawberries, two peaches, and one more bottle of champagne. Boyd barely had the fruit sliced and soaking by the time she finished drying her hair.

"Oh sweetie, you shouldn't have!" Krystal launched herself at him, arms and legs clutching eagerly as she wrapped herself around him from waist to shoulders like a skinny pink koala.

They sprawled across the rumpled bed; fed themselves and each other, smothering their giddy nouveau riche laughter with kisses sweet and sticky, wondering how best to spend the money.

"Remember the night we first met, and how I said the only shortcoming you had was that you weren't twins?" he asked. "Well, for starters, I'm thinking of having you cloned."

"That's so amazingly adorable, nobody's ever wanted to clone me before." She offered him a slice of peach from her own lips, licking away the stray drops of champagne. "Umm . . . why, exactly?"

"I'd think the answer is obvious." He slapped the mattress. "Just imagine a three-way under circumstances like that . . . both of you knowing what the other was thinking and feeling at any given moment. Haven't you ever wanted to make love with yourself?"

"Wow. Oh, wow." From the misty look in her eyes he could tell she was halfway to bliss already. "I have to confess I've had that fantasy. But I always imagined it happening on, like, more of an astral plane."

"Well, we'll work on that too," he said, and then, speaking of astral, let his head wobble back and forth, light as a helium balloon on a dandelion stem. "Champagne and codeine. I am feeling *damn* good this morning."

"No comas," Krystal warned. "That would be such a downer at this point."

"Not to worry. My judgment remains as sound as ever."

Agog with wonder and thanksgiving, Boyd gazed down into his lap as Krystal suddenly squirmed her head into it, poured herself a half-mouthful of champagne, then treated him to an astonishing display of oral coordination as she took him past her lips without spilling a drop. Like cool, effervescent velvet, it was, a galaxy of tiny stars bursting across his tumescent skin. Here was an entirely new frontier in sparkling wines—clearly, he had not known it all. The explosive revelation left him so drained he couldn't even find his voice long enough to propose they consider holy matrimony the instant they hit Las Vegas again.

Reverie shattered only when he checked the clock and realized how much time had elapsed, so he called the Wainright home again, without success. After two more calls throughout the morning, he began to get the feeling that Constance was a stay-at-home mom with too few outside interests.

"We'll give her another couple of hours, and if she's still there, fine," Boyd explained. "We'll revert to our backup plan."

"There's a backup plan?" Krystal sounded mildly concerned.

"Well, there will be in a couple of hours." Now she *looked* mildly concerned. "You have nothing to worry about. I have total confidence in myself."

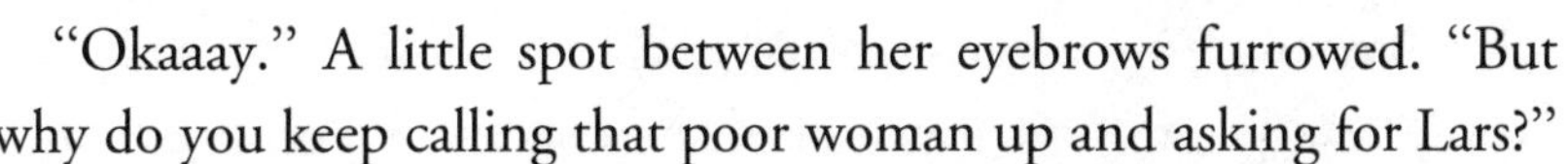

"Okaaay." A little spot between her eyebrows furrowed. "But why do you keep calling that poor woman up and asking for Lars?"

"We can't very well sit out on the street in broad daylight and wait to see if they all vacate the house at once. So that leaves the phone. But it's going to strike her as odd if she gets a string of hang-ups with nobody saying anything. That happens too many times, it starts to creep people out. But play like you're some yutz who can't dial a phone, all you do is annoy them, instead of turning on their radar."

Krystal nodded. "So, with all these calls for Lars, is she getting annoyed?"

"No! She's got to be *the* most understanding person on earth! The last time, she offered to check the phone book for me. She's too nice, I can't stand it." He sank onto the bed and sighed. "I got half a mind to call her up again, tell her it's Lars, and ask if there are any messages."

In midafternoon, he made one last call and got the welcome sound of the other end ringing away unchecked. Triumphant, he seized Krystal around the waist and twirled her off the bed. It was finally time to go endorse that check of destiny.

"I know the way this woman thinks," he told Krystal in the car. "I'm almost certain she's one of these old-fashioned trusting types, still leaves her doors unlocked. But even if she's not, then sure as Buddha's got droopy earlobes she leaves a key out on the porch somewhere. Under one of those flower pots, probably. So, either way, we basically let ourselves in, find the boxes Allison shipped, and correct this misunderstanding between her and me, without inconveniencing extraneous bystanders. I think it's damned considerate of us, taking everything into account."

"And suppose she's back home again by the time we get there."

"Then we employ our backup plan, and its beauty lies in its bold simplicity." It had settled upon him not ten minutes ago, as if gently blown by the inspiring holy breath of God. He didn't know why he fretted so over these things. "You, my love, are Allison's new roommate up from Jackson to pick up her stuff while she's out on job interviews. Oh, you two go way back, when she used to live in Seattle, except you lost touch after she moved to Vegas. But now you're here, you just got engaged—that's where I come in, I'm a medical intern by the way—and damned if you don't need a responsible roommate to help you save on expenses until the wedding."

"And what am I supposed to say when she wonders why Allison didn't even call to tell her we were coming?"

Boyd shrugged it off. "I think the phone's out or something."

Krystal probed him for a few extra details, most of which he extemporized as she steered the car past those glorious old houses he remembered from last night. Between her sweet-faced sincerity and his own inside track on the details of Allison's life, he had no doubt that they could not only walk out of there with boxes and Constance's blessings, but maybe persuade her to advance Allison a modest cash loan, as well, until that first paycheck came through.

"Umm, Boyd?" Krystal said. "What if nobody's there and we've let ourselves in, and *then* she comes home?"

"That *would* be a faux pas, wouldn't it?" Three blocks away. It was good Krystal was thinking ahead like this. "Okay. Okay. The backup plan still holds, except now you're pregnant and you can't wait out in the heat any longer. She's a mom, remember. Play your cards right and she'll probably pour you a nice foot bath."

"This may sound strange, coming from me," she said, and Boyd assured her that was quite impossible, "but I'm going to be sorry when all this is over. This is, like, *the* coolest vacation I've ever been on. Except for when you almost got killed the other morning. Oooo, I just love these old houses, don't you? They have so much character."

"Oh yeah. It's like we fell asleep watching an old movie and woke up inside *To Kill a Mockingbird*."

Krystal nodded. "After we leave here, what then?"

"We'll hop back across the country to L.A., go see my giant-headed brother Derek. He's brokering the deal with the guy who'll get this money transferred back onto U.S. soil for us."

"Giant-headed?"

"Hugest head you've ever seen on a human being. It was like growing up with the Elephant Man. And hard, that big noggin of his? God have mercy." Boyd shuddered. "When we were kids, my other brother was buzzing us with a radio-controlled airplane and lost control. I thought Derek was dead for sure when that thing went slamming into the side of his head." He looked at Krystal with undiluted awe. "*It shattered.* Derek, the most he lost was a patch of hair where the propeller chopped it away. In fact, my other brother? He lost more blood than Derek because Derek beat the snot out of him, right there in the car on the way to the hospital."

Boyd realized then what a formative experience this had been. As he recalled, he'd tried to make a bet with a total stranger in the emergency room over which brother would need more stitches. Clearly, everything he was today he had family to thank for.

Krystal eased off the gas as they neared the Wainright house. No one was moving on the porch or in the yard. No black vans with Florida plates. No psychopaths with eye problems. No former lovers howling for his emasculation.

They parked two houses down, then backtracked toward the Wainrights'. When Krystal gazed intently down the street where they'd just come, he feared someone had been following, until she pointed halfway up the block, at a preschool-age child meandering across his yard atop a tricycle.

"I know it's all so totally conventional," she said, "but do you ever sometimes wonder if you might be missing out on something by not living on a street like this?"

"The way I figure it, it's like having a third eye. It might work out great, but it isn't anything I actually desire."

While he supposed he meant it, Boyd wondered if, even more, this wasn't something that Krystal truly needed to hear from him right now—assurance that they were both okay being who and what they were. That they weren't missing anything they couldn't have anytime they wanted.

"That's what I thought," she said, relieved. "And if I ever decide

I want things to be, like, more normal, I know I'll be all the better for coming to it later in life. Like, I'll be bringing in so many more experiences I can draw from. Maybe that way I can be more understanding and not so scared, or judgmental. Isn't that the way you look at it?"

"Absolutely," he declared. "Say life is like a library. How can you know what you want until you've stolen enough books?"

She squeezed his hand and stared at the boy on the tricycle again, smiling to herself, or at some piece of herself she'd only just recognized. For a pensive moment of his own, Boyd wished she had never brought it up. Wishing, too, he could see the future, all possible futures, the lives in those alternate universes he'd been thinking about the other night. It would make decisions so much easier.

They walked up the steps to the Wainrights' porch. He pushed the button and they could hear its insolent buzz inside the door. When neither voice nor footstep responded, he pressed again, and finally the conclusion was inescapable:

"Free lunch." Boyd waggled his eyebrows.

"That's a relief. I'm not the most comfortable person when it comes to lying and keeping it all straight."

"Nothing to it, really." He opened the screen door, gripped the knob of the inner door, gave it a twist. "It's primarily an organizational skill. And mnemonics can help." The knob turned easily. "What'd I tell you? I cannot express how heartening it is to still find trust in this cynical age."

Boyd led the way in, Krystal shutting the door behind them as they stood in the high-ceilinged entry hall. He called out in case Constance had missed the buzzer, or was slow to answer, but his voice fell on deaf walls. The air smelled of old plaster and wood polish, potpourri and children. He pointed directly ahead, where just past a cross hall a wide wooden stairway with carpeted runner led upstairs; it turned in right angles at two separate landings, the newel posts as blocky as railroad ties.

"We'll forget the upstairs for now," Boyd said. "We'll start looking in corners and closets, like that—anyplace out of the way, but handy."

There was nothing inside the coat closet to their right, so Boyd steered them ahead and to the left, into the family room, where he'd seen the flickering television last night. He noticed an oddly haphazard layout to the furniture, as though most of it had been cleared out of the middle, then neglected before it was in place again, on the bare wooden floor.

"I think she might benefit from a course in *feng shui,*" said Krystal. "You know—the Chinese art of arranging your surroundings to maximize the harmony they bring you. She could use that."

Boyd glanced over his shoulder. "Maybe you can leave her a note."

Another doorway looked like it might lead through a short hall and back to the kitchen, and Boyd was moving for it when he realized why the family room appeared so off-kilter. It looked as though someone had taken up a rug, one of those heavy wall-to-wall designs that some people preferred over carpeting.

When he reached the hallway and peered back, Boyd halted, everything going hinky. The rug lay across the kitchen floor in a lumpy, uneven roll. The sight itself was unexpected enough without the head protruding from the end of the carpet.

From this angle, Boyd could clearly see the top of the head and its early onset of male-pattern baldness. The face, looking off toward the right, appeared loose, jowly, although given the damage sustained, it would be tough to say where jowls ended and swelling began. This face could easily have belonged to the potbellied silhouette seen in the window last night. Nickel- and dime-sized spatterings of blood congealed on the linoleum beneath him. Jefferson Wainright? Probably so. Somebody had given him a severe work-over, then rolled him up like a tamale.

"Oh shit," Boyd whispered as he felt Krystal's chin craning over his shoulder to see. She made a tiny squeaking noise deep in her throat. "I think we've really stepped in it this time."

From behind, the arresting metallic click-clack of a pump shotgun. When he turned, the only thing that surprised him was spiky black hair where the other day there had been blond.

"I love that fucking sound," Gunther said. "The way it just grabs your attention by the 'nads and won't let go? I love that. Sounds like . . . truculence."

That word again. How this guy must love that word. Boyd began to feel ill. Too much champagne, too much codeine. And Gunther looked to be in no mood to play cards.

"About a half hour or so ago, that cousin of Allison's? She happened to mention to Madeline that some numbnuts'd been calling all day, asking for Lars." When Gunther slowly leveled the shotgun at his middle, Boyd felt all sphincters contract. "Maddy *knew* that had to be you. Said it was just your style."

He took a couple steps toward them, curdling with fury and deranged anticipation. The sweaty, bottle-black hair began to leak blue-gray trickles down around his head. Between that and the giant suckered abrasion on his face, Gunther looked as though he'd just wrestled a squid.

"See these bruises? See this bloodshot eye?" He angled to show them the colors. "These became extremely motivational over the past few days. Oh, you got no fucking idea. 'I'm gonna see him again,' is what I told Madeline. 'Someday I'm gonna see him again. And when I do, I'm gonna be on him like a pit bull on a baby.' "

Then, for some reason that Boyd suspected would make sense in the end, Gunther began singing the first lines of "Mr. Sandman."

chapter twenty-two

When they left Willoughby's house, they left with no fingers pointed at them by the neighbors, and Tom thought that maybe this hateful house was strong enough to protect for a change, rather than imprison. They retraced the two sweltering blocks back to the van, while clouds continued to gather and seal off the eternal sky from those insignificant and bloody goings-on beneath it.

"You know I can't go right on to my cousin's now, don't you," said Allison. "And I'd just as soon not stay anywhere else in town either. Not for tonight."

To the city limits and beyond. A dozen and a half miles east lay the interstate, and when midway between they came to a fork in the highway they chose the southern branch. It led them to a motel struggling through its last inferior years, designed like cabins in a chain, surrounded by willow and pine. Tom asked for the room farthest from the road, and when they carried in their bags it felt as if the days had been turned back, that he and Allison had slipped once more into their roles as total strangers. He did not know her. He did not know himself.

Fathers left behind much more than sorrow when they vanished and took their meager love with them. They left behind unanswered questions that could wait years before they were even posed. They left behind riddles and doubts and guilty hatreds.

Too restless to sit around just yet, Tom took the van back to the tiny hamlet of Benton, where he bought a bottle of rum, and bread and cheese and the makings of sandwiches for later if they wanted.

The thunderheads had nearly caught up to them, banking low over the woodlands and fields. Along the horizon, blue-white jags of lightning leaped from cloud to cloud, or turned to ignite them from within, and they would flicker from black to a sentient gray, as though suddenly alive and cognizant of their own evil.

Allison was lying curled on the bed when he returned. She'd unpacked nothing in his absence, except for her tape player and the cassettes that lay scattered before it on the scarred dresser. One of her early blues tapes was playing now, stark and primeval, as haunted as this land that had inspired such a resonant sound, where the only things once grown in more abundance than cotton were misery and the will to survive.

He fetched ice from the office, brought glasses from the bathroom, broke the seal on the rum. Filled one glass for himself and when he looked at Allison, she nodded, so he made it two.

They sat at the table and drank, listening to the soft earthy gliss of slide guitar. The rain came down in a hard, steady wash, pecking at the roof like handfuls of gravel while the sun-beaten blacktop steamed. And when at last they spoke, they spoke of small things that needed no thought, as though the sound of their voices was all that either of them truly wanted.

Willoughby had played each of them like a pro, in the ancient game of divide and conquer, his instincts honed shrewd and cunning and malicious. As rum burned its way down and simple words slipped from his mouth, Tom told himself that all the old man had wanted was to rob them of everything he could.

Maybe Willoughby had known that Allison really would have pulled the trigger in the end, and forced Tom's hand instead to deny his daughter that last violent redemption. Or maybe he had known she couldn't, but was ready to die anyway. Or maybe, given the chance and a faster hand, he'd have shot them both.

Only one thing did Tom know for sure: Willoughby had taken him from a man who'd hoped to spare a life and turned him into the one who had taken it. Nothing else was quite so clear.

"It was self-defense," Allison finally said, as if she'd had her fill of trivialities, "wasn't it? It *was* self-defense."

Tom laced his fingers around the glass. "That'd be hard to claim. I mean, when you walk into a man's house the way we did . . ."

The rain beat down and the steam rose up. For an instant he imagined that Willoughby and the devil might be laughing so hard by now that they had to hold each other upright. The devil, being the father of lies, would surely appreciate the joke.

Allison and I, we can't be related. This he told himself more than once. That Willoughby wanted to poison their future, if they had one at all. That Willoughby was only trying to get to the gun.

As daylight dimmed and every minute brought a new shadow, Allison sat contained and pensive in her chair. He hunted for some telltale feature in her face that he'd worn all his life; knowing that if he saw it, he would argue it away as a trick of dying light. And then watch for the next. And the next.

"Tomorrow," he said, when he'd had rum enough to say it, "after you see your cousin . . . do we keep going?"

"Going where?"

"The rest of the way."

He could not look at her, terrified of what might be there to see. The wrong kind of familiarity would surely breed contempt. And if she looked upon him with love, could he ever be certain it wasn't for who he was, rather, because down in some deep and unacknowledged cleft inside her, he reminded her of her father?

"How many of us," he tried again, "are going on to Florida?"

She waited for the thunder, a low, rolling grumble.

"How many of us *are* there, inside?" Allison said, and pushed her hair back from her bruised but healing face.

She left the table then, crossing the room to their luggage and taking from it that travel-worn monument to failure that he'd carried for so many miles. She carried it to the bed, where she lay on her side and opened it—the small, flat box filled with small, flat books. When she'd held them long enough, Allison began to weep over them, in painful, racking sobs.

And if happily-ever-afters were more elusive than the books would lead you to believe, perhaps the possibility of them was enough, so long as you were willing to turn another page.

She came violently awake in the night, spit forth from dreams like Jonah spit from the whale's mouth. Her father's friends had been waiting for her again, as they so often had over the years, sleep the only doorway through which they now walked.

A creaking hinge and a silhouette in the doorway: familiar, but not as instantly familiar as the man of the house. A pungent smell of smoke and spirits, and he was sitting on the edge of the bed with a sanctioned hand clamping hard on her coltish thigh. The world was ending again, and it would do no good to keep her knees locked, her mouth shut. There was always a threat, a loss of house and home that she alone could forestall by making it easy on all concerned and keeping their secrets. Only one had ever threatened to hurt her personally.

"It's all right, sugar, I'm a friend of your daddy's, and he told me how much you want to help the family," said this visitor, and when he leaned forward into moonlight she could see that she'd been fooled again. Because this time it was Tom.

Awake. Awake in the dark and the cool, dripping calm after the storm. Allison wondering if they would leave her alone if she tried hard next time to dream herself a clear conscience and a loaded gun.

Tom lay sleeping on his side, nothing of him to see but his shoulders and the back of his head. Not the enemy, yet she felt overwhelmed by his thievery. She surged onto her knees and seized his arm, shaking him roughly, and when he rolled onto his back in confusion, she battered her fists down upon his chest and screamed that the man had been hers and hers alone to kill, no one else's, and damn you to hell for stealing that from me.

Tom caught each wrist and restrained them in the air, until she relented and remembered who she was and why, and that he was not blameless, but he *was* hers if she wanted.

And she did. For tonight and tomorrow and the next day, she did. Her fists unclenched and when he let her go she sank atop him, let him hold her, cheek to chest.

"I'm sorry. I woke up, I was . . . confused," she said. "I can't promise it'll never happen again."

"I know. So what are you trying to do, anyway?" He laughed with soft reluctance. "Give me gray hairs?"

They coiled like this for a time, listening to the silence of night and the wet earth. Finally, sensing the imminence of sleep, Allison slid from him so that they might sleep unentangled. She'd felt last night, in the bunkhouse, how unaccustomed Tom was to spending a night with someone in the same bed.

And sometime later she touched his turned back, lightly, with the tips of her fingers, feeling him tighten in response. She knew that no good could come of it, but had to ask anyway:

"When I got sick today, when I had to go running off to the bathroom," she said. "Did he . . . say much of anything? Did he beg? Because he's such a manipulator, you know, I recognize that now that I'm . . . older. But I need to know. What did he say to you?"

"You couldn't hear anything from in there?"

"Voices. Just voices. No words, really, just . . . voices."

Tom was silent for a long time, long enough for her to wonder if he'd not fallen asleep. Finally, "It wasn't much. He asked me if I'd ever killed anyone before. I don't know how, but he seemed to guess I'd been in the military, so maybe that's what gave him the idea. Asked me if I'd ever killed anyone."

He's lying, she thought. *He's lying.*

"How did you answer that?"

"I told him I had."

"That's not true, is it?" Thinking of the wife, the embryo, that she wasn't even supposed to know about. "It wasn't true?"

"I don't know," said Tom, from beside her and from far away. "I wish I could be sure. I think I must have. But I don't know."

She touched her lips between his shoulder blades, over the knobs of spine; tasted the salt of his skin. "I don't think you did," she told him. "I would've seen it in your eyes. So let it go if you can. Let it go, for me. Because I don't think you did."

Awake in the night, she remembered some story she'd heard of the creation of the world, some other culture's lesser-known ideas on God and the beginning of human affairs. Persian, maybe, Allison could not remember, but in their eyes God was a far more pragmatic sort than the white-bearded, thundering meddler she had grown up learning to live in terror of. Perhaps more like the capricious playwright she imagined now.

Adam and Eve, there they had been at the dawn of time, as God had shown them the Garden of Eden and all its splendors, but at no time was any mention made of fruit and taboos.

"Take what you want," this God told them, "and pay for it."

While Allison preferred to think of it all beginning this way, better by far than blaming serpents, she recognized how much more subtly devious it was at heart. For while you can take only once, the terms and currency of payment are never-ending.

We took today for ourselves and we have tonight, she thought, the last thoughts before sleep. *And if we start paying tomorrow, I guess that won't be too soon.*

chapter twenty-three

Midnight came and went, taking with it the last of Gunther's hope that they might get this situation mopped up tonight.

"What's keeping those two, anyhow? I can't believe this, we beat them here by an entire day, and *we're* the ones got our faces on billboards, just about." Gunther scowled with ill intent and disgust for humanity. "Some people, they got no concept of the importance of time."

"Importance of time?" Madeline rolled her eyes. "Oh, *that's* rich, coming from a man whose foreplay technique has sunk to the phrase 'Aren't you wet *yet*?' "

"Would you get off of that? Once. I said it *once*." Gunther quit pacing and swung around, shotgun and all, to explain himself to this cousin of Allison's, this Constance person, as she cowered in the upstairs hallway corner. "I was feeling a modicum of stress last night, so maybe I was a little impatient. Now I'm supposed to hear about this the rest of the year?" To Madeline, then, who sat on the floor with her back to the blue-papered wall: "I know what your match is in the animal kingdom now. You're an oyster. Just like an oyster. Get one grain of sand in you, and you work that thing and work it until you got a pearl as big as a jawbreaker up your ass."

Maddy didn't bat an eye, just smirked. "Which explains why a day with you is like a day at the beach."

"What a mouth you got on you." He turned again to the cousin. "You. You're native southern, right, you got that accent? Maybe you could give this ballbuster of mine lessons. Southern women are sweet to their men, right? Stand by them, don't always talk such trash to their men? Think you could give her some pointers?"

She appeared not to have heard him. Her eyes were red-rimmed in darkened hollows, and she sat in the corner with her knees hugged up against her chest. Her short brown hair had, over the course of the day, become a tangled mop.

"May I please see my kids one more time tonight?" she asked, in a steady voice that did not match her eyes. The begging she'd gotten out of her system hours earlier. "I just want to make sure they're sleeping sound and all."

Gunther saw no harm in it, if it would keep her calm. He nodded, and Maddy picked up the Browning and escorted her down the hall, to a door across whose top half was taped a misty-toned poster of a prancing unicorn, hooking a rainbow with its horn.

The second floor had become everyone's temporary home in case some nosy neighbor happened to come along and take a look through a first-floor window. The layout proved more functional as well, bedrooms and bathroom branching off a hall that was wood-floored along each side, with a thread-worn runner of blue floral carpeting anchored down the middle. The consolidation was ideal, no one more than three seconds from either end of the shotgun.

The kids they'd confined to the girl's room. Lainie was five and Randy two, neither old enough to wholly grasp the situation, and the cousin had so far been able to keep them convinced it was some sort of game. Earlier, their curious faces peered from the doorway, as though trusting that their mother was still in charge, even if they'd not yet figured out all the rules. What they probably wondered most was why their dad wasn't playing.

Gunther had checked the guy an hour ago. Still out of it, in a bad way. Unemployed slob, the man had no pride, nor any worth to his life beyond insurance policies, so far as Gunther could tell. Sitting on his fat can watching TV talk shows when the cousin had let them into the house this afternoon, he'd looked as useless as a ruptured appendix. While Madeline, in her blond wig and casino blazer, pretended to be from a real estate agency and spun her lie about representing a buyer interested in the acquirability of the house, Gunther had picked up a train engine made of cherry wood and walloped the slug across the head. In hindsight, the next several blows might have been above and beyond, but the man's existence—like that of all the deadbeats from whom he'd collected over the years—was so loathsome that Gunther couldn't contain himself.

An hour ago, still constricted by the rug in which Gunther had wrapped him in the event of his waking up with heroic notions, Jefferson Wainright's left pupil was fixed and dilated.

Yet for all that, he still looked better than Boyd.

The unicorn girl's door reopened and Madeline returned the cousin to her place in the corner at the opposite end of the hall. The cousin thanked them, calling them "sir" and "ma'am," then sank back to the floor, where she fixed her gaze on the unicorn. They'd decided that she, unlike Boyd and the hooker, needed no rope from the utility room to keep her restrained. So long as she stayed in their sight, the cousin posed no threat, for fear of endangering the kids, and it was vital she remain free to maintain illusions, in case someone came to the door or she had to answer the phone.

"Won't either one of us be much good tomorrow, we don't get some sleep," he said to Madeline. "Who goes first, you or me?"

"Last time he asked me that," she told the cousin, "he was talking about orgasm."

"I never said that!" Gunther cried. "I never *once* said that!"

"Oh, calm down, you big baby." Madeline tickled a fingernail along the length of his jaw. "Can't you tell I'm only teasing?"

He nuzzled the stiff copper of her hair. "All I can say is, there's a fine line between teasing and all-out, trash-talking nastiness, and in you that line's gotten awful blurry."

"Blurrier by the day, too," she said. "Get some sleep, I'll be fine. But before you dirty up *my* pillow, go wash yourself and put down a towel to sleep on. Your hair's running again."

He left her the shotgun, along with the Browning he'd given her earlier, after going out at dusk to search the coral Mazda and park it behind the house. Its glove compartment had returned to him the Glock that Boyd had taken from him Saturday. So happy was Gunther to see it again that he kissed its hard polymer skin. Add to this the Smith & Wesson .357 Magnum revolver he'd found in the master bedroom and they were set up better than ever for truculence.

Gunther brushed his teeth with one of the kids' toothbrushes, scrubbed away the latest trickles from his jet-black hair. Caper of his life, and he was a human inkwell.

When he stepped back into the hall, he saw that Maddy was sitting on the floor with the Browning in one hand and, with the other, turning pages in the photo album she'd packed for the trip. He'd not even known it existed, much less that she had brought it, until running across the thing by accident two nights ago, while lying low in western Louisiana. He had sensed that it was nothing he'd been meant to find, ever, making no mention of it, keeping it to himself while wishing, even though he'd never been one given to regrets, that he had moved to Las Vegas years earlier.

He went to stretch out on the bed, and did not interrupt her.

As a last act, Gunther paged through his well-worn dictionary and stabbed a random finger into the P's. "Propinquity," he read, then decided it was a silly word and he wanted nothing to do with it, and he yawned, and in the last few instants before dozing off, he heard Boyd again, groaning on the other side of the wall.

In the years when her faith in most things meant to sustain hope began to crumble, Madeline supposed that belief in miracles had been the earliest to go. Maybe she'd been hasty, for a miracle was the only thing that could've gotten her and Gunther this far.

They had fled that Texas diner hoping the lack of witnesses would get them down the road before anyone knew what to look for. They'd assumed that, despite Allison's refusal to stick around, she and Thomas St. John would be calling the law the first chance they got, but would at least call believing all that was needed was to swing by for a simple arrest. Under such an impression, why bother giving descriptions for a manhunt?

Madeline had worn the blond wig, driving from the parking lot in the car of a dead man. They switched plates several miles away, then to another car entirely when they could. Enduring the hours of slow roast with a bottle of water and towels soaked through in a gas station sink, Gunther had ridden for most of the afternoon and evening—and through two roadblocks—in the stifling oven of each trunk, after first shooting in a few discreet airholes.

Throughout her solitary hours of driving she replayed it over and over: Gunther in his armored vest, striding with the shotgun toward the diner, wading through the man left to guard them, then disappearing within. She had stood outside in the heat and dust, listening to the rolling boom of the shotgun, and during those eighty seconds of blood and smoke and thunder had come the certain knowledge that her life had ceased to resemble anything it'd been before, with no going back, and that she would miss none of it.

Stolen cars and black dye for Gunther and back roads and idle hours hidden in copses of trees listening to a police band scanner and dim motels far off the beaten path—this was not the good life but it was better than it had been, for what had been was but a sad, pale remnant of what had been long before that.

In the hallway floor of the Wainright house, Madeline turned another album page, to examine the evidence for herself.

"What is it there you're looking at?" Constance asked. The hostage hoping to ingratiate herself with the holder, perhaps. "Is it pictures of your kids? Do you have kids?"

"I have a daughter. Tiffany." Madeline closed the album. "But these were all taken before I had her."

"How old is she?" The awful thing was, Constance appeared to genuinely want to know.

"None of your business." Very firm on that. "She hasn't been in my life now for a while. That's better for both of us."

"Don't be so sure. Little girls need their mothers even if they turn up their noses sometimes and go wrapping their daddies around their little fingers. They need us." Constance nodded down at the photo album. "May I see that, would you mind?"

Madeline slid it toward her using the barrel of the shotgun, pleased to have someone to show it to. Who might appreciate it. A drab little country mouse who'd stuck close to home, what had she seen of lights and glitter and celebrity, other than what she'd seen on TV, and magazine covers while in line at the supermarket?

"These are you?" Constance said, and Madeline said they were, if neglecting to mention that the earliest pictures went back over twenty-five years. But Constance cared nothing for dates, absorbed by the elaborate costumes, their brilliant colors and the towering headpieces that capped them off. Madeline remembered them as having turned her from a young woman who was merely lovely into one who'd been stunning, with the graceful stature of a heron and the plumage of a peacock.

And look at her now, stuck with a dodo.

"Oh, the Tropicana, Caesars Palace, Bally's, Stardust," she said. "I danced on some upscale stages, you'd better believe it."

"And just look at some of the people you got to meet!" For a moment, you'd never know that Constance had two guns on her and a legbreaker in her bed. "Is that who I think it is? Is that . . . Frank Sinatra you're with?"

"The Chairman of the Board himself. Oh, I met some names, all right. Wayne Newton's in there. Buddy Hackett. Dean Martin. Joey Bishop. Phyllis Diller. Don Rickles. Anybody you don't recognize, feel free to ask."

"Elvis?" she said, with hope.

Madeline shook her head. "Him I missed."

Constance paged through to the end. When she gave the album back, Madeline glimpsed a look on her face, as if in contrasting the glimpses of then with the reality of now, Constance could ask only one thing: *Whatever could've happened to you?* To answer would be fatuous. She could figure out time, the simple passage of time, easily enough.

"I should be looking like that again before the year's out," Madeline said. "New Year's Eve, you won't know me to look at me. Which isn't a bad idea at all, considering how I've spent the last couple of weeks."

She lit a cigarette to keep herself busy, awake, then cocked her head toward the room where Gunther lay sleeping.

"I used to attract smart men. Maybe not geniuses, but smart. I think what they appreciated was that I actually *could* carry on a conversation. The average man? If every showgirl in Las Vegas went mute overnight, you think he'd care? So it was always a pleasure to surprise them. Smart men," she said, and shook her head. "You can't help but wonder, when gravity really starts to hit home, if they think it goes for the mind, too. They should know better."

She thought of yesterday, how much she had become willing to put up with—to crave, even, in a sick way—and wondered if she wasn't kidding herself; if her sense hadn't gone to hell the same as everything else except her legs.

She'd thought that Gunther had done them in for sure yesterday, in the middle of Louisiana, that his brain had been baked beyond repair while in the car trunks. For all the good it would've done them, they might have reached Yazoo City one day sooner, had it not been for Gunther and the Whack-A-Mole game.

They'd walked into a truck stop and near the front had been a group of video games and the like. Gunther stopped before one, doubtless attracted by its more kinetic nature. He watched as a young boy stood before two rows of four holes each, while plastic rodents randomly popped their silly heads from the holes. The boy beat wildly at them with a padded mallet chained to the console.

Gunther watched, intrigued. "So the object is, you pound the shit out of the moles. That's it?"

"Uh-huh," said the kid. "Only afore they hunker back down in them holes."

"Well, how hard can *that* be?" he said, and slipped a quarter onto the game to reserve the next.

She rolled her eyes and left him to his innocent diversions while she went to place a carry-out order. Behind her rose the dull, frantic thudding of the mallet, then a venomous blue streak of swearing, and a chilling bellow of rage. Upon hearing the first gunshot, Madeline believed that the manhunt had ended, and whirled to deal with it, only to see that Gunther had abandoned the mallet and was now jamming the muzzle of the Browning down each mole hole and pulling the trigger as fast as he could. The red video display went berserk, and the game began to thump ominously.

Their food order forgotten, she'd rushed over to Gunther and given him a roundhouse slap across the face, dragging him out by the arm as he continued to curse the spiteful moles. Another quick exit with squealing tires and dust clouds.

"Low profile?" she screamed from behind the wheel. "What the hell kind of low profile was *that*!"

"Little bastards, they're faster than they look," he said, turning sheepish, then sullen. He stripped the gauze bandage from his eye socket. "And I've about had it with this fucking thing."

The stunt had necessitated a brand-new round of car stealing, plate switching, and cost them a full afternoon of travel time, as well as another possible pushpin on a law enforcement map. Yet for all the inconvenience and risk, it was the most alive she'd felt all day.

And now, sitting on the hallway floor at the Wainrights', she rethought the episode, wondering instead if it wasn't just the way Gunther was hardwired these days, that he could no longer consider himself finished with anything if he hadn't first left everything dead in his wake.

When he could string thoughts together again, Boyd wondered, considering how gruesomely awful he felt, if it might not be even worse had he not gulped all that codeine earlier.

"Can you hear me now?" Krystal's voice, from far out in the prickly red haze. "How . . . how are you feeling?"

"Like if you could go to work on me, we'd need a rock the size of a basketball." To his ears it sounded mumbled, forced past swollen lips. "How do I . . . look?"

Boyd met her eyes with the one he had left, the right nearly hidden behind puffy folds. She sat trussed into her chair, green sundress lashed and wrinkled against her body, and looked him over with a sickly cast to her face, until the expression began to quiver, as if all that remained were the tears.

"Oh, sweetie," she pleaded, "don't . . . make me . . ."

"That's okay, I get the idea."

Krystal brightened with a tiny spark of optimism. "At least Madeline talked him out of using the drain cleaner first thing."

"Ah," he said. "Well, that's some good news, isn't it? And for a minute there I thought we were screwed."

"I've been focusing," she told him in a sudden whisper. "And I mean hard, too . . . *really* hard. I've been focusing for hours and hours, Boyd. Visualizing us walking out of here and everybody okay and nobody else hurt. You've got to put the vibes out there to get them back."

"Power of positive thinking," he mumbled, "like that?"

"It got me out of jail once, when the vice squad cracked down last election year. Usually they don't hassle working girls except for the streetwalkers downtown, and then it's mostly a racial thing. We're just another part of the local economy. Except when election time comes around, then they do it for appearance."

"And you just pictured yourself walking out of jail without arraignment." Intrigued as he was by this prospect of the power of her will, he had to clarify matters. "That's all you did."

"Well, that, and give head to a detective lieutenant. But I'm pretty sure I *created* the opportunity to begin with."

"No doubt," he moaned.

The room where they were being kept must have belonged to Allison's nephew. The windows had been blacked out with newspaper, so no one could see in. From each side, he and Krystal were watched by a malevolently gleeful crew of wallpaper clowns, juggling and turning cartwheels and puttering about in tiny cars, unleashing their ghoulish painted grins as though they were delegates dispatched from the twisted depths of Gunther's mind.

"God have mercy, I hate this room. How does her kid sleep in here without having nightmares?"

"There, there," Krystal soothed. "I'm sure they look entirely different to him."

"At least there's one bright side to that beating I took," he said. "I can only see them with one eye."

Gunther had done it downstairs with the butt of the shotgun, slamming it across his face without warning, with glaring bursts of pain, huge and repetitive, until unconsciousness had overtaken him as the last defense. Codeine could carry you just so far.

Boyd's only clues to the horrors of his face lay in the pity on Krystal's, the throbbing sensation of swollen mass where once had been contours, and the broken, pulpy textures he found while exploring the inside of his mouth with his tongue. The right inner cheek was raw as an ulcerous boil. Three teeth along the side were gone, broken off and jagged, a fourth loose enough to wobble if he wished; he'd cut his tongue already on a spiny ridge. Of those missing entirely, he assumed either they were on the family-room floor or he'd swallowed them.

At least he'd not had to contend with the Drano. This had been Gunther's original intent, as Krystal explained, turning into a loud debate between him and Madeline, who'd been pragmatic if not sentimental in sparing Boyd's sight. She'd argued that the last thing they needed was a lot of screaming emanating from this happy southern home.

With coils of clothesline they'd been tied into heavy chairs brought up from the dining room. While their upper arms had been pinioned, their right lower arms were oddly loose, sticking out before them. He could scratch his groin, but that was about all.

"What I can't understand," she said, "is why they left our right hands free like this. Not that it does us any good."

"I feel like a T. rex," Boyd groaned after he gave it more thought. "If he's remembering what we talked about Saturday, I can guess what he has in mind for later." He would explain no more, so as not to worry her, adding only, "If he comes at you with a deck of cards and has you cut high-low, start visualizing like crazy."

Pitfalls of unconsciousness opened beneath him now and again, when the pain gathered as if by tidal cycles. He would sink into fitful dreams, hazy red, to be tossed there awhile, then deposited back into the hard chair later on. Through the open door he could sometimes hear voices in the hall, at other times noticing Gunther or Madeline checking on them, but immediately on each awakening he would seek Krystal, at his left, thinking that if he awoke to find her gone, he would just give up and somehow let himself die.

Most often she was waiting for him to rouse again. Twice he caught her awake but with her eyes half lidded and her lips softly murmuring, as though she'd entranced herself before some court of higher appeal to petition on their behalf. Finally, very late, he found her slumped in sleep like a normal person.

He watched over her, an impotent guardian, as flickers of bad dreams twitched at her features. He dwelt on an argument against her continuing in her chosen line of work that he had come up with yesterday, with his usual pretzel logic, but hadn't gotten around to presenting: that if she was karmically atoning for the pain inflicted in a past life, of what benefit was that when this call-girl thing caused him such fresh pain every time he thought of it?

Stating his case didn't seem quite as important now.

Morning came, daylight seeping around the edges of the papers covering the windows, and soon there came a stirring in the hall. Gunther filled the doorway, toting the shotgun, two handguns stuck into his waistband.

"Looking good, Gunther," Boyd told him. "Couple ammo belts across your chest, maybe an NRA hat, and nobody could tell you from the *native* rednecks down here."

"Redneck—get the fuck out of here." He took a step back and called down the hallway. "Maddy? I don't look like a redneck, do I? Carrying these guns around?"

"*Red*neck?" Madeline called back. "You? Whatever gave you that idea?" A pause. "You're not listening to Boyd again, are you? I'm warning you, you better not forget what happened the last time you listened to that weasel. Is that what you're doing again?"

"No!" he shouted angrily, then ducked back into the doorway, glaring, and shook a finger at Boyd. "Blow me. *Blow* me."

"Sorry. Didn't mean to cause trouble," Boyd told him. "Look, could you send Constance back in with my piss cup? I really have to go again."

Gunther balked, then went to fetch her from the kids' room. Boyd had voided his bladder once this way, hours earlier, and it was completely humiliating, having to fish himself out of his pants and aim into a plastic cup that she held. Better, though, than the position in which Krystal found herself. They had refused to untie her, even to go to the bathroom, and she'd held it in and held it in, until she could hold it no more, and had to let go in the chair. As the room warmed and her urine cooled, soaking her dress, Krystal sat in the indignity and the rising stink as if none of it could touch her anywhere that mattered.

Gunther marched Constance through the doorway, and she held a large plastic cup with dinosaurs on it. She knelt, held the cup in place. Boyd paused with his hand on his zipper, scowling at Gunther with all the annoyance left in his ravaged features.

"Do you *have* to watch this?" he said. "Is this something that *arouses* you? Because if it is, just get it out in the open and hold the cup yourself."

"Maybe I'll cut you off at the root instead. Give you a dress and let you piss yourself from now on, like her." He pointed at Krystal, then backed out into the hall.

"I'm sorry," Boyd told Constance. "I'm sorry to make you do a thing like this. . . ."

She shook her head. "Not as bad as dirty diapers, overall."

A night of little or no sleep had left her face drawn and pale, her brown eyes darkly rimmed. The beginning of a soft little double chin seemed tauter than it had earlier, but underneath she was far harder than she looked, and bearing up well.

Boyd glanced at the doorway, then riveted her gaze and leaned forward as he began to urinate. The first chance they'd really had to talk, and it could last only the duration of his flow.

"Listen to me," he whispered. "What they want. Computer disks of Allison's. I think they may be here already but those two don't know it. In the boxes she shipped ahead. Where are they?"

"The garage," Constance whispered back. "You mean what they want's been here all along? Then why don't we give it to them?"

"They'll leave a houseful of dead people as soon as you do. I don't know how, but if you could get to them first, that'd be our only leverage."

"This is the most they've let me out of their sight since they got here," she said, and Boyd could feel his flow starting to dwindle. "They'll *never* let me outside."

"I'm just saying *if*," he said, and then heard slow footsteps approaching in the hall, beneath tart-tongued bickering between Gunther and Madeline. "Listen. Don't ask why, just do what I tell you. I have a loose tooth. Right side bottom. In back of the hole. Pull it, but leave it in my mouth."

Constance looked at him with horrified eyes.

"Reach in and *pull* it. *Now.*"

He gaped like a bass with his dribbling penis in hand. As the footsteps came closer, and a nauseated look washed over her face, Constance plunged her fingers past his swollen lips. In the course of his life he could recall no moment more absurd than this.

Constance seized the tooth, with a twist and a yank. Nerve endings squealed. Broken edges grated with a rasp that conducted through jawbone, and the edge of his gumline tore like a split cuticle, while hot tears squeezed from the corners of his eyes and ran down the lumps and valleys of his face. She withdrew her hand from his mouth, wiping blood on her blouse, and he swallowed a salty sip of it, feeling the free tooth on his tongue like a chip of porcelain. He tried to ignore the throb, shifting the tooth beneath his tongue and leaving it there for now.

Constance backed away from him with the cup held in two shaky hands. Gunther stepped into the doorway, sensing something amiss, sniffing tension in the air while his eyes flicked from one to another to the next. His grip on the shotgun tightened.

"Boyd," said Krystal, sharp as an icepick. "*That* wasn't nice, you can't say whatever lewd thing you want just because you've got your pants open. She *is,* like, a married woman."

He loved her then, truly, swallowing more blood, and Gunther relaxed and told Constance to feel free to empty the cup over Boyd's head if she wanted.

"Not anymore I'm not," she said to Krystal, with a spare and chilling resignation. "Married, I mean. Not anymore. Jeff died sometime in the night down there. Alone. He died."

Constance looked at Gunther as the origin of miseries great and small, then brushed past him and went to rid herself of the waste.

chapter twenty-four

They dawdled beneath the sheets as though reluctant to leave the bed, then dawdled about the room as though reluctant to leave the motel. And when they finally did, it was with the sense that up until now this journey had been a fantasy, sometimes violent and sometimes redemptive, and now had come the moment to begin living within the confines of their deeds and of each small day.

Tom drove them back to town and Allison thought how unchanged it looked, as if yesterday's killing might never seep past those childhood walls. A false hope—he would be found eventually. But for today she liked to believe that her father's body would remain upon its chair, preserved by the air-conditioned chill, and when at last the power was turned off, the enveloping heat would cure him and dry him, making of him a leathery mummy left to sit alone in the loveless tomb he had created.

While she went on, forgetting him a little more each day.

"You shouldn't keep that gun," Tom said. "We get caught with it, that's it, all it'll take to convict."

"I know. I hid it, back at the motel. I put it in the shell on back with the spare tire."

"It needs to disappear better than that."

"It will. But not today. Tomorrow, maybe."

Allison watched the passing houses along the way to her cousin's—the biggest, oldest, grandest homes, whose balconies and cupolas harked back to a time that was only half a myth. When they were growing up, it had been Constance's wish to someday make her home in one of them, tending its gardens and raising children who would respect their heritage and traditions. It had been all she'd wanted, and she'd only missed it by a few city blocks.

"I'll get rid of it," she said of the gun, "but I want to do it right. I want to wait until Florida. I want to go for a walk on the beach, just myself, and find the most secluded spot there is. And around sunset I'll wade as far out on the flats as possible, then I'll throw it as far out into the Gulf as I can. And that'll be the end of that."

Allison thought she recognized Constance and Jeff's house when she saw it, working from the memory of old snapshots, then confirmed it by the address. They parked along the curb, in the shade, having decided to stay only a few hours. They would eat and drink and talk. They would pretend yesterday never happened. And then they would return to the road, all the way to Panama City.

She pressed the buzzer, and they waited, then the door opened with a peculiar slowness. The moment she saw Constance, Allison thought with a shock that something must have gone badly wrong since they'd spoken last. She smiled and tried not to let it show.

"Guess who," she said. No change in her cousin at all. "If we came at a bad time . . ."

"It's all about the same now, Allie Cat," Constance said.

After they walked in, the door shut, shoved by another hand, and only then did she see Gunther behind it. He racked the slide of a shotgun that had been aimed at her cousin's head, then pushed her aside, bulled past Allison as well, and flung Tom unsuspecting to the floor of the entry hall. Gunther spiked the shotgun down, butt-first, into the small of Tom's back, over a kidney.

"Be pissing blood for a week, you lived that long," he said.

Madeline came next, rounding the corner from the parlor with a pistol in both hands. Allison wondered how this murderous pair had anticipated them here, then dismissed it as irrelevant. *Take what you want, and pay for it,* God said.

"You," Gunther said to Connie, pointing toward the door. "You bring in their luggage. And if Maddy sees you even *look* at anybody outside, I'm going for a steak knife and I'll be all over your cousin like stink on rice."

"White!" shouted Madeline. "*White* on rice! Stink is on *shit*!"

"Don't you start up with me, you skanky old troll, not this time!" Spittle flecked from Gunther's mouth, and in his rage he stomped on Tom's back, then began to kick him in the ribs while continuing to rant—"You keep *track* of these things, is that what you do? Can't you just once let something go? Finally get this business taken care of, I'd think you'd cut me some slack, but no, I still gotta hear about every fucking wrong word comes out of my mouth, like this is what you live for, you diseased harpy, you!"—kicking, turning Tom into a curled ball with both arms wrapped about his head, until he shouted himself out and stared down at Tom with glazed and unappeasable eyes.

"Watch yourself, Gunther," Madeline said. "She was carrying the other day."

"So get on it yourself, why don't you."

He knelt, pressing a knee into the back of Tom's neck as he ran a hand over him. Madeline took Allison's purse, pushed her against the wall to frisk her too, that hard hand like a claw. A bitter smell of cigarettes and coffee rode on Madeline's breath and in her hair and seemed to exude from her pores.

"Where is it?" she asked.

"Where's what?"

"You need a hint, I'll give you a hint." Madeline thrust the gun beneath Allison's chin, jabbing up, until her throat stretched taut. "Like that, the other day. Except mine holds more bullets."

"I got rid of it in Texas," she said to the ceiling, "because I was afraid we'd get stopped."

"Bullshit. But as long as you can't reach it, then it might as well be in Texas."

Gunther yanked Tom to his feet, and with his arms dropped now from around his head, Allison saw that his face had gone as hard and blank as slate—no hint of pain, nor anger, nor even will. He had become unreadable.

"You. Luggage. What are you waiting for?" Gunther said to Constance, then prodded with the shotgun to get everyone moving.

Allison led the way down the second-floor hall, and time felt as though it were doubling back on itself—twenty years come back around, sent up to her room again to await the worst, and if she was taller now, this was the only thing that had really changed; that, and her willingness to now look her violator in the eye.

Allison was more surprised to find him here than Boyd was to watch her walk in. Nearly as bad as seeing her at the end of the gun was the look she gave him—not of accusation, rather, at first she didn't even know him. Recognizing him only because of Krystal.

"Oh, Boyd," Allison said, with such pity that only now did he grasp how bad it must truly be, if it made her overlook what he'd put her through. "You never could leave well enough alone."

"You know me." He felt the cracking of skin stretched to its limit. "Always looking for an easier way."

Krystal gave him a smile filled with her peculiar faith that the worst was behind them. How could it be that she had not once averted her eyes, still seeing something within him worth smiling *at*? Never in any lifetime had he deserved this.

After Constance brought up more chairs from below, Gunther made a circle of them and took over with his supply of rope. He tied St. John first, then Allison.

"Look at you people. Have you really seen yourselves?" said Constance. "Y'all were covered in cuts and bruises even before you got here . . . except for you." She pointed at Krystal. "You've been beating each other up from one side of the country clear across to the other?"

After the luggage was dumped into the hall, from its other end came the sound of an opening door and a small voice—Lainie, the five-year-old—crying out that she wanted to go outside, she didn't want to play this game anymore. By one arm, Gunther pulled Constance from the chair she was about to be tied into.

"You quiet her down," he said in a low voice. "One minute I'm giving you. You quiet her down and you keep those two in that room even if you got to strap them to the bed."

He sent her down the hall, and Boyd didn't know but that each of them in their chairs began counting privately, praying for a hush of silence before the count of sixty.

And with no one's attention on him, he continued to work with the broken tooth.

When Constance returned, she halted and looked up at Gunther, nearly backing him off a step with the unexpected hatred in it.

"I saw a ghost once, on an old plantation estate," she told him. "Saw it just as plain as day, same as you're looking at me now, and I think if I hadn't been so shook up, we could've carried ourselves on a nice conversation, him in his Confederate uniform. They say there's ghosts all over the south."

Gunther's eyebrow cocked. "Am I missing the point to this?"

"I can't hurt you," she said, "and I know you probably will kill me. So before you do, I just want to let you know: I'm going to haunt you. Every day of your life I'm going to scream in your ear till you jam one of those guns of yours in it and decide you'd rather hear that, instead. I just want to let you know right now who that's going to be."

Gunther blinked with hesitation, then pushed her toward her chair and tied her. When he drew back his hands, he rubbed them on his shirt, as though she'd already leached past his skin. Then he watched as Madeline, in the hall, began searching the luggage.

Only Krystal knew what Boyd was up to, as he sawed discreetly at one more section of rope, using the broken edge of the tooth Constance had pulled. Three hours now, since he had spat it and a puddle of stringy blood into his one free hand. A first molar, it looked like, minus one crooked shard still left behind. Most of the root was attached, the rest shattered at an angle, its edge serrated and flintlike.

He'd cut himself through in fifteen or more places; done it between increasingly brief look-overs from their captors. Once his right arm was free, he'd been able to reach anywhere across his body, and each loose end he had tucked beneath the slack coils so that everything looked the same.

"Wow. Oh, wow," Krystal had whispered when he'd begun. "That is so amazingly resourceful."

"Got our two-week anniversary tomorrow," he'd whispered back. "You think I want to spend it here?"

Now she watched him, watched out *for* him, being his eyes in case Gunther looked his way. Her focus was starting to draw the curiosity of the others. Krystal gave her head a furious shake.

Don't watch him, she mouthed. *Don't . . . watch . . . him.*

He wanted to laugh. When a captured animal chewed its way out of a trap, ordinarily its teeth were still in its head.

Madeline's voice from the hall: "They're not here."

"What do you mean they're not here?" Gunther said. "*She's* here, that's her stuff, how hard can it be?"

"What didn't you comprehend? I'd let you look through these bags for yourself but I'm afraid you'd get caught in a zipper, so just take my word for it: *They're not here.*"

When he slammed his hand against the wall, the entire room shuddered. "Drano," he declared, stalking off toward the bathroom, then back in, shaking the can. "You assholes are putting me in a Drano mood like I never been in before. Now, who wants their baby blues looking like a couple of runny eggs?"

Boyd held the tooth immobile in cramping fingers, had only wanted more time to cut through a few more coils.

Gunther set the shotgun aside and wrapped one arm around the nearest head, and St. John's face purpled as he thrashed against the enclosing arm. Chair legs shuddered on the floor, St. John like a hooked fish whipping whole-bodied against the force drawing him in, eyes crushed shut. He snapped, sank his teeth into the meat of

Gunther's biceps, snarling through jacket and shirtsleeve, fierce as a cornered wolverine, and Gunther yelled and began to flail with the can until he dented it on the crown of St. John's head, tearing free with a grimace.

"So everybody's wanting to play this the hard way," Gunther said, "is that where we stand here?"

"And what's it change if we don't?" Allison asked.

Madeline plunged her hand in one of Gunther's jacket pockets and came out with a straight razor. "Well, you might help avoid the worst for whichever of those two brats at the other end of the hall I get my hands on first. Quit rubbing your arm, Gunther, he didn't even break the skin. Now *I'm* going to finish this up before we waste any more of the day."

Razor in hand, she left the room and the shouting behind her. The truth about the disks, if she was even listening. Boyd knew that she would do it. Never knew she was anywhere near this vicious, but Madeline did not bluff.

And Gunther went after her.

"Stop," he said. "You stop right there! That's not the way it's done, you *don't* go after kids! You hear me, Maddy? You leave them out of this!"

The hallway went abruptly silent.

"You go right ahead, Maddy. You take your best shot with that thing, and I'll break your fucking nose." Gunther's voice lowered with disgust. "What's the matter with you, anyway? Kids? This shit's not done that way, I never hurt one kid in my life."

Her laughter was abrasive. "That's why you always would've been a bag man, Gunther."

Carrying the razor now, he marched her back into the room and pointed at Allison. "You. I heard you shout loudest a minute ago."

She took a deep breath. "I said I'd shipped the disks ahead. To here. I was never traveling with them in the first place."

"See how easy that was?" Gunther pointed next to Constance. "You. You were shouting too, but your cousin's got just a little bit bigger mouth than you."

"Two boxes, they came about a week ago. We put them in the garage, along the back wall, so Randy wouldn't get to tearing into them. Randy, he sees a box, he . . . he thinks it must be for him."

"Just take the disks and go," Boyd said. He felt an immense sorrow, then the strange solace of abandoning hope. "If you need to kill somebody, then kill me, but leave the rest of them out of it." He shook his head. "Can't believe I'm saying this." Sighing. "I'm the only one here who knows where those deposit records point to, offshore. So there's no advantage to killing anybody else."

They all stared at him in awkward silence.

"Now I *know* you hit him too hard," Madeline told Gunther.

"I'll check the garage," he said. "Don't go all screwy. Can I trust you five minutes alone up here?"

She blew him a kiss, then slouched in the doorway with her pistol and hooded reptilian eyes.

"I can't believe you'd've done that to my kids," Constance said. "After last night? You showed me those pictures. Told me you had a daughter of your own. I thought you had a heart somewhere in you."

"If my man hadn't stopped me, oh, I'd've done it, all right. And you know why? Because of you." When she lit a cigarette, she let the lighter burn and stared into the flame. Let the flame die, then nodded at Allison. "At least *she* left here. At least she tried. What did you ever do? Stayed behind and behaved. You risked nothing, you gambled nothing. In the end you gained nothing that couldn't be taken away from you in one day." Madeline sucked a scorching drag off the cigarette, then with jittery fingers dropped the unsmoked length of it to the hallway runner, to stub it out. "And as little as that is, you still ended up with a lot more than I did."

She scarcely looked at them now, while clocks ticked and verdicts were awaited. Boyd did what he could with the tooth in the little time he had left to do it. Footsteps sounded down the hall, and for once they telegraphed no rage.

When Gunther crossed the threshold, Madeline slapped him on the rump, and he grinned, raising one hand and waving a stack of

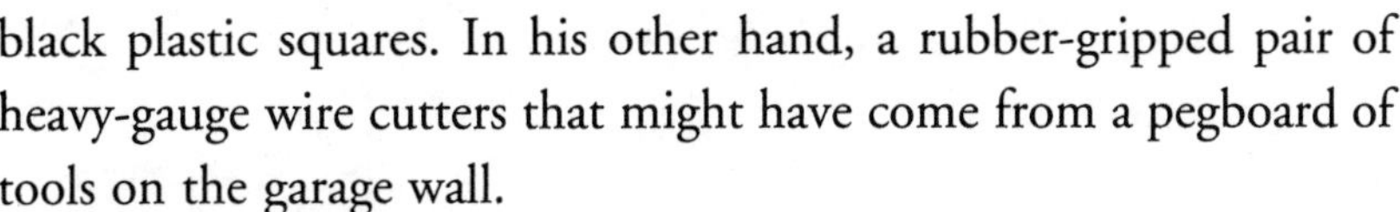

black plastic squares. In his other hand, a rubber-gripped pair of heavy-gauge wire cutters that might have come from a pegboard of tools on the garage wall.

The disks he set aside, then slipped a deck of cards from one pocket. Ran them under his nose and sniffed.

"I know you were just talking trash to me the other morning," he told Boyd, "but I been thinking on it ever since. Maybe you're right, my image does need a little more flash. Maybe I could still push this Vegas thing a little harder."

Gunther tested the fit of his own pinkie in the juncture of the beveled shears, nodded with satisfaction when he got a solid grip, then slipped his finger free.

"So as long as we got some time to kill, now I'm thinking the other morning wasn't a total loss after all."

He looked about the circle and clicked the cutters together.

"Anybody feeling lucky?"

chapter twenty-five

While he walked among them with the cards, loose-shuffling from one hand into the other, Allison summoned the horses as she had learned to many years before, to carry her beyond the hurting.

"Simple high-low cut," Gunther was saying. "All of you got those loose hands I left you, so you get to draw your own, just so nobody can bitch I cheated them. Draw low card, it's your own damn fault when you lose a pinkie."

The stillness was shattered moments ago, Madeline turning on the stereo downstairs, loud, for the benefit of any neighbors who might otherwise notice cries of pain and pain to come.

"And since this Mr. Las Vegas routine was your idea," Gunther told Boyd, "you go first."

Gunther pried Boyd's little finger from the sweaty fist he'd made, notching it into the V of the blades. Allison held her breath, knowing how still he must be trying to hold himself, that he could risk no movement that might dislodge those severed ropes.

"Ten of spades for me," said Gunther, then pushed the rest of the deck to Boyd's fingertips. Over the music, droning organ and sinewy guitar, she could hear the chattering of his teeth.

Jack of diamonds.

"Got a little luck left after all, don't you?" said Gunther. He moved on to the next hand, Constance giving him her finger freely, even boldly. When he showed the seven of hearts, she took a deep breath, then beat him with a queen.

Allison looked into her eyes as she was next, Connie forcing part of her spirit through the air between. Allison felt the cold metal bite over gristle and bird bone, Constance refusing to let her go, nodding calmly to her—

"Eight of diamonds for me," said Gunther.

—and when the horses were no longer there, her cousin was. Connie's eyes her world now, Allison could not look down even to see the card she'd drawn, then the pressure lifted from her icy hand, and she remained intact.

Tom next, then Krystal, back to Boyd, and around the circle again, and Gunther could not win. When he drew low they drew high, when he drew high they drew higher. When once he drew an ace, Krystal tied him, then beat him in the redraw.

"This isn't possible!" he screamed. "Nobody can lose this many times in a row! Nobody! *Nobody!*"

"Except you," Madeline said from the doorway. "So snip one anyway and get it out of your system, I won't tell."

"That's not the point! The point is style. The point is, they let themselves down by their own low cards. I go cheating on the rules I set up, that defeats the whole purpose of the game!"

They bickered and they swore, and finally Gunther dashed the wire cutters to the floor and flung the deck of cards at Madeline. She ducked the blizzard they made, still laughing.

Allison noticed Boyd's face, the love and amazement it yet managed to convey . . . and not for her. He was watching Krystal as if some secret triumph had passed between them, in which he'd had no prior faith. As if she'd carried them all through on her narrow shoulders. Allison could not fathom why Boyd should think such a thing, yet she knew his eyes, knew his heart . . . knew that he was.

"We'll be fine," Krystal whispered to him, and Allison wanted desperately to believe her.

For anyone could see that the game was about to change.

Madeline had taken the large Magnum revolver from Gunther and swung its cylinder open to eject the six bullets into her hand.

"Only chump losers cut cards in Vegas, Gunther," she said. "Roulette, on the other hand . . ."

She chambered one and pocketed the rest. Gunther told her to wait a minute, disappearing downstairs, returning with a handful of heavy plastic supermarket bags.

"You see the way those two cousins were looking at each other earlier?" he said. "They got some kind of funny vibe going. That one, she's *spooky.* What she said about haunting me? Threw off my game, I think is what happened."

One by one, he yanked the bags over their heads like hoods before an execution. Allison was there for Tom when the bag came down, as Constance had been there for her. His brown eyes filled with yearning, then he was taken from her—the shoulders that strained at their ropes could have belonged to many men.

Her turn came next, and the bag descended, a veil of white, leaving her blind and alone with the smell of plastic.

She could only hear the rest—the crinkle of bags, Gunther's heavy tread, and Madeline's lighter steps. Her own timpani heart.

"You want a game, Gunther, I'll give you the real thing," she said. From out in the void came the spinning of the cylinder, the hard slap of it back into the revolver's frame.

So your life didn't turn out the way you wanted, and that's your excuse? she wanted to say to Madeline. *Yeah—so whose does?*

Madeline's footsteps, the whirring, the crisp clicks of the hammer drawing back. Allison flinched each time it snapped on an empty chamber. The inside of her bag grew thick with moist heat, her breathing loud, trapped close to her ears.

The grooved cylinder was pressed to her fingers, then yanked up and away—tricked into spinning for herself. She could not breathe, knowing the gun was aimed at her head, even knowing which spot, a crawling at her scalp like the touch of a ghost's finger.

Daddy, I am so sorry for yesterday, so sorry, because we were no better than this—

Another dead snap. Every muscle loosened.

On it went, while Allison tried to follow. She lost track, lungs recycling her own stuffy air, then grew light-headed, only to plummet sickly when the shot resounded like a crack of thunder.

And nothing and no one moved.

"It wasn't hard," Madeline said moments later, as if it had taken her a while to realize what she'd done. "Not a bit hard."

"Okay. So you did somebody, finally. Now you know," Gunther said. "Is that what you been trying to prove all along?"

"I don't know. How . . . how can I tell from only one?"

Who was it? Allison couldn't stand it any longer. If they killed her too, she would at least make them look her in the eye. She strained her head down, clawing with her free hand until her nails snagged the bag, and tore it stretching from her face like a caul. The air was rank with the smell of gunsmoke and human waste and, now, much blood.

Allison let loose a sob, wondering how she could feel such grief for the person here she'd hardly known at all. She had a flash of Saturday morning, talking with her outside the trailer. Krystal had been the only person she'd ever met who'd looked at her and simply *known* what she had carried with her from this town. Recognized it as only one who carried it herself might.

And look at her now. Oh, just look at her now.

Boyd suspected. He ripped his own bag away, looked with dread to find Krystal limp in her ropes, the bag melted and blackened with cordite residue, and the blood gathering into her lap.

"Always another one where she came from, Boyd," Madeline said flatly. "You just call the escort service."

A wail ripped from the ruin of his mouth as he surged against the sectioned ropes. They fell away like dead snakes, hung webbed between him and the chair. He thrashed free of those that clung stubbornly, and for a moment Madeline and Gunther could only stare in astonishment.

Boyd would have killed her, Allison had no doubt, had he only gotten close enough. Gunther reacted first, drawing a pistol and firing once. Boyd's head snapped, some indistinct but solid tatter spinning from the side of his skull and slapping the wall. He tumbled backward over the chair, to land in an unmoving sprawl.

"Twice!" shouted Gunther. "That's twice he's got out of a chair on me! I don't understand how he does that!"

Madeline nudged his foot. "I don't think he'll be doing it anymore."

Constance and Tom had rid themselves as well of the makeshift hoods, ashen as Madeline swung open the Magnum's cylinder to let the single spent brass casing ping onto the floor.

"Haven't you had enough yet?" Allison screamed. "Two aren't enough for you?"

"Allie," Constance said. "Don't, Allie. She may have ears but there's nothing left in there to hear you with. It's all in this album full of old pictures, that's where she left it."

Madeline uprighted the fallen chair and sat after reaching into her pocket for the rest of the bullets. Bright and shiny as new pennies, they clicked in her palm while she stared at the roulette-wheel face of the cylinder.

"Five," she counted. "Let's reverse the odds, why don't we. I know what you're thinking about me. But you should be *thanking* me, instead." She looked back at her palm. "Five. That should work out about right. . . .

"Allison," she said, and chambered the first.

"Thomas," she said, and chambered the second.

"Constance," she said, and chambered the third.

"Burn in hell," Connie spat.

And when the next two names were spoken, and Gunther voiced no objection, Allison wondered if his earlier defense of the kids hadn't been part of some prescripted drama played out to inspire a misguided faith that if they cooperated he would at least ensure that the most innocent would survive.

"Randy," she said, and chambered the fourth.

It was the worst headache of his life. Boyd came to, amazed that he was still in the room, neither moving nor knowing if he could. He let his eyelid roll open and this boded well for the top end; flexed both sets of toes to confirm hope for everything else in between. Fabulous.

"Constance," he heard through the ringing in his ears.

It felt as though a band of fire encircled half his head, with patches of raw cold front and back. Clearly, Derek wasn't the only Dobbins to possess a skull of uncommon hardness.

"Randy," Madeline was saying.

Likely the bullet hadn't hit squarely; had hit instead at an angle, penetrating his scalp and burrowing wormlike beneath, to curve along his skull between bone and flesh until exiting through a second wound. He'd heard of it occurring before.

"Lainie," Madeline said.

Yet through it all, he'd never lost his grip on that tooth.

His mouse-level view of the room was blurry, but he was close enough to Madeline to discern the backs of both seated legs. He lunged upright onto jellied knees and, while he had the surprise of resurrection still going for him, lurched the rest of the way.

He threw one arm around Madeline's shoulders, hanging on for support as he slashed the tooth's filleting edge down the right side of her face. From eyelid to jawline, the flaps of skin peeled wetly apart, splitting like the rind of an orange.

Madeline shrieked—such terror he had never heard—and dropped the gun she'd been loading. He clung tighter, and reached across her face and gouged the tooth under her left eye and held it there.

"Do I do this side too?" Boyd rasped in her ear. "Or does he start cutting them loose?"

The shotgun was just out of reach in the doorway, but Gunther already had the Glock in hand. He jammed its muzzle into Allison's head. Her eyes drifted shut as though she were dreaming.

"Gunther?" Madeline wailed. "Gunther!"

"I'll do it!" Gunther shouted. "You know I'll do it! One more scratch and I'll leave her like the other one!"

"You'll do what you'll do," Boyd said. "First rule of Vegas is 'Scared money always loses.' " Madeline's blood was spilling across his wrist. "*I'm* not scared anymore."

"Gunther!" she pleaded. "He's going to do it! Don't let him cut my face anymore, *please,* Gunther!"

He stood his ground, ripped with uncertainty. The gun wavered from Allison, was then aimed at Boyd as though Gunther thought he might try slipping one past Madeline's ear. She pleaded with him not to—what if he missed? Boyd thought of Krystal and slit half an inch down Madeline's cheek, while Gunther squeezed both eyes shut.

"Aw, Maddy," he moaned, "what he's done to you . . ."

Boyd told him to put the Glock in St. John's hand, and he did it. Told him to take the razor and cut St. John loose, and Gunther did this too. As St. John shrugged off the coils, Boyd watched to make sure Gunther had no tricks left, thinking no, he couldn't be this compliant.

Madeline must have regained her wits as soon as she ceased howling about her face, from beneath her shirt pulling the pistol he forgot she'd been carrying earlier. Her arm twisted back and Boyd felt a poke between the slats of the chair. Twice she gutshot him. He toppled backward and, though it was not intentional, still held fast to the tooth and drew it back with him, laying open her face from the left cheek, across her nose, and around and down to her right earlobe. She turned to shoot him again and was instead shot from across the circle by St. John.

Boyd looked to see the extent of the damage he had wrought, and hoped she wouldn't die, wishing her a long, healthy life—just her, and her memories, and the thick and shiny scars.

. . .

Tom hadn't wanted to take his eyes off Gunther for so much as an instant but could not look two directions at once. He hit the floor after felling Madeline, rolled to his side, and swung the Glock around to discover that Gunther had vanished, the open razor dropped in favor of the shotgun on his way out the door.

Had it not been for Constance's children, Tom wouldn't even have considered going after him; would've been happy to wait for the police. He recalled from his stint in the Marines that anyone with sense and combat experience ranked houses as dead last in preference. No jungle could conceal as many hazards as a plain, ordinary house; worse when you fought room to room. And matching pistol against shotgun verged on insanity.

Body memory. Unending hours of torturous drills, imprinted into muscle, imbedded into bone. You could almost forget it was all there, until it awoke, and drew the first fiery breath it had taken in years.

He crawled to the doorway so he could peek along the length of the hall at floor level. All clear. Now he had to decide which tactic Gunther might have adopted: if he'd fled outright, if he'd gone straight for the kids' room, or if he was waiting in between to ambush Tom on the chance he would rush directly there himself.

"Tom," Constance whispered. "That last time he sent me down to quiet them? I hid them in the back of Lainie's closet."

He nodded, saw Boyd doing his best to crab his way across the floor. With his boot Tom slid the razor to him so he could cut the others loose, then thought of the noise those boots would make on the floor and took them off. Socks too, for traction. He ejected the Glock's clip to count the remaining rounds—thirteen, plus the one in the chamber.

"Stay low along the floor," he told them. "I don't know how solid these walls are. Bullets might go ripping right through."

He slipped out the door to glide flush against the wall.

Every tactic they'd trained into him for a house fight required things he did not have. A grenade to lob into each room before rushing in to finish the job? Fresh out. Stupidity would have to suffice.

The master bedroom came first, on his left; across and down was the bathroom, and across from this was a guest bedroom. Tom was betting against the bathroom—too confining, not enough cover.

He streaked low past the master bedroom doorway, tensed for reflex fire that did not come. He doubled back and swung in his gun hand, swept it across the room, then bounded through the doorway toward the bed. He rolled off the mattress onto the floor, then saw the doors of a ransacked closet standing open along the wall shared with the guest bedroom.

A pair of Jeff's shoes strayed from beneath the bed, and he grabbed them, hurling one after the other at the closet wall. They struck with heavy thuds, and a heartbeat later two shotgun blasts came ripping back through. Heavy-gauge buckshot fragmented a lamp and glass picture frames behind him, and with a burst of confetti shredded through a case of comic books sitting on the dresser.

From the floor, Tom snapped off three shots back through the perforated wall in hopes of getting luckier than Gunther. From the steady footsteps pounding toward the hall, he didn't think he had.

Eleven, he told himself. Easiest thing in the world, losing count of how many shots were left.

Hearing Gunther's mad rush down the hall, Tom hopped over the fractured glass, and when he came through the doorway dropped low again, spotting Gunther from behind. Gunther swung around and fired, while Tom hugged the floor to let the charge pass overhead.

When Gunther rammed through the door with the poster of the unicorn and the rainbow, Tom held his fire just as they both knew he would. Tom prayed for the kids' unswerving obedience, that they hadn't left the closet, and that on rushing in, Gunther could react only with indecision.

Gunther slammed the door shut behind him, and the blast he fired back into the hall punched a hole through the door as big around as a dinner plate, showering splinters and tearing through poster to gut the unicorn.

Tom scrambled forward, hugging the hall baseboard, wondering how much he should gamble on having heard nothing out of the kids. One would think, if they'd left the closet and seen Gunther charge in on top of them, they would at least cry. That's what children did when the bogeyman came to call.

These two hadn't made a sound.

A clear field of fire. It had to be. *I think . . .*

He dropped on the run and slid to the floor, on his butt, as though to straddle the doorjamb, half aligned with the doorway, half shielded by the wall, and kicked out with his bare foot. The sprung door shuddered open to reveal a widening slice of young girl's room. Gunther fired again to rain down more chunks from the blasted door. In silhouette against the curtained window, he ran for it as if to leap through the glass, heedless of the fall. Tom knew with all his heart that Gunther was the only thing moving.

He tracked the shape, squeezing careful shots; could tell he was missing every time more glass shattered. He counted down each until he had four rounds left, and dared waste no more.

Gunther staggered and ripped aside curtains and newsprint to flood the room with sunlight, then began, for no reason Tom could fathom, to whirl in a mad and contortive frenzy. He slapped at his hip, bellowing like a bull, waving the shotgun but only because he hadn't thought to drop it.

"Shit! Shit! *Shit!*" he cried, then fell against the wall, tearing furiously at the side pocket of his sport coat, the bulge within. He flung aside the perforated can of Drano in a shower of blood and crystals, and slapped again at his steaming hip.

When Tom shot him the next four times it seemed almost the humane thing to do.

He got to his feet and crossed the room, filled with frills and tomboyish touches alike. Although he would later undoubtedly shake until his joints rattled, he felt steady now as he plucked the shotgun from Gunther's lap. He waited for those still-open eyes to turn upon him, but they did not, and the blood-speckled neck gave no hint of pulse. Gunther was as dead as men ever got, just not soon enough. Tom stripped a sheet from the unmade bed and draped it over him to spare others the sight.

The closet door remained closed, covered with another poster that might appeal to a young girl's fancy: a serene and soft-focus picture of a young woman with face averted, caught in ephemeral grace upon the burnished floor of a dance studio. He opened the door and told those within that it was safe now, that they had to leave the room, that he would take them to their mother.

Out they came, wary and frightened as rabbits, rumpled and hungry, red of eye and wet of pants. The boy toddled into his arms but the girl did not. Tom followed her gaze across her room, to the dead heap against the wall. She looked upon it, then upon him, making connections with a heartbreaking acuteness that belonged on no five-year-old face.

He wondered if yesterday and today would end soon for her, or if for years to come she might dream of strange men in her room, and of the violence they brought with them.

Madeline hung on past the last gunshots as if by some miracle she might find herself able to keep going.

Allison watched the final hopes dim in her eyes as soon as Tom called down the hallway that it was finished. Madeline had been gazing toward the door, but she now let her head loll to the other side and shut her eyes and bled during each shallow breath.

Connie sprang to her feet, then rushed into the hall.

Allison sat on the floor with the confiscated guns, but they were not needed. Madeline's breath wheezed and rattled. So Allison held Boyd's head in her lap as she used to weeks and months ago, at the end of long days, even after suspecting that they each had made a mistake in the other and that both knew it but were too curious or stubborn to say so, and would rather hurt than admit being wrong.

Love—lust, even—was no different from any other game of chance, in that true skill meant knowing when to leave the table.

His open eye roved about the room. She had positioned herself so that her body blocked anything he might see of Krystal. Boyd nodded toward the wall, any wall, and she assumed that he meant those hideous and inescapable clowns.

"Wasn't it, like, Oscar Wilde's last words," he murmured, "something like 'Either that wallpaper goes or I go'?"

"Curtains," she said. "I think it was the curtains."

"Close." He sighed with the rank breath of swallowed blood. "This is a bitch. . . ."

"You're not . . . going anywhere . . . are you?"

He told her he didn't know, they'd just have to wait and see; that he hoped not but couldn't explain why, not with the condition of his body and his life. Soon he looked up at her, gripped with a terror that she could not name, and that he had no time to name for her. She wept for their wrongs and held him tighter until the fear subsided in his eye, then he touched her wrist, and went.

Allison turned to find Tom watching from the doorway, and he nodded and, just as he had yesterday, knew when to turn his back and give her the gift of solitude.

Although with Madeline in the room it was not the same.

"Gunther's not coming back," Allison told her. It seemed very important she understand this.

"Yeah," Madeline grunted. "I got the idea already."

"So die, why don't you? Just die. You know you want to."

"I did what I can, the rest isn't up to me." Madeline lolled her head back this way. "I wouldn't mind . . . some help."

Allison shook her head. "I don't think I could do that now."

Madeline's gaze settled on the pistols. "One of those . . . and I'll do the rest."

"I'm not giving you a gun, either."

"Well that, then." She crooked a finger toward the razor.

Allison stared at the obtuse angle it made on the floor. This far, at least, she could go. Madeline was better dead for more reasons than she could count. Allison laid Boyd aside and stood, kicked the razor to Madeline's side, watched her turn it as though mesmerized by the blade's keen edge and its possibilities, then Allison gathered up the guns and left the room to the dead and the deserving.

She found Tom trembling against the banister, midway down the first flight of stairs; told him she'd be back in a moment.

On leaving the house she could hear sirens outside, perhaps a few blocks away, no more. So she worked quickly, running to the van, opening the spare tire case, taking out a small rag-wrapped bundle hidden there earlier. Then back she ran into the house.

The rags were peeled aside by the time Allison met him on the stairs again, and she made sure Tom saw it: the revolver, fired yesterday by both their hands.

"Gunther." She pointed up to the shattered door. "In there?"

Tom nodded.

"When it comes up . . . when they ask . . . he took this from me on Monday. In Texas. Do you understand?"

Tom said that he did.

"Because if he could find out things about you the way he did, he wouldn't have any problem finding my father. That's where they must've gone first, yesterday. Doesn't that sound right?"

Slowly, he nodded. And said that it did.

While the sirens drew near, and Tom watched her ascend the stairs; while Constance kept the kids in the guest room out of sight of things they should not see; while Lainie asked why her father was not there for her and when he would be . . .

While all these things swirled about her, Allison entered the room where Lainie had slept and dreamed and trusted, and found it not unlike the room across town where she herself had grown up and also been forced to learn some things too soon. And if the power of lies was among them, then that was only fitting, and in some small way was one accountability for other days settled at last.

She drew the sheet aside and found Gunther stinking beneath it, and wiped the revolver clean, bullets too, before pressing it once into his hand, then tucking it behind his belt. When she left the room she felt that she should close the door, as though latching a secret inside a heart-shaped locket, but on second thought she couldn't see the point, because in their zeal and in their thirst for one another's blood they had filled it with so damned many holes.

chapter twenty-six

By the latter half of October, Tom found that the middle of the previous month had come to feel like a dream, in which he had said and done things that bore no likeness to the life he knew or the man he thought he was. And so, having returned to that man's life in Panama City, it seemed that those words and deeds, like any dream, should be of no concern to anyone but himself. But this was not so.

Many of those exploits were known to others—certainly among those he employed and those who were his neighbors, but also among voracious strangers who watched their TVs or read newspapers or gossiped with others over drinks or fences.

They knew him now, or believed they did, even when their faces stirred no recognition and even less desire to accept their accolades or satisfy their curiosities. They made him nervous. It felt as though they had insinuated themselves in his soul and been somehow privy to those parts of himself that should have remained protected by the impermeable boundaries of the dream.

I'm no hero, he could've told them, *because what you know is only the part that looked the best. The rest of it we left out.*

The greatest refuge was his work, as it had always been when times turned cruel. Beneath his hands and blades and needles the leather drew its first breaths of new life as he awakened all the potentials that lay dormant inside each swatch of once-dead hide.

ST. JOHN'S APOCALYPSE, read the labels. Under the lettering a highway vanished over a fiery horizon streaked orange and red, where an immense black sun had newly set. *Clothing for the End of the Road.* And he realized that he was there.

Aunt Jess phoned frequently from South Carolina to check on him. As always she called him Tommy, and told him how proud his mother would've been of him, saving those two children. He must have put it off for four or five calls before working up nerve enough to turn to the past and blow away its dust.

"Do you remember much about my father?" he asked. "Not the big things, more . . . the little things."

"We're very few of us big people, Tommy. We're mostly all of us made of little things. Yes, I have memories of the man."

"Do you remember," he began with tremendous hesitation, "what kind of pet names he had for me when I was little? If he ever called me anything like 'Tom-Tom'?"

She thought about it, then told him she recalled having heard nothing of the sort, but this didn't mean it had never been used.

Missing nothing, Aunt Jess picked away at pretense with her septuagenarian grace. "After he left the family, you told your mother more than once that someday you'd just strike out on your own until you found him. You've not been making good on foolish old promises, have you, Tommy?"

"Probably not," he said, then asked if she had any pictures of the man lying around in drawers or boxes, taking up space. His mother, after all, had done such a thorough job eradicating every trace of the man she'd married—all but his son—that Tom was left with no memory of his face. Jess told him that she could probably scrape up a few, and send them in a day or two.

"That'd be good," Tom said. "I'd appreciate that. But . . . if you would? Could you double-wrap them? Because I might not want to look at them right away. And there's no reason for me to open that package and have them falling out all over the place. I might want to keep them around awhile, so that should keep them safe until . . . until I'm ready to look."

"I'll tell you what I'll do. I'll triple-wrap them," said Aunt Jess. "That'll give you an extra chance to change your mind."

He told her that would be fine, and looked forward to the day when it wouldn't matter what the photos had to tell him, for only on that day would he feel certain that, whoever else he was, he was no father's son that he didn't want to be.

Because she was family and because she was now alone with her children and because sometimes people need the presence of someone who remembers them from long ago, Allison decided that she should stay with Constance awhile after all.

Her cousin decided that for her and for the kids, the house was forever ruined, and nearly as soon as the holes were patched and the glass replaced and the blood mopped up, it was put on the market. As went the house, so went the town itself—when Constance announced she could no longer live there, Allison told her it was a smart decision, and helped her pack, and they moved to Jackson. Ten times the size of Yazoo City, it was a land of opportunity to Constance, to Lainie a world full of large and unfamiliar threats, and to Allison merely the latest hostel in a string of hostels, from which she would one day surely move.

Jefferson's life insurance paid off handsomely, with double indemnity. Money would be no problem anytime soon.

With children in bed and autumn stars in the sky, Allison and Constance would some nights spread a blanket on the back lawn of the rented house and share a bottle of wine and occasionally something stronger, and deep into the night they would talk as freely of mid-September as Allison knew that Tom, most likely, was not.

"That marriage wasn't going to make it, Allie," Constance admitted, for some reason waiting until they had moved to speak of it aloud. "Jeff . . . I've never seen a more unhappy person with any less idea of why he felt that way. I think he'd decided it was the rest of us."

"You never let on to me." But Allison wasn't surprised.

"It's the way we were raised, you know. Don't let anybody see that smile slip, even if it's no more real than a Halloween false face." Constance raised the wine to the face in the moon before she drank. "And as far as the bedroom was concerned, forget it. Whenever Jeff had trouble falling asleep, I'd tell him to pretend he'd just come. That usually did the trick."

They laughed long and hard, once Allison got over the shock; it had come from a Connie whom she'd never really heard before.

"You must've had some idea what was wrong with him," Allison said, "even if he didn't."

"Oh, sure. Sure. I don't think there's anything sadder than watching someone come to realize that the best time they ever had in their life was over before they really understood much about it. No matter what Jeff did, I don't think one bit of it made him half as happy as the things he did when he was eighteen. Get together with his friends, and that's all you'd ever hear about. 'Remember when . . . ?' Like every one of them was so busy keeping yesterday alive they forgot about today."

A common human failing, although Allison couldn't decide which yesterdays were harder to let go of: the best, or the worst.

But Constance was right—it was no true life, holding on to your past so fiercely that you denied yourself a future. And so Allison wondered if, when tempted to live like that, the best way to treat your yesterdays wasn't simply to kill them all, and let the playwright sort them out.

She came one evening, finally, from the near northwest, and when she did, the days were getting shorter, and Thomas St. John cherished the lengthy nights as though the darkness were a friend, because the worst things he had ever seen people do to each other had been done in the light of day.

She came without promises and with few expectations. It was the way survivors lived—betting no more against the world than they could afford to lose. She came only agreeing to try, and learn if the way in which they'd touched each other during those last few hundred miles had been genuine, or only inspired by the fear of death, and enchantment by an ever-changing road.

She came for a week and the week became two, and by early December the northern Gulf shores felt the gray and cheerless grip of an otherwise mild winter.

Late one afternoon she trudged alone down a grassy slope that fell away from his house, past spiky thickets of palmetto, then on to the deserted beach. Until now he had forgotten the way she'd told him she wanted to rid herself of the revolver used to kill her father. She left with the same sense of purpose, even if she didn't have the gun anymore. Tom watched her shrink at the end of a meandering line of footprints dimpled in the sand, a slim figure in leather, her wheat-colored hair snapping behind her on the frigid Gulf winds, until he lost sight of her altogether. Gulls circled and screeched, swooped low and soared high.

It was too cold for the ritual as she had described it three months ago, the water gray as iron and unfriendly for wading, but the rest of it he imagined she might just as easily go through with, so long as she had something to throw. And when she came back, after a good long brooding time, she looked as though she might be free of one more clanking old chain.

"What was it?" he asked. "What did you throw in?"

She merely smiled with serenity and intrigue. She touched a finger to her lips, then kissed his, and went to hang up her new jacket. He recalled that he'd never been sure what had become of those sought-after disks. But whatever she'd thrown, he decided it was best not to know, for it was natural that men and women have their secrets from one another, and make of themselves mysteries that were better for remaining unsolved.

She'd come for a week and now it was five, and finally Tom

decided that it was time for the trip he'd yet to suggest. They went to the cemetery and walked among its stones and its tattered shrouds of dead leaves, and they stood before the newer of the two graves marked ST. JOHN.

"I'm sure Mom would've preferred meeting you before now," he said, "but you do what you can."

At his side, unmoving, she gazed upon the headstone, its graven masks—one in laughter, one in tears. She stared so long it was as though they held some special meaning for her already.

"Dwight told me about it," she finally admitted. "I knew all along what you'd done here."

"Dwight," he said. "What else did he tell you?"

"More than you probably would've wanted him to. Don't be mad at him. He loves you and he just wanted me to make an informed decision."

Tom nodded, sidestepping for a moment the issue of informed decisions. "So. The headstone. You like it."

"I think it's perfect. More than you probably ever intended," she said. "I think those masks belong on every single one of these stones."

He decided that she was right, for while few would ever set foot upon a stage, there was a greater truth that cut to the heart of each of them, player and audience alike. That we are born, and that we laugh, and we cry, and if in the end we've managed to do the former a little more often than the latter, then we can have achieved no greater triumph over the script and scripter of our lives.

"That decision you were talking about," he said, thinking he knew the verdict already, still wanting to hear it from her lips. "Are you staying?"

She looked at him with most of her mysteries intact, from past and present and future, and he would take them, good and bad. Take them one and all.

"Wild horses couldn't drag me away," she said.

He thought for a time of taking her to visit the other graves that had brought him here before—Sweetwater, and the other St. John—then decided to leave them for another occasion, or perhaps none at all. Because the dead were at rest, all of them, for the first time in forever so far as he knew, so maybe for today it would be best to leave them that way.